ONE MANHATTAN

TENLEY SERÉ

TS WRITING

it clear he wasn't aligned with the future I'm trying to build.

But it seems like tonight my luck is about to change. At least for one night. I am here to make poor choices, *dangerous* choices. Starting with this one. This incredibly handsome one.

"I guess you could say I'm celebrating good company." He says with a wink that I wouldn't normally find sexy, but somehow on him, I do. *Damn, he's smooth.*

"Well, let's see just how good this company can get," I counter, tapping my glass gently against his before taking a sip, holding his gaze over the rim of my coupe as my heart pounds.

Did I really just say that? Out loud?

"I'll drink to that, too," he says with a smile so charming it shouldn't be legal, but there is a twinkle in his deep blue eyes that sucks me right in.

Is he flirting with me?

He puts down his drink and offers his undivided attention as he asks, "So, what brings you here, alone, on a Wednesday?" He's fishing for personal information, and I plan to give him as little as possible.

"Wanted to grab a drink or two after a rough meeting." Vague, but truthful. "Though I could ask you the same thing." I attempt to turn this conversation back on him.

"You could," he says.

"Could what?" I take the bait.

"Could ask," he smiles. Now I'm wondering whether he is actually flirting with me, or whether he's just an asshole.

Honestly, do I even care?

The answer is no, I don't. As long as that body ends up on top of me, and whatever he's packing under those pants ends up inside of me, then no, it doesn't matter. Because if he looks this good with his clothes *on*, then... Fuck. Me.

No, literally fuck me.

Oh shit, he's waiting for me to ask. God, I've really never been good at flirting.

"So, what brings *you* here, alone, on a Wednesday?"

"I thought you'd never ask," he flashes me a teasing smile that makes my stomach do strange things. "I'm meeting someone for dinner, but I wrapped up my workday before him, so I decided to come early for a drink. Plus, I had to get the hell out of the office after a disagreement I had with my boss about the amount of time and resources he's spending on a questionable *investment* of his."

And he just confirmed that my initial assessment was spot on; he is a finance bro.

Tailored suit. Ferragamo loafers, I clocked those immediately. Classy, but not flashy. That absolutely tracks, considering he didn't start the conversation with the cliche, *So, what do you do for a living?* line.

My hopes fall, though, as his response starts to sink in. He's meeting someone for dinner. Which means, he's unavailable after this. Which means my plans, to allow him to take me home and do unspeakable things to me, just fell apart.

Just my luck.

You know what, fuck that. I came here determined to be *reckless,* and I'm going to shoot my shot because why the fuck not.

"That's too bad," I smile coyly as I take a sip of my drink, looking at him through my lashes.

"What's too bad?" He asks, brow furrowed. *God,* he's sexy.

"That you have dinner plans," I casually shrug, though my heart is pounding at my brazen behavior.

"Oh?" He asks, a curious smile tugging at the corner

purpose of doing something absolutely reckless, or should I say *someone*. And that's what I'm doing.

I just agreed to go home with a man I do not know.

This is a terrible idea.

A dangerous idea.

A reckless idea.

And it is exactly what I need.

CHAPTER 2

HADLEY

"Ready?" The sexy stranger I've just picked up at the bar throws on his blazer and reaches for my leather jacket, holding it out for me as I slip my arms into the sleeves.

He looks like he was AI-generated for a luxury fashion campaign, *and* he's a gentleman? Okay, something has to be wrong with this man because, *really?*

He reaches out, taking my hand in his as he leads us out the door into the chilly night air, which does very little to cool my desire.

"Can you walk in those?" He's looking down at my stilettos.

No. But I am not going to tell him that.

"How far?" No chance I'm walking more than a block in these Louboutins.

"You're selling yourself just as much as you're selling your company." The words of my oldest friend, Jade, play out in my head. *"It's why realtors and pharma sales reps drive BMWs and shit, you need to look successful, Hads."*

She can be pretty overbearing, but she also bought me the $800 shoes. I insisted she was just fronting me the money, but we both know they were a gift. The same way she and her boyfriend are currently letting me live with them in Manhattan, rent-free. I can't afford the increasing rent in Bushwick, let alone rent in Manhattan.

Not yet.

Success came easily to Jade - not that she doesn't work her ass off for it, but I wish I had even a fraction of her confidence sometimes. Unlike me, who chose to pursue a tenuous career in niche tech, Jade always knew she wanted to be a lawyer. She never worried about her grades or getting into Columbia; she just *did*. She knew she'd get in, just like she knew she'd ace the LSAT and kill it in law school, and even now, she knows she's really damn good at what she does.

And she'd better be, I don't even want to know how many hundreds of dollars she gets paid per hour to argue with people, but it's a sizable figure. Enough that she didn't have to think twice about *investing* in a pair of designer shoes for me. But that is also the type of friend she's always been, more like a sister, really.

I know I've created something brilliant with Trueno, my app, my company, my baby, but I struggle with showing other people how the technology that powers my product is truly revolutionary.

Jade insists that being confident is a choice she made, and assures me that embracing confidence, even just dressing the part, is a choice I need to make as well. *Dress for the job you want*, as the saying goes. From the way she styles her hair in a clean, crisp bob, down to her shoes - Louboutins - Jade exudes a bold sense of self-assurance that I have always found enviable.

And so here I am, wearing my own pair of red-soled pumps. Purchased for me by Jade. For confidence. Definitely not for comfort.

These are easily the least comfortable pair of shoes I own.

They are also by far the sexiest.

"It's not too far," he replies, "just four or five blocks."

Well, shit.

My face must say it all, because the next words out of his mouth are, "Don't worry, I'll call Emilio to take us back to my place, he can be here in less than five."

Does this guy have a private driver? And the way he says it so casually, *I'll just call Emilio.* Like it's the most normal thing in the world to have a personal driver on speed dial. It feels highly probable that I am going to die tonight. Preferably of ecstasy brought on by the man standing next to me, but actual death seems plausible too. I shoot Jade a text while he is calling Emilio.

> Hadley: May not come home tonight if things go well ;)

> Hadley: I've shared my location with you.

True to his word, a black SUV pulls up not even three minutes later, and a gentleman I assume is Emilio, hops out and opens the door for us. I climb in, hoping I look comfortable in one of the captain's seats while trying to act like getting picked up in a private car is a completely normal occurrence for me.

The ride is short, yet it feels like an eternity. Emilio's presence only heightens my awareness of how much I crave a physical connection with this handsome stranger, and maybe it's the anonymity of it all, the thrill of not knowing where we are going or who I am with, but I am so outrageously turned on. I cross my legs in an effort to alleviate the ache pulsing between them, the anticipation of what's to come hanging in the air between us like a promise we both yearn to fulfill - well, at least I definitely do. I cannot help but wonder how much longer I can endure the suspense.

Just as I begin to consider reaching out and touching him, the car stops, pulling up to what looks like the facade of an exclusive downtown apartment building. He quickly ushers me past the doorman and into the elevator. I watch as he pushes the button for 6A.

The doors on the rear side of the elevator open directly into his living room. He owns half the floor? It's clear he has money, but I can't say I saw that coming.

"Can I offer you a drink?" He asks as we exit the elevator. The casually charming way he says it tells me that bringing home a woman is likely not a rare occurrence for him.

"Sure." A little liquid courage can't hurt.

"What would you like?" He gestures for me to follow him deeper into his living room, where he pauses in front of a vintage steamer trunk that has been repurposed into a chic, custom bar - its worn leather exterior adding warmth and character to the otherwise contemporary space. Inside, it contains an enviable collection of what looks like top-shelf bourbon and a few pieces of crystal glassware.

"Whatever you're having is fine." A lame answer, but it's the only response that comes to me.

"On the rocks okay then?"

"Perfect," I smile. The stronger the better.

I watch him pour the contents of a crystal decanter into two identical tumblers before picking them up and offering one to me. My fingers graze his as I take the glass of what I assume to be very nice whiskey, sending a little jolt of anticipation racing through my body, electrifying the moment. He clinks our glasses together.

"To good company," he echoes his toast from the bar with a wink and a playful smile.

"I'll drink to that." I take a hearty swig from the crystal

glass, feeling his eyes on me as I do. The amber liquid burns a path down my throat, despite its chilled temperature, as I swallow it and slowly lick the remnants off my lips.

A thick haze of anticipation wraps around us, and I can't help but wonder if he feels it too, this desperate need to close the distance, to shatter this tension between us and embrace the inevitable. That's why I came here, isn't it?

He must be feeling it too because his eyes lock on mine, narrowing as his gaze heats and subconsciously drawing me towards him. One step closer is all it takes. He doesn't take his eyes off me as he removes the tumbler from my hand and sets it down beside his.

Mere inches separate us now, and I catch a whiff of his cologne - it smells of warm honey and smoke, like temptation made tangible. My eyes gently flutter closed. I know what's coming, and I melt into his touch as his arm wraps around my waist, pulling me flush against his hard body.

Only then do his lips finally meet mine. It's like a spark igniting into a kiss that sets everything ablaze, filling the space with a heat that leaves us both breathless and desperate for more.

His other hand cups the back of my head, fisting my hair as he holds me firmly against him. Then, without warning, he spins me around and props me on the back of his couch. The hand wrapped around my waist begins to wander, tracing its way to the slit in my skirt, and following the opening up my thigh. I let out a little gasp when his fingers reach the sensitive peak between my legs.

"Are you sure you want this?" He asks.

"Yes," I gasp, already desperate for more.

"Good," he says, "because I've been fantasizing about this since the moment you walked into the bar."

Holy shit.

No man I've been with has *ever* spoken to me so

directly, and fuck if that confession, coming out of his mouth, isn't the hottest thing I've ever heard.

Need erupts from every pore in my body as I kiss him back with everything I have. It's hot, hungry, and demanding. My hands are roaming, frantically clawing at his jacket as he helps me out of mine in a frenzied attempt to get undressed as quickly as possible while I remain perched on the back of his sofa.

His hand wastes no time reaching under my skirt again, instantly finding that sensitive spot between my legs, stroking gently as my back arches and I gasp from the contact.

Fuck, that feels good.

Too good.

I need more.

I rock my body against his fingers, seeking more pressure as I moan.

"I can feel how much you want this," he growls against my lips as he dips beneath the lace fabric of my underwear and slips a finger inside. "So ready for me already."

"Oh God," I moan.

"You like that?" I can feel him smiling against my lips.

"Fuck," I breathe. It feels so impossibly good, and I struggle to catch my breath as I involuntarily clench around him, pressure coiling and building within me. And just as I feel like I'm about to fall apart on his fingers, his *magical* fucking fingers, he stops.

"Not so fast," he whispers against my neck before nipping at my ear, and fuck if that doesn't leave me trembling for more.

"Please." I am not above begging, desperate for his touch and the impending promise of release.

"Shhh." He presses his finger against my lips before trailing his tongue from my collarbone, along my neck, and up to my ear, sucking my lobe gently between his lips. "I'm going to take care of you," his hot breath causing goose-bumps to rise along the back of my neck as a shiver dances down my spine.

He claims my mouth with another hungry kiss, applying pressure to the seam of my lips with his tongue, requesting access which I readily grant. The kiss quickly grows frantic, insistent, his hands running down the length of my back and cupping my ass as he lifts me from the back of his couch.

My legs instinctively wrap around him, and we're a tangled mess of tongue and teeth and roaming hands as he carries me down a small hallway and into his bedroom.

"Now," he gasps as he deposits me on his bed, climbing on top of me and gently pushing me onto my back. "I'm going to kiss you."

I smile as his lips gently graze mine. "Here," he says before his mouth trails down my neck. "Here," he says again, kissing me gently. His lips land on my collarbone, and I can feel his smile against my skin as he says, "and here." Then he lifts the hem of my camisole as he kisses my abdomen. "Here too." He keeps moving lower until his fingers find my skirt's zipper, tugging it down before he pulls it right off my body.

Oh.

Wow.

"Here," he says, and my body trembles as he places a soft kiss on my inner thigh. The whisper of his breath tickles my sensitive flesh as he moves higher, "And here."

My whole body tenses in response. He must sense my discomfort because he pauses, rising so that his gaze catches mine, a brow raised as if to ask if I am okay.

"It's just," I can't think of the words, how to say it. God, I feel so *awkward*. "I've never, nobody has ever –"

"Nobody has ever gone down on you before?" His tone is filled with astonishment, but coated in warmth. No judgment, but maybe a little pity. And I don't know why, but suddenly, I feel comfortable enough to open up to him.

"No," I whisper, propping myself up on my elbows to look at him as I feel my cheeks heat. "My exes never offered, and the one time I asked Ca– my ex, he declined, saying he didn't enjoy it." *God*, how embarrassing.

"I told you I'd take care of you." His smile is somehow both mischievous and tender. "But if you aren't comfortable, we don't have to do this. Just let me know what you want."

I came here tonight looking for a little adventure. Hell, I came looking for danger, and the hottest man I have possibly ever seen is between my legs, offering me *that*. Something I've *definitely* been curious about, but never really experienced. There is absolutely no turning back now.

"I want this," I say, trying to sound more confident than I feel as my *entire* body flushes.

"Good," he smiles, "because you deserve to be worshiped, and that is exactly what I am about to do to you."

A sudden, intense wave of desire tears through me like a rising tide as I throw my head back onto his bed. This can't be real life, yet somehow, I don't think I'm dreaming.

His fingers hook onto the fabric of my underwear, gently pulling them off before tossing them aside, leaving me quivering and bare as he slowly spreads my legs, humming gently against the soft skin of my inner thigh as he kisses his way up each side, finally settling in where they meet.

Oh.

My.

God.

I instinctively roll my hips towards him at the first moment of contact, the rush of pleasure almost too much.

Almost. I need more. So much more. And he is about to give it to me.

Tension coils within me, growing tighter with each taunting kiss, every flick of his talented tongue that he has just weaponized against me, relentlessly teasing, flicking and kissing *everywhere*. Except he is careful to avoid the one spot that is so desperate for contact.

Then finally, *finally*, he hones in on it, careful not to give me enough to push me over the edge, but just enough to cause my entire body to tremble with tension.

"Oh God," I stifle a scream, as the pressure grows within me, every moment building toward the inevitable explosion of ecstasy that he promised.

"Patience," he hums between my legs, causing another current of pleasure to ripple through my body as my fingers fist the sheets and my toes curl.

"Please," I'm begging now. I need release like I need air.

He lifts my legs, draping my knees over his shoulders as he lowers his mouth back to me, and it feels so good. *So* fucking good. But he still doesn't give me what I need most, careful not to give me the one thing I so desperately crave.

I think I might die here.

Right now.

And just as my life begins flashing before my eyes, he brings his tongue directly where I need it. One flick and I unravel. I come undone. *Completely* undone.

Never. I have *never* experienced an orgasm like this. It consumes me completely as swells of pleasure crest and crash over every inch of my body, drowning me in this endless chasm of euphoria, and all I know is I am crying out while my body writhes, gripping the sheets as I ride out each wave of the very ecstasy he promised me.

But it's better. Even better than I imagined.

He continues working me through the seemingly never-ending surges of pleasure that continue steadily pulsing through my body, and only once I've finally come down does he rise, smiling as he kisses a trail back up my body.

"See," he teases. "I promised I'd take care of you."

I am a puddle of bliss, melting into the mattress. I have no words, so I simply smile back appreciatively at him. He responds by leaning over and fusing his mouth to mine in a gentle, but charged kiss.

My fingers begin undoing the buttons of his dress shirt, and the kiss instantly grows more frenzied, more urgent as I frantically work my way through every one of them. I reach for the hem of his undershirt, eager to reveal what hides beneath the white cotton of his fitted tee.

Slowly, I lift the material, the fabric sliding up to reveal a chiseled abdomen that seems to have sculpted itself to perfection. Each muscle is defined and pronounced, each ridge sharp and contoured. His obliques curve gracefully, forming a powerful V that draws my eye downwards to the waistband of his pants.

Suddenly, I am desperate for those to come off too, eager to explore what lies beneath them.

This man's body is *unreal.*

And he fucking knows it.

"Like what you see?" He smiles as I pull his shirt over his head, revealing his broad, well-defined pecs as they rise prominently, showcasing the strength and athleticism that he possesses. Yep, he definitely goes to the gym at 5:00 AM every morning. And to answer his question, yes, I very much like what I see.

"So much so that I need to see more," I reach for his belt and begin unbuckling.

Who the hell have I become?

Suddenly, his hands are *everywhere.*

Roaming.

Grasping.

Raking.

The kiss, the *everything*, grows wild and chaotic as a primal urge to suddenly strip him naked and have my way with him consumes me. At some point, he pulls my camisole over my head and unclasps my bra with impressive ease, but I barely notice as I undress him with a lot less grace, but equal enthusiasm.

Now he's as naked as I am, and *holy shit*.

He is *more* than I imagined, more than I fantasized.

The corner of his mouth lifts into a cocky smirk, revealing his apparently unshakeable confidence. It shouldn't be, but it's such a fucking turn-on.

"Still like what you see?" His blue eyes sparkled teasingly, though there was a warmth behind that mischievous gleam.

Yeah, yeah I really do.

"I assume you have a condom?" I ask, trying my best to sound nonchalant, but holy shit, *that* is presumably about to be inside me.

"Give me a second," he responds, leaning over and pulling open the drawer of his nightstand. Not surprisingly, he has a healthy stash of condoms. I feel an unexpected pang of jealousy over those who came before me, but it melts away as soon as he turns back towards me, offering me his undivided attention.

"You are stunning," he murmurs, running his fingers through my hair. "You absolutely deserve to be worshiped, and *that* is exactly what I plan to keep on doing." I can't help but swoon.

He makes good on his promise as he gently pushes me back on his bed, positioning himself on top of me, dragging his fingers along my leg and pausing only as he adjusts himself at my entrance.

The rush of anticipation I feel is electric, firing every nerve ending in my body until I'm practically vibrating.

His hand dips between my legs, and I feel him smile against my mouth as he settles in on top of me.

"Is this okay?" He asks, and I nod before he pushes himself in with a soft roll of his hips, inch by tight inch.

Oh God. The feel of his weight on top of me as I sink into the mattress below. The pressure. It's divine. And for the second time tonight, I see my life flash before my eyes as he takes me fully, slowly allowing himself to ease all the way in.

And then he begins to move.

Gently at first, rolling his hips with a slow, steady cadence that leaves me hungry for more.

Starving is more like it.

His breath is hot on my neck as he sucks and kisses a trail from my collarbone to my jaw before plastering his mouth onto mine with a tender yet bruising kiss.

"You feel so good around me," he growls against my neck, causing a series of shivers to race across my body as I shudder with pure desire.

"More," I gasp as he begins to increase his pace, taking me harder with each thrust. I need more of him. Always more.

"You're fucking perfect," he groans, each thrust hitting deeper, causing pleasure to ripple through me with every one. But it's still not enough.

I rock my hips against him, still seeking more. He responds to my need, his hand running up my leg, grasping it beneath my knee and lifting it towards my chest, pushing my leg farther back with every thrust as he takes me even deeper.

I cry out in pleasure. I can't help the sounds that escape me because, damn, it all feels so fucking good.

I am so close now, and I can sense he is too as his

breathing becomes ragged and shallow. His fingers grasp my breasts before returning to that sensitive spot between my legs. One touch and I'll be done for, every bit of me coiled so tightly, already on the precipice of my impending release.

His fingers make slow, deliberate circles as my whole body seizes, anticipation building within me like a storm ready to unleash its fury.

And then, it's as though I've been struck by a bolt of lightning, a sudden rush of white-hot pleasure surging through me, wild and untamed, heating every inch of my skin and heightening every sensation. I have never fallen apart so completely, and yet tonight, I've done it twice.

He cries out and shudders as I ride out the climax of my own simultaneous release. Finally, he collapses beside me, pulling me so that I face him as he claims my mouth in a soft, lingering kiss.

"That was –"

"Perfect," he cuts me off, tucking me into the crook of his arm as I settle my head against his chest and begin to drift off, wrapped in a soft glow of contentment.

Shit.

Shit. Shit. Shit.

What time is it? How long have I been asleep?

Holy shit.

I just slept with a stranger. It was easily the best sex of my life, sure, but I am still in his apartment. I cannot believe I slept here.

I can't explain it, but there was something oddly comfortable about him, something that made me feel safe amidst my ardent desire to do something reckless last night. Something *dangerous*. Well, mission accomplished. I let my guard down. Apparently, I felt safe enough with a total stranger to fall asleep in his bed? I am smarter than this.

I look towards the window, the sky is turning a deep pre-dawn indigo, transitioning from the inky blackness of the midnight sky.

Okay, so I still have a chance of sneaking out of here, I think to myself as I stealthily gather my discarded clothes and haphazardly dress myself.

I pick up my shoes, tiptoeing out of his bedroom and back towards the living room before putting on my leather jacket and reuniting with my phone.

5:45 AM.

Three missed calls and a series of texts from Jade. I'm sure she's going to have a field day with this one, but I'm a grown-ass woman. I'll deal with her once I get out of here.

I grab my bag, do a quick scan of the space to make sure I didn't forget anything, then hit the elevator call button, eager to escape before my beautiful stranger wakes up. I still cannot get over the fact that this elevator opens directly into his living room.

Who *is* this guy?

A console table sitting just to the left of the elevator catches my eye. His mail is neatly stacked there, and it suddenly dawns on me that we never exchanged names. He didn't ask, and I didn't offer. How is that even possible? I don't know, but I just had sex with a man, without even bothering to learn his name.

I need to leave.

Suddenly curious as I wait for the elevator, I pick up what looks to be a bill off the top of the stack, hoping to learn the mystery man's name.

William Eskridge III. Of course, it's something pretentious.

The elevator dings, signaling its arrival, and I place the

envelope back in its tidy pile before stepping inside and pressing the button for the lobby.

Well, William, whoever the hell you are, thanks for the best sex of my life, even though I'll probably never see you again.

I realize, just as the elevator's doors begin to close, that I spoke too soon.

Because across the room, I'm drawn to a flicker of movement, and there, a pair of haunting blue eyes catch mine, holding my gaze. I momentarily lose myself in their depths; they are the last thing I see as the elevator door closes, leaving him standing naked, and very alone, in the middle of his living room.

CHAPTER 3

TREY

You coming, man?" Lex asks, noticing I hesitate on our way out of Brawl & Order. It's shortly after 7:00 PM on Friday as we leave the boxing gym, and normally I'd be joining him and Jaxon for drinks.

"Yeah, just going to drop in at home first. I'll catch up with you." I need to clear my head a bit; I'm not sure why, but I'm not really in the mood to go on the prowl with the boys tonight. I shake my head. I've been hanging out with Jaxon and Lex, and a fuck-ton of other men in tailored suits all day. I *need* to go out. Set my sights on some beautiful women, that will help.

It always does.

I'm standing in my room forty minutes later, trying to determine whether I can still smell that fresh, floral scent that's been lingering on my pillow, haunting me since early Thursday morning, when a text comes in from Lex reminding me they are waiting for me at the Bar Room and wondering when I'll be there.

Images of the woman from Wednesday night flash across my mind, and I feel my heart rate increase. The moment I saw her, she looked out of place, not because she couldn't mingle with that crowd, but because she was far too beautiful, far too pure, to be associated with the usual downtown scene. I'd already been determined to take her home, and then, after that brazen declaration, her *radical* candor, I couldn't get her out of there fast enough.

And I still can't get her out of my mind.

Maybe she'll be there again?

I know the chances are slim, but I am suddenly very eager to get to the Bar Room. I respond to Lex's message, letting him know I'm on my way.

When I arrive fifteen minutes later, I find the guys already seated at our usual table. It's apparently not enough that we all work together; the three of us spend most of our time outside the office together too. It's always been this way – me, my stepbrother Jaxon, and his cousin Lex Sterling. Well, legally and professionally, Lex goes by Alastair, but socially, he prefers to be called Lex, despite Jaxon's refusal to address him as such.

A waiter appears with a platter of caviar, a brussel sprout salad, and braised pork belly nachos. I guess they got started without me, but I can't really blame them. We all order our entrees and another round of drinks.

"By the way, nice mention by Aria Thorne, Jax." Lex chuckles, knowing it will get a rise out of Jaxon. Jax doesn't really care for the spotlight, and he especially hates when he gets written up in Manhattan's most popular society gossip column, *According to Aria.*

"Oh, really?" Jaxon's tone is unamused. "I don't read it, so I wouldn't know."

Just the usual. A picture of you looking as handsome as ever in a tux, talking to some woman who *isn't* Kit." Lex raises his brows. "Aria wonders if you've moved on." And apparently so does Lex. And me too, if I'm being honest.

"Aria Thorne really just needs to learn to mind her

own business and quit publishing her speculations about my personal life." He grumbles through gritted teeth.

"So, who was she? The woman in the picture. Was she one of the ballerinas? I could see that for you, actually." I tune into the conversation because honestly, I'm all ears if it means Jaxon has moved on from Kit.

I cannot *stand* that woman.

"I have no idea. I haven't seen the photo, and I talked to a lot of people last night." He's intentionally vague, per usual. Jaxon attends so many events and fundraisers, I'd forgotten he was attending the Season Opening Ballet Gala last night as the guest of one of our limited partners.

"Well, until you tell me otherwise, I'm just going to assume you've moved on with a stunning ballerina. I love that for you, man." Lex smiles smugly before taking a healthy drink of his old-fashioned.

"Here is me, telling you otherwise." Jaxon picks up his cocktail, leaning back in his chair as he takes a long, slow sip, signaling that he's done with this conversation. Lex visibly deflates, focusing his attention instead on the brussel sprout salad while eyeing the nachos that I'm currently enjoying. The man maintains one of the most stringent clean diet regimens I've ever encountered. His self-control is honestly impressive, though he claims his affinity for high-end bourbon is an approved exception.

I change the subject, mumbling something about how I am starving after my workout. Lex offers me some of the caviar, but I decline - I hate caviar - and just continue digging into the nachos Jaxon ordered for me.

"You might as well eat some of the salad then. You're paying," Lex smiles deviously as he slides the bowl of shaved brussel sprouts in my direction.

"The fuck I am. You *know* I don't like either of those." He does know.

"Maybe you shouldn't have stood me up Wednesday

night then, I've been craving this caviar for two fucking days." I cringe watching him devour the stuff. Gross.

"I did not prevent you from venturing out for caviar, that's on you, man." I'm distracted tonight, my mind still stuck on Wednesday's mysterious woman. Of course, he had to go and bring up Wednesday night.

"Fine. But why did you stand me up??" He raises a brow at me, and I know he's not going to let it go. "It was for a woman, wasn't it?"

I can't help but sigh.

"It was definitely a woman." Jaxon makes his first contribution to this conversation, his tone matter-of-fact. As if there is no other possibility, and he knows it.

Of course, my step-brother reads me like a book. Not that I've ever seen him bent out of shape over a woman. Never. But he's watched our parents - and they are definitely sickeningly in love.

My mom and his dad, Kenneth, got married when I was only twelve, Jax fourteen - the perfect age for us to be grossed out by their constant displays of affection. Once we realized they'd been sneaking around for years, it kind of made sense they'd want to be able to finally *show off*. Though I think we both could have done without their endless indulgence in over-the-top PDA in front of us.

If it hadn't been for Jaxon, I don't know if I'd have ever forgiven my mom for having an affair with Ken. And honestly, I'm not sure Jaxon has ever really forgiven his dad for moving on after his mom died; he really doesn't talk about it. In the end, it worked out for everyone I guess. Even my own dad seems happier now with his new wife. Though, thanks to living through all that family drama, Jaxon and I both have a healthy aversion to the prospect of marriage, or even falling in love for that matter - that shit fucks people up. It's easier to keep things strictly physical.

Speaking of physical... I smile at the memory of the

woman from Wednesday. "Lex," I address him by the nick-name he adopted when he left home for college, the one Jaxon still refuses to use, emphatically stating it is a terrible rebrand of Alastair. But Lex hates his given name, claiming Alastair sounds too pretentious. Kind of like my own name, *William Eskridge III*, though I've been going by Trey for as long as I can remember, so nobody ever had the chance to call me William. "You know I wouldn't have canceled on you if I hadn't had a very good reason."

He leans closer. "And? Was she a good reason?" His eyes are twinkling, a smile tugging at his lips.

How do I even begin to describe her?

Good definitely doesn't cut it. Not even close. She's stunning, but Manhattan is full of gorgeous women. It's more than that. Her beauty lacks that air of pretense that so many women put on these days. I picture her, the way she turned to me when I ordered her drink, eyes wide. Her hair was loose, and she wore minimal makeup, but somehow her big almond-shaped eyes stood out, blue-green or gold-gray, depending on the light - and now, come to think of it, how aroused she was. I distinctly remember the steel blue color in them deepening as I *took care of her*. Twice. Her lithe, little body, all curves and edges, trembling beneath my touch.

"Like I said. Very good." I bite back a grimace at my weak words. Instead, I catch myself laughing at the way Lex's eyes widen. He clearly wants more.

I sigh. Again.

"Oh shit." He grins, popping a forkful of brussel sprout salad into his mouth - how can he eat that crap? "You okay there, Trey?" he teases.

I glare at him. "Fine. She was just… incredible. Hot, obviously. At first, I thought she seemed uncertain? Nervous? I don't know, but then she told me she wanted me to take her home and…" I shrug.

Jaxon is frowning at me. "So what? You've had plenty of women proposition you before. You are a master at turning them down with a smile. What makes her so astonishing?"

"Do you even know her name? I want to Google this incredible woman of yours. Or at least check out her Instagram." Lex joins Jaxon in his skepticism.

"No." I wish.

"Not different then," Lex says it like it's decided. "Admit it Trey, you were just horny. You ditched me so you could get laid. You could have just said so." He chuckles to himself.

"Fuck off, Lex." I glare at him.

I want to come to Wednesday's defense, make them understand she *is* different. She didn't just *proposition* me. I mean, she did, but the *way* she did it. Her honesty, her countenance, her quiet confidence, or lack thereof. There's something innocent, yet feisty about her. I can't articulate it, even to myself.

With nothing else to offer about my mysterious Manhattan mistress, the dinner conversation moves on to Lex's upcoming meeting with our colleague Genevieve. She's a real cutthroat with strong instincts and opinions - and to be honest, she's usually spot on. She is one of the youngest partners at AVC, which in Manhattan venture capital terms means she survived the gauntlet in a male-dominated field - and then some. At Avenier Venture Capital, performance is the only currency that matters, and Genevieve, with her sharp instincts and equally sharp demeanor, consistently delivers wins.

Right now, she's apparently all worked up over an upcoming pitch from some start-up with potentially extensible technology. AVC isn't so much interested in the app itself, but the application of its tech to our other ventures. I haven't been privy to the details, nor have I really paid much attention since I don't handle potential new business. Lex seems unfazed by the conversation - he usually is. Jaxon doesn't outwardly show any reaction, but I notice him sipping his old-fashioned quietly. He is paying much closer attention to everything Lex says than he's letting on.

I vaguely follow their conversation, but my mind is elsewhere tonight. Besides, it seems unlikely we will invest in the weather app they're discussing, despite its technology's potential. Especially given Genevieve's apparent resistance. From what I gather, she has an issue with the founder. I can't quite tell, but it sounds personal. I only get involved with businesses we actually fund.

Finally, the work talk wraps up, and Lex turns to me with a conspiratorial look. "Enough business for tonight," he says, eyeing the crowd gathered along the ornate wooden bar. "I'm thinking about the one with the long brown hair in the tight leather pants. She looks like she's got a bit of an edge to her. What do you say? Looks like she's here with friends. There are three of them." He looks at me first. "Purplish hair? Or Goldilocks? Take your pick, Trey."

I spot the trio of women Lex is talking about. I can't help but smirk. "Go for it, Lex. I'm pretty sure Goldilocks is hitting on the one with the purplish hair. You probably have a good shot with the third wheel though, that brunette that caught your eye." Then, because I can't help myself, I add, "I bet you get lucky and she has a tongue ring too."

Jaxon is not even engaged, focused on his phone instead. He's texting - it better not be - "Yeah, I think I'm just going to send a driver for Kit."

Lex slaps his hands down on the table in disappointment. "Come on man," Lex's shoulders fall.

"What? She's reliable. Discrete enough. Good at what

she does. I don't have to worry about her business." Jaxon attempts to defend himself.

"Because she *is* a fucking business." I never understood why Jax would go the escort route. High-end, very exclusive escorts, sure, but still. It's not like he can't get any woman he wants.

"I would be worried if I were you. That fucking *Kitty Cat* is definitely trying to sink her claws in you." Lex is not wrong. That bitch makes me uneasy every time I'm around her.

"She's practically feral." I catch Lex's eye as I grin at my own joke.

"Maybe that's how I like it." And with that, Jaxon stands up to leave.

Lex rises at the same time to pursue the edgy beauty, laughing alongside her friends at the bar.

Guess that leaves me with two options. Prowl like Lex and join him at the bar, or leave alone. I scan the Bar Room again for the girl from Wednesday, even take a tour around the place. But she's not here. I *should* take someone else home; maybe it would help get her out of my system. But when I catch myself looking for a woman who *looks* like her, I shake my head and stride purposefully towards the exit. These women deserve better.

I don't even bother saying goodbye to Lex. I walk the five blocks home and lie in bed, waiting for sleep that doesn't come easily. It's still there, that sweet, seductive scent of her alluring perfume.

How am I so fucked over a one-night stand?

CHAPTER 4

JAXON

I sigh at the text message that just popped up on my home screen. Kit. Again. I am starting to regret reaching out to her last Friday after the Bar Room. The whole point of our arrangement is that she should be drama-free, but this is the fourth text in as many days, confirming whether I want to see her again.

I ignore it, like I have the last two messages, especially as I see my colleagues, Genevieve and Alastair, arriving for the pitch meeting we've all been anticipating.

"What are you doing here?" Genevieve is surprised to see me hanging around for a 5:00 PM meeting. Her blonde hair is pulled back into a severe low bun at the nape of her neck, making her appear even more intimidating than usual.

I raise an eyebrow, questioning her tone. She may be my Managing Partner overseeing strategic investments, and she may also happen to be my cousin Alaistair's best friend from grad school, but nobody, not even Genevieve, gets to talk to me like that in the office. Like it's not my fucking company. Alastair just rolls his eyes and chuckles to himself. Typical.

Alastair met the ruthless Genevieve Fontaine at Harvard Business School almost a decade ago. Even then, she was a force, and Alastair insisted she come back to the city with him to work as a summer associate between their first and second years. My father was the CEO of AVC at the time and, based on her performance, she was offered a job upon graduation. Along with Alastair, of course. My stepbrother Trey joined the firm as an intern that summer as well, fresh out of undergrad. He's been here ever since.

Dad always prided himself on this being a family business. Which is exactly how I found myself in the position of CEO at barely thirty-years-old. And how Alastair found himself in a Managing Partner role, overseeing portfolio management. *The board unanimously approved the appointments,* my father told me proudly last year at his retirement party. In hindsight, it's clear now that their unanimous approval had less to do with the board's faith in me and more to do with my age. They thought I'd be easy to manipulate, but much to their disappointment, I've worked my ass off to prove them wrong.

One of my first moves as CEO was to promote Genevieve. It didn't take long for her to earn her reputation as one of the most ruthless executives in the company. She'd already risen rapidly through the ranks and now she is second only to myself, in both title and reputation.

"Jesus, Gen," Alastair mumbles under his breath.

"That's Elizabeth Aldridge's daughter in there," I gesture towards the conference room where that new temp - Joe or Beau or George - some godforsaken name I'll never remember, recently showed the founder of a startup called Trueno.

"Exactly my point," Genevieve scowls.

Ordinarily, we likely wouldn't have even taken a meeting with a company like Trueno, but a long-time stakeholder, Sebastian Devereaux, called in a favor and vouched for the tech. He also happens to be a central figure in Russell Artanza's professional circle, Russ being one of my biggest investors, and an even bigger pain in my ass.

"Don't worry, Genevieve Fontaine," I smirk. "I'm not here to take over. You can be your usual terrifying self in there. I'll watch through the window."

My father had a two-way mirror installed in a number of our conference rooms to discreetly observe potential clients and, honestly, some employees. The man could be paranoid sometimes, but I have to admit, I have used them more than once. And I'm not sorry about it.

"I hate that we are even considering funding that bitch," Genevieve folds her arms across her chest. "And you're actually on board with this, Lex?" She gives Alastair her most intimidating glare, but he knows her well enough that he is unaffected.

"That's not Elizabeth Aldridge in there, Genevieve," he interjects. "We don't know anything about her daughter." I silently thank him for proactively backing me up. He relayed the message more eloquently than I would have.

"We are considering her *company* and her *product*," I assert firmly. "Which has nothing to do with her mother's business or her mother's feud with my father."

I fully understand Genevieve's animosity towards the Aldridge name. There is a part of me that wants to rip this Trueno start-up away from Elizabeth Aldridge's daughter solely for revenge, but I'm willing to hear her out, even if only as a favor to Sebastian. If the technology truly holds the promise I think it does, we can still take control and use the technology to our full advantage. Profiting off of Elizabeth Aldridge's own daughter? Well, the cruel irony of that offers an even sweeter type of revenge.

"You looked it over Gen," Alastair steps in again. "It's some weather app. Can we just leave The Rebel Media drama with her mother in the past for the duration of this meeting?"

We both know she won't.

Despite acting like he doesn't take much time to get to know the files he is working on, my cousin Alastair is always well-informed and very reasonable. He has talked me off a ledge on more than one occasion, and I'm confident he'll go into that conference room with an objective, business-minded approach.

Genevieve will never be objective; she is ruthless and trusts her gut. Which I can appreciate, but sometimes it steers her wrong, and this might be one of those occasions. Not that I fucking blame her. I looked over the file myself the moment I saw the Aldridge name cross my desk. I also looked into its founder.

It seems Elizabeth Aldridge's daughter rejected the opportunity to work at her mother's lobbying firm, instead choosing to start her own business, building a technology company that more closely aligns with her late father's meteorological background. Her tech could be a real disruptor in the industry if applied creatively. And it could have applications far beyond what she has ventured into so far with weather satellites. She's a fucking genius, and she's decided to apply this groundbreaking tech to a weather app?

Naive little thing.

If she's built what I think she has, we can stand to profit substantially off Trueno. Especially considering some of our other investments involve more private applications of satellite technology, and this tech, if it works the way I assume it does, could make us a shitload of money when applied to other ventures. Which we may or may not choose to tell her. Most likely not.

If we even invest.

That being said, Genevieve's antipathy is not

misplaced. Rebel Media Group was one of the first digital disruptors in the online streaming industry. And one of my father's largest investments several years ago, back when he was still the CEO of AVC. It was the first account Genevieve ever worked on, fresh out of business school. She was assigned to research and draft the early regulatory and risk analysis and flagged some vague noise about upcoming privacy legislation, but she'd judged it low risk.

The partners, led by my father, wanted the deal. He was under a lot of pressure from the board, so no one asked too many questions. Then Elizabeth and her firm successfully lobbied for legislation, rallying support for content regulations and privacy rules that changed the industry overnight. The Rebel Media business model fell apart, costing AVC hundreds of millions of dollars. Many, including my father, largely blamed Elizabeth Aldridge and her targeted lobbying efforts. But internally, investors and executives were looking to point fingers. Genevieve hadn't even been senior enough to make any decisions about the investment, but her name was the one on the risk assessment memo. In any other firm, it would have ended her career before it got off the ground. The only reason she didn't crash and burn is that Alastair went to bat for her. I'm fucking glad he did, and that my father listened.

Some called it nepotism, but I saw it for the strategic long-term investment that it was. The move bought Genevieve's loyalty to AVC, that's for damn sure.

AVC has slowly built back our portfolio. As Alastair said, the drama with Elizabeth Aldridge is in the past. But I haven't forgiven and certainly haven't forgotten; I'm not the fucking CEO of AVC because I *forget* about the people who fucked us over.

"Let's just get this over with," Genevieve sighs before spinning on her heel and stomping towards the conference room.

"Have fun," I smirk at Alastair, making my way to the small, private office on the other side of the two-way mirror, curious to watch the pitch unfold. This should be entertaining at the very least.

As I step into the office, I look through the glass and stop dead in my tracks as my eyes fall on the most alluring woman I have *ever* seen standing alone in the conference room. I don't know what I expected the apparent tech genius behind Trueno to look like, but never had I envisioned *her*.

She's smaller than I imagined she would be, and she looks nervous, adjusting the skirt of her tailored black suit.

She stands facing the mirror, because that's all it appears to be to her, a mirror. She has no idea that I stand on the other side, watching her. She pauses in front of it to check her reflection and smooth down the jacket of that form-fitting suit. As she does, a glimpse of soft ivory lace peeks out from beneath her blazer, kissing the edge of her defined collarbone.

I watch as her chest rises and falls with every steadying breath. She's anxious. And for some inexplicable reason, I want to reach through the glass and offer her my reassurance.

Get a fucking grip, Jaxon.

It's not just her beauty that has me mesmerized, though that in itself is impossible to describe. No, it's the way she carries herself. Despite her obvious nerves, every inch of this petite woman exudes confidence, and there's a quiet determination behind those grayish gold, almond-shaped eyes, the ones that flicker with shades of blue and green when the light hits them just right.

Not that I notice.

I've used this two-way mirror countless times. In moments like this, when potential, or frankly, current, clients prepare. They really reveal things about themselves when they think nobody is watching. Secrets. Weaknesses. Things I can use to my advantage. It's one of the things I learned from my father. It's never fucking bothered me before, yet the intimacy of this moment somehow feels wrong, like an invasion of her privacy. I want to look away. I *should* look away, but I can't fucking do it. The pull to stay outweighs the instinct to stop myself, and I let it.

Then Genevieve enters the room, and Hadley Aldridge turns away from me.

I take a deep breath, reminding myself why I'm here. I *never* allow myself to get distracted like this, and I'm not about to start right now.

I've also never been so taken by anyone in my life, and I haven't even heard this woman speak. I'm struck by the way she carries herself, especially as Genevieve stares her down. I can feel the fight in her, the resolve beneath that delicate exterior. And I'd be lying to myself if I didn't admit that it is a fucking turn-on.

As I watch her face Genevieve's ruthlessness without so much as a flinch, I realize I'm at a loss. I've never been so captivated, so *disoriented.* She's done something to me, and I don't know what to do with this tight, restless coil in my gut that refuses to ease.

Ignore it, that's what I should do with it. Suppress whatever the fuck that is.

But I don't know if I can.

Her pitch hasn't even begun, yet somehow I feel like she's already won.

I shake it off and finally remember to flip the sound switch, allowing me to hear what is going on in the room. Genevieve's voice, in her acerbic tone, floods in, and I can't help but smile. A part of me still takes satisfaction in seeing Elizabeth's daughter cowed under Genevieve's wrath.

But the way Hadley lifts her chin in defiance

completely captivates me. She marches to the center of the room to start her pitch, and I am fucking *entranced*.

Genevieve never lets up, Alastair only asking the occasional question, nodding approvingly at Hadley's responses to Genevieve's inquisition. And Hadley Aldridge responds coolly and confidently to every question and thinly veiled dig thrown her way. At most, she might pause or blink before decisively responding, not once losing her composure.

She truly is *astonishing*.

I hang onto every word she says. I *try* to listen intently to her pitch, I can understand the basic foundation of her work, but once I realize the true potential of her product, most of the technical nuances slip past me, drowned out by the sight of her. Despite the nerves she initially displayed when she thought nobody was watching, she is poised in the confident, yet graceful way she presents herself now. And her body language matches the confidence in her tone.

Once again, I catch myself noticing more than just her poise as my eyes are drawn to the subtle curve of her chest, the lace of that camisole that peeks out occasionally as she moves, taunting me nearly as much as the way her eyes flicker with that fire I desperately want to understand.

Genevieve begins throwing some inappropriate questions her way, clearly trying to dig deeper and determine what Hadley's relationship with her mother is. And that grabs my unwelcome attention. There are much better ways, more subtle ways, to ascertain this information, but Genevieve is like a dog with a bone sometimes. I swear, she doesn't know when to call it quits.

Thank God Alastair does. I see him shifting and can tell the meeting is over before either of the women do. He stands up without warning and extends his hand towards Hadley. "Thank you, Miss Aldridge. We'll be in touch."

I watch her closely, noting that the abrupt dismissal by my cousin has thrown Hadley more than any of Genevieve's questions did. She gasps and sputters, and I have to tamp down the urge to… reassure her? Storm in there and offer to fund her company myself just so I can erase that sad, confused look of disappointment from her face?

Fucking hell. This woman is going to be trouble. That alone should be reason enough for me to stay far the fuck away.

But I don't.

I step into the hallway as I watch the three of them exit the adjacent room. My eyes are on Hadley as I watch her walk towards the elevator bank. She pushes the button, then glances back as she is waiting, her gaze catching mine for a moment, and I swear I watch a surprised flicker of what looks suspiciously like recognition flash across her features. Seconds later, her elevator arrives, and she steps inside, leaving me gawking like a fool in our 57th-floor lobby.

Alastair clears his throat next to me, and I swear I can *hear* Genevieve's eyes rolling. "We're funding her company," I say without preamble.

The side of Alastair's lip turns up, like he knew what my decision would be already. As expected, Genevieve starts to argue.

"You can't expect me to work with her. Have you forgotten what her mother did? That bitch almost ruined my career." I clench my jaw in an effort to stop myself from rolling my eyes at her melodrama. Even if she'd lost her role at AVC over the Rebel Media debacle, there is no way she wouldn't have found her place among Wall Street's elite.

"I don't expect you to have anything to do with her, Genevieve. This account is *mine*."

"Uhh..." Alastair is almost certainly about to say something reasonable and logical about how unusual it would be for me to be personally involved in one of our ventures, especially one as niche as this one. Which is why I deliberately ignore him.

"Joey," I snap my fingers at the new floppy-haired temp sitting outside my corner office, signaling I'd like him to join our conversation. "Cancel any remaining appointments, I'm going out for dinner."

"Actually, my name is Beau, Mr. Avenier." I have no patience for these antics.

"That's what I said. Joe." I stare him down, reminding him that *he* works for *me*.

"Okay. So like *out* out?" He frowns at the screen on the tablet he holds in front of him. "Cancel tonight's reservation at Cubed too? With Russell Artanza?"

"Jaxon..." Alastair cautions. He knows we need to be there tonight. "Russ was one of our biggest investors in the Catalyst fund last round, and you know we need him for the new Echelon fund. And as you probably recall, he wasn't initially thrilled with his investment, given that Catalyst's returns didn't fully materialize until very recently."

I don't need Alastair to remind me of the number of years the Catalyst fund probably stripped from my life. It was a risk, investing in convenient health food and related technology, but we're in the business of risk, because without it, there is no reward. I put together an impressive portfolio of compelling businesses at the forefront of the newly emerging industry. My father offered his advice, but largely just watched to see whether I had what it took.

The concept for that funding round was a tough sell, focusing on high-growth consumer and wellness ventures, but Russ saw the value in it. He was its largest investor by far. And the last month finally showed returns that exceeded our initial estimates, which means we finally have Russ's attention. His *positive* attention.

Alastair is right, we have to strike while the iron is hot if we want Russ Artanza to join the Echelon fund as a limited partner. I fucking hate that we need Russ's investment to close this new round, but Echelon is quickly becoming our largest funding round to date, venturing into new territory for AVC as we try to ride the AI tech boom in a much more intentional way. The Catalyst fund proved we can spot the companies shaping culture through technology. Echelon is taking that thesis upstream - now we're backing the platforms and systems that will power the next major breakthroughs.

Still, it's degrading having to suck up to Russ. The man may be one of the wealthiest investors in Manhattan, but he still reeks of last night's cigars and desperation. Regardless, the Echelon fund represents AVC's riskiest move yet, but the potential payoff is also by far our greatest.

"I'll still make Cubed. You too, Genevieve." I give her a pointed look.

"No chance. I got dragged to your late-night erotica club for *networking* last month, and I do not need to go again. Not tonight, not ever. Not my scene. You boys can handle it just fine."

Genevieve is being a real pain in my ass, but if I don't leave now, I might not catch Hadley Aldridge before she exits the building. I walk away, leaving Alastair to persuade Genevieve to be there tonight. Or not. I don't really care.

I smile to myself as I spot Hadley striding away from the concierge desk after returning her visitor's pass and signing out. My timing is fucking perfect. But then again, it almost always is.

She walks out the door and turns right. I follow, maintaining a careful distance.

CHAPTER 5

HADLEY

"One Manhattan, please," I order from the hotel lobby bar as I pull out my phone to text Jade. "Rail is fine, assuming it isn't terrible," I add, almost as an afterthought.

Given how that pitch just ended, I need a strong drink, and honestly, even if the rail liquor is terrible here, I don't actually care. The Manhattan worked out well for me the last time, the only other time I've ever ordered this cocktail, so I've now dubbed it my lucky drink. After that pitch, I can use all the luck I can get.

Hadley: That sucked.

Jade: That bad? Chances?

Hadley: Not good. They grilled me and I think I answered the questions well. I felt OK until they just abruptly ended the meeting.

Jade: Did they say when you might hear back?

I do love Jade's optimism. She's always been my biggest cheerleader. But she wasn't there. The two representatives from Avenier Venture Capital, Alastair Sterling and Genevieve Fontaine, were ruthless. Sterling's easy smile was disarming at first, especially next to his colleague's menacing glare. Damn, that woman was terrifying, and there was something about her blonde hair and dark brows that made her appear even more so. With Sterling, I quickly realized his initial charm covered a keen intellect that he effortlessly wielded like a weapon, asking only occasional, but very insightful questions. I felt like I had all the answers to everything they threw at me, but still none of them seemed good enough. There was hardly any affirmative head nodding or brow raising, no acknowledgement of anything really. Genevieve Fontaine remained disinterested in my product the entire time, asking occasional questions with no more concern than if she'd been inquiring about the weather.

Except when she asked me about my mother. She seemed to be more interested in my relationship with her than with Trueno.

The bartender places the Manhattan in front of me. "Room number?" he asks. Yeah, I'm not staying here. I could never afford to stay at the Four Seasons. I can't even afford a drink here, but I tell myself I deserve it. I just wandered into the first upscale place I knew I could grab a good drink and wallow in self-pity after that abysmal ending to the pitch. It also happens to be one of the nicest hotel lobby bars in all of downtown Manhattan - I suppose there are worse places to wallow.

"Oh, I'm not a guest. I'll just pay," I respond sheepishly, reaching for my wallet and cursing the fact that my one *rail* drink just cost me forty fucking dollars.

"I've got it," says a deep voice behind me. Normally, I might welcome the attention, particularly after last week at the Bar Room, but I'm just not in the headspace for that kind of distraction.

"I appreciate it, but you might as well move on. You're not going to get anywhere with me tonight," I say, turning around. I am in a mood; I am about to give this presumptuous prick a piece of my mind and –

Oh.

Shit.

The absolute smokeshow standing behind me tosses his head back and laughs. And God damnit, he is *beautiful*. I should really learn to look before I speak.

Fuck me.

The voice belongs to Jaxon Avenier, CEO of AVC.

Damn, I'd recognize that face anywhere. I forgot how attractive he is. Nope, that's a lie, I absolutely know how attractive he is - his face regularly graces the cover of magazines, staring at me while I wait in the Whole Foods checkout line. I could have sworn I saw him in AVC's lobby, but I was too unnerved from that abrupt dismissal to do the double take I'm giving him now. He's even more attractive up close and in person. Holy hell, he may actually be the most exquisite man I have *ever* seen.

"My, you are feisty, aren't you?" The corner of his mouth turns up in amusement, and I feel my face flush. Actually, I'm pretty sure my entire body flushes.

I have to swallow before replying.

"Yeah, well, you don't exactly get ahead in a male-dominated industry without learning how to stand up for yourself when you look like me," I bite back.

"Like what? Beautiful?"

I blink. I meant small, petite, average. My 5'3" frame doesn't exactly command attention. But seriously? Beautiful? Fuck this guy.

Actually, I wouldn't mind that. I'm not in the mood for his antics right now, but I'm not blind either.

Wait, what? No. My future, my *life*, is quite literally in his hands. Well, his company's hands.

"Never mind," I sigh.

"So you're going to let me buy you that drink now?" I mean, that's not the only thing I'd let this man do to me, but yeah, let's start with a drink.

Besides, at this point, I am way too embarrassed to protest, not that I even want to, so yeah, of course, I let him throw down some plastic and buy my overpriced cocktail. My *Manhattan*. Apparently they are my lucky drink - bringing me a very specific sort of luck.

He produces a fucking Amex Black Card. Of course he does. After our awkward exchange, the bartender just looks relieved and moves to process the payment.

Jaxon clears his throat, causing me to look directly at him.

He holds my gaze with those intense eyes he is so famous for. And when they lock onto mine, the air around us thickens, charged with an electric intensity that is impossible to ignore. I can't look away, and I don't want to. Every inch of me suddenly feels alive, and every inch of my body tingles; it is like his gaze alone is pulling me closer, drawing me into a storm I don't want to escape.

"I'm here on behalf of AVC. Hadley Aldridge, allow me to properly introduce myself. Jaxon Avenier, CEO." He extends his hand. I am clearly too distracted by this absolute adonis standing in front of me because it takes me more than a few beats to reciprocate, tentatively shaking his outstretched hand.

"You followed me?" I lift my chin defiantly, not that I feel confident, but I'm not going to let *him* see what he does to my nerves… or the rest of me, if my rapid pulse and that blooming ache between my legs are any indication.

"Follow you?" He smirks, and my knees nearly buckle, I cling to the edge of the bar for support. "I prefer to think of it as being where I need to be to make sure the right person gets the right opportunity." He winks. "As I said, I came here on behalf of AVC. I'd like to personally congratulate you, Ms. Aldridge. But if you don't want the opportunity…" his voice trails off as a smug smile tugs at the corner of his mouth.

Is he serious?

Jaxon Avenier is everything the tabloids say… and about ten *thousand* times more.

He's here to congratulate me? I blink, unable to hide my confusion. If he's implying what I think he is, I need to hear him say it. "Congratulate me for what, exactly?"

"For your brilliant pitch. If you're open to a conversation, Hadley, AVC would like to extend you funding." Surely I've just misheard him.

"But… your executives."

"What about them?"

"The meeting ended abruptly. They ended it mid-pitch, I hadn't even finished demonstrating Trueno's most compelling capabilities."

"And?" he gives me a sly grin. "They saw all they needed to see." He pauses, "And so did I." His eyes don't just pass over me. They stay. Like he *sees* me. Like he wants to see *more.*

I now fully appreciate everything the tabloids say because fuck me if I don't want to bare it all for him.

"I was watching you," he continues, "Not from the room obviously, but I saw what I needed to see. It's my firm, I have the final word." He doesn't offer more information. Which is probably a huge red flag, but I blink at his words, trying to compose a response. Are they giving us the funding?

"So, this means..." I hesitate to ask, the idea that this might be some cruel joke ringing alarm bells in my brain.

"We'd like to fund...Trune-"

"*Tru*-en-o," I enunciate the syllables. "It means thunder." Shit, I didn't mean to cut him off like that.

"Yeah, that name's going to have to change," he scoffs. The *audacity* of this man. Doesn't even bother learning how to pronounce the name of my company, yet he came here to tell me he's going to fund it?

I take a deep breath - it's just a name.

"At what valuation?" I ask.

His gaze settles on me. It's steady, assessing, and something in my legs goes soft, like they've forgotten their job is to hold me upright. I can't tell if it's nerves or the sudden, slightly disorienting awareness of how closely he's watching me.

Definitely both, I think, as he tilts his head ever so slightly, scrutinizing me further, and in his one subtle movement, I feel like he has stripped me bare.

His brows knit together as if he doesn't understand my question. "You asked for $25 million," he says in a tone that feels way too casual to be discussing that kind of figure. "We're prepared to lead the round with that number."

Holy shit.

"You'd cover the full raise?" That comes out breathier than I intended.

A slow smirk spreads across his face; it's not smug exactly, but certain. Like it belongs to a man used to outcomes bending his way. A part of me wants to punch that smug look off his face, but I'm simultaneously overcome by the overwhelming urge to jump into his arms and kiss him.

"Why are you so surprised? AVC is investing in exactly this kind of tech. Your pitch was very thorough," he picks up my Manhattan and hands it to me, his fingers brushing against mine as he does, the touch landing like a live wire against my skin. I shiver.

With a shaky hand, I lift the glass, meeting his eyes over the rim, as I take a respectable sip.

"Your colleagues..." I stutter.

Jaxon is smirking again - is this man always this much of an asshole? I mean, he looks like *that* and runs Avenier Venture Capital. Why would I expect anything else? "Alastair and Genevieve can be intimidating in a pitch." He chuckles to himself. "Well, Genevieve is absolutely terrifying all the time. But you must know that's how it is at these things?"

"So what, they don't let you in the room because you bring too much friendly charm?" I ask sarcastically. *Or maybe he's just too distracting because, well, fucking look at him.*

"Something like that," Jaxon takes the now-empty glass from my fingers. Shit, did I finish it already? "Shall we talk terms, Ms. Aldridge?" And the way he says my name causes my head to spin.

God, I am so fucked.

Jaxon places his hand gently on my lower back and guides me towards the exit, letting me know he's taking us next door to Slice, downtown's hottest new steakhouse. I've heard of it, I'm pretty sure everyone in Manhattan has heard of it. It's impossible to get a reservation there, so I'm not sure how he thinks we can just waltz right in, but I'm not about to correct him. I can't focus on anything but the intense heat flaring from the spot where his hand rests on my back.

"Welcome back, Mr. Avenier," the maitre d' greets us as we step inside the sexy, dimly lit downtown hotspot. "Your usual table?"

Jaxon just nods.

"Right this way." Okay, then. Glad I didn't say anything, or I'd surely be putting my foot in my mouth right about now.

It's not long before we're settled into a cozy corner booth upholstered in a deep turquoise velvet. It's luxe, that's for sure, and set back in a dimly lit alcove of the restaurant's main dining space. It feels both intimate and private, and I'd be lying if I said my heart wasn't racing at the thought of spending time alone with him in this secluded spot, away from all prying eyes other than, of course, his.

"So, does the CEO of AVC always spontaneously take new ventures out to dinner?" Maybe it's the Manhattan I just downed, but once again, I feel bold enough to just go for it.

Jaxon laughs as the waiter pours us each a glass of brut champagne from the bottle he ordered when we sat down.

"AVC wasn't your first choice for funding. Why?" Is he deliberately avoiding my question? Or is this question in response to my question? Either way, he's clearly done some research. On *me*.

"I honestly didn't expect AVC to be interested," I answer truthfully.

He looks at me like he's trying to see right through me, and I feel the hairs at the back of my neck stand on end in response to his scrutiny. It takes all my focus not to squirm as he eyes me carefully.

"You didn't run to Mommy for help securing funding? You actually want to work with AVC?" Ouch.

So apparently, he's done more than just a little research. Though I expected this, and prepared for this very question. Well, not exactly *this* question, I didn't expect to be asked it quite so directly.

I take a deep breath and look him in the eye. I need to choose my words carefully, the same way I did during my pitch. It takes everything in me to maintain focus, to ignore all the wicked thoughts I keep having about him. I take a deep, steadying breath before I respond. "I don't want to take money from just anyone, and after Bash suggested I consider AVC –" I pause, noticing the way his brow furrows in confusion at the mention of Bash.

"By Bash, I assume you mean Sebastian Devereaux," Jaxon clarifies.

"Yes." I attempt not to stammer over my next words. "After *Sebastian* suggested I consider AVC, I did my own research." I pause for effect, holding his gaze as my heart thrums beneath my ribs. "AVC's innovative investment portfolio aligns with my own values, so I see no reason why Trueno shouldn't be among those ventures. This isn't my *mommy's* company. It's mine."

"I tend to agree with your assessment." He brings his glass to his lips, eyes scrutinizing my reaction as he does.

It's true. Despite his ruthless reputation, a vast portfolio of AVC's ventures trend towards advancements in technology, particularly where innovation intersects with culture. I was genuinely surprised to learn this when I first looked into funding options. I hadn't even considered AVC, given the rumors about my mother's bad blood with the firm and its founder, Kenneth Avenier. That is, until Jade's boyfriend, Bash, encouraged me and made the initial introduction.

Jaxon asks some follow-up questions throughout the meal that seem tangentially related to my company, but I struggle to concentrate. My mind won't stop spinning, distracted by the way his voice wraps around me, low and smooth and oddly comforting. I answer him, but my words are tumbling out in a rush, all jumbled together, nothing coherent. At least it feels that way. It's like I can't form a cohesive response before I am distracted by the way his gaze lingers, how his lips twitch like he's holding something back - something I can't pinpoint, but I swear I can feel.

This electric tension. Does he feel it too?

I'm certain I'm rambling, but he is leaning forward like he is hanging onto every word that drops from my lips. He's staring so intently I almost feel self-conscious. His eyes never leave mine, and I can't stop fidgeting in my seat, crossing and uncrossing my legs beneath the table in an effort to alleviate the ache that pulses between them, trying not to think about how badly I want him to reach across the table and touch me.

The more we talk, the more the tension thickens. It's like we're both caught in it, pulled by an invisible thread that ties us together. And I wonder if this dinner, this celebration, is some kind of cruel game where he's the predator and I am his prey, already falling into his trap.

Maybe it's all the champagne, I didn't even realize we'd moved onto a second bottle, or maybe it's the white-hot gaze of the very sexy man sitting across from me, but suddenly, I feel like I am overheating. Placing my napkin next to my plate, I excuse myself to the ladies' room.

Once there, I check my phone for the first time tonight. Shit, how did I just spend four hours at dinner, and why does it feel like time just stopped? Forget that, how did I just spend four hours at dinner *with Jaxon Avenier?* Hard stop.

The curl in my hair is starting to loosen, but other than a few stray wisps, everything is still in place. My minimal make-up doesn't need touching up, though another round of lip gloss couldn't hurt. I give myself a nod in the mirror and a little pep talk. That's the fucking CEO of AVC out there, and *he* is paying rapt attention to *me*.

Because of my company.

Because of my tech.

Because of its potential.

That doesn't stop me from fantasizing about what it would be like to have that focused attention on me in other ways. *Hadley, stop. This is Jaxon Avenier you're fantasizing about,* I remind myself. I need to get him out of my head, right now. This is a dangerous game I cannot afford to play.

I give my head a shake before pulling back my shoulders and striding confidently out the bathroom door and directly to our table, where I find Jaxon settling our check as I slide back into the booth.

I pull my phone out and order myself an Uber. This night is over. It's almost 11:00 PM. This man is *funding* me. Well, his company is. This is a business dinner. God, this is so inappropriate. What the hell is wrong with me? I have one single, albeit very steamy, one-night stand, and now I want to jump the bones of every hot man who buys me a Manhattan? Granted, this man is doing a hell of a lot more than buying me a drink. And he looks like he could give the man from Wednesday night a run for his money. But no, I remind myself, this one is off limits.

Very off limits.

My Uber is three minutes away. I stand at the same time as Jaxon, and he leads me out of the restaurant. I feel his warm hand on the small of my back through the thin silk fabric of my camisole. Apparently, it found its way beneath the hem of my suit jacket, and I have to resist the urge to arch against his touch as my traitorous body reminds me *exactly* how much I want this.

"I'll have my driver bring you home. He can be here in ten," Jaxon is frowning at my phone.

"Thanks, but my Uber is a minute away." Thank God, I don't trust myself to stay here much longer. A cold wind rushes down the street, tangling my hair across my face. My Uber can't get here fast enough.

I notice Jaxon's jaw clench. At the idea of my getting an Uber? I almost roll my eyes, but his hand comes up then to brush the hair away. Fire races along my skin from the feel of his fingers as they linger on my cheek. I'm pretty sure I visibly shiver. And it's not from the chill in the air.

Jaxon's lips part as if he is about to say something. Then he leans in ever so slightly, and my pulse skitters. Is he about to kiss me? I look up at him and see a hunger in his eyes that mirrors my own.

Every instinct screams at me to run, but I cannot look away. My lips part ever so slightly, an involuntary response, and I watch his gaze fall to my mouth.

Mercifully, my phone buzzes in my hand notifying me that my Uber has arrived, immediately interrupting whatever the fuck that just was. His gaze is drawn from mine as a car pulls up beside us. I sway ever so slightly, off balance and dazed from the interaction. My ride arrived just in time because something tells me I almost made a serious mistake.

Or maybe I'd just imagined it.

"I'll see you again at AVC, Ms. Aldridge." He smiles, but there's something dangerous in it, something playful. My chest feels tight, my breath shallow, and I can't think of anything to say in response. Each thought for the right words feels like it's coming from somewhere far away. I blame the champagne, but still, I know I must look like a fool. At least I'm a fool with funding. "My assistant will be in touch."

We got the funding.

A slow smile spreads across my face as I settle into my Uber, reminding myself that I now have 25 million reasons to resist Jaxon fucking Avenier.

CHAPTER 6

JAXON

I watch Hadley's Uber pull away.

Fuck.

I shouldn't have touched her.

I don't know what the hell came over me, but if her car hadn't arrived at that moment, I'm not sure my renowned self-control would have been enough to keep me from kissing those perfect rosebud lips of hers right there on the middle of the fucking sidewalk.

My phone vibrates in my pocket. Again. I steel myself as I pull out my phone for the first time in hours, knowing there is undoubtedly an onslaught of angry messages demanding to know where I am.

Eleven text messages and two missed calls from Alastair. Several more from Trey. And another one from Kit. She really has been needier than usual since the stupid *Aria Thorne* column featured me the other day. That woman is becoming a thorn in my side. Frankly, both of them are.

Trey's last text actually asks if I'm okay, which honestly, is fair. I never ignore my phone for five minutes, let alone five fucking hours - and that includes when I'm sleeping.

But I didn't even think about my phone, or Alastair, or Russ fucking Artanza, or Cubed.

I send a quick text to Trey letting him know I am on my way. Thank God Cubed is on the Lower East Side, and I'm already downtown. My driver, Emilio, gets me there in barely ten minutes, and I bypass the line without issue. The show hasn't even started yet. I head straight for the table directly in front of the stage. It's the only table I ever reserve. They know me here, and they know what I expect.

"Jaxon! Jesus fucking Christ dude, where the hell have you been?" Okay, Alastair is understandably pissed, but he wouldn't normally be so aggressive. I want to remind him of his place, but I am fucking late. Russ can't know why, though. I don't want him to know I was with a woman. Though I wasn't with just any woman, I was at a business dinner. To that end, I also don't want him to know about Hadley Aldridge being the latest addition to AVC's roster. And I definitely don't want him anywhere near her soon-to-be-renamed tech company.

"I was at dinner… learning about a new investment opportunity." I offer, aware that Russ is likely listening.

Alastair seems to realize it too because his voice drops so it can barely be heard over the music pumping out of the speakers. The sound system is made to allow for close conversation, while still feeling immersive. "Aldridge?" The surprise in his voice is genuine. "Fuck, man. That was over five hours ago!" He searches my face, which I keep perfectly still and indifferent. "We will talk about this later. Right now, you need to get in there and fix this shit with Russ."

I raise my eyebrows at him. "You couldn't manage that on your own? Trey is here too." I'm being an asshole, I know. Russ responds to power, and the more power, the better. My showing up late is rude in his eyes. My showing up late without so much as a text message expressing my apologies, well, that's rude in anyone's eyes. To suggest it's Alastair's fault he didn't close the Echelon investment is a dick move, and I know it. He gives me a look that says he knows it too, and I don't push back.

"Russ. Enjoying another fantastic night at Cubed?" I take a seat next to him and signal the server - Bethany, the only one I will allow to serve us - to fix me a drink.

"You're late, Avenier." Russ's tone leaves no room for argument. He's pissed. And he's not wrong. He wanted to talk first, over drinks, before the real fun, the show, begins. Russ takes a healthy sip of his cognac as he stares me down. Is he trying to be intimidating? Because it is not working. I silently judge him, wondering who the hell sips cognac at a place like Cubed. "Alastair said you had some problems with a new account?"

I sigh. Hadley Aldridge is definitely a fucking *problem*. But not the kind he's thinking of. No, *he* is the real problem. I decide to ignore his probing question.

"You know, I still remember the night you said yes to Catalyst. You called it a test." I watch as he sips his cognac. "I'd say I've more than proven myself, wouldn't you?"

"It bought me a new building, I'll say that much," He raises his glass in a toast.

"And a new yacht, if the rumors are true." I hedge, carefully toeing the line of power and reverence.

"Rumors are their own kind of currency, Jaxon. You of all people should know that." I am not quite sure what he is implying, but I choose to ignore him for the time being.

"Catalyst proved that we both saw it before anyone, the IPO, followed by the recent acquisition - those weren't flukes, Russ. We read the room, we saw the direction things were heading and put capital there first."

Russell doesn't say anything, just nods, forcing me to keep talking, forcing me to make the ask he knows is coming. I remind myself why I'm here. I *have* proven myself.

Catalyst was initially pitched as a $150 million early-stage fund focused on a new, rapidly-growing consumer class of young, health-obsessed, and convenience-driven, individuals. The biggest investment within the fund went to a chain of farm-to-table salad shops that masqueraded as a popular restaurant, but functioned as a data operation. Every location acted as its own adaptive node, quietly tracking consumer preferences and reshaping its menu accordingly - cutting waste, optimizing spend, and collecting far more than just orders.

Most of the ventures we supported through that fund have failed to turn a profit, and Russ has not been shy about letting me know he was only taking a chance on me because of his relationship with my father. He also likes to remind me that he is not in the business of giving second chances.

It took some time, but that once-little chain of salad shops finally went public six months ago, and Catalyst's modest early payout turned into a significant windfall. Suddenly, the Catalyst fund, the very same one that critics were calling *too lifestyle, not enough innovation,* looked visionary, proving that betting on the fund was paying off for its investors. The numbers spoke first, and my reputation quickly followed.

Then, just a few short weeks ago, when news of another successful venture within Catalyst broke, it meant another surge in returns.

I remind Russ as much. And then I press further.

"Just think of what we could do through Echelon. I'm done focusing on feeding people, and I think you are too. Let's take this concept to the next level, together, focusing on feeding algorithms instead."

Russ smiles at me as he leans away. "Compelling, I'm

sure. But I'm not in the mood for such serious conversation at this hour of the night. Really, it's poor etiquette to discuss business at a place like this now that the performance is beginning. Besides, aren't we here for *pleasure?*"

He gestures at the act just starting on stage. Three women are *getting ready* for a night out. But instead of putting clothes *on*, they are taking each other's clothes *off*. I look over at Russ. He may be pissed at me for showing up late, but he's sure as hell enjoying the show.

Good.

Three women sit in front of a series of large mirrors, their hair wild and makeup glamorous. They're dressed in edgy outfits, leather jackets with studs, corsets, and dark lace, all wrapped in a mix of glam rock and biker chic. Russ fucking loves this shit, and so do I.

I could use a momentary distraction from Hadley Aldridge.

I refocus on the act playing out in front of us under the moody stage lighting. As the music kicks in, the three women move with calculated precision. With the first heavy strum of the electric guitar, slowly, they pull at their costumes in a choreographed routine that mimics the energy of the song, a hard rock cover of some classic rock shit that I can't quite place. But it's fantastic. It's an act of undressing without vulnerability, it's bold, and it's hot as hell. Yet despite these incredible women on stage, all I see is Hadley.

I've never been hung up on a woman, and I'm struggling to understand what exactly is happening to me right now.

I try to focus on the women in leather and lace. Their costumes continue coming off layer by tantalizing layer, but they're always in control, never rushed, and always in sync with the hard rock soundtrack.

And as my eyes trace the curve of their necks to the

swell of their breasts, I can't fucking help it; I am only picturing Hadley Aldridge on the stage, dressed like the ladies there, in nothing but a leather corset, lacy bottoms, and thigh-high stockings.

The energy of the music only drives my fantasy as I visualize Hadley in this provocative dance unfolding in front of me. I look over and see Trey and Alastair, both entranced, as each layer of clothing is discarded, though the objective is not for titillation, but rather an act of empowerment. I see it for exactly what it is; everyone in the crowd is captivated.

Some may not read much into these burlesque acts, but I sure fucking do. I've seen enough of them. And fuck if this one in particular doesn't embody everything I feel about Hadley Aldridge, that defiant little minx who's crawled into my mind and decided to make herself comfortable. That brilliant mind of hers shattering every expectation I had about those who carry the Aldridge name.

One thing is for sure: I want her. I want everything about her.

And I cannot have her.

The music shifts, and for one brief moment, it draws me out of Hadley's spell.

Then all of a sudden, the light turns off as the music simultaneously ends. The crowd goes wild. Including Russ, who sets down his cognac to clap excitedly like the tool that he is.

"Hell of a show, Avenier, but I'm disappointed in you." I frown in response, and he continues, "You know how important punctuality is to me; it's a sign of respect. And I don't take kindly to being disrespected."

I may have actually fucked this up. I know that this is Russ bluffing, but it isn't entirely an act. He's holding out solely for the sake of teaching me a lesson, and I'm almost certain no amount of haggling is going to sway him tonight. All because I lost sight of the bigger picture, so wrapped up in a woman.

Hadley. She has a name.

That brilliant woman - she's going to fucking ruin me if I'm not careful. And maybe I want her to.

I know I should regret it, but I feel absolutely no remorse. Instead, I find myself wishing I was still with her. I think back to the quiet heat in her gaze when presented with AVC's offer. I can't deny how satisfying it felt to give her everything she'd asked for. I could almost hear the gears turning in her head, realizing what I was handing her. I know my gut is right about this one. She's feisty and determined - she knows she's built something powerful. And just as importantly, so do I.

But as it stands, she is not here. Russ is. And I need to salvage this fucking Echelon deal. "You're right. This isn't the place to talk business." I raise my glass to him in a reconciliatory toast. "We should have done dinner, let's just enjoy the show. I hope you find it *pleasing*. The acts will only get more erotic as the night goes on, so perhaps it's best we forget about business and just enjoy tonight. "

"Happy to hear it, Avenier. This place is absolutely charming, and I'm thrilled you invited me," He says, raising his own glass in response to my peace-offering before turning to Trey. *Charming* is not a word I'd ever use to describe Cubed, but I know he enjoys this place. The man loves nothing more than a good show, the more outlandish, the better. "Though I'm not entirely ready to abandon our business conversation. Now, why don't you all tell me about this problematic account that kept our boy Jaxon here out so late?" His eyes sparkle with mischief.

Our boy? I raise my drink to my lips, taking a sip before I say something I'll end up regretting later. Trey offers the most basic information. "Some weather app, right, Lex? Uses AI with weather satellites or something."

Russ purses his lips in a discerning way. "How does it do that?" He inquires. Trey shrugs in response. "I'd be interested in what *other* applications this AI might have on some of our satellites. And I'm suddenly curious, is this new app going to be part of the Echelon fund?" Of fucking course he asks, Russ and his data mining.

"No." The word is out of my mouth before I even realize it. Fuck. The slow smile that crawls across Russ's face tells me I've shown my hand way too fucking soon.

"And why not? Didn't you just say that you were ready to, what was it you so eloquently said, *stop feeding people and feed the algorithm instead?*"

Alastair's eyes widen for a beat, then narrow as he glares at me. Trey has a small frown on his face as he looks between the three of us. Yeah, I'm going to fucking hear about this.

"I thought we weren't talking business tonight?" Alastair's shoulders slump, but what am I supposed to do? I signal for our waitress to come make him another drink. This conversation is over. Probably just as well, because the music fades as another act begins.

Twenty minutes later, I look over and see Alastair and Trey both smiling and talking happily with a group of women who clearly came in without table reservations, inviting them to join us in the VIP section. One of their classic moves.

There are now a pair of very lithe, very flexible acrobats on stage. The only thing they are *wearing* - if it can be called that- is the aerial silk suspended from the ceiling, and its placement on their bodies is both highly strategic and very seductive. The show is starting to heat up. Good.

Russ is busy with something on his phone. I know I should try again, but I honestly just want him to leave so I can give up on this whole night. Though he certainly won't be leaving while an act like *that* is unfolding before him. We're not closing his Echelon investment here, not tonight.

I do manage to lock in a dinner with Russ for next month before he leaves, we'll go to Opus. He fucking loves that lavish place. It oozes old school extravagance, which is the opposite of my taste, but this dinner isn't about me, it's about wooing Russ, and all that jacket-required, white tablecloth bullshit he enjoys.

Alastair confronts me as soon as Russ is gone.

"What the hell was that? We were supposed to secure the Echelon funding tonight." It seems my customary irritation has transferred to my usually cool and aloof cousin. Fucking great.

"Yeah, well, that wasn't happening. I'm not going to appear desperate. Relax. I have dinner scheduled with him next month." I try to soften my tone as much as I can. He narrows his gaze at me. I'll have to offer to take the dinner without him. Fine.

I'm not off the hook yet.

"And why were you being so cagey about the new Aldridge account? What happened to using her to our advantage? Suddenly she's off limits?" He leans closer, getting in my face as if he has something to prove. "This is *Echelon* we're talking about." My cousin's voice is gentle, as always, but there is a bite to it. He doesn't like how things panned out this evening. Neither do I. I do not want more schmoozing with Russ fucking Artanza on my calendar.

"I was discussing Hadley Aldridge's tech and initial contract terms with her."

"Oh yeah? And what did you learn?" He isn't going to let this go.

I'm quiet. What did I learn? I learned that she gently bites her lower lip while she's thinking of a response, and that it's fucking adorable. I learned that her eyes light up a brighter blue when she's talking about something she's passionate about. That her brain works faster than her mouth sometimes, her tongue darting out when she's trying to find the perfect word to describe her ideas. I learned that she is smarter than even she realizes, and she knows she's fucking smart. I am confident AVC struck gold with her and her company. And yet, I am filled with the urge to keep her all to myself.

But I can't say any of that. I look at Alastair, my jaw clenched.

"That's what I thought. Nothing. You want to inappropriately involve yourself with our newest venture? No fucking way, man. You are not going anywhere near that account."

"Fine, assign Trey to it." It's a feeble attempt to prove I'm unaffected by Hadley Aldridge. I know Alastair is right, and I know he's not going to let this one go. I trust my stepbrother with my life, and apparently, to protect Hadley and her company from Russ.

"Hmm?" Trey turns towards us at the sound of his name.

"Trey, you have a new account," Alastair tells him.

"Sorry ladies," Trey gives both women sitting with him a dazzling smile, removing his arms from around their shoulders as he flashes his dimple and turns to join the conversation I'm currently having with Alastair.

"New account? Does this have anything to do with why you were late, Jax?" His smile grows even wider.

I sigh. Am I that fucking obvious? "I'll fill you in tomorrow. Come by my office around 11:00."

"You got it." Trey glances back towards the girls still loitering at our table. I can tell he is assessing them, but he seems to lack his usual enthusiasm. He's been like this since last week.

"Jesus man, you've got to fuck that mystery woman out

of your system," Alastair says it before I can, but clearly he sees it too.

"Yeah. Maybe." Alastair raises a brow at Trey's resigned response. "Okay, yeah, I definitely do. But give me a break, it's 2:00 AM on Monday night, well technically early Tuesday morning, actually." Alastair shrugs, like that shouldn't be a deterrent. It wouldn't be for him. And the women are *right there.*

Which reminds me - I pull my phone out and see a message from Kit. My brow furrows as I purse my lips.

"Kit?" Trey asks, with more venom than I've ever heard him use in a single syllable.

"Yeah," I grimace. I don't even want to get laid tonight, which is unsettling.

"You're leaving us then to go see her." He doesn't even try to hide the disgust in his tone. This is why he doesn't run point with Genevieve and Alastair. The guy has absolutely no poker face. None.

"Not tonight," I say more to myself than anyone, giving Trey a quick shake of my head while I send Kit a message telling her the same.

"Wow." Alastair's eyes narrow. "Obviously, I am thrilled about this turn of events, but you still need to turn her down gently, Jax. The last thing we need is *Uncle* Russ to catch wind of it, especially when he's already pissed at you." My stomach churns at the way Alastair emphasizes the word *uncle,* echoing Kit's pet name for her godfather. I shudder. Russ, the fool that he is, has no idea what line of work his precious goddaughter is really in, or at least, I assume as much. If he does, he's never let on.

Alastair scrutinizes me, contemplating the situation. "I have mixed feelings about this Aldridge situation. On one hand... it's completely inappropriate." His expression is dead serious as he pauses for dramatic effect. "But on the other hand... she's not Kit."

I roll my eyes, I am not even dignifying that assessment with a response.

"I support whatever is happening here if it means you're dumping that demonic bitch. I don't even need to know the context." Trey is completely serious as he says it. "I promise to help make whatever *this is* work." Trey doesn't hate anyone, except, apparently, Kit.

It's settled then. Trey will manage Hadley's account. He can meet her engineers, attend every business meeting, and review every document. And report it all back to me. I'll have Joey arrange for her to meet Trey tomorrow morning after I've filled him in. 11:30 AM. That means I'll be seeing her again in less than ten hours.

I need to focus on the meeting tomorrow, on the plan for her account, but I know I'll just be watching those damn eyes of hers. Their color never the same, shifting from a blueish green to a golden gray depending on what she's saying. Tomorrow can't come soon enough. I need to see her again, to feel gravity shift when we're in the same room. I can't place it, but she has this pull, this energy that's impossible to ignore. Fuck, she still has it, and she's halfway across Manhattan for all I know.

My phone buzzes in my pocket, and I decline the call from Kit before texting Emilio for a ride home.

"You need a ride, or are you going to stay and play?" I ask Trey. Alastair has *gallantly* taken both of the women who'd been sitting with us to a recently vacated corner booth. Honestly, good for him. It wouldn't be the first time he ended up with more than one partner at the end of the night.

"Normally I'd stay, but you've just given me an important meeting to prepare for." He gives a last wistful look towards Alastair's booth, and my cousin gives Trey a nod in response, an understanding passing between them.

And they accuse *me* of being down bad. At least this

infatuation with Hadley is just that - a brief infatuation. She's a novelty is all, brains and beauty, the prospect of a fat payday. I'll be over it in a couple of days. Whereas Trey is apparently still hung up on a one-night stand from almost a week ago. We both make our way to the exit, where Emilio is already idling.

I ignore another text from Kit as I make my way into my building, Hadley's face still on my mind.

I'll take care of things myself when I get home. Alone.

Chapter 7

ACCORDING TO ARIA

NOT ALL THORNS SPILL BLOOD…

…SOME SPILL SECRETS.

WHERE VENTURE MEETS VOGUE

BY: ARIA THORNE

Welcome to the sharp edge of society, where beneath all the polished petals, the thorns never stop growing.

Last night at Cubed, Manhattan's elite erotica nightclub, billionaire playboy Jaxon Avenier made a not-so-surprise appearance. Dressed in tailored black and his usual swagger, Avenier arrived solo and, more intriguingly, left the same way - igniting whispers that maybe he has moved on from his year-long relationship with Collette (Kit) D'Vesle.

Though sources say her godfather, business tycoon Russell Artanza, was spotted at Avenier's table. This begs the question… is Mr. Avenier seeking permission to make his relationship with Kit a more permanent situation, or has the city's most notorious libertine finally found a new muse?

Because word around (down)town is that Jaxon Avenier was allegedly getting cozy at culinary hotspot Slice for an hours-long dinner with an anonymous woman - and it looked anything but professional.

However, the real story of last night wasn't the lack of a particular leggy brunette on Avenier's arm. Readers, it's time we shed a spotlight on the broody billionaire's very own cousin, Alastair Sterling.

Sterling was spotted deep in conversation - and even deeper in flirtation - with none other than Vera Norvelle, the runway-walking phenom with soul-piercing eyes and cheekbones so sharp that they could slice glass.

Did they arrive together? Sources say Norvelle was at the club with a group of friends for a birthday bash - but by 3:45 AM, she and Sterling were seen canoodling in a shadowed corner before slipping into an idling black SUV. Together.

Was it a coincidence? Or was it the first glimpse of Manhattan's most dangerous new duo?

The nights may be getting cooler this time of year, but the city's social season is just heating up.

Stay Sharp,
  Aria Thorne

CHAPTER 8

TREY

"Hey, Mr. Eskridge! Thank God you are here," Jaxon's assistant jumps up to greet me with far too much enthusiasm for my current state.

I was rudely awakened by my alarm after only three short hours of sleep. And when I got to Brawl & Order for our 7:00 AM workout, Lex wasn't there. Not that I expected him to be, he only shows up for our morning training sessions about half the time after a late night. I'm surprised I made it, though I'm glad I did. A workout always helps clear my head a little, and it probably helped sweat out the hangover too.

I smile at the man. He's been here two weeks, currently holding this quarter's record for the longest a temp has lasted as Jaxon's assistant. Maybe this one will actually stick. He seems pretty unflappable.

"Beau, right?" I am definitely right because the man *beams*. This is why I make a point to remember people's names. "Is Jaxon in there?"

"Yes, go, go, he is... especially Jaxon-y today." I chuckle at Beau's comment. He's lucky he didn't have to endure teenage Jaxon. "Can I get you a coffee? Espresso? Anything at all?"

"A dry cappuccino, more foam, less milk. One lump of raw brown sugar. Thanks." I smile appreciatively, and he nods in affirmation before rising from his desk chair. "Oh, and could you add an extra shot of espresso?"

"Late night?" Beau's eyes sparkle with curiosity.

"Something like that." Beau is still watching me expectantly. Like I have something in my possession that he's hoping I'll share.

"What's she like?" He finally caves, whispering as he leans across his desk.

"Who?" I legitimately have no idea who he's talking about.

"Vera Norvelle." He says her name in an exaggerated whisper, even though there is nobody else around.

"The supermodel?" I'm not sure why he thinks I know her.

"Weren't you with Alastair last night?" He is buzzing in a way that has me wondering how much caffeine he's already consumed this morning.

"Yeah…" His brow furrows at my response. Apparently, I'm not giving him what he's looking for.

"Have you not seen this morning's *According to Aria?* Alastair went home with her!" Beau overly enunciates the last sentence. "And since you were with him, presumably you met her too? Mr. Sterling is not in yet, which, given what I read in the column, is not surprising." He wiggles his eyebrows suggestively.

"Oh." No, I had not read about that yet, though now I am curious. When I left Lex, he was wedged between the two women he'd invited to our table. "I went home earlier than he did. I guess I'll have to ask him about that later." And I *definitely* plan to. But first, I need to get this meeting over with.

Finally accepting that I have no more information to offer him, Beau excuses himself to make my cappuccino and gestures towards Jaxon's office.

I push open the door without knocking. Jaxon is standing in his classic broody I'm-a-billionaire pose, looking out his floor-to-ceiling window at the NYC skyline. Hands on his hips, shirt sleeves rolled up. His black vest and pants are perfectly tailored to his powerful frame, and even I have to admit, he looks pretty damn sexy, in an imposing sort of way.

And a three-piece suit? I can't remember the last time I saw Jaxon wearing one of those. Shit, he really must be trying to impress this Hadley woman if he's pulling out his black custom Zegna. *With* the vest.

I know he hears me enter, but Jaxon doesn't turn around or otherwise acknowledge my presence. Fine. "Are you brooding? Scheming? Or looking at your reflection?" I can feel the restless energy radiating off of him.

"This new account. I need you to prioritize it." He's strictly business this morning and remains as serious as a heart attack.

I wait for him to elaborate, but he doesn't say more. "Sure," I respond as I move to join him at the window, taking in the view, and letting him know the CEO act doesn't work on me. "Care to share more, or is this one of those meetings that could have been an email?" I barely got three hours of sleep, which is fine, but not if he's going to give me the silent treatment. I can't successfully manage this account if he gives me nothing to go on.

"The thing about this account. It's Hadley Aldridge." Not new information.

I nod. "Elizabeth Aldridge's daughter." I know this. Jaxon knows I know this. It would make this account dicey to begin with, but I know there's more to it than that. So much more. Enough to completely rattle Jaxon Avenier.

I've never seen him like this, certainly not over a woman. I want him to admit it though. I want to hear him say it, but I'll have to draw it out of him.

"Okay, are we suspicious? What's the catch?" I ask tentatively.

Jaxon sighs, and I watch his jaw tick.

A slow smile spreads across my face. "Wait. Last night you were late. Were you really at dinner for over four hours? How involved are you?" My tone is soft, gentle.

He shakes his head, finally turning away from the window and striding over to his desk. I stay where I am but watch him discerningly, arms folded across my chest.

"Too involved. But not *that* involved." I hear the hesitation, the unspoken *yet*. "Look. Genevieve is being a pain in my ass; she wants revenge on Elizabeth through her daughter. There's a lot at stake here for AVC - and for me personally - in how this account is handled."

He's not wrong. On the heels of our recent success with the Catalyst fund, there are a lot of eyes on him. Many would love nothing more than to watch him fall. Logically, his argument is sound, but I know him well enough to know there is more to it than that. He sighs, and I swear there is *longing* in his expression. I'm reading between the lines here, but I think Lex is right. There is no fucking way Jaxon should be allowed anywhere near this account.

"Her tech is promising," he continues. "But she hasn't even begun to realize the impact it could have." He eyes me carefully to ensure he has my undivided attention. "Or the money we could make," Jaxon pauses, "though we do not need to be so transparent with her yet about our intentions there." He offers me a stern look. *Keep all intentions for how we plan to utilize her tech confidential.* Got it. "I want regular status reports on this one. I want you to meet her team. Attend meetings with her. Look over her docs. And everything that goes on - you let me know about it." Interesting. He has never been *this* invested in an account before. Ever.

"Okay, there are *status reports*, and then there's whatever this is you're asking me to do. Which sounds a hell of a lot more detailed than *status reports*," I give him a concerned frown. "Jax. What is this really about?"

Jaxon looks me dead in the eye, and his expression is almost pleading. His lips are drawn into a thin line. I feel my eyebrows shoot up; I know the shock must be plain on my face. But he still won't *say* it. "So what? You're hot for Elizabeth Aldridge's daughter? Go for it, then. You're Jaxon fucking Avenier. If Genevieve wants to get back at the Aldridges, that'll do it." I scoff below my breath, "What do you need me for?"

He breaks eye contact and turns away from me.

Shit, this is worse than I thought.

He looks out the window again, absently running a hand through his hair. "You don't understand. Hadley, the founder, she's… she's actually brilliant. She will go far. Her product, I mean her application of the tech, is completely naive, but it's fucking incredible the way her mind works." I hang onto every word, the wistful way he talks about her. This isn't Jaxon Avenier, billionaire CEO of AVC. This is simply Jaxon Avenier, my stepbrother. And he is falling. Hard. For a woman he's met once.

"Okay," I say gently. "I see, you actually admire her." Jaxon grimaces at my words, as if *admire* somehow isn't deferential enough. I get it though. He wants her, in more ways than one. "I'll handle the account with the care you desire." I *will* protect this account, and by extension, her. And I'll keep her *available*, for when Jaxon is ready to admit how much he clearly wants her.

"I know you will." There's a certain finality to his tone, one that leaves no room for argument.

"So, when do I get to meet this astonishing woman?" I'm more than a little intrigued now. Because I have *never* seen Jaxon hung up on a woman before, and I can't help but wonder what makes her so special.

Jaxon looks up. "Now." He says as Beau knocks on his door.

"I have your cappuccino, Mr. Eskridge. And uh, Hadley Aldridge is here?" Beau places a ceramic cup and saucer on the desk in front of me, and I give him a half-smile, nodding in thanks.

"That will be all, Joe. Send her in." *Is he so caught up in this Hadley woman that he forgot his own assistant's name?* I watch him as he waits for Beau to send Hadley in. Jaxon is staring intently at the door. His jaw clenched. He's nervous. About a woman. Never thought I'd see the day.

I hear the door open again and his jaw ticks at the sound of her heels clicking. I watch his gaze drink her in the moment she enters, roaming up and down in a blink, like he is taking a mental snapshot. His face barely moves, but I see it. The man is bewitched.

I turn my head towards Hadley Aldridge to get my first look at the woman of the hour. Her pace slows as she walks in, her eyes immediately locking with Jaxon's, widening slightly. I watch as her lips part, hear her breath catch at the sight of him.

Her eyes.

Her lips.

My heart stops beating beneath my ribcage, and my chest tightens as if a vice has clamped down, squeezing the air out of my lungs, each breath suddenly a struggle.

No.

I stand there frozen, a prisoner of the moment as I watch them both. The worst part isn't even the shock of seeing her. No, it's the feeling of my heart sinking into the pit of my stomach. I see the way she looks at him; it's the way she is just so effortlessly *his*.

And though the world suddenly feels much, much smaller, the space between us now feels impossibly wide. *I never got her name. I never got her number.* Every inch of me is trapped beneath the pressure of a thousand unspoken words, a thousand silent regrets.

Their gazes are still fixated on each other. She is so clearly just as captivated by Jaxon as he is by her. They don't even seem to realize I'm here.

God, I wish I were anywhere *but* here.

All my dreams from the last five days have come true, except it turns out I'm now living in a fucking *nightmare*. The woman who has had me drowning in a sea of endless fantasies is the very same woman my *stepbrother* is already falling for. The woman AVC is funding. The woman I just promised I would keep safe, keep tabs on, keep under my watchful eye. For Jaxon. So that *he* can have her.

"Hadley," I test it out on my lips. She turns at the sound of her name, a small frown marring her brow. Did she think she was alone with Jaxon? Or did she recognize my voice?

Hadley stops with a gasp. Her eyes widen further, like a deer caught in headlights, and when her green-gray eyes meet mine, it feels like the ground beneath me is caving in.

And that is the moment that I decide Jaxon absolutely cannot know. I school my face, hoping not a trace of recognition shows in my eyes as I move my lips into my signature disarming smile.

"Hadley Aldridge," I say her name again, moving forward to stand in front of her. I swallow as I extend my hand to shake hers. "Trey Eskridge. Pleasure to meet you." I watch her glance briefly back to Jaxon before reaching out tentatively.

My grip almost falters as her fingers meet mine. Her

palms are warm and soft, her handshake firm. I can't help but remember how those slender fingers trembled as she undressed me, on my bed, not one week ago. I can feel my pulse quicken as I try to keep my face void of emotion or any sign of familiarity.

I don't have a convincing poker face at the best of times, and the way she looks back at me threatens to crumble my self-assured façade. I can feel my cheeks flush as I wonder, *is she remembering too?*

We appear to be on the same page though. At least when it comes to not wanting to reveal to Jaxon that we know each other already. Intimately.

"Trey Eskridge," she nods.

God, that voice. Again, I'm taken back to last Wednesday. I swallow, struggling to maintain composure.

I can't speak. My mind is racing, but my mouth won't move. The sound of my name rolling off her tongue hangs in the air like a cruel joke. An ugly, jealous knot rises in my throat, twisting tighter as I force it down, force myself to breathe, force myself not to let Jaxon see. He *can't* see.

"Trey will be managing your account, Hadley," Jaxon's voice infiltrates my senses, loosening the haze of my shock. She blinks and releases my hand, which I realize I still have gripped in mine. I drop my hand quickly to my side, flexing it against the urge to make a fist at the loss of her touch.

Instead I stand there, still as stone, watching my step-brother gaze at her like he's seeing the sunrise for the first time.

CHAPTER 9

HADLEY

"Trey will be managing your account, Hadley." I hear Jaxon, but I still cannot process what he is saying. I remain temporarily paralyzed, my eyes locked onto the very tall, very handsome, very *familiar* blue-eyed man standing directly in front of me.

"Hmm?" It comes out sounding strangled, but God knows I can't possibly manage actual *words* right now. I try to at least *appear* calm and unaffected even though, internally, I am very much freaking the fuck out.

There. In front of me. Having just released my hand, is the man from the Bar Room. William Eskridge III. Apparently he goes by *Trey*.

The man I shamelessly threw myself at - though it was definitely a mutual kind of interest if you ask me. The man who took me home and did *unspeakable* things to me. *Reckless* things. Amazing things. The man who said he would worship me, and then absolutely did. The one who made me feel like I was the center of his world, his only interest bringing me pleasure. The man I was never supposed to see again.

Yeah, *that* man.

Is right here.

Handling my fucking account.

This cannot be happening.

And Jaxon Avenier is introducing us, as if he has no idea we've – *shit*. Right, he doesn't have any idea. Why would he? How could he?

Oh God.

He cannot find out. He absolutely *cannot* know.

I silently will Trey not to say anything. Not to acknowledge that he recognizes me. Not to make this awkward situation any more painful than it already is.

Fuck me.

Nope, he already did that.

Trey, to be clear, not Jaxon.

Jaxon…

"Hadley?" Jaxon's deep voice cuts through my spiraling thoughts as my gaze shifts uneasily between the two men.

"Sorry," I offer Jaxon a tight smile, "I don't know why I assumed I'd be working directly with you." Although, who am I kidding, that's probably just as *reckless*. Why the hell would the CEO of the company be handling my account directly? What was I thinking?

Jaxon looks almost amused, his lips curving ever so slightly. God, I must sound naive. "Trey is the best business manager at the firm. Statistically, the accounts he manages have seen the most success. You will be his top priority, which means daily interactions. He'll attend all meetings and events with you." His tone is assertive; meanwhile, I feel like I might hyperventilate. I'll be seeing *Trey Eskridge* every fucking day?

"Every meeting and event?" I barely choke out the words. I don't risk looking at Trey, instead keeping my gaze locked firmly on Jaxon's. I shouldn't worry about hurting Trey, but dammit, there is a part of me that feels a tiny bit guilty for being so rude about spending so much time with a man I've *allegedly* only just met mere minutes ago.

"Yes." Jaxon moves closer, leaning into my space. My nails bite into my palms as the low pitch of his voice sends a shiver down my spine. It takes everything in me not to visibly tremble. "Trey is overseeing *my* investment. AVC's investment. You managed on your own for years, until you found yourself in need of funding, isn't that right? And I can't manage your account myself. Trey can, he has the time, the knowledge and the resources. You'll get used to him. Soon you'll probably wonder how you ever *managed* without him."

If only he knew just how much innuendo was buried in those words.

I force myself to look directly at Trey, and I am reminded how soulful his eyes are. I take a deep breath. "It's lovely to meet you, Trey." I try not to blush as his name, *Trey,* rolls off my tongue. "I look forward to working with you."

He offers me a dazzling smile in response, but there's an uncertainty there, hiding behind his charm. I can sense it.

"Now that we've settled that, let's go over some basic logistics, then we will have Joe set up some meetings for you and Trey." He pauses, glaring at his closed office door, and it looks like he is debating whether to yell for Joe - whoever that is - or go open it himself. Instead, he picks up his phone and hits a few buttons, presumably dialing Joe's extension.

"Joe," he says into the receiver, "I need you to coordinate some meetings for Hadley Aldridge's account, and I need you to join this meeting and take notes." His tone is commanding, and while it shouldn't be, just the sound of his voice is a turn-on. Suddenly, I'm wondering what it would be like if he were commanding me in the bedroom rather than the boardroom.

God, I'm grateful Jaxon wasn't in my pitch meeting, because apparently I cannot control my own thoughts around this man, let alone form a coherent sentence.

As we stand before him, watching him converse with Joe, I finally allow my eyes to drink up every bit of Jaxon Avenier in his element. He is easily the most captivating man I have ever seen. And very, *very* off-limits, I remind myself.

I watch his mouth move as he talks. His jawline could cut glass, and it clenches, ever so slightly, in response to whatever Joe on the other end of the line just said. Every sharp line of his face looks as though it's been carved from stone, sculpted to perfection. I find myself staring at his mouth. There's something about it, the way the corner of his mouth turns up in a subtle smirk as he hangs up the phone that only makes him hotter. Scorching hot. Dangerously hot. Gets-you-into-trouble-and-you-like-it kind of hot.

I can't help the way my eyes fall to his arms. He looks like he spends every morning bench pressing steel I-beams or something equally absurd. His broad shoulders stand out in his perfectly-tailored black dress shirt, as if every bulge in his bicep was measured explicitly for the creation of this shirt. And you know what? It probably was. The man just exudes confidence. And that vest, the way he so effortlessly carries it on his frame, makes me think about three-piece suits in a whole new way because, *damn.* There's something about the way the tone on tone of the black vest with his black, obviously custom, dress shirt just works so damn well. It's a little edgy, and it's sexy as hell.

And it is exactly what I should not be focusing on.

I shouldn't be thinking about him this way. I mean, I have *literally* 25 million reasons not to, and yet, here I am.

Every time he catches my gaze, that pull, the one I keep trying to pretend is not there, tugs harder. It's inappropriate.

It's *reckless*.

I am a lot of things, but reckless isn't one of them.

Until last week.

I was reckless that night. Intentionally. And look where that got me.

"Agreed." Trey's smile is genuine and so disarming. Shit, what was Jaxon just saying? I completely spaced. "I'll need to meet your team, Hadley. Let's start by scheduling a meeting with key members of your senior leadership team."

He is strictly business. So matter of fact. His expression betrays not even a flicker of recognition. Is it possible that *he* doesn't remember *me?* Maybe, and that's likely for the best. He probably brings home a new woman every night. A man who looks like that and knows how to utilize his wicked tongue for a hell of a lot more than conversation? More likely than not, he doesn't remember me.

You know what, Trey? I think to myself, *maybe it's better if you don't.* It'll make things cleaner. Easier.

Logic, however, does not ease the pang of disappointment that I feel for being so… forgettable. I give myself a mental shake; this whole meeting is giving me whiplash, but if there's one thing that can ground me, it's focusing on my work with Trueno.

"Of course," I smile back. "We're a relatively small operation right now, but we're proud of what we've accomplished so far."

That's right, Mr. Eskridge, two can play this game. I'll just act like I'm not affected by our *history* at all. It was just one night. One *incredible* night, but just one night. I can go back to trying to forget it ever happened.

Because, if I'm really being honest with myself, what I

felt with Trey was real - electric, unforgettable, *incredible.* But standing this close to Jaxon makes whatever I had with Trey feel like static before a storm. And Jaxon Avenier is that storm. A dangerous storm, not waiting on the horizon but already breaking overhead. And, I'm realizing, there's no escaping it.

"I'd like you to meet with everyone Hadley considers senior leadership to start, then you can work out what makes the most sense moving forward." Jaxon addresses Trey. "You'll need to work on a roadmap for key deliverables, set up regular meetings with Hadley and her team, and develop a reporting matrix. I'd like you to get a stronger understanding of her product and its capabilities." I'm glad I met with the team to assign all these C-suite titles before going out to secure funding. We barely have the staff to warrant it, but this is exactly why I decided we needed to make our roles more official on paper.

"Understood," Trey responds, sounding deferential, but somewhat defeated.

"I'm trusting you to ensure this remains a sound investment, Trey. You're the only one I trust with this account," he deadpans. Is this something he says in front of all new ventures to make them feel important? Because if so, it's definitely working.

"Hadley," he turns to me then, and the moment his eyes meet mine again, my thoughts scatter, and my breath catches.

"You're in excellent hands with Trey," he says. Yeah, no shit, if only he knew how *excellent* this man's hands really are.

I swear Trey flinches as Jaxon proudly claps him on the back. There's a weird energy passing between them, but I cannot put my finger on what it is. Maybe I'm just imagining things in my state of hyper awareness and excruciating discomfort.

This meeting cannot end fast enough.

A knock on the door has all our heads swiveling towards the sound.

"Come in, Joe," Jaxon commands. *Command.* That's what it is; even when he's offering just a simple response, he *sounds* commanding. And it's sexy as hell.

"You wanted me to take notes?" I am all out of sorts today. I swear I thought the man's name was Beau. *Joe,* I make a mental note, correcting my mistake.

"I did five minutes ago," Jaxon snaps at his admin, though Beau - *Joe?,* seems utterly unaffected. "I'd like you to work with Trey to sync up our calendars."

"Yes, Sir," Joe says with military precision.

"Trey, stay." Jaxon asserts. "There are a few things I'd like to discuss with you." I watch a look of understanding pass between them before Trey nods. "Joe, please see Ms. Aldridge out." Jaxon extends his hand to me, offering a curt goodbye.

His grip is firm and certain, and the second our hands meet, it's like an electric current arcs through my entire body. My heart skips a beat, maybe two, and for a split second, the room feels charged. I can't tell if it's the static that's common in the air this time of year or the electricity sparking between us, but I feel it all the way to my toes and fight their urge to curl.

"Welcome to AVC, Hadley." Jaxon smiles at me, but it reads as more of a smirk, the corner of his mouth turning up only slightly. Whatever it is, I offer back a thin-lipped smile, attempting to hold his gaze as my traitorous body reacts in a thousand different ways.

And it's the way his deep brown eyes hold mine - so dark I feel like I could drown in their cavernous depths - that nearly steals my breath. It's like he's peeling me open with just a look, and suddenly I feel naked and exposed.

Frankly, I wouldn't mind being naked with him.

I need to get out of here before I do something stupid like allow him to ruin more than just my composure.

"Thank you," I hate how shaky my voice sounds. Jaxon's mouth twitches ever so slightly in response, and as my eyes inadvertently fall to his mouth, I once again find myself thinking about what it would feel like to kiss him.

"If you'll come with me, Ms. Aldridge," Joe's voice mercifully cuts through the growing tension, drawing me away from my own dangerous thoughts.

"Of course." I move to follow him, eager to extract myself from this situation. "I'm grateful to be working with AVC," I say to both of the executives, doing my best to avoid looking either of them in the eyes on my way out.

I can feel Trey watching me, like he's waiting for me to look at him. But I can't, not with *Jaxon* right there. Jaxon's mere presence is exhilarating.

Then those sable eyes meet mine. The same ones that have stared at me so many times from the cover of various glossy magazines - only in person, their power is undeniable. It's sharper. Harder to escape. My breath catches beneath the intensity of Jaxon's gaze. He only holds it for a second, but it's enough; I almost don't know how to leave the room, it feels like the air's been cut off, but I'm not even sure I want to breathe again.

"Likewise, Ms. Aldridge," he smirks, and suddenly the room is spinning. "Joe will set up your next meeting with Trey on your way out. He has access to all of our calendars."

"Okay, great." I manage a pathetic response. Really? *Okay, great?* God, I need to leave this office before I say something truly idiotic like *sorry I'm just in shock because I had a one-night stand less than a week ago with the guy you just assigned to my account and I never thought I'd see him again, but surprise! Here he is.*

I'm in way over my head, but I'm not about to let any of them see it.

I follow Joe into the hallway and watch him shut the door to Jaxon's office behind him.

"Are you okay?" If even he can sense my discomfort, Trey and Jaxon *definitely* could.

"Fine," I offer a clipped response.

"No offense, but you don't look fine. I've literally seen corpses look more okay than you do right now. And I mean that with all sincerity, my uncle Buck was a very talented mortician." My first inclination is to slap him, but his tone is so genuine, and his eyes carry so much kindness that I think he really is just legitimately concerned about leaving me without at least trying to help. And let's be honest, currently, no, I am *not* okay.

"Where's the ladies' room?" As kind as he may be, I just need a minute alone to compose myself.

"Right this way," he gestures for me to follow and leads me through a maze of hallways and modern glass conference rooms until we stop in front of the women's restroom.

I push open the door and to my absolute horror, Joe follows me inside.

"Excuse me?" I turn and face him.

"Yes?"

"This is the ladies' room," I stare at him.

"I know, but nobody ever comes into this one," he smiles conspiratorially at me. "I just wanted to make sure you're okay. Mr. Avenier can be really intimidating. And honestly, he's kind of a dick."

Oh.

Oh.

He thinks I'm upset, *flustered*, because Jaxon was a jerk? This, yes, this I can work with.

"Yeah, but I'll be okay," I reassure him.

"Yes you will. He's an asshole, but whatever, it's not like he's a murderer or anything."

I snort a little at that.

"I'm sorry," I say, suddenly realizing I've been meaning to apologize to Joe for calling him by the wrong name.

"For what?" he asks.

"I'm sorry that I've been calling you Beau. I swear, I thought that was what was written in your auto signature, but I must have misremembered, because when we met earlier it's also what I thought I heard you say."

He lights up like a Christmas tree, beaming. "Oh, no, that *is* my name!"

"It's not Joe?" I'm now really confused.

"No, Mr. Avenier just can't keep it straight." Beau, *not* Joe, is much more understanding about it than I would be. "He's a busy man, goes through a lot of temps from our agency, from what I understand. Mr. Eskridge told me that I've lasted longer than anyone, and I've only been here a couple of weeks!" He seems oddly delighted by this.

"And you haven't corrected him? Mr. Avenier, that is, about your name?"

"Oh, I tried in the beginning. But he's set on calling me Joe, can't be bothered to get it right. I'm not even sure he hears me half the time." Well, if I were looking for more reasons, besides the 25 million I already have, to stay far, far away from Jaxon Avenier, this is a good start. That level of arrogance is a massive turn-off.

"What an asshole," the words escape me before I even realize I've thought them out loud. *Shit.* Instinctively, I clap a hand over my mouth, but to my immense relief, Beau only smiles. "What I mean is, that isn't a very kind way to treat you. Especially when it seems you're really on top of everything. He's lucky to have you, Beau. But I have to ask, why do you bother staying?"

He laughs, more like chuckles to himself, before responding. "Well, for starters, I need the paycheck. My last off-Broadway contract ended a couple of months ago and, well, it's not exactly easy to find the next gig. It's a cutthroat world and I've got to pay the bills, you know?" I can totally relate to that, as someone who is barely scraping by, living out of my best friend's guest room. Thankfully, she and her partner, Bash, have been really accommodating, but still. I'm a grown-ass woman, I should at least be able to pay my own rent.

"I see, but surely your agency can place you somewhere else where you're treated better?"

He laughs again, this time more heartily. The man seems genuinely amused, totally unflappable.

"Ok, real talk," and now the twinkle in his eyes feels almost conspiratorial. "Have you *seen* the men who work here? Holy shit, Hadley." He fans himself.

"Seriously?" I try to sound nonplussed, but I can't disagree with him.

"Oh, *come on!*" He sounds incredulous. "You cannot possibly tell me you haven't noticed that the men you've been meeting with here look like, well, *that!*" I've been trying to remain professional, but he does have a point.

"I mean, sure, but that's no reason to let them treat you like you're anything less than. The least they can do is learn your name."

"Oh, Mr. Eskridge knows my name." He smiles and I swear his cheeks flush. "Swoon. Mr. Baby Blues is just as sweet as he looks." He gives me a knowing look, and I feel my cheeks heat. I am treading in hot water here, I cannot imagine what would happen if Beau found out about that night. If he found out that I know exactly how *sweet* Mr. Eskridge tastes too.

Fortunately, he doesn't seem to notice as he continues rambling. "And oh my God, have you *seen* Mr. Sterling?

He's just as hot as his cousin, Mr. Avenier, but not nearly as terrifying."

Cousins? I knew AVC was supposedly a family business, but I thought that just meant it had been passed down from father to son.

"Oh, I didn't realize they were related." I feel like this is something I should have known.

"Are you blind? They could practically be twins!" Twins is a bit of a stretch, but now that he mentions it, yeah, I guess I can see the similarities between Alastair Sterling and his cousin - same warm, golden-brown skin, the defined, angular jawline, and that dark, impossibly perfect hair, though Alastair's is longer, more wavy. Alastair's eyes are several shades lighter, too, and he's shorter than Jaxon - but not by much. I didn't really pay attention at first, probably because I was so fucking nervous during my pitch, and whatever intense chemistry I feel with Jaxon just doesn't exist with Alastair. Or Trey, if I'm really being honest with myself. Not that it matters, all three of them are very, *very* off limits.

"I guess so," I offer, wondering how I ended up talking about how attractive the senior leadership team is at AVC. In the *women's* bathroom. With Jaxon Avenier's very male, very unprofessional, but very friendly executive assistant.

"You guess so? Ok, so tall, dark, and devastatingly handsome is not your type. Got it. Then *surely* you noticed Mr. Eskridge today. Hello, gorgeous!"

I sure as shit noticed *Mr. Eskridge*. The problem is, I noticed him *last Wednesday*. His deep, blue eyes, his perfect smile, complete with that dimple that forms in his cheek.

"So I see you *do* have a type. Daydreaming about the new lead for your account? Good thing for you, you'll get to spend *plenty* of time with him." He wiggles his eyebrows suggestively.

"What? No!" But apparently nothing gets past Beau,

and judging by the way his eyes widen and sparkle mischievously, I know he can see how affected I am. Great, this is *not* how I wanted this morning to go.

"You dodged a bullet there, by the way. Rumor has it, Mr. Avenier was trying to involve himself with your account. Working directly with him would be terrifying. Don't worry, his brother is easily the nicest guy in the whole office." And he leans in closer to me, as if he's about to tell me some secret. "I call him 'Sunshine' - not to his face, obviously, but when I talk about him with my partner."

Brothers? What exactly am I missing?

"Brothers?" To my absolute horror, the word comes out as a squeak, but I need clarification because I have yet to meet a third person who looks like they come from that insane Avenier gene pool.

"Mr. Eskridge," Ridoc explains. "He and Mr. Avenier are stepbrothers. So not *technically* related or whatever but yeah. Their parents got married when they were teenagers. It's amazing how much you can learn about people just from listening ..."

I don't hear the rest of what he says, bracing myself on the countertop as the floor beneath me seems to vanish. The moment the words register, realization hits me with a crushing blow. This is worse than I thought, and the weight of the truth sends me into a dizzying freefall.

"I know, I know, it's a lot to process, but I promise once you've gotten used to everyone, you'll find it easier to keep track of everything," he smiles. "I swear though, you've got the *best* of them on your account." And he crosses his hand over his chest in a gesture I don't think I've seen since junior high school.

"Good to know." I hope I don't sound as hopeless as I feel. *Brothers.*

"Anyway, too bad for all of them, I'm taken." He

flashes me a charming smile. "Though, probably for the best, those three are total womanizers, so I likely wouldn't stand a chance. Not that that would stop me from trying."

Right. Of course they are. And my mind drifts right back to last Wednesday. Of course he doesn't fucking remember me. I'm just one of probably a dozen from this past week alone.

It's better this way, I remind myself. Cleaner. Easier.

Not that it matters. Because I'm not seriously considering a potential - what? Relationship with Jaxon Avenier? Based on everything I've read about him in the tabloids, the man doesn't *date*. So he took me to dinner. A *business* dinner. So I felt an insane connection to him. I could barely take my eyes off him today, not even when faced, literally, with last week's one-night stand.

Google is free, and I've certainly gotten my money's worth. It taught me that Jaxon Avenier is a player with a list of conquests a mile long. A certified bachelor. A *notorious* bachelor.

Beau must mistake my disappointment, or whatever this feeling is, for concern because he continues, "Not that I'd try anything inappropriate while working here. Or at all, since I am very committed to Victor. That's my partner, by the way, you'll meet him one of these days." His smile is impossibly wide as he talks about Victor, and this seems like a good time to finally end this conversation. "Maybe at the holiday party next month. I'm sure you'll be invited!"

I nod distractedly. "Well, thanks for the pep talk, Beau. But maybe we should move to your desk? Actually work on setting up those meetings?"

"Right-o!" Seriously, who is this guy? He wears a suit, looks sharp as hell in it, but has his floppy coif styled in an unconventional way that you'd hardly expect to see in a place like this. He doesn't exactly exude the Wall Street vibe, but he wears the uniform well in his own way.

He waits outside while I freshen up, and I follow him back to his desk. We arrange a series of meetings, more than seems necessary, but he's following the instructions laid out in the memo from Jaxon.

My head is still reeling as I make my way out of the office and to my Uber. Normally I'd take the subway home to Jade's, but I forgot to pack a spare pair of shoes. I can barely stand, let alone walk, in these stupid Louboutins.

CHAPTER 10

HADLEY

"How was it?" I hear Jade greet me from the kitchen as I return home from the most uncomfortable meeting of my entire life. And that includes the one where I was brought in for the sole purpose of being denied funding in person.

"You're not at work today?" What is she doing at home in the middle of the day? Though I'm not mad about it. After that shitshow of a morning, I could use a distraction.

"Nah, technically I'm taking a remote day; I needed to get shit done around here." She takes one long look at me and then her tone shifts, "So, the meeting didn't go well?" I swear she can read me like a book. "I know it's barely past lunch time, but you want to go down the street, grab a bite and a glass of wine and tell me about it?"

"I'd rather just stay in," I say, defeated.

"That bad, huh?" She says, grabbing two wine glasses and setting them down on the counter in front of us before she opens a bottle of red, probably something expensive.

"No, the meeting was fine, it's just... ugh, I don't even know how to begin."

"Okay, so not work-related." She looks me over, brow

furrowing in concentration. "Is it a guy? God, I hope it's a guy. And it better not be your clueless ex, David. He's still your ex, right?" I nod. "Thank fuck. How many times have I told you that you need to move on, get thoroughly fucked, have a little fun after Lame Dave and Vanilla Sex Calvin? You'd better not be getting back together with Cal." I almost smile, I can never get anything past her.

I chew on my bottom lip for a moment before deciding how much to tell her. I *need* to tell someone before I really start spiraling. "What if I told you I did get *thoroughly fucked?* Kind of." I can feel my cheeks flush. Jade has a healthy sex life and has exactly zero qualms about oversharing all the *exciting* things she does with Sebastian - *Bash* - Devereaux. *He's even sexier than his name implies,* she always shares before going into a far too detailed account of their exploits. Though, that's always been her M.O. She routinely shares things I can't un-hear and really don't want to talk about right now. For once, I think I'd actually rather talk about my own sex life.

"I knew it!" The fact that she seems more invested in how much sex I'm having than I am is probably concerning, but I'll deal with those feelings another time. "Last week, when you told me 'nothing happened,' and you were 'too hungover' to talk. It was that night, wasn't it? Was he hot? Where'd you meet him?"

"Yes, very. Hot, that is. I met him at the Bar Room." Short answers, sticking to the bare minimum here.

"Jesus, Hads, that finance bro watering hole in the financial district? Really? I told you to go looking for good sex, not a one-night stand with some pinstripe-clad douche canoe who wouldn't know where to find your clit if you gave him a map." I barely manage to stifle a laugh. I really can't with her.

"Fine, if you want to know the truth, yeah, I got picked up by a smoking hot guy. Maybe it was the other way around, I don't know. And no, he wasn't wearing *pinstripes*. I went home with him - to his very nice apartment, by the way - and he had no trouble at all finding my clit. No trouble with his fingers, or his tongue, and yes - after he got me off, he fucked me into oblivion." Her jaw drops, and I smile smugly in response. I have finally managed to shock my best friend, who is usually much more daring than me. "Happy now?" I ask.

"Delighted," she cannot conceal her grin, "so what's the problem?"

"I snuck out of his apartment the morning after, thinking I'd never see him again," I admit, sheepishly.

"Ok, we'll get back to that in a minute. You finally find a man who knows how to properly take care of you and you… run away?"

"I just wanted to do something reckless for once, I don't know, Jade." I'm exasperated, and I haven't even gotten to the worst part yet. I stare into my wine glass before taking a healthy sip.

"Ok, so what, you ran into him at a coffee shop or something on your way home from the meeting? Ran away again?"

"Not exactly," the words are escaping me. How the hell do I explain my predicament to Jade?

"So, what then? You saw him on TV, and he committed some kind of crime? Jesus, Hads, you look like you just saw a ghost!"

"Worse," I whisper.

"Worse? What the hell happened Hadley? Did he hurt you? Threaten you?" Now she's getting worked up.

"No no, nothing like that. It's just… okay I'm just going to say it. I met my account lead at AVC today, and… it's *him*."

"Oh shit!" She slaps the counter with her hand. It feels like she's enjoying this.

"Yeah, no shit. What are the fucking odds?"

"Wow, okay, I was not expecting that." She sighs, the gravity of the situation sinking in as the initial humor she found in my predicament slips away. "What did he say?"

"Nothing, just that it was nice to meet me. Extended his hand. I don't think he remembered me."

"I see," she says. "I mean, ouch, but probably for the best. At least you got one night of mind-blowing sex out of him. That counts for something." And she raises her glass to meet mine.

"Yeah," I sigh. She's echoing my own thoughts from earlier. But my mind keeps wandering back to thoughts of last Wednesday, the way his touch made me feel, how his lips felt against mine. I can still feel the heat between us, the trails his fingers left along my body, as if it's burned into my skin. The sex had been *good*. But he isn't the only man in Manhattan. And I refuse to pay any attention to the nagging thought tickling the back of my mind. *Jaxon Avenier is probably even* more *amazing in bed.*

I take another sip of wine, a mix of wistfulness and confusion swirling within me. "It was just a one-night stand." I force a smile, but I know, deep down, this isn't the end; it's just the beginning of a tangled web I never saw coming.

CHAPTER 11

HADLEY

The office Trey assigned to Trueno is technically temporary. I'm not an employee of AVC, but I have no proper office of my own for taking meetings so they offered me a no frills space with glass walls, no name on the door, and a quad of desks. I've only been here a week, but it already feels lived-in. I've been here every day and already I've found it to be a far more productive space than the rent-a-desk spots or coffee shops I've worked in when I've needed to get out of the apartment.

I've been laser focused, and I already feel like I've made progress. Other than being distracted by Jaxon's presence in the building - and the fact that he seems to be intentionally avoiding me.

Papers are spread across the surface of my desk in loose, chaotic stacks. I know where everything is, but to the outside observer, it probably looks more like a crime scene investigation than a CEO's workspace. My laptop hums, overheated and overworked, half-buried under the most recent set of printouts I'm reviewing. Two empty takeout containers from the Thai place across the street sit near the window, waiting to be thrown away, but I'm too focused on analyzing this data to be bothered to take care of it at the moment.

I'm mid-note, pen circling a figure I want to review further, when I feel it.

That awareness. A subtle prickle along the back of my neck. Like someone's stepped into my orbit. Like someone is watching me.

I don't look up right away. People pass through all the time. Analysts. Associates. Trey. Someone is probably here to check in on the report that I'm currently updating.

When I finally do look up, my breath catches. Jaxon stands in the doorway in all his imposing glory - I didn't even notice him pull open the sleek glass door - one hand still on the frame. His suit is crisp and perfectly tailored. Not a wrinkle in sight. For a split second, neither of us speaks, we just lock eyes.

Then he clears his throat.

"I didn't realize this space was occupied," he says finally, voice even, professional.

"Yes you did," I respond, unable to help myself. Then I wince, biting my tongue to prevent myself from saying anything else.

His mouth twitches, like he's amused despite himself. "No. I didn't mean to *interrupt*," and that twitch turns upwards into a smirk. "Sorry if I startled you."

"Trey usually knocks." The words are out of my mouth before I can take them back. "Do you need me to relocate?"

A flicker of some indiscernible expression flickers across his face, but it's gone just as quickly as it came.

I close my laptop a little too quickly.

"I'm not here for any kind of formal review," he says. "Or to ask you to leave. Relax."

"I am relaxed." I lean back in my chair, crossing my

arms over my chest just to prove a point. Though I'm pretty sure *relaxed* is the opposite of how I come off.

His mouth curves, just barely. "Hadley."

The way he says my name does something inconvenient to my pulse.

"I was on my way out to a meeting," he continues, his voice measured and careful. "I glanced in as I passed by and noticed you frantically scribbling away. Thought I'd check in." My temporary space is tucked away down an unoccupied hallway - most certainly not on anyone's way out of the AVC offices, but I'm not about to remind him that I know that. Especially now, the first time he's spoken to me since I've taken up residence here at Trey's insistence.

I've seen Jaxon from a distance over the course of this past week, but this is the first word he's spoken to me. He seems to disappear into his big corner office or turn the other way the moment he sees me approaching. I can't help but feel like his avoidance is intentional, which I know is ridiculous. I need to get out of my own head.

The silence stretches between us, growing thick enough to feel intentional.

"You always work like this?" he asks finally, eyes pointedly dragging across my desk's chaos. "Or is this a special occasion?"

"Always," I say. "But the mess is structural." I know where every report, every chart, every scribbled-on post-it note is.

"Interesting."

I open my mouth to speak in defense of the way I work, then stop myself. His eyes dip, not quite to my mouth, but something in his expression tightens anyway.

His gaze shifts to the now cold cup of black coffee cup on my desk. "That looks like it's been there a while. No oat milk today?"

"Are you judging the way I usually take my coffee?"

"Observing," he corrects. Then, quieter, "It's a habit."

I don't ask how he knows. Or what else he has *observed*. I'm not sure I want the answer. Despite the thrill I feel at being noticed by him.

"The coffee station was out of oat milk," I reply matter of factly. "I prefer it black over using the artificial flavored creamer, which was all I could find."

His gaze falls to my desk and lingers on the papers there before sliding to the empty containers near the window.

"This," he says, nodding at my work, "looks intentional. That," he lifts his chin towards the takeout, "looks like you forgot to take out the trash."

"If I stop to clean, I lose momentum," I admit, feeling self-conscious about the state of my workspace as a vision of his spotless, almost sterile, corner office flashes across my memory. "I'll deal with it later."

"Later has a habit of not coming," he chuckles. Then he steps back. "I should go, I can't afford to be late to my meeting."

"Of course." I suddenly feel flushed.

"And Hadley," he pauses at the door, "Trey says he's impressed." Then almost as an afterthought he adds, "and so am I."

Before I can even reply, he's gone.

I stare at my notes and realize he didn't ask a single question about Trueno.

Only about me.

Chapter 12

Trey

"Come in," I call out, surprised that Jaxon bothered to knock. It's only Hadley and I in her small office space today, so we chose to take the meeting here as opposed to one of the board rooms. The space is built for four, and Trueno's CPO or Chief Engineer are often here, but they both chose to work from home today where their desktop set-ups are more advanced and geared towards the work they do. I suspect the two week review meeting with Jaxon is part of it too - they are intimidated by him, unlike Hadley.

If anything, Hadley brightens whenever Jaxon enters the room. He doesn't normally get that reaction from people and he knows it - but with Hadley, he seems to enjoy it. I can see the difference in both of them. Honestly, it's impossible *not* to notice the way they orbit each other, drawn in tight, almost like gravity decided for them.

"Hi, Jaxon," Hadley smiles up at him, her eyes bright and eager. Most start-up CEOs are either over-confident, or nervous to discuss their progress with Jaxon - not that he regularly takes this level of interest in an account, but Hadley seems down-right excited. Though I imagine she was the kind of student who got excited for report cards too.

"Hadley, Trey." Jaxon takes a seat at one of the empty desks. He scans the office discerningly, a look of approval playing across his features. And it's then that I notice the surfaces are devoid of the usual empty take-out containers and cups that often litter the space. Jaxon's gaze finally lands on Hadley's coffee mug. "Oat milk?" he asks, the corner of his mouth quirking upwards as he gestures to her cup. Almost as though he is trying to suppress a smile.

Hadley beams. "What else?"

I suddenly feel out of place, like I'm missing some sort of insider information. "Shall we get started?" I ask in an effort to gain control of the meeting. It's already 4:00 PM and Jaxon has never been one for small talk before business meetings.

"Yes, of course," Hadley straightens up in her chair, sending me a quick smile. "Trey has been so helpful already," she directs towards Jaxon. "Let me show you what we've accomplished in just two short weeks."

Hadley launches into her update while I sit quietly observing. She hardly needs me here, and I start to feel like a third wheel. She answers all of Jaxon's questions with barely a glance my way.

"You would like that, wouldn't you?" She retorts to one of Jaxon's more pointed questions about expansion.

"I would. That's one of our primary objectives," he says firmly, but he's smiling at her playful response. She clearly values his input, his attention, and his expertise, but she doesn't automatically defer to him the way so many others do. What's more surprising though, is that Jaxon is apparently okay with it, even enjoys the witty way she pushes back.

Jaxon and Hadley continue their banter, both clearly testing each other's boundaries, and I can't deny that they are equally matched. Their words are strictly business, but there is so much more brewing beneath the surface that neither of them seems willing to acknowledge. At least not in front of me.

I decide to excuse myself. "You two clearly have this under control," I say as I stand. "I have to take a call." I gesture with my phone before leaving the room. Lex is going to give me shit for leaving those two alone, but they're both adults. And I was contributing next to nothing in that *meeting*.

It shouldn't bother me, their connection is so goddamn apparent, yet I can't help but feel like they are rubbing it in my face when I see them like *that*. I'm not jealous exactly, I refuse to be jealous. If Jaxon were behaving this way with any other woman, I would be thrilled. He needs this. And I want this for him. I want this for them.

I should be happy for him. I *want* to be happy for him. Hell, I *am* happy for him. And that means I need to figure out how to truly let Hadley go.

CHAPTER 13

JAXON

Once again I find myself reluctant to leave Hadley's presence. I've been here for over an hour already, and Trey left almost thirty minutes ago. I'm genuinely starting to feel hungry, but Hadley keeps talking, and I'm in no rush for her to stop. She's asking questions, good questions - about business, about AVC, even about me. And I am surprisingly eager to give her answers.

I don't have any more meetings today so there's nothing stopping me from staying.

Except maybe my basic human need for sustenance. But that problem is easily solved. "I'm famished - and it looks like we'll both be here late. I'll have Joe order us some Thai, from that Khao San place you like?"

Hadley blinks twice before giving me a smile. "Okay," she says quietly. "How did you know that place is my favorite?"

"I told you, I'm observant," I hold her gaze in a way that feels intense, but not uncomfortable. We aren't exchanging any witty repartee right now, but she doesn't break eye contact, still testing me in a way no one ever has before. "I don't know your order though, so you'll have to tell me that."

"It's Beau, by the way."

"Your order is what?"

She tilts her head, a contemplative expression crossing her face. "No, not the order. Your assistant, his name is Beau. Not Joe."

I feel like I knew this, and her unapologetic correction lands harder than it should.

"Beau," I say. "You're right." I make a note to commit his name to memory and wonder why nobody else has bothered to correct me all this time.

Her shoulders ease just a little and a satisfied smile pulls gently at the corner of her mouth. It's fucking adorable. And I realize this about her then, that she notices things that other people overlook - or choose not to confront - and she won't let them slide just to be agreeable.

Not even with me.

We place our order with my assistant, *Beau*, and Hadley quickly gets back to business by asking about AVC - how my father started it, and how he began preparing me to take over, starting a few years ago. We break only when the carry-out order arrives, and we eat at her desk, sitting across from each other. I'm sure eating like this is a regular occurrence for her, but this is unusual for me, and it feels oddly intimate.

"Thank you," Hadley says suddenly, chopsticks still grasped between her fingers. "Truly. I know it's probably unconventional, you have more important things to do than go over what you probably consider basic business strategy with me."

I study her for a moment. She's so genuine and authentic in her gratitude, it's incredibly refreshing and such a contrast from the crowd I usually find myself dining with. "Time is an investment too, Hadley. AVC has invested money, and I consider investing time with you to be just as valuable."

She smiles and looks down at her green curry. "So, is Trueno going to be part of this Echelon fund?" I feel my jaw clenching as I frown at the question. Hadley glances back up at me, catching my reaction. "I heard talk of it. It sounds - "

"I don't know," I interrupt. I don't offer an explanation, and I don't want to.

"Okay. That's fine. I just, I don't know, you seemed to imply that you found my tech innovative, and the fund sounds right up our alley." Fuck. She's disappointed. This is not how I wanted this evening to go.

"Your tech *is* innovative, Hadley. I said *I don't know*, because nothing is set in stone yet."

What the fuck am I saying? I don't like the prospect of Russ profiting off of Hadley in any way. But it's not like I even have Russ' commitment to Echelon yet, I remind myself, so anything is possible.

Hadley merely nods as she takes another bite, followed by a healthy swig from her water bottle.

"Spicy?" Hadley nods again. "I'm pretty sure I can smell how hot it is from here. God, I don't know how you eat that."

Hadley laughs. "I'm impressed you're willing to admit you like it mild. Most men like you would pretend they can handle my spice level." She takes another bite as if to prove her palate is stronger than mine.

"Most men are *not* like me," My voice drops lower as I say, but I can't fucking help it when I'm around her. "I don't need to prove myself by eating something that I know is going to make my eyes tear up." I notice her eyes are barely even glassy, nor is her nose running, though her cheeks are flushed. But is that from the food? "Seriously, how do you handle it?"

Hadley shrugs. "I've always been able to, I guess? My father's nanny was West Indian and dad developed a love of spicy food as a child which he must have passed on to me. When he realized I did too - I was a toddler - he fed my craving for spicier and spicier dishes. Now it's almost nostalgic." She looks down at the food again, moving it around in the container without taking a bite. "He passed away in my junior year of college."

"I'm so sorry." I want to reach out and comfort her somehow, but I resist it, reminding myself where we are. *Who* we are.

"Thanks." She gives me a small smile.

"You were closer to him than your mother then?"

"Understatement of the year," Hadley rolls her eyes, before focusing her gaze on me. "What about your mom? Everyone knows of the infamous Kenneth Avenier, but I don't think I even know what your mother's name is."

I sigh. Of course everyone knows my dad, the founder of AVC, polished businessman, charming and sociable. "Her name was Nasim. She died when I was young." Hadley is watching me, I can tell she's waiting for me to share more. And I can't help but give her what she wants. "She was wonderful, she could work a room with my dad when he had to network more than I do now, and yet she always had time for me. She read me books, so many books. And sang to me."

The wistful smile on Hadley's face makes me consider leaning over and kissing her as my heartbeat kicks up a notch. I distract myself by picking up a skewer of chicken satay and sinking my teeth into it instead.

"She sounds like a wonderful mom." Hadley has a way of choosing words that coax things out of me, because now I find myself wanting to tell her all the ways in which my mom was wonderful.

"She was. She made me a rum cake every year on my

birthday, because I loved it so much." I don't tell her I haven't had a bite of my once-favorite dessert since my mother's death.

"Your favorite childhood dessert was rum cake?" Hadley barely conceals a giggle as she takes another bite of curry. "Sorry," she covers her mouth with her hand, "but that's just so unusual."

"Yes. Not exactly conventional for a child, I know. But someone sent my father a rum cake one year as a holiday gift. He wasn't much of a dessert guy, and so it just sat under a crystal cake dome on our kitchen counter taunting me. After a day of staring at it, I couldn't resist ripping off a handful of cake." I rarely talk about my past, and I surprise myself as I continue sharing one of my most cherished childhood memories with Hadley. "Mom caught me, of course. Shoveling fistfuls of that sweet, buttery rum cake into my mouth. It was unlike anything I'd ever tasted, and I told her as much. She didn't punish me, laughing as she cleaned me up. Instead, she cut us each a proper slice and we enjoyed it together as our dinner that night while dad worked late." I take a slow breath as I feel a swell of emotion rising in my throat. "And four months later, when my sixth birthday rolled around, she surprised me with a homemade rum cake. Made one for me every year after that until she got sick."

"Oh Jaxon." Hadley's eyes are glassy now, and the expression they carry tells me the water in her eyes has nothing to do with the spice in her curry.

"I miss her every day." I sigh, realizing how *good* it feels to talk to Hadley about my mom.

"Of course you do," Hadley places her small hand over mine, only briefly, but it's enough. Enough for my pulse to quicken, for my senses to heighten so that I catch the floral scent in her perfume over the Thai aromas. Enough for me to realize I've just admitted something to her that I've barely even acknowledged to myself, let alone anyone else.

Not that I'm ashamed, or embarrassed, she was my mother. Of course I miss her. Mostly I avoid talking about her. Except, apparently, with Hadley. Somehow she has me opening up about my past over Thai takeout in a poorly ventilated office.

Hadley removes her hand before I can even thank her and the rest of the meal passes comfortably as conversation moves on to current events and other safe topics, boring topics, before I finally force myself to take my leave.

As I make my way home an hour later, I can't help but ponder the way Hadley has cracked open something that I normally keep shut. She's broken through the granite business exterior I always maintain, and somehow touched a side of me that I normally keep locked away, under heavy guard.

This is dangerous. I should call Kit. I should shut down whatever this feeling is that Hadley uncovered, buried deep within my heart. But for some reason I can't bring myself to do either, relishing instead in the sudden rush of exhilaration it brings.

Chapter 14

Trey

I find Hadley in the kitchenette the following morning, making herself a coffee. "So, how late did you stay last night?" I can't help but ask.

"Oh, I think it was past 8:00 PM before I got home," Hadley says. "Well, to Jade's, which is my home right now, I guess." She wrinkles her nose as if she is annoyed to admit she's living with her friend. Though she could probably afford to move out now, I get the feeling she enjoys the company. The start-up world can be a lonely place for anyone, let alone a CEO.

"Talking to Jaxon the whole time?" I'm not sure why I'm torturing myself this way. I tell myself I'm just gathering intel, gauging Jaxon's interest. Which is true, even though I've already decided Jaxon will never find out about our one-night stand, and I'm determined to follow Hadley's lead and continue pretending like it never happened.

"Oh no, he left after we finished eating. Maybe 6:30?"

"So you *did* have dinner with Mr. Avenier?" Thank God for Beau, the office gossip, taking one for the team and asking the questions I wish I could. I pretend to busy myself with the coffee machine as I listen for her answer.

"Yes, Beau," Hadley laughs at the way Beau waggles his eyebrows. "It was all business. No tea to spill, I'm sorry to report."

"Hmmm," Beau sounds unconvinced. "So it's just business as usual, Mr. Avenier rather assertively making sure I understand that the fridge is always to be well-stocked with oat milk? Do you expect me to believe that the man who only takes his coffee black as midnight suddenly developed an infatuation with plant-based milk? I know that's for *you*, Hadley."

She practically preens. "He was the one who made sure of that?"

"That's right," Beau winks. I watch as Hadley bites her lip before realizing how obvious she's being. I now understand the oat milk comment from yesterday.

"Do you want to meet quickly in your office, Hadley?" I ask, eager to steer this morning's chatter in another direction. We typically do a quick stand-up style meeting every morning before I let her team get to work.

"Sounds good." She picks up her coffee from the counter and offers Beau an apologetic smile as she follows me out of the break room.

As we're walking to her office, Hadley suddenly asks, "Did you ever know Nasim?"

The name sounds familiar, but I can't place it. "Who?"

"Jaxon's mother," Hadley explains. "She died when he was young."

I almost trip over my own feet. Jaxon told Hadley about his mother? I don't even think he's ever talked to me about his mother. Though maybe that has more to do with the fact that my mom had an affair with his dad, even if it didn't start until after his mom passed away. Regardless, they clearly didn't only talk business last night after all.

"Uh, no," I have to clear my throat before continuing. "Our parents met shortly after she died. Jaxon and I didn't know each other before that."

I pull out my phone to text Lex - he asked me to let him know if Jaxon ever ventured into dangerous waters as far as Hadley is concerned, and I'm pretty sure this qualifies as something Lex would want to know about.

Trey: Heads up, Jaxon and Hadley "worked" late last night.

Lex: What's that supposed to mean?

Trey: Dude, they talked about his mom.

Lex: Please tell me that's code for something.

Trey: Nope. He actually talked about her.

Trey: And he's making sure we never run out of oat milk.

Lex: I'm not following.

Trey: Apparently, it's how Hadley takes her coffee.

Lex: Shit.

Trey: Yeah. Shit.

Lex: Thanks for the heads up. I have a meeting with him early next week. I'll find a way to bring it up.

CHAPTER 15

JAXON

"One last thing," Alastair looks at me seriously. We've been going over some of the numbers before the year's end, and I fucking know he's about to bring up Russell Artanza. "Russ wants you to bring Hadley to his holiday party next week." He doesn't need to remind me. "And he wants to hear more from her about her company. I think he's operating on the assumption that Trueno will be part of the Echelon fund." I've been thinking about this dilemma for days. Thinking about *her*. It's been almost a week since we had Thai food in her office together. I've only seen her in passing since then, and I've avoided mentioning the Russ Artanza holiday party. I just need to figure out how to play this.

Alastair gives me a pointed look as I start shaking my head. "Jaxon, it's been almost a month since you fucked up our meeting with him at Cubed. He asked about her account then, and you evaded his questions. You've got to give him something."

"No." I've been firm on this. The man makes me uneasy in the way he's showing an interest in Trueno. I've seen Russ mistake proximity for entitlement before, and the way his attention keeps circling back to Hadley tells me I'll need to manage him just as carefully as the investment. The language in the contract for limited partners was drafted specifically for men like him - but he hasn't committed to Echelon yet.

"Dude, do you want to lock down his Echelon dollars or not?" Alastair isn't letting up; he's been hounding me relentlessly for the past few weeks about this. I get it, he's the one who has primarily been managing Russ, but still, my answer is, and always has been, no.

"There has to be another way." I know there isn't. I'd have thought of it by now. I know Russ, and he's not going to let it go. The problem is, Alastair knows him too.

"Fine. I'll tell him you don't want her there. Which, of course, will only make him more curious. Men like Russ don't back off. Especially when they think they're being denied something you're protecting." Fucking Alastair, he has a point.

"I hate that you're probably right about this," I sigh as I contemplate the situation. I've been so focused on how to get her out of the event that I hadn't even thought about how to make it work if she *is* there. This might not be as catastrophic as I originally thought. "We'll tell Trey to take her as his date," I conclude. He'll stick to her side like a bodyguard.

"Well, at least you have enough sense not to bring her as *your* date," Alastair offers a smug chuckle, his eyes sparkling mischievously.

I exhale, refusing to even dignify whatever it is he is suggesting with a response.

"I'm serious," he adds, the grin lingering but softer now. "You've taken an interest."

"Relax," I mutter. I don't like the direction this conversation is headed.

"I would," he says lightly. "If this looked like you were just having fun."

I glance at him.

"Fuck off." I rise from my desk and walk towards the well-stocked bar cart I keep in my office. He follows. Clearly, this conversation isn't over.

"I haven't heard you say her name in almost twenty years, Jaxon." He's talking about my mother, and somehow, he must know that I opened up to Hadley about her. I don't respond, and Alastair doesn't push, silently letting the implication of his words sink in.

I pour two fingers of Avenier 23, the parent liquor company being one of my father's earliest and surprisingly profitable ventures. I offer the crystal tumbler to Alastair before pouring a second glass for myself and taking a seat on the leather couch next to my cousin.

"So tell me," I need to change the fucking subject. "When can I see a report on the pitch you sat in on today? What was the group called? Genevieve tells me you plan to recommend them for the next round of funding." I need to keep Alastair focused on business and far the fuck away from the subject of my personal life. Alastair's been checking in on me every fucking day, making sure I'm keeping a safe distance from the Trueno account and, more specifically, its founder.

I've made a point to try to avoid her as much as possible, keeping my eye on her from a careful distance. Though I'm admittedly not doing a spectacular job of staying out of her orbit. Never have I struggled to maintain control around anyone before. *Never.* This is new fucking territory for me.

At the end of last week, she caught me as I was heading into my office, thanking me for ensuring the fridge always had her oat milk. I had to clench my jaw to stop myself from smiling; so she noticed. *Beau said you asked him to make sure it was regularly stocked. That was really sweet, thank you.*

I wanted to argue with her, tell her I'm not *sweet*. No one has ever called me sweet. But between her hand on my elbow and the adoring smile on her face, I was rendered speechless. All I could manage was a nod and a tight smile in return.

It's just fucking oat milk.

It's not just the way she looks, though it's not like I can ignore the way her tight, perfect ass fills out those skirts she wears most of the time. The way her legs look as she wobbles a little in those ridiculous heels she insists on wearing. It's something in the way that gentleness, the graciousness, contrasts with the way she defiantly combats any criticism I throw at her product or her process. Like the *structural mess* of her office.

It's infuriating how much she affects me. What it does to me when she acts like she isn't intimidated by the fact that I'm the CEO. She isn't afraid to call me out when I question her, clearly lacking her technical expertise, or when I cave and seek her out for some made-up business reason. It's like she knows I'm there for her, not Trueno.

She's right too. Of course she is. She's a fucking genius. She's smarter than me, I can admit that to myself, though never aloud; I pride myself on my intellect. But Hadley… she is simply *astonishing*.

But then she'll defer to me, ask for my advice on the things where my technical knowledge supersedes hers - like how to grow her business or ways she can more effectively streamline her quarterly budget forecasting - like she did the other night over dinner.

And I can see how far she'll go, how far AVC could take her. She's open to input, confident in her area of expertise, and willing to take risks. I've caught myself pondering the risk of pursuing something beyond business with her more than once. Which is exactly why it can't happen.

"Shit!" Alastair's outburst interrupts my thoughts as an intense bolt of lightning streaks across the sky. Not long after, a clap of thunder, long and dramatic, shakes the building.

"Need a ride?" I offer, knowing he usually walks home, but I'm not going to leave him to his own devices in weather like this. The inevitable downpour is imminent.

"Nah," he smiles, "Saul has me covered with the corporate sedan tonight. Heading uptown to see a show. Your new assistant, Beau, his boyfriend is some kind of producer? Investor? Not sure exactly, but he has some connections on Broadway and secured me a pair of great tickets to that show that just opened, the new musical headlined by Hugh Greenley." He seems abnormally enthusiastic about seeing a Broadway production on a cold, rainy evening.

"You seem way too excited about a fucking musical. Is it a girl?" I give him a look that says I know there's more than he's letting on. He's been quiet about his social life since Aria Thorne made his hookup with Vera Norvelle very public information.

"Something like that," he can't hide his grin, and wiggles his fucking eyebrows at me. I just roll my eyes in response. At least someone's getting laid tonight.

"So, Russ's holiday party," he isn't going to let this go, even though I thought we'd moved on from this subject. "I think it's safe to assume Kit is going to be there."

"Of course she is. It's her godfather's party." I stand to pour another finger of bourbon. "Her dear Uncle Russ undoubtedly extended an invitation to her."

"Right, and her *Uncle Russ* is one of our biggest investors." He sighs. "Which is why it's so dangerous to mix business and pleasure. Russ thinks you and Kit are, what? Dating? He has no idea what she really does, *does* he?"

"Obviously not," I confirm. I'm not even sure Russ would care if he did know. Hell, maybe he'd be proud of her prowess - she definitely caters to a very exclusive clientele. And knowing Russ, I'm sure more than one of her *colleagues* will be at his party.

Alastair's expression grows serious, and I know I'm getting one of those lectures where my cousin proves to me that, despite the fact that I am older, he is by far the wiser one. "Look, nobody is more thrilled than I am that you've moved on from her."

"Who says I've moved on?" I cut him off.

"Well, your actions do. The fact that you haven't seen her for a month is pretty telling, for starters." *Yeah, because I can't stop thinking about Hadley fucking Aldridge.*

I knew this conversation was coming. I need to break it off with her formally. Not that our relationship, or whatever you want to call it, has been anything more than a business arrangement. And I'm the fucking client, I have no obligation to her. But I've been avoiding Kit, and she's not happy about it. Therein lies my problem. If it weren't for her godfather, for his pending investment in the Echelon round, I wouldn't give a shit about the Kit situation. I'm just not interested in what she has to offer right now. I should be, she's great at what she does and looks good on my arm at all the insufferable social functions I have to attend, but I can't seem to think about anyone else except the one woman who is totally and completely off limits.

I run my fingers through my hair as I stare out the window. A few fat drops of rain have started pelting the glass. The loud, rhythmic patter echoes through my office in the same way Hadley constantly hammers at my thoughts. This is just the beginning of the storm rolling in, forcefully overtaking the island. I have a bad feeling that this preoccupation with Hadley Aldridge is only beginning to pick up speed and force as well.

"Okay, well, wish me luck," Alastair jumps up, taking his leave. And whether he means luck with his date or with the weather, I'm not sure.

CHAPTER 16

JAXON

I toss back the rest of my drink in one swig and stand in front of the floor-to-ceiling window as I watch the rain's intensity increase, each drop spattering against the glass before cascading downward like a torrent of silver tears. Just before I turn to walk away, the sky cracks wide open with a violent light, mesmerizing me as it forks across the sky, turning the city below into a shadowed sea of steel and flashing lights.

I fucking love Manhattan.

I set my drink down on the bar cart and make a mental note to have Joe see that the glassware is cleaned tomorrow. He'll be long gone by now. The office is eerily quiet, empty this time of night. I always take comfort in the stillness, walking among the shadows as I make my way to the elevator bank and –

Movement.

Someone else is here. Standing in the brightly lit bank of elevators, staring at the illuminated downward-facing arrow.

Hadley Aldridge.

My heart stutters. There is no avoiding her. And if I'm being honest, I don't want to.

"Late night?" She startles at the sound of my voice, and I can feel that involuntary smirk pull at the corner of my mouth. I'd say I didn't mean to alarm her, but that would be a lie.

"Trey had to leave a while ago, something about catching a game?"

"I'm surprised to see you're still here, given the storm currently raging outside."

"I had work to wrap up," she challenges. "Not all of us have the luxury of a window office to keep tabs on the weather."

"Yes, well, doesn't your app predict these sorts of weather patterns?" I respond, keeping my tone light. I've seen how protective she is of her company, and I'm not questioning Trueno's capabilities.

"It does, but the storm doesn't faze me," she holds up her chin as a clap of thunder outside rattles the entire building, but I'm not buying this act of bravado for one second.

"If you insist." I watch the nerves, the uncertainty flash across her eyes, despite her defiant tone. I know I'm being an asshole, but I can't help from riling her up.

She narrows her eyes at me, and I feel a slow smile tugging at the corner of my mouth. She's infuriatingly adorable when she's frustrated.

The elevator dings and the doors open, drawing her eyes forward and allowing me to catch a glimpse of her perfect ass in that pencil skirt as I follow her inside.

I watch her unlock her phone and open the Uber app. I decide I'll wait with her until her car comes. No way I'm leaving her alone in the lobby on a night like this.

"Damn it," she grumbles to herself.

"Trouble getting an Uber? There's a downpour. In

Manhattan. And it's forty-five degrees outside, what do you expect?" I really can't help myself.

"It's fine, I'll just take the subway." She's stubborn, that's for damn sure. Then, rather sheepishly, she adds, "I'm just angry with myself for forgetting my umbrella. I *knew* this storm was coming. I didn't mean to stay so late."

The way she looks at me, those almond eyes flickering between a honeyed gray and a dark stormy blue, filled with a pleading she refuses to acknowledge, like it would pain her to ask for help. *She won't ask for help,* I know she won't. She doesn't want to appear vulnerable. She doesn't want to need my assistance. But right now, in more ways than one, she absolutely does.

"I can give you a ride, my driver is waiting outside," I say, the words tumbling out of my mouth before I can stop them. *Fuck.* I want her to say yes, *need* her to say yes, to let me pull her into the warmth of my car, where the cold and the rain can't touch her.

She holds my gaze for a moment, biting her lower lip as if pondering her response. God, those lips, I feel my eyes drop to them, lingering for a beat too long. *Shit.* When my eyes return her gaze, there's a stubborn tilt to her chin and my heart fucking sinks.

"Thanks, but I'll be fine," her defiant rejection stings more than I expect it to.

"Don't be absurd," I bite back, regaining control of the situation. "Emilio is outside, waiting, and he'll drop you off before he takes me home. As long as you don't live in Jersey or some other impossible location. Then he'll be dropping me off first." She laughs at that, and my heart fucking skips a beat as I watch the blue in her eyes lighten with laughter as she throws her head back.

"Fine," she says. "West Village. And to be clear, it's only because you're so insistent." Relief washes over me, drowning out the anxiety that had been gnawing at my insides. I ignore it.

"It's just common sense," I tell both her and myself. It's common sense, completely reasonable, to care for the well-being of someone who is leaving *my* building, to face this raging storm. To want to make sure she gets home safe. I wished Alastair luck after all, even offered him a ride as well. This is no different.

As we exit the elevator, I instinctively place my hand on the small of her back, and not only do I feel her warmth, but I feel her breath catch at the contact. I leave my hand there, savoring this moment of physical connection as I lead her out the front door of the office building and into the driving rain.

I guide her gently to the idling car, grateful for Emilio as he rushes from the black SUV with an oversized umbrella to greet us at the entrance, shielding us from the curtain of water falling from the sky as we swiftly make our way to the car.

"Thank you," she says once we're both securely inside, rain relentlessly pounding against the glass of the window that frames her face. And the way she is looking at me. I *know* it's not just gratitude. It's something else, something she can't say, neither of us can, but I can *feel* it. She needs me. She might not *want* to need me, but she does.

This. This moment feels like the start of something dangerous. And it's something I am not sure I can resist. It's something I'm not sure I *want* to resist.

I nod in acknowledgement, but I can't think of anything to say. Instead, we sit in silence, listening to the hum of the car's engine and the rhythmic beat of the wipers as they dance back and forth along the windshield. She's so close to me, close enough that I can feel the heat of her body, yet it feels like there is a chasm between us.

I want to say something, anything, to bridge the space

between us. But it's not just that space I so desperately want to close.

It's even more than that. It's everything *unsaid*, the way I can feel her gaze flicker to mine and then away, like she's holding back, like there's a wall she's built that she isn't ready to let me through yet. Maybe she's better at this than I am; the control, the restraint. I've never let anyone in, never let anyone past my carefully constructed walls, so why is she so different? Why do I feel so compelled to lower the drawbridge and grant her entrance to the fortress I've built around me?

Breathe.

I have to remind myself to breathe.

She doesn't say anything either, and the air lies thick between us, as if we're both waiting for the other to break the stillness – it's fucking killing me. All I can think about is how much I want to reach out and touch her. How I want to run my fingers through the long, loose strands of her hair. How silky those strands felt when I did just that a few weeks ago. When I almost made a colossal mistake. When I almost *kissed* her.

And I haven't thought about anything or *anyone* else since.

There's almost no traffic tonight, the ride passing with cruel haste. I want to make this moment last, but at the same time, I don't know if I can handle this kind of restraint much longer. There's an un*fucking*deniable magnetism between us, a pull that neither of us seems ready, or willing, to give into. And the harder I try to resist, the stronger the force that draws me to her tugs on me, like an invisible string.

"Hell of a storm, came out of nowhere." Emilio cuts the tension with a banal comment about the weather, and I can't decide if I should thank him or fire him.

I wonder if she can feel it too? The tension. The static.

"Not out of nowhere," she says, and I hear the pride in her voice.

"Right. The forecast called for rain. But we typically get more warning for something this intense." Now I'm making small talk about the weather?

"Maybe if you used my app, you'd have been better prepared," Hadley's tone is smug, and it earns an incredulous huff of laughter from me.

"I'm always prepared," I turn to meet her gaze, which is a fucking mistake. The look in her eyes is daring, challenging me to question her.

Maybe small talk about the weather is a good idea after all.

I swallow. "Is this something Trueno predicted?" I made a point to learn her company's name - and how to pronounce it. She never changed it.

"Yes." She lifts her chin defiantly, which just draws my attention to her lips. "And I can do a hell of a lot more than predict a storm. Though most of the more precise capabilities aren't available to our users. It requires more isolation on things like location, segmenting vast satellite images, and categorizing distinct patterns with precision."

I don't understand the technicalities of what she's talking about, but I'm taken back to her pitch in that boardroom. Her knowledge, her confidence, her *passion*.

"But the load on the server to do that for every location of every user is not feasible. My system at home is set up to run predictions for Manhattan, though. The technology I built can—"

"Show me." The words are out of my mouth before I can reconsider them. I want to see her *system at home*. It's a bad fucking idea. I know it. The way she's looking at me says she knows it too, but I hold her gaze. Her chest rises and falls with her breath - she's breathing as hard as I am. I don't miss the way her tongue skims her lower lip.

"Okay," she breathes. "I'll show you."

I nod once, lost in the deep pools of her eyes, now more blue-green than golden-gray. She breaks the gaze suddenly, peering over my shoulder out the window.

"This is me," she says, and we slow to a stop along the cobblestone, pulling up in front of a red brick apartment building.

Emilio once again leaps out of the car to escort us one at a time to the front door. There's no overhang, though the doorman anticipates our arrival, swiftly offering us refuge from the sheets of rain that still manage to soak us despite the oversized umbrella.

"Shit," Hadley curses as we're making our way through the lobby. And before I can stop her, before I can offer to help, she runs back out into the deluge, towards the car. And without thinking, I follow.

Ten seconds. That's all it takes.

She's soaked. Completely, fucking soaked. The rain clings to her skin, running off her sleeves in rivulets. The perfect, silky waves of her hair are now flat and matted against her head, hanging in heavy, wet clumps around her face. Her body briefly turns, facing mine, as she pulls open the door of the SUV. The silk camisole she's wearing beneath her open blazer is now practically transparent, sticking to her body, and outlining every curve with perfect clarity.

God, she's fucking beautiful.

I follow after her without thinking. If she'd forgotten something in the car, does she not realize I could have called Emilio to bring it inside?

Water runs off my hair and down my neck, dripping from the sleeves of my overcoat. The storm feels personal now, though if I'm being honest, it always did, a metaphor for these chaotic emotions that have been swirling inside of me since the moment Hadley Aldridge walked into my life.

Every drop of water seems like it has a grudge to settle, and it is taking no mercy on either of us.

I can't take my eyes off her as I close the distance between us, the pull towards her stronger than ever, crackling with the same intensity as the electric charge in the air.

I reach her just as her fingers land on the folder she left beside her seat.

"Give it to me," I offer, holding open my wool dress coat. I'm the one in outerwear; I can at least protect its contents from the torrential rain. Realizing this is the best option, she nods, handing it to me and watching intently as I tuck whatever precious papers it contains into my jacket. She slams the door shut and runs back towards the lobby.

As I follow her all the way up to her apartment, all I can think about is how completely fucked I am.

Her fingers, frozen with the wet chill of the night, tremble as she unlocks the door and pushes it open.

Inside, it's dark. And silent.

Nobody's home.

It's just us.

I should go. I need to go. But I know I won't.

I don't *want* to.

I choose to stay.

The only sound is the rain pounding against the windows as we enter her dark, empty apartment. Lightning streaks across the sky, illuminating the space. Cozy, modern, and distinctly masculine.

Masculine.

Does she live with a male roommate? A boyfriend? The thought never even crossed my mind, and, well, *fuck*, it shouldn't, but the mere thought of someone, *anyone* else's hand on her ignites a flare of something way too close to jealousy.

"Looks like Jade isn't here," she says as she flicks on the lights. "My best friend," she clarifies. "I'm crashing with her for now. She lives here with her boyfriend." My blood pressure instantly normalizes as I release the breath I didn't realize I was holding. Her *friend*. That's right. She lives with a friend, Jade Corven. I know Jade's partner - the one who vetted Hadley's company, suggesting we look at it in the first place. Sebastian Devereaux, one of our industry partners I know through Russ.

She shivers as she kicks off her shoes and peels away her soaked blazer like she's trying to escape a grip that just won't release, the wet fabric sticking to her arms and fighting her as she wrangles herself free.

God, I'd like to help her out of more than just that jacket. It takes every ounce of my will not to reach out and touch her. Instead, I remove my overcoat and hang it by the door, placing her precious folder on the console table as I do.

"You're soaked," she says apologetically as her eyes follow my coat, drops of water falling from its hem.

"I'm fine," because compared to her, I'm relatively dry.

I shouldn't, but I allow my eyes to rake over her body.

Her clothes cling to her, the fabric so wet that it molds to every perfect curve, every sharp line. The creamy silk of her now-sheer camisole sticks to her like a second skin, the delicate lace of her bra plainly visible, taunting me from beneath it.

I can't stop looking at her. I don't even try.

My body feels like it's frozen in place, my throat dry, every inch of me aware of the way she looks right now. The rain has made her pale skin glow, slick and flushed rosy pink with cold. Something about this storm seems to electrify the air between us. I swallow, trying to still the desire that's creeping up my spine.

But it's impossible when she's standing there in front of me. Looking like *that*.

She starts walking into the kitchen, filling a kettle with water and placing it on the stove.

"Tea?" she asks. I just nod, looking for any excuse to stay here. Stay with *her*.

"I'm pretty sure I can handle making the tea if you need to change," my eyes can't help but drift lower, noticing the way her silk camisole is practically painted onto her skin, accentuating the outline of her breasts, the firm buds of her nipples, the delicate curve of her waist.

Every drop of water on her seems to highlight her pebbled skin, leaving me aching to reach out and touch her, to provide her the warmth and comfort she so clearly needs. I want to be that comfort. But I know I can't.

"I'm fine," she says, shivering. She's not fine, but she's better at resisting this than I am. Or maybe she knows exactly what she's doing to me.

Is she really not going to change? She must be freezing. God, she's so stubborn, and so fucking distracting. I feel my resolve slipping. I should leave, but we both know I won't.

Her eyes meet mine, and she shivers. Whether from the cold or a mutual desire, I'm not sure. But one thing I am certain of is that this storm raging outside is tame compared to the one that is now brewing between us.

I can't fucking stand it, seeing her there, her clothes clinging to her, and revealing the body I've spent weeks trying not to think about. I tell myself it's for her own good, that it has nothing to do with my desire to be near her, to touch her, as I walk over to the sofa in the open concept living room and grab the first throw blanket I see.

"Oh." She smiles at me as I stride back to her, wrapping the blanket around her shoulders like a cape, and I fucking melt as she looks up at me, her eyes meeting mine, revealing a desire that mirrors my own.

"You're welcome." I smirk, tugging on the fabric of the blanket.

"Thank you, Jaxon." Her gratitude sounds genuine, and the way she says my name causes my chest to tighten with something fiercely protective. My *name* on her lips pulls at something I've always kept buried within me, and I realize I'm starting to fall in a way that fucking scares me.

"I look out for the people I care about," the words just tumble out of me, the admission that I *care* about her.

The gray fades from her eyes, suddenly overpowered by a greenish-blue as she gazes back at me with, what is that, hope? Yearning? Anticipation? I don't say anything, I can't say anything.

My hand reaches out and brushes back a wet strand of her hair as my thumb strokes the soft skin beneath her ear. Time seems to slow as I grasp the blanket in both hands, instinctively pulling her towards the warmth of my body until she's flush against me.

Fuck, every inch of me instantly heats in response as desire shoots down my spine and straight between my legs. I lean in, my eyes dropping to her lips, watching as they part further on a sigh, feeling her breath now barely an inch from mine.

Fuck, I can't do this. *We* can't do this.

"Damn it," I say, abruptly taking a step back. "I shouldn't have touched you like that."

"Probably not," she whispers, watching me through hooded eyes as she drags her teeth over her bottom lip. I need to walk away and right out that door, but I remain frozen, drawn to her, trapped in her orbit, unable to escape.

"And I definitely *shouldn't* kiss you." I don't mean to, but I groan. I can't help it, I've never been this pained, this desperate, this *transfixed*.

"Definitely not." Her words are breathy, as she rolls her lips together and her eyes shine a deep, dark blue, drowning me in desire.

"We can't," I remind myself, more for my own benefit than hers.

"Of course not," she whispers, though her words are barely audible, and her gaze is so heated it burns through me like a wildfire, the last of my resolve reduced to nothing more than useless ash.

I am hers.

She tests me, taking a step closer. And that's all it takes; any remaining control I had instantly evaporates from the heat radiating between our bodies.

"Fuck it."

I close the distance between us in an instant.

CHAPTER 17

JAXON

My mouth crashes into Hadley's with reckless abandon. Finally, fucking finally, I taste her as her lips part eagerly for me.

My tongue slides into her mouth, and it's fucking *delicious*.

It's like tasting something I've wanted my entire life but never thought I could have. It's intoxicating. I savor the sweetness of her mixed with the bitter edge of guilt and the tang of knowing we're doing something we shouldn't. It's fucking irresistible.

I can't stop, and I don't want to.

Her mouth is warm and soft and fucking perfect.

Desire burns through me like she just set my world on fire, and, fucking hell, she absolutely did. It consumes every bit of me until everything else disappears, reduced to this one moment.

Reduced to nothing but this kiss.

My arm instinctively wraps around her waist as my other hand cups her face, angling to deepen the kiss as I pull her closer. All I can think about is how I want more of her, how I need to taste every part of her.

My fingers tangle themselves in the wet strands of her hair as I pull her harder against me, sucking on her bottom lip and grasping it between my teeth like I'm starved for her.

I know this is wrong. Spectacularly, dangerously, wrong, but her sweetness and the desire that floods through me feels so fucking *right*. I am lost in her. Drowning in her. Wholly consumed by this kiss.

I already know, I will never get enough of her.

"Hadley," I groan against her mouth as her hands find my chest, gripping my shirt with a force that suggests she's afraid I might leave, that she's not willing to let me go. I'm not fucking leaving.

I've wanted this for weeks, resisted this for too long. This is something I'm not supposed to want, I am not *allowed* to want, and yet it tastes so much more delicious because of that. When have I ever played by the rules? No, this forbidden fruit that's been just out of reach is finally within my grasp, and I'm willing to take a bite, even if it means risking everything. Because it's worth it. *She* is worth it.

She lets out a breathy moan that fucking undoes me. I kiss her back with everything I have, as the hunger I've suppressed for weeks finally breaks free, overwhelming every one of my senses.

You're going to fucking ruin me, Hadley.

My hands begin their exploration of her body, running down the length of her back, sticking to the cool, damp silk of her top before finally cupping that perfect ass of hers. I need to be closer. I need *more*.

I grip the backs of her thighs and lift, pulling her against me as we crash against the door of the wood-paneled fridge, and I pin her against it as she wraps her legs around my waist for stability. Instinctively, I roll my hips into her, craving contact. The fabric of her skirt rolls up to her hips, and I can feel the heat between her thighs.

The kiss grows deeper, more frantic, and I let myself surrender completely. I'm in a fucking freefall, and there's nobody to catch me as my mouth begins to roam, wanting to explore every single inch of her exposed skin. I begin kissing a trail down her neck, and she audibly gasps as my lips reach the spot where her neck meets her collarbone. She arches against me, her hands gripping my shoulders.

Our breathing is ragged, chests heaving as my mouth finds hers, her arms wrapping around me as her fingers rake through the damp strands at the nape of my neck. I groan against her mouth as her body presses against mine.

I thrust my hips against her with each breath, groaning and gasping as my tongue dances with hers, my lips sucking and kissing her with an ever-increasing fervor. I can't help it, an animalistic instinct consumes every bit of my consciousness, it's chaotic, primal and urgent. I growl against her neck, unable to hold back. Not with her. Not anymore.

Her fingers rake through my hair, tugging and grasping as I lose myself in the sweet, fresh scent of her - warm, sweet, and a little wild - like spun sugar melting in the rain.

I am so lost in this moment, in this kiss, in *her*, that time fucking stops; I don't even want it to start again. I want to stay here, completely immersed in her. She sucks my tongue into her mouth, and that fucking does it - I lift her and place her on the countertop, her legs never breaking their embrace around my waist.

The marble island is large and empty, beckoning me to stop wasting time and take her now as the last of my control vanishes. A rush of desire, hot and desperate, rips through me with the force of a tidal wave. I push her backwards, bracing myself on the counter's edge as I prepare to take her, right here.

There is no holding back. I am hers. I've always been hers. And I fucking *need* her.

Her cold fingers tug at my shirt, untucking it as her hands slide beneath the fabric, tracing my abs. Her hands are fucking freezing, but I don't care. I want to be the source of their warmth, and I crave her touch.

Then slowly, her fingers move downward, slipping just beneath the waistband of my dress pants, and it completely unleashes something in me. I fucking pounce. One second, my feet are on the floor, the next, I'm on the counter; like a starved predator, desperate for its prey.

She slides back, pinned beneath me, as she eagerly pulls me down on top of her, her hands now gripping the lapels of my blazer, tugging me closer as I straddle her on the island, bracing myself with my arms as my mouth finds hers. I press one of my legs between hers, grinding into her hip and kissing her with every bit of the ferocity that this primal power has torn out of me.

Mine. She is *mine.*

"Jaxon," she gasps between kisses, her fingers gripping my hair now as my hand skims her thigh, tracing her delicate skin just beneath the hem of her skirt.

My mind and body respond in unison as my mouth fuses to hers. The kiss is hungry and frenzied and completely desperate. We both know where this is going, but we're powerless to stop it as need consumes us both.

A whimper escapes her as my lips find that sensitive spot at the base of her neck. I suck on the tender flesh there, feeling her shudder beneath me. Whether it's from the cold slab of marble beneath her trembling body or arousal, it doesn't fucking matter. We're both about to set ourselves ablaze with this fire that is devouring us with a feverish determination.

She arches herself against me, parting her legs as my fingers climb higher along the inside of her thigh. I feel like

I'm about to explode as she grinds her perfect body against mine. Then, at the moment my fingers climb well past the hem of her skirt, at the same moment her breath hitches in anticipation, lightning streaks across the sky, and a powerful clap of thunder shakes the building.

Damn.

If that isn't some kind of divine fucking analogy for everything I'm feeling in this moment. Everything I'm about to release.

Shit.

What *am* I feeling? What am I *doing*?

The kettle whistles on the stove, screaming at me to stop, that I'll regret this, that *she'll* regret this.

I abruptly tear myself away, pushing my body up and off of her as I slide from the counter, my feet, once again, firmly planted on the floor. The kitchen floor. Of her *best friend's* apartment.

Fuck.

I'm *funding* her. I have a fucking stake in her company. She's my... shit. I run my fingers through my already-tousled hair. This can't happen. This didn't happen.

It was just a kiss.

Then the dread settles in, crushing me beneath its weight. What if it's not *me* she wants, but she feels like she has to because I'm... *oh God.*

I've fucked up.

This is why I don't allow myself to fall.

I need to go.

But I can't make my feet move. I can't walk away from her as I look into those eyes, staring back at me with confusion.

I grab the kettle and forcefully remove it from the burner, slamming it down before shutting the stove off. I can't listen to it screech for another second as the world, perfect for a few brief minutes, comes crashing down around me, realization setting in.

"I have to go," I mumble, I can barely get the words out. My chest is heaving as I tear my gaze from hers. She's sitting now, legs hanging over the edge of the counter, and it takes every ounce of my focus to carefully weave the tattered remnants of my control back together.

"Why?" She asks, reaching for my hand. I so desperately want to let her take it, let her pull me back towards her so I can taste her sweet lips again.

No.

I deliberately take a step back, dragging my fingers down the sides of my face and burying my face in my hands as I try to hide my shame.

"Because," I take a deep breath. I have to choose my words carefully. Do the chivalrous thing, the *noble* thing. I've never been any of those things. But for her, I want to be. "Because, Hadley. AVC is the lead investor in your business. I'm a primary stakeholder. This isn't appropriate. This can't happen," I pause, letting that sink in. "This isn't what you want." I force the words out because no matter how fucking inappropriate it is, she is *everything* I want.

"I think I am perfectly capable of knowing what I want, Jaxon," she counters, like she always does, only this time the hunger in her eyes beckons me, and I feel my resolve start to crumble once again.

I am barely hanging on, and if I allow my eyes to wander, to take in that thin camisole that still clings to her, the swell of her breasts beneath that delicate lace, visible through the sheer, still-soaked silk—

No.

I focus on her, her hair, damp and untamed, her kiss swollen lips, her almond eyes, locked on mine, betraying her hurt and confusion. I swallow and take another slow, steadying breath.

"I have to go," I say again. Firmly, convincingly.

I watch the blue drain from those beautiful fucking eyes as they dull to a deep golden gray. The pain of my chivalrous rejection is evident in her expression. *Fuck.* She thinks I'm leaving because *I* don't want this. But I'm leaving *because* I want this. Because I want this too badly to think straight.

What a fucking mess.

"But what if I don't want you to go?" She pleads, and her words cut like a knife, slicing a deep, painful slit across my heart. I don't want to go either. I need her to know this. But I can't fucking tell her that. I don't want to be the source of her pain, but I know nothing good will come of this. It's already gone too far. This is for her own benefit as much as my own.

"You don't want this, Hadley. Trust me." I exhale. "And right now, neither do I. This can't happen again, nothing but regret will come of this..." There, I fucking said it. The lie rolls off my tongue. Because if I stay, I know *exactly* what will happen. I'll worship every inch of her, and I'll regret nothing. That's the fucking problem.

We just look at each other as an uncomfortable silence settles over us both. I watch her chest rise and fall, her breathing still heavy. I can feel the rhythmic pounding of my own heart beneath my ribs, so loud it's ringing in my fucking ears. This isn't what I want. This isn't what either of us wants. But this is what it has to be.

"Good night, Hadley." I force the words out, trying not to reveal the pain I feel, the way something inside of me is cracking wide open at the thought of leaving her alone, at the thought that she now believes that I'm not interested in her.

Because nothing could be farther from the truth.

I am hers. And only hers.

There is no one else.

But I can't have her.

Slowly, I turn and walk towards the door. Leaving her sitting, stunned and silent, on the kitchen island. I can feel her watching me as I leave, and I hold her gaze for just a beat, glancing her direction as I grab my coat and exit the apartment, closing the door behind me.

CHAPTER 18

HADLEY

I want to talk to Jaxon about what happened last night, but he's locked away in his office when I arrive, the door closed. And I'd made a point to get here a full hour earlier than usual, hoping to catch him.

"He's preparing for important investor meetings," Beau shares when he sees me glancing at Jaxon's closed door. "He told me to hold all calls and not to let anyone enter under *any* circumstances." Beau leans across the desk, beckoning me closer. "He's in a real mood this morning. Came into the office looking like he'd barely slept."

Well, that makes two of us.

I spent the night tossing and turning, replaying that kiss over and over again as my fingers drifted between my thighs. More than once.

"Well, I should get to work. I came in early to get some reporting done ahead of today's meetings." I smile at Beau, hoping that I am convincing enough.

I walk down the hallway feeling defeated and a little bit deflated. What was I expecting would happen? If I'd gotten Jaxon alone, what exactly was I hoping he would say? What was *I* planning to say?

When I get to my office, I step inside and pause.

On my desk sits a large black umbrella, neatly closed. It looks expensive. And brand new. Beside it is a small paper bag from the café downstairs, the top folded once. Next to it sits a small to-go cup of coffee, the word *oat* scribbled across the cup in Sharpie.

My pulse skitters as I walk towards my desk. I open the bag first and find an almond croissant inside.

My favorite.

Beneath it, a simple note written in precise block letters.

You forgot this yesterday.
Now it won't happen again.
And something in case it kept you up all night, too.
– J.A.

I smile before I can stop myself, warmth settling over me.

I am treading in dangerous waters, but just for the moment, I close my eyes and take a sip of the now lukewarm latte as I let the current carry me away.

CHAPTER 19

TREY

Four weeks.

It's been over four weeks since I started handling Hadley Aldridge's account. Not *her* account, I remind myself, the Trueno account. That means it's been over a month since I took Hadley home from the Bar Room.

I need to get over it, but that has proven impossible; I see her every fucking day. I let out a long breath as I step out of the elevator and slip on my metaphorical mask. Bright smile, confident saunter.

"Morning, Beau." The way Jaxon's assistant beams at me does lighten my mood - the man is so cheerful all the fucking time. "Congratulations on two months with AVC. You are Jaxon's longest-lasting executive assistant this year by far."

"Thank you!" Beau gushes. "Make sure to tell Mr. Avenier I deserve a healthy holiday bonus, would you?" He says this with a wink, and I can't help but chuckle at that. I do not doubt that Beau will be getting a bonus that will make him squeal.

"You can go ahead." Beau nods towards Jaxon's door.

I steel myself as I prepare to give Jaxon my weekly

report on Hadley's account. I've managed to keep it strictly professional so far. Jaxon warned me off her on day one, and I'm not fucking stupid. Nor do I have a death wish. Not that he'd actually kill me, but he could fire me.

"Hey Jaxon," I flop down on his couch. I never sit in the chairs that face his desk. He says he got comfortable looking, but actually uncomfortable feeling chairs on purpose. Some intimidation tactic? Like he needs intimidating *chairs?* Yeah, that's why people do whatever the fuck he tells them. His chairs.

"Where were you last night? What was so important that you had to leave early?" He's in a mood this morning, and he looks uncharacteristically unkempt. To anyone else, he would still seem impeccably composed, but I can tell he likely didn't sleep at all.

"I went to a hockey game with Genevieve because she hates going to those things alone. We were guests of our outside counsel - they hosted us in their suite. I filled in as a last-minute replacement for Lex, who apparently had something come up."

"Yeah, a fucking Broadway show with some woman he was trying to impress." Jaxon rolls his eyes, but seems to relax a little.

"Like Vera Norvelle?" I add with a wink.

Jaxon sighs, and I see the edge of his mouth quirk up - it's as good as a smile from him.

"That's not even what I really want to discuss." He takes a deep breath, which tells me either he's unhappy about the news he's about to share, or he knows I will be. "I need you to take Hadley as your date to Russ's holiday party next week."

The confusion must be plain on my face because Jaxon continues. "You heard how interested Russ was about Trueno at Cubed last month. I need you there. By her side. Guarding her." The way he ends the statement as if he's not finished talking makes me purse my lips. There's an *and* coming.

Jaxon looks at a spot behind my left shoulder. "Also, Kit will obviously be there."

Damn. This could get messy.

Who am I kidding? It's already messy. Jaxon just doesn't realize that. He has no clue about my tryst with Hadley. It's not his fault that he's fallen for the same girl I took home last month. And now he's asking me to take her to Russ's holiday party as my date? Why doesn't he just have me rip out my own fingernails while he's at it - it would probably be more comfortable.

"Got it," I say, aiming for casual. "So basically keep her away from Russ and Kit?" Two people I'd already planned to avoid like the plague.

"Should be easy enough. Hadley's friend Jade will probably be there anyway. Sebastian Devereaux's partner. Romantically. He's worked closely with Russ on many ventures over the past few years, so surely Russ invited him."

I don't respond other than to nod. I know this already. I do spend *every fucking day* with Hadley. I know about Jade and Sebastian, whom she calls *Bash*. Because Hadley *lives with them*.

"Anyone else from Trueno coming?" I ask, partly to say something, but I'm also hoping that if I have to be Hadley's shadow all night, I might at least have an extra buffer.

Jaxon shakes his head. "No. Hadley wouldn't even be there if I weren't so certain that her absence would only pique Russ's curiosity in an unwelcome sort of way. I'd rather control the situation as much as possible, so I'm really counting on you here."

Fucking great.

Chapter 20

I stayed late last night, burying myself in my work - the way I always do when I need an escape from life. Jaxon kept his distance all day, despite the thoughtful gift that I found waiting for me in the morning. And it wasn't for nothing, I made real progress on something that's been knotting up my team and I for weeks, and didn't leave until I'd untangled it.

Late enough that I felt justified in taking an Uber home instead of navigating the subway. I couldn't help but notice the light spilling out from beneath Jaxon's closed office door, and I hesitated on my way out, wondering if it was an oversight - or if he was just a few feet away on the other side of that door.

I nearly knocked, hand hovering for just a second before I let it fall. Then I told myself not to be ridiculous, he probably has better places to be after ten. Besides, if he wanted to talk to me, he'd had all day to find me himself.

I tossed and turned again despite the exhaustion, and when I woke up early, once again to thoughts of Jaxon, I decided I might as well just come in early.

Not even Beau is here when I scan my key card, letting

myself into AVC's executive offices, and making my way to my temporary space. I freeze as soon as I reach my desk. Sitting on it is a spectacularly green smoothie, and a note in the same tidy handwriting I've come to associate with Jaxon Avenier.

You're overdue for something green.
Consider this a strategic upgrade.

P.S. Try to go home before 10 PM tonight.

– JA

So he *had* been behind that door. Watching the clock. Watching me.

My pulse stutters at the implication.

I open my laptop, sipping the *green ginger* smoothie as I catch up on all the emails I ignored yesterday while buried in my work. I have to admit, it tastes surprisingly good for something so healthy.

An hour or so later, a notification pops up on the office chat app from Beau, requesting my presence at his desk as soon as I am available. He must know I'm here already, and now seems as good a time as any for a break.

"What is *that?*" He eyes the smoothie as I take a sip.

"The smoothie?"

"The exact same smoothie from the exact same place Mr. Avenier always has me order from. Ginger Greens with an extra scoop of protein powder. Only, he didn't ask me to place an order today." He eyes me suspiciously. "It's not even that close to the office. I didn't realize it was such a well-known spot."

"Mmm, hmm." I bite my inner lip to suppress a smile. "You said you wanted to see me?"

"Oh, yes. I just sent you a calendar invitation for Russell Artanza's holiday party next week. According to Mr. Avenier, your attendance is mandatory. You're to ride there with Mr. Eskridge. I'll send you an itinerary shortly with other important details like timing, what to wear, that kind of thing."

Whatever warmth had just been blooming in my chest cools instantly. Jaxon wants me to attend Russell Artanza's holiday party - but he wants me to go with Trey?

My stomach knots, my fingers itch, my lungs suddenly feel too heavy to fill with air.

What the hell?

I can still feel the ghost of Jaxon's lips on my mouth from just two nights ago, when he kissed me like he couldn't help himself, like he wanted me in a way he'd never wanted anything before.

And now this.

I want to scream. I want to cry. I want to smack him.

And the smoothie, perfectly chilled in my hand, is suddenly unbearable.

He knew I'd see it, he knew I'd notice, and that tiny, simple fact made my heart flutter in a way that now feels entirely unfair.

But I can't let Beau see any of that, so instead, I smile politely at him and hope I'm convincing as I tell him I'll be there.

"Of course you'll be there! I've heard his parties are lavish and outright outlandish. I looked up last year's event online; several society bloggers covered it, and the evening culminated with an indoor fireworks display! I'm counting on you to give me a full report."

"Looking forward to it." I flash Beau a smile before making my way to the break room and throwing whatever remains of the smoothie in the trash.

CHAPTER 21

TREY

I arrive to pick up Hadley on the night of Russell Artanza's holiday party, stepping out of the idling car to see Hadley sweep out of her building. We'll be riding together - Jade and Bash having arranged their own transportation through Bash's company. Evidently, they were invited to some sort of pre-party event that AVC was not.

As I watch Hadley approach the car, my breath catches. She is stunning. And off limits, which only adds to her allure.

The rich fabric of the black velvet gown she wears flows over her subtle curves. The plunging neckline reveals just enough to steal my breath, reminding me that I know *exactly* what lies beneath. She is classic, elegant, and absolutely breathtaking.

I have to clear my throat before I can speak. "Hadley." I extend a hand to help her into the vehicle and climb in behind her. "You look beautiful." My tone sounds stilted, almost clinical. But it's either that or I risk pulling her into my arms and reminding her of the way I drew so many gasps and moans from her the first night we met, Jaxon be damned.

"Thanks, Jade let me raid her closet," Hadley responds demurely, gesturing to her dress. "And you look nice, too." It comes out almost as a whisper as she turns away from me to buckle herself in.

Our ride to the event is spent in mostly companionable silence. I'd briefed Hadley earlier in the week on the players at Russ's party. Russ himself, of course, and his unsavory interest in Trueno. Hadley seems reasonably wary of Russ now that I've outlined his past precedent for crossing professional boundaries as a limited partner working with other investment teams. She understands why we want to protect our investment in Trueno. I also briefly explained that we do want to work with him on other ventures, so we're treading a fine line as far as he is concerned. I didn't go into it further, nor did she ask.

Kit, though, I didn't bother going there. What is there to say? Kit and Jaxon are certainly not an item. Neither are Jaxon and Hadley, but I have a feeling Kit won't see it that way. Hopefully, she and Hadley don't even cross paths.

We quickly settle in at the cocktail hour after checking our coats, scanning the room for familiar faces. An hour of small talk and introductions later, Lex finally finds us, a festive-looking martini in hand.

"Thanks, Sterling." I snatch the cocktail for myself.

"Easy there, Eskridge." He holds my gaze for a moment, eyes sharper than they need to be. Then a small smirk. "Try not to spill it."

He claps me on the back as he laughs hard enough that I do spill it; but his fingers stay there on my shoulder, steadying me as I compose myself enough to take a good sip of the frosty cocktail. I shift a little, leaning into his familiar touch without thinking, already feeling a little lighter.

He looks sharp tonight, like all of us from AVC do, in a

tailored black tux, skinny tie, and a pair of perfectly buffed patent loafers - all swagger and style. Classic Lex.

We laugh about how Russ somehow manages to spend a fortune on these lavish parties and still every one of them is a supremely tacky affair, it's a skill, really. Though I am enjoying this candy cane martini. I notice Hadley likes the signature drink too - she grabbed one off a passing tray shortly after Lex joined us.

"I've managed to avoid Russ so far," Lex grins. "It's easy to spot him in that red velvet tuxedo." He visibly shudders. "You haven't seen Kit yet, have you? She's harder to avoid than her godfather and a hell of a lot more stealthy."

"Who's Kit?" Hadley asks as my eyes widen at Lex. He gives me a frown that says *you didn't tell her?* I merely roll my lips in response.

"No one to worry about," Lex shakes his head. "Just someone looking to… bag an investment of her own. You know what? Just forget I even mentioned her." He looks back towards me at that last bit, and I just roll my eyes and smile.

"Let's grab another drink?" He eyes Hadley's now-empty martini glass. "Or maybe some food," Lex quickly shifts gears. He gestures towards the glowing, backlit bar on the far side of the room.

"You two go ahead, I'll meet you at the buffet. I'm gonna grab another one of those signature cocktails." Hadley will be safe with Lex for a few minutes. I could use a break from babysitting for a minute.

I do another quick scan of the room, my eyes, of course, falling to Hadley like they always do. I watch her, her gaze flicking over the crowd as she stands at Lex's side, and I know who she is searching for. She's looking for *him*. And it stings, because I know it isn't me she is trying to find. No, she forgot about me as soon as she left my apartment all those weeks ago. She'd been looking for a one-night stand, and that's exactly what I gave her. Still, it's hard not to feel the bitter pang of rejection when I watch her pine for someone else day after day.

Her eyes light up, and I follow her gaze the second I notice. I see the way she looks at him as he stands there next to Genevieve. His eyes are already on Hadley, even from all the way across the room, and how could they not be? Most people wouldn't notice the shift, the way he gravitates towards her, but I do. I've never seen him this fixated on a woman, watching her like she's the only one in the room.

I grab a festive-looking cocktail from one of the dozen or so sweetly provocative candy cane girls wandering the party. They're dressed in festive red and white striped corsets and flared mini skirts that flutter like ribbons. Each one actually wears a round, white tabletop like a hoop, the surface dotted with martini glasses so that guests can serve themselves if they please, never having to wait in line. In true Russell fashion, they definitely give off a vibe that is distinctly more Vegas flash than Manhattan class.

I linger near one of the over-the-top cocktail displays featuring a massive tower of pink martinis, each glass garnished with peppermint sprinkles. I can't tell if they're meant for drinking or purely for display, and I try not to roll my eyes at the absurdity of it all. I need to compose myself again before rejoining Hadley and Lex. After a few minutes, while a fast, annoying Christmas jingle is playing, I make my way around the circumference of the room and

—

Oh shit.

I find her immediately, only she's no longer with Lex. Hadley is leaning up against the bar, full glass of wine in hand, and Lex is nowhere in sight. But I know that vicious vixen in the red dress: Collette D'Vesle - *Kit*. She has a menacing gleam in her eyes and a sly smile on her lips. It's impossible to tell what she is saying to Hadley, but I doubt it's pleasant or complimentary.

Hadley looks deeply uncomfortable. There is a beseeching look in her eyes as she does a quick scan around her. I cut through the crowd, not even bothering to apologize as I bump into a toy soldier on stilts in my haste to get to her. Goddamn Russ and all his over-the-top *entertainment*.

"Collette," my voice is low, threatening. I address her by her formal name. I hear Hadley gasp as her gaze lands on me. I place a hand on her lower back, subtly pulling her towards me, and she leans in immediately. I feel her body relax as I slide my arm around her waist, allowing her to settle into my side.

"Trey Eskridge. Hello, darling," Kit purrs. Just the sound of her voice makes the bile rise in my throat. I can feel the hairs at the back of my neck stand on end. "I was just getting acquainted with your newest little *investment*, and now I understand why this one has been keeping Jaxon *so distracted*."

"So I see you've met my date," I emphasize the last word of that sentence and don't miss the way Kit's eyes narrow suspiciously. "And yes, Hadley is important to us at AVC," I add fiercely, hoping my words and my tone end her line of thinking, that Hadley is somehow Jaxon's, because it is absolutely and very dangerously true. I don't wait for her response, instead turning towards Hadley. She now has a faraway look in her eyes. "Come on, Hadley. Jade's around here somewhere, and I know you wanted to see her." I turn away from Kit, somewhat abruptly, and it causes Hadley to stumble slightly. I tighten my hold on her waist as her hands come up to grasp my arm. I can feel Kit's eyes boring into my back as we take our leave.

I remove the wine glass from her hand and discard it on the bar as I lead her away. The glass was still mostly full. How many drinks could she have had in my absence? She was fine when I left her, but now she seems unsteady on her feet.

"Trey?" Hadley leans hard against my side, almost pushing me into one of the poor waiters. "Why-a she sayat? Wassit Kit?" Whoa, okay. The line about Jade was a ruse, but now I'm legitimately scanning the room for Hadley's friend.

"Jade!" Hadley suddenly calls, flailing one arm wildly. Fuck, she's plastered… or something? I make a beeline towards Jade, who stands with Bash at a cocktail table. Jade initially smiles at the sight of her friend, but the smile fades quickly as her eyes narrow and focus on me.

I have never met Jade Corven, but I've met Bash a handful of times, and knowing him, Jade must be a force. I like Bash well enough - he actually reminds me of Jaxon in some ways. Which means any woman who manages to capture his attention for anything resembling a long-term basis must be formidable, impossible to intimidate, and able to meet him toe to toe without backing down.

He glances briefly at us before continuing his conversation with the gentleman standing at their table. Jade brushes a hand down his arm and, with a nod, moves away to join us. She grabs Hadley's other arm and starts maneuvering us towards a corridor that leads to some couches and a restroom.

"Hadley! You're drunk. You've been here, what? Two hours, not even!" Clearly, Jade is annoyed.

"Noooo," Hadley tries to wave a hand, but even her *no* is somehow slurred. Jade glares at me in a way that makes me feel like a puppy that got into the trash.

I shake my head at Jade. "I swear, she hasn't had more than two, maybe three drinks. She was with my colleague,

Lex Sterling, for a bit, and then… I found her with Kit." I have no idea if Jade knows Kit well, or at all, really. The way her eyes widen and her lips purse in rage, however, tells me that she knows *enough*.

"And you are?"

"Trey Eskridge," I respond quickly, realizing Jade only knows me as the man currently escorting her very intoxicated friend around the party. "I'm from AVC, and I've been the lead on her account for the last month." The looks she gives me then is… not exactly recognition, but I get the sense she recognizes my name, or at least she knows *something* about me. Her lips part, as if she's about to say something, but I'm saved from whatever she's about to say next when Hadley hiccups next to us.

Jade turns towards her friend, expression laced with concern. "Come on, Hads," she leads her towards the ladies' room. "Don't go anywhere, Trey Eskridge." She throws over her shoulder.

Fuck.

I sit down on one of the couches across from the ladies' room door and pull out my phone.

> Trey: WTF Lex? I found Hadley with Kit. She's a mess.

> Trey: I swear to God if you left her alone to pursue some candy cane bimbo, I'm throwing YOU under the bus.

No response. Not that I expected one, but fuck. Where is he? It's not like Lex to let me down like this. Though it's more than likely Kit swooped in the moment she saw Hadley alone. Even if she doesn't know who Hadley is to Jaxon, whatever the fuck that is, Kit has a way of finding shit out. Knowing Jaxon hasn't reached out to her in a month… there's no way she is just letting that slide, no way she is letting him out of her grasp without a fight.

And Hadley had no idea she was being thrown into the ring.

I should have told her about Kit. Not everything, but *something* to prepare her better.

Jade storms out of the restroom then, with a pale-looking and glassy-eyed Hadley in tow.

"I'm taking her home," Jade insists. Yeah, she's just like Jaxon. "I'm pretty sure she was drugged."

"Hadley," I pull her close, and look at Jade over her head. Jade is glaring daggers at me, but I hold her gaze. "It's okay, Jade. I've got her." Jade can trust me. I don't know what it is that convinces her, maybe whatever it is Hadley has told her about me over the past month, but she tilts her head slightly and nods.

"Give me your phone. I expect an update." I pull my phone out and unlock it before passing it to Jade. She places a call to herself, reaching into the pocket of her gown and pulling out her own phone to confirm the call comes through. "You have my number. Use it." Damn, that is the least sexy, and most terrifying way any woman has ever said *those* words to me.

Jade's expression shifts into one of tender, worried compassion as she rubs Hadley's arm. "Trey's going to take you home, okay? I'll see you in the morning." Hadley's head lulls against my shoulder as she mumbles some affirmative gibberish. I hold her a little tighter to my chest, wishing I could go back in time and undo whatever Kit just did to her.

I call Emilio to come with the sedan, and we're in the car heading home a few minutes later. "Where to Mr. Eskridge?"

My mind blanks. I don't have Jade's address, though I could easily get it. But I'd have to figure out how to get inside, get Hadley into bed and then... I can't leave her alone if it's possible she's been drugged. Just the thought of bringing her to her bedroom... seeing *her* space when she hasn't invited me in. And then what? Sitting on the couch in her friend's apartment?

Fuck it. Jade said *bring her home*. She didn't specify *which* home. I have a spare bedroom. It's the safest option. The easiest option. "My place, Emilio. Thank you."

By the time Emilio pulls up to my building, Hadley is curled up on my side, barely conscious and mumbling something inaudible. I extricate myself from her and climb out of the car, only to watch her slump over across the seat. Shit, she's worse than when we left the party.

"Hadley, hold my hand." I lean in and try to guide her out. But she just looks at me, her gaze dazed and beseeching. As if moving her limbs to get out of the car is an astronomical feat.

So I carry her, one hand under her knees, the other under her arms as she drapes herself around me, head on my shoulder, arms folded loosely around my neck. I hold her close and breathe in the subtle floral scent of her hair. She is barely coherent when we get to my apartment, so I carry her straight to the guest room and lay her gently on the bed. Her eyes are hooded, almost closed as I take off her shoes.

"You're m'best fren," she mumbles before her eyes drift closed. *Friend.*

I find the zipper on the back of her dress and gently remove it from her body, sliding my hand down her ribcage. I try to avert my eyes, but it's impossible. She is completely limp, and I'm now more convinced *someone* tampered with her drink. I pull one of my old t-shirts over her head, guiding her flopping arms through each of the sleeves, and tuck her in, brushing her hair back from her face.

"Good night, Hadley," I whisper as I step away, feeling

like a failure. I had one job tonight: to protect her. And I failed.

But it's more than that, it's not just that she so obviously wants Jaxon - though that part stings enough - it's that in her eyes, I'm somewhat invisible. Like that night we had together never happened. It's as if it was erased from time, a memory she chose not to carry.

CHAPTER 22

TREY

Jade's at my place before Hadley even wakes up the next morning. She wasn't exactly thrilled that I brought her back to my apartment, but there wasn't much she could do when I messaged her last night. Jade said she'd be here at 7:30 AM to retrieve her best friend, and sure enough, she is marching into my apartment at 7:29 AM to make good on that promise. She brought a change of clothes for Hadley and some choice words for me. Hadley is still in rough shape, though, so I'm spared the full extent of Jade's righteous wrath as she practically carries a semi-conscious Hadley into the elevator.

And once again, Hadley Aldridge leaves my apartment before the sun is fully risen. At least this time, I know her name.

It's now two hours later, and I'm just not in the mood to see Lex - or anyone for that matter. I woke up to some apology texts from him. He swears he got caught up in a productive Echelon discussion with Jaxon and Russ, and did not, in fact, run off with some *candy cane bimbo*, but I have nowhere else to direct my frustration, so Lex feels like a convenient target.

I suppose it's a good thing we are meeting at Brawl & Order. Some good old-fashioned sparring is probably exactly what I need to work out all these feelings.

When I emerge from the locker room and make my way over to the boxing ring, Lex's smile is as genuine and authentic as his warm greeting, but I struggle to return it. "Let's go." I jump into the ring without even a hello. Lex just raises his eyebrows but doesn't argue.

I'm immediately on the offensive, never even allowing Lex to get in a hit, a kick, a punch. Nothing. He is blocking and deflecting, dancing backwards around the ring. Ten minutes in, he puts his hands up, signaling he needs to take a break. Lex eyes me from the corner of the ring, where he reaches down for his water bottle. He takes a long swig.

Keeping his bottle in his hands, he brings his gaze to mine. "What's up with you this morning? I don't think you're mad at me about last night. You know full well I ran interference with Russ. I kept him away from Hadley; he barely got a glimpse of her all evening. I know Kit had a *moment* with her, but… that doesn't feel like what this is about either." He gestures between the two of us with his water bottle at *this*.

"That moment with Kit… I don't know exactly what happened, Lex, but I think someone tampered with Hadley's drink. We left less than two hours after arriving. She stayed in my guest room."

"Oh, *shit*. Seriously? Does Jaxon know? Hmmm, maybe don't tell him." He lets out a long sigh. "Thank God you took her home with you." I huff a humorless laugh. *Thank God you took her home with you.* He has no fucking idea. Nobody does.

Thank God I took her home with me…

"Trey? Dude. Are you okay?"

I shake my head. *No, I'm not okay.* "Jaxon doesn't know," I say instead. "I don't see any advantage to telling him my suspicions either." Lex nods once. He's good at this. Waiting for answers to his questions.

I know he won't let up, so I sigh and grab the water bottle from him. I take a drink as I lean against the post of the boxing ring, considering what exactly to tell him. I slowly slide my back down the post until I'm sitting, elbows on my bent knees, feet flat on the mat. I stare at the water bottle in my hands.

"She's everything I can't have." I let out a heavy sigh. It's a loaded statement, I know that, but it's all I can force past my lips.

"Who? Hadley?" Lex's voice is calm, concerned, and completely non-judgmental as he sits down next to me, facing away from the mat, his legs dangling over the edge of the ring. He sits close, closer than usual, his shoulder gently brushing against mine. "Shit, man. And all this time I've been wondering why you were still pining over a fucking one-night stand you had a month ago, but all this time you've been, what? Developing feelings for Hadley? This makes *way* more sense, explains a lot more about your recent demeanor."

I need to tell someone. I need to get this weight off my chest so I'm not carrying the burden of this impossible secret alone. "No," I sigh. "She *is* the mystery woman, Lex. The one last month, that Wednesday. The night I bailed on you… it was Hadley."

"No!" The color drains from his face. "Oh, fuck." Lex grabs my bicep. "Trey." The sympathy in his voice tells me everything. Even he realizes how hopeless this whole fucked up mess is.

"Yeah," I grumble, eyes downcast.

"Jaxon doesn't know," I state the obvious. "He can't," I add softly

"No. He can't," Lex agrees, releasing his grip on my arm as his hand remains there in a gesture of comfort.

"Jesus fucking Christ." I can feel Lex looking at me, but I don't lift my gaze from the water bottle. "I'm sorry, man. What can I do?"

I shrug. "I have to get over her." I glance up then and meet his gaze. "But how do I do that when I have to see her every day?" I sigh, defeated. I don't fucking care if Lex sees me like this. I needed to open up to someone before I imploded. It's been eating at me for too long, the way she's always there, always just out of reach.

I feel him move closer, his arm settling around my shoulders, a solid weight of support. I'm not sure what I want right now, but his touch feels more comforting than I expected, like he's offering me more than just pity, and I rest my head on his shoulder, grateful for his presence and his friendship.

"I've got a few ideas, Eskridge," he says, winking before shrugging me off and jumping up as he offers me his hand. "Tonight, you, me, and our usual table at Cubed. No business this time, just pleasure."

CHAPTER 23

HADLEY

I crawl out of my room feeling like I've been hit by a truck. My eyelids are still heavy and my head throbs; a dull ache pulses at my temples with each heartbeat. My legs are stiff, struggling to make the short walk to the kitchen. It's like my blood hasn't properly flowed through them in hours, and they've now forgotten how to function. It's dark outside, and I'm confused by the clock in the kitchen. Is it 6:34 AM or PM?

I need water. My mouth is so dry it feels like fine sand is coating my tongue, and my throat has been scraped raw. The bright overhead lights slice through the fog in my brain, but not in a good way. Ugh. It's sharp, like it's boring into my skull. My eyes squint involuntarily; the glare feels like a thousand tiny needles stabbing my retinas. I blink hard, trying to adjust, but my vision feels clouded. *Every-thing* feels clouded. The light doesn't help; it only makes the pounding in my head worse.

I grab the counter to steady myself, breathing in and out slowly, trying to push through the fog and gather my bearings.

The *counter*.

The events of the past week come rushing back. *Jaxon*, the way he looked at me, like his eyes were speaking directly to my soul. The tender concern, the hungry kiss, the way we almost… *right* here.

The way he abruptly left.

And then last night. The party. The way he ignored me.

The way he's spent the past week ignoring me.

Kit. The woman who called him *hers*.

I turn to see Bash and Jade sitting at the dinner table, the remnants of some pasta concoction Bash probably ordered from Carlina's, his favorite neighborhood Italian, on their plates. So, it's 6:34 *PM* then.

"There she is," Jade's voice holds a gentle command, but I also know she's concerned.

"Hi Jade. Bash," I croak out. God, I sound as bad as I must look. Water. I need it. I turn towards the cabinet and fill myself a glass, needing to soothe my parched throat.

"I'll just leave you ladies to it. I have some work to catch up on anyway," Bash loads his plate into the dishwasher before hightailing it down the hallway to his home office.

Jade gets up to shovel some pasta from a to-go container into a bowl and gestures for me to sit. I've got a lot of explaining to do, so I might as well get this over with.

"I don't know what happened, Jade. I'm sorry if I ruined the party for you," I say, because I can feel her disappointment from here. "I swear I didn't think I'd had that much to drink. I'm so fucking embarrassed."

"Hadley," she reaches across the table to take my hand and looks into my eyes with a serious but compassionate expression. "I think someone tampered with your drink. Trey said you only had two, maybe three drinks at most. I know you barely drink, but not even you are *that* much of a lightweight. You were… God, Hads, you were out of your mind last night."

Trey?

I must appear exactly as confused as I feel because Jade gives me a discerning look. "How much do you remember?"

Oh God. I know Trey wouldn't ever… I mean, we'd never. Not again, not after… right? But what did I *say* to him? What happened? Did I leave with him?

What do I remember?

Him. And Lex. Jaxon wasn't with us. He barely even acknowledged my presence all evening. I was with Lex. But then Lex left me when Genevieve waved him over to talk with the guy in the red velvet tux. The guy Trey warned me about, Russ Artanza. And then… Collette, *Kit.* The impossibly beautiful vixen in the red dress. Of course, she belongs to Jaxon. I feel like such a fool.

So you're Hadley Aldridge. The woman who's been keeping my
Jaxon so preoccupied.

Her Jaxon.

You went with a basic black dress tonight, I see.
I would have chosen something more colorful if you wanted to capture
Jaxon's attention. That's why you're here, isn't it?
He bought me this red dress, in fact. And the lingerie I have on
beneath it? That's from him too.

"I remember meeting someone named Collette," I tell Jade. "I think Trey swooped in before we talked much, but my memory starts getting hazy around that time. She was not friendly, that much I definitely remember. And then I was in the bathroom with you?"

"Yeah, she's a real piece of work. Anything else?" Jade

asks, trying to access exactly when my memory starts to fade.

Emilio. The driver. I vaguely remember Trey saying he was calling him to pick us up, and getting in the car. That guy is *everywhere*. The things he must *see*. The things he must *know*.

"Things really start to get fuzzy after that," I admit. "I mean, I remember leaving with Trey. Kind of. A car came to get us."

"So you don't remember going back to Trey's? This time anyway?" There is a hint of a teasing smirk on Jade's lips. *She* obviously remembers who Trey is.

I feel the heat spreading across my cheeks, painting them pink as mortification sets in.

"No. I woke up in his guest bed, though." God, what a fucking mess.

I ponder my last hazy memories of last night and conclude that Jade's assessment of the situation - that something was slipped in my drink - is probably correct. "I think you're right. I don't remember drinking that much. But I don't understand? Why would someone drug me?" I wonder out loud.

Could it have been Collette? Kit, I think they called her. Did she find out about Jaxon and I? About our kiss. About us. Not that there is an *us*. There absolutely could have been. Is *she* why he pulled away that night? Was *I* almost the other woman?

Jade's expression is filled with rage. "That's what I want to know. I have my suspicions, and yes, that bitch, Kit, is at the top of my list. I've already interrogated Bash about her, as I'm pretty damn sure several of his colleagues are well *acquainted* with that harlot. He agreed he wouldn't put it past her, given what he knows of her. The problem is, there's no way to prove it was her. Yet."

"Did you ask Trey?"

Jade looks at me sympathetically. "I did. I grilled him, but I can appreciate that he got you away from her and out of that situation as soon as possible. To his credit, he came straight to me as soon as he realized the *condition* you were in." She must have noticed the panicked look in my eyes when she said she grilled him because Jade let out a short laugh.

"I didn't grill him about *that*, though God knows I wanted to," Jade smirks. "And I get it, honestly, Hadley. He's gorgeous. And that apartment. Very nice. I'm starting to think maybe you should just lean into it. So you had a one-night stand, and he's now your account manager. Why not get him reassigned and just go for it? It was pretty obvious he cares about you." I can't tell if she's being serious or not.

"Other than the fact that he doesn't *remember* me?" Really, does she have to rub it in? I'm already feeling all kinds of shame and rejection today.

Jade gives me a considering look and lets out a long sigh. "I think he remembers you, Hadley," she says softly. "You don't give yourself enough credit."

I want to ask her what she means by that, why she thinks I should pursue something with Trey, but before I can say anything or even finish my train of thought, my eyes fall to the kitchen island, and suddenly, I'm pulled right back to the other night with Jaxon. I can't escape it, I can't escape *him*.

The memory hits like a jolt. His presence, the way everything between us crackled with an undeniable tension. My body heats instantly, a warmth blooming between my legs as the electric charge from the moment he kissed me rushes through me all over again. He's not even here, and I can feel my pulse kick up, the memory so vivid it feels like he could walk in the door any second and pick things up right where we left off. But we can't, and I know he won't. "It doesn't matter." I sigh, shaking my head.

Jade raises her eyebrows as I suddenly become extremely interested in my pasta. I take a bite - it's really fucking good, I can outlast her.

"Okay, spill. *It doesn't matter?* That statement was fucking loaded, and you know it."

Oh my God, it was, and I want to tell her - though not the part about making out with Jaxon in the exact room where I'm currently eating my paperadelle. I should have known better than to think I could outlast Jade; she's not going to let up until I give her what she's looking for. She is relentless. Which is probably also why she's so damn good at her job.

"I might have kissed his boss." *Kissed.* Yeah, that's all it was.

I can see the gears in Jade's head turning. "His boss..."

"The... CEO," I sheepishly admit.

"No. Nope. Hadley. You did *not* just tell me you kissed Jaxon fucking Avenier."

My cheeks flush hot, pink splotches rapidly spreading like a fire across my skin with a warmth I can't put out.

"Hadley. Jesus. There are so many things wrong with this. For one thing, his company is funding you. Objectively speaking, this is bad. Secondly, and trust me on this, you do not want to run with this crowd. You are too smart, too pure, too *good* for this shit, Hadley." She reaches out to take my hand, and I swiftly pull it back.

"Oh, so you can *run with this crowd*, but I can't hang?" I snap back. She's probably not wrong. I'm not as socially savvy as Jade; I never have been, but it still stings to hear it from her.

"Hads, come on, you've been involved with these guys for barely a month now, and you've already slept with one of them and, what, made out with the boss? And do I need to remind you that you're just now rejoining the world of the living because you were quite possibly *drugged* last night? At a party *they* brought you to?" And there's the lecture I've been dreading. "So yeah, forgive me for being protective of my best friend."

"Fine. You might be right, Jade. I can't deny any of those things..."

"I know I am. So stay the hell away from Jaxon Avenier," she demands. I nod, but she tilts her head like she doesn't believe me. "Stay. Away. From. Him."

I sigh. "Your opinion has been noted."

We'll see, I guess.

CHAPTER 24

ACCORDING TO ARIA

Not all thorns spill blood...

...some spill secrets.

VENTURES EN VOGUE PART DEUX

By: Aria Thorne

It's not uncommon that Cubed - that seductive sanctum - plays host to a true Manhattan moment. And last night it once again delivered.

Because when supermodel Vera Norvelle walks into any establishment, people notice. The aisles of Cubed became her own private catwalk - even in a club that caters to the ultra-rich, the beautiful, and the barely clothed - people can't take their eyes off of her. Dressed in a backless black number, the supermodel made a stunning entrance shortly after midnight together with none other than Alastair Sterling, the impossibly tall, maddeningly private venture capitalist.

Yes. Together. As in: arrived together, left together.

Let the record state that you heard it here first, because According to Aria, first reported Manhattan's hottest new duo just a few short weeks ago, when they were spotted leaving the very same club together for the first time.

Is it official? According to inside sources: not quite. But his hand on her back said claimed, *and the heat between them could've set their booth ablaze. Sterling is notoriously tight-lipped about his love life, but the way his eyes never left Norvelle sent a very clear message - she isn't just a casual* plus one.

And Sterling's table, filled with models and Norvelle's industry friends, delivered more than one coupling last night.

Also in attendance? Sterling's longtime friend and colleague, William (Trey) Eskridge III, another one of AVC's elite. It's very much a family business over there, isn't it? Trey, the step-brother of Jaxon Avenier - yes, that *Jaxon - appeared besotted by a woman in Norvelle's company.*

Practically drowning in a sea of models, Eskridge seemed only to have eyes for one of them. Who is she? I can tell you this, readers, she looked an awful lot like Norvelle's closest industry friend, recently signed to the same New York-based agency that represents the famed supermodel.

By the end of the night, the two were practically stitched together, lost in - let's just call it conversation - until the venue's lights came on around 4:00 AM.

Notably absent at last night's gathering? Jaxon Avenier. Which only begs more questions.

Was he spending an uncharacteristically quiet night in with long-time flame Kit D'Vesle? Or has someone new captured his attention? Perhaps the stunner he was spotted with at last month's Ballet gala? Either way, his absence was noted by this thorny journalist.

One thing is certain: when the city's power players start shifting priorities, it means a storm is brewing on the horizon.

And you know I'll be the first to tell you when it strikes - thorns and all.

Stay Sharp,
Aria

CHAPTER 25

HADLEY

Shortly after lunch on Monday, I'm doing exactly what Jade told me not to do - standing outside Jaxon's office. But I'm here to try and catch Trey before we head into our weekly strategy meeting.

And yeah, I'm maybe hoping to catch a glimpse of Jaxon. I know he's off limits, but I can't just turn off the attraction I feel. He might be physically off limits, but that doesn't mean I can't enjoy the view every now and then.

Hopefully Trey will finish early, not that there seems to be any movement in Jaxon's office. I need a minute to talk to Trey, thank him for helping me the other night, saving me really. And also… maybe figure out what I said.

"Do you know how long they are supposed to be?" I ask Beau when he gets off a call.

"Let me check." Beau stares intently at his monitor, presumably having pulled up Jaxon's calendar. "An appointment labeled *Cipher acqui-hire* is blocked until 2:00 PM. Sterling and Eskridge have both been in there since before I got back from lunch. Genevieve left the meeting about thirty minutes ago, though she was there too."

I decide to use this moment alone with Beau to ask the

one question burning a hole in my brain. I tried googling Collette and Jaxon, as well as his name paired with her moniker Kit, but the only hits that appeared were tabloid-style gossip articles, and I've never been one to give them much credence.

Checking first to make sure no one else is nearby, I lean in. "Do you know Collette D'Vesle?" I ask. The way Beau's eyes widen tells me he absolutely does. "Is she Jaxon's… Jaxon's something?"

"Oh, Kit? She's Jaxon's *something*, alright." I must look seriously confused, because half a beat later, Beau clarifies. "She's an escort," he says in an exaggerated whisper. I can feel the way my jaw falls open. "Oh, you can't let that surprise you. These billionaire types and their escorts - it's not a big deal. They need arm candy that knows how to rub shoulders at their elitist events, and not some air-headed bimbo that can't engage in intelligent conversation."

Wow. Okay. That… shit, I really am as naive as Jade claims. Although I guess it kind of makes sense.

"So not his girlfriend. Got it. So is he dating Genevieve Fontaine then? I saw them arrive together. Is Kit mad that Jaxon is now with *her?*" I ask, trying to sound as casual as I can.

Beau laughs and then abruptly stops. "Oh my God, you're serious." He places his hands gently on his desk as he works through another round of laughter. "Oh God, Genevieve Fontaine and Mr. Avenier. That's hilarious. Babe, they came together because they both left for the party from the office. Got ready here and everything."

"Oh." I feel silly now for even asking. "That makes sense, I guess."

"Wait, why are you asking about all these women being with New York's most terrifyingly eligible bachelor?" He asks with an absolutely mischievous grin.

The look Beau gives me says he knows exactly why I'm asking, and I don't hide the expression of longing on my face as I stare at Jaxon's office door. "Oh, babe, I get it, trust me, I do. But do you really want to go there?"

I purse my lips as I give Beau an appraising look. We've definitely developed a friendship over the past month, and he's been discreet about everything I've told him so far. And Jade's ardent insistence that I *stay the hell away from Jaxon Avenier* is proving kind of impossible. "It might be too late for that," I admit.

Beau's jaw drops, his eyes sparkling with pure delight. "Stop. You've already *gone* there?" His tone drips with disbelief.

"I guess it depends on your definition of *there*. But yes. Jaxon gave me a ride home the other night, a little over a week ago, and we kind of, I don't know. Kissed?" More like ravenously swallowed each other whole while somehow remaining fully clothed, but once again, I find myself downplaying our encounter to *just a kiss*.

"Just kissed? Was he into it?" Beau is practically draped across his desk, laser-focused like I'm unwrapping the rarest gift for him.

"More or less, and," *was he into it?* I remember the way he pounced on me, the feel of him pressing against me. I swallow. "He was into it."

"So..."

"So, he pulled away. Said we couldn't. That it would be a conflict of interest."

"Hmmm," Beau narrows his eyes, considering me. I don't know whether to be afraid or excited. "I mean, that tracks. Mr. Avenier is kind of a dick, but he is professional. I don't really get it, though. Sure, you have AVC funding, but that's a contract, right? It's not like you work for him. Or even directly with him. So. What's stopping you two from… ?"

I shrug. "Honestly," my cheeks flush even at the thought of admitting it. But it's Beau, there's no judgment here. "I absolutely did not want to stop. We were in the kitchen about to …"

Beau's eyes shine gleefully at my confession, and he cuts me off. "I've got it!" He even claps his hands a couple of times. "Do you want to make him regret holding back? Show him what he's missing?" The corner of my lip curves up because, yeah, I kind of do.

Beau catches my smile. "Yes! That's what I'm talking about. You and I are going shopping after this, and we are going to find you something to wear at the AVC party that Mr. Avenier will not be able to resist!" Beau is a very enthusiastic man, but I don't think I've ever seen him this excited. I'm not sure whether I should be flattered or concerned.

Moments later, Jaxon's office door opens, effectively ending our plotting, but Beau gives me a quick wink.

"Okay, I'm going to go call my contact at Cipher this afternoon. I'll keep you posted," Lex is saying as he exits the office, offering me a brief smile as he walks past. Something about the way he looks at me feels different, and I'm awash with shame all over again. I must have been such a mess Friday night. How many people saw?

"Hi, Hadley. " Trey's tone is polite, but it lacks its usual warmth. "We have a boardroom on the south side of the building." And just like that, I'm being ushered away.

Trey begins outlining the meeting's objectives as we walk down the corridor, and I can't help myself, I throw a glance over my shoulder towards Jaxon. We lock eyes for the briefest of moments, but that one second is all it takes; the heat of his gaze sets my blood to molten fire, sliding beneath my skin like lava. He turns away almost immediately, retreating into his office, ignoring me like he has largely been doing for the past week.

But surely, he must have felt it too.

We make our way to the boardroom, where I sit down at the table with Trey. We are still waiting for a couple of junior associates from AVC who will be strategizing with us on some performance metrics for Trueno.

I glance over at Trey, deciding to take this opportunity to speak with him now. "I've been meaning to thank you, Trey," I say softly. "I wanted to talk more about Friday night." I reach out to put a hand on his forearm resting on the table.

Trey stares at my hand so intently that I remove it after a second. "Hadley, you don't have to thank me. I should be apologizing to you for letting –"

The door to the boardroom opens without so much as a knock. It's one of the junior associates arriving for the meeting. "Hi, I'm Taylor. You must be Hadley Aldridge.""

Trey throws me an apologetic glance. "Come in, Taylor, we're just waiting for Rachel and then we'll get started."

We spend the next forty-five minutes focused on Trueno with Rachel and Taylor, developing a go-forward plan that Rachel will flesh out further with our teams. Trey leaves the room before the meeting is done - Jaxon apparently needing him for something.

It's still mid-afternoon when the meeting ends, but I'm eager to go shopping with Beau. I desperately need a shot at redemption at this AVC holiday party because right now, after everything that's happened this past week, I feel like a walking poster board for humiliation.

Beau is ready and waiting when I stop by his desk. "Mr. Avenier just left with Mr. Eskridge, and said he won't be returning to the office today, so whatever, I'm letting myself off early. Let's go!"

God, I'm so ready.

CHAPTER 26

HADLEY

"Everything looks great on you, Hads. Can I call you Hads?" Beau is fawning over the latest dress I'm trying on. It's a midnight blue satin gown with a back that is so low it barely kisses the base of my spine.

"Of course you can," I smile at him, glad I finally have a friend who is supportive of my complex *situation*. Though, I admit to myself, he doesn't know the half of it. Literally.

The *Trey* half. I sigh.

"Like I said," he continues, "everything looks amazing on you, but this is not it either. We can do better." He smiles mischievously before declaring, "We're going to Bergdorf's!"

"Oh," I tell him, my face falling, "I can't afford that. I don't have *that* kind of money." Jade's words, that I don't belong with this crowd, cut through me again, a sting that refuses to fade every time I realize how out of my league I really am.

"Nonsense!" Beau demands. "We're going. We'll figure it out later. Besides, I've already made an appointment, and you don't want me to be disappointed, do you?" He bats his eyelashes wildly at me, and I can't help but laugh.

"Ok, fine," I sigh, resigned. "You win." Besides, even if it's only window shopping, it does sound fun, and I'm not ready to give up my bonding time with Beau just yet.

We walk the five or so blocks from Zara to Bergdorf's, and Beau laughs at me as I pause to take photos on every street corner. I hardly even notice the cold, distracted instead by the magic of Fifth Avenue during the holidays.

This is a part of the city I rarely visit, and everything feels different here. The holiday spirit is overwhelming, but in the absolute *best* possible way. Giant wreaths, each one the size of a small car, hang in the windows of multi-story department stores, their glossy red ribbons curling in perfect spirals as the lights twinkle in the twilight. I feel like a tourist in my own city, because that's exactly what I am. It's like walking onto the set of a Hallmark Holiday movie; the only thing missing is a dusting of snow and a hot cocoa in my hand. No photo can truly capture the beauty, the absolute magic of Midtown Manhattan in December.

"Oh my God!" I can't help myself as I point at Bergdorf's.

"I know, isn't it fab?" Beau replies, completely unfazed, as if he's already seen it a thousand times before. Of course, he probably has. "This way," he says, and he drags me, from where I stand gawking, across the street before we miss the light.

Suddenly, we're directly in front of the most exquisite store window display I've ever seen, showcasing an elaborate holiday feast. On a lush velvet cloth rest gold-rimmed dishes piled high with sweets and champagne flutes overflowing with baubles that resemble bubbles. The next window has a lavish showcase of jewelry, displayed like ornaments in a sparkling winter forest, with trees flocked in silver and white. We have, apparently, arrived.

A man in a tailored wool overcoat opens the door for us. This department store evidently has a doorman. I follow my new best friend inside.

"Beau, lovely to see you," an associate greets him as he drags me through a section of women's shoes en route to wherever the hell he is taking me. "This must be the lovely young woman you texted me about. I've already pulled some dresses and reserved a table at the cafe so you can celebrate when you've made your final selection. Champagne is on me, of course."

I have questions. How is a semi-employed off-Broadway actor a regular at a place like Bergdorf's? Beau seems to make fast friends wherever he goes. I mean, look at me, suddenly finding myself in his orbit and loving every second of it. I decide to let it go and just enjoy the experience.

"Thank you, Dylan." Beau flashes him a dazzling smile. "You are the absolute best, as always."

"And you must be Hadley," the gentleman smiles at me. "Beau told me all about your quest for the perfect dress, though he didn't tell me how *striking* you are. Goodness, you're going to have that man eating out of the palm of your hand in no time."

I blush.

We're ushered off to the private, personal shopping quarters where a plush, richly appointed fitting room the size of my bedroom has been prepared for us, a rack of gowns in my size just waiting to be tried on.

Moments later, Dylan returns with a silver tray, two glasses of champagne and two mini bottles of sparkling water sitting on top of it.

"May I offer you something to drink?" I smile in thanks as Beau picks up the two glasses, handing me one. I take a sip as I silently pray we don't get billed for it, though Dylan did say champagne was on him.

I try on designer dress after designer dress, and I'm not going to lie, even though I know I can't afford any of these gowns, I feel like a princess. Having Beau fawn over each one only adds to the excitement.

This. This is exactly the evening I needed to take my mind off of, well, *everything*.

"Try on the two-piece number!" Beau demands as I stand before him in the most spectacular jumpsuit I've ever seen, let alone *worn*. I really thought this was going to be it; everything about the rich forest green velvet screams holiday elegance, and it needs no tailoring, as if it were made for me.

"Ok, but last one." I'm having fun, but this whole exercise is starting to seem silly. I'm nearly done with my second glass of champagne, and Dylan keeps returning with spectacular shoes that perfectly complement each garment.

I wrestle myself into the two-piece gown, refusing to even look at the price tag. I'm just trying this one on to humor Beau. But then I turn and catch a glimpse of myself in the mirror, and my heart skips a beat.

Oh.

Shit.

This dress.

I step out of the fitting room, my heart racing as I await Beau and Dylan's reactions. This dress - *the* dress - looks like it was custom-made for me. It's a sleek black gown, simple but flawless, the kind of elegance that feels effortless but still turns heads. The high-waisted skirt hugs my hips before falling into a daring slit that runs the length of my leg, showing just enough to captivate, but not too much. The cropped halter-style top fits perfectly; it's like this dress was designed to accentuate all my best features. The back dips low, highlighting the length of my spine in the most graceful way. I can't explain it, but it just feels so… *me.*

I stand there frozen for a moment, waiting for Beau's reaction as he just stares, silently. I've apparently rendered the man temporarily speechless, and I hope that's a good thing.

His eyes scan my body before he suddenly gasps, causing me to jump. The sound that comes out of his mouth is so sharp and astonished that I almost laugh.

"Oh my God," he whispers, stepping closer, his voice heavy with awe. "Oh my fucking God, Hadley. He won't be able to look away. Not for a second. Nobody will."

"Do you think he'll…?" I start, but he cuts me off.

"He won't be able to breathe. He'll *worship* you in this. You're… you're untouchable, but like in a way that means he'll want to do nothing *but* touch you." He is positively beaming.

"So you approve?" I ask.

"Approve? Shit, Hads, you're going to turn more heads than Vera Norvelle at the party." Is he talking about the supermodel? Because comparing me to *her* is just laughable.

"Vera Norvelle?" I ask, curious.

"Oh my God, Hadley! Have you been living under a rock? I need to catch you up on all the AVC gossip, apparently." I stare blankly, having no idea what he's talking about. "Mr. Sterling, he is *dating* Vera Norvelle! Finally introduced her to Mr. Eskridge over the weekend, so it's definitely official. They were all photographed together, and it showed up in Aria Thorne's column!"

He pulls open his phone, scrolling until he finds the article. I've never kept up on society gossip, certainly not the kind he's referencing. But sure enough, there is Lex, standing with his arm around Vera Norvelle's waist. I feel a pang in my chest as

I look at him, and the way he's gazing at her, smiling. He looks so much like Jaxon, and I once again find myself fantasizing about last week in the kitchen and what *almost* happened.

"And look! There's Mr. Eskridge!" Beau shoves the phone in my face, finger pointed at a couple in the background. I recognize Trey immediately, talking closely with a different, very leggy, very beautiful woman. Suddenly, unexpectedly, my stomach lurches with an unwelcome and entirely unwarranted pang of jealousy.

"Oh," is all I can manage.

"But I digress, back to you, and that dress, and the things Mr. Avenier is going to be fantasizing about doing to you all evening."

And just like that, the ugly green monster trying to crawl its way out of my gut and into my mind has been tamed.

Jaxon. It always comes back to Jaxon for me.

There is nobody else. I might as well admit it to myself. Regardless of what I am to him. Beau insists he'll take care of the dress, and for once in my life, I don't argue, I don't push back, and I just allow someone else to take care of me as I take his arm and he guides me to the cafe where champagne awaits. Friday's holiday party cannot get here soon enough.

CHAPTER 27

JAXON

I've been at the AVC holiday party all of five minutes, and Genevieve has already cornered me. Something about a potential issue she's just uncovered heading into the next round of negotiations regarding the acqui-hire of Cipher Group - I swear the woman works more than I do. I try to tell her it's nothing that can't wait until Monday - or at the very least, tomorrow - but she is insistent that it is urgent.

I'm about to suggest we table it, offer to meet her at the office first thing tomorrow morning, even though it's a fucking Saturday, when I stop mid-sentence.

Because my gaze lands on *her* walking into the party. I can't explain it, but it's like she is a magnet, and I am instantly drawn to her presence.

This is definitely going to be a problem.

It's as if the world is suddenly reduced to just her. Hadley Aldridge. She moves with effortless grace, her presence commanding attention. Or at least *my* attention.

Her hair falls in soft waves around her shoulders, and I swear it's like the room's temperature instantly rises the moment she enters.

As she glances around, taking in the atmosphere of the party, our eyes briefly meet, and an electric jolt races through me with lightning speed, nearly striking me down. She lifts her chin ever so slightly as she holds my gaze, and I can see a hint of intrigue in her eyes; a flicker of defiance, perhaps, or maybe a challenge.

As she takes a step forward in a dress that should be fucking illegal, I notice the way it exposes her leg. That slit is criminal, running all the way to the top of her thigh.

I can't help but stare.

And that fabric, a black satin, the kind that glows under the lights, sleek and dangerous like liquid mercury.

Black suits her.

Hell, everything suits her. At least in my eyes, it does, and that's the fucking problem.

"So, you and the Aldridge girl?" Genevieve follows my gaze; she doesn't even bother to hide the judgment in her tone.

"Not funny," I take a slow sip of my old-fashioned, hoping she will take the hint and drop it.

"Is this going to be a problem?" She asks it like she already knows it is.

"No." I respond too quickly.

"Right." The word drips with sarcasm.

"I'm fine." I scan the crowd.

"Careful, Jaxon. You look like you're forgetting where the power actually sits." Genevieve has never been subtle about her feelings, I'll give her that.

"Oh, I'm well aware. Which is precisely the problem." The universe just handed me Hadley Aldridge, and for professional *reasons*, I am totally fucked. Because I have no choice but to stay far the hell away from her. It feels like some cruel test of my control. One that I'm already failing.

"You're better than this," Genevieve follows my gaze, which I cannot seem to take off of Hadley. I can feel

Genevieve's eyes narrowing in disgust. "Just don't make me clean up your mess later." The statement is quiet. Flat. Like she's already decided how this ends and is giving me the courtesy of course correction.

"Noted," I grit out through my clenched jaw.

The word lands evenly, but I already know Genevieve isn't going to be satisfied. There's a pause beside me. I can feel her deciding whether to leave it there. She never does.

"I see the way you look at her." That one hits. Because I can't fucking help it. "I don't approve," she adds, as if it matters. "But I'm not blind."

I meet her gaze, hold it. She's right. She usually is. She studies me for a second longer, then nods once and looks back at the screen of her phone, already moving on.

And my eyes are already moving back to where Hadley stands.

I don't fail to notice that she is standing with my executive assistant, Beau, and some man in a perfectly tailored tux. Beau's partner? If I recall, he did mention he was bringing someone. He looks vaguely familiar, but I can't place the man in the fitted navy blue velvet-trimmed tuxedo, not black, I note. Not my style, but I can appreciate someone with an air of importance when I see them.

Hadley walked in with the two of them. Which means she didn't come with a date. I already know this, however. I scanned the guest list, confirming she was not bringing a plus one.

Just as I'm debating how to approach Hadley, a brief hush falls over the room before the din of conversation picks up again. Turning towards the entrance, I see Alastair has arrived, looking pleased as shit with Vera Norvelle on his arm. They are followed immediately by Trey and a woman I've never seen before. She looks like the type of woman who belongs on the runway right beside Vera

Norvelle. It doesn't take much imagination to guess where he picked her up.

I start to make my way towards the foursome when I notice Hadley heading in the same direction. She reaches them before me. I'm sure as hell not about to look like I'm in a rush as I cross the ballroom.

I saunter up just as the group is finishing introductions. I hear Hadley first, and why does my heart start racing at the sound of her voice? Light, and a little bit throaty. I want to hear her say my name with that voice again. She sounds both amused and surprised as she turns to Trey's date.

"It's nice to meet you," Hadley smiles at the woman on Trey's arm.

I stop next to Hadley, almost too close for propriety, but I forget I am supposed to care. It's like my feet propelled me to her side and refused to stop a moment sooner. I swear I see her stiffen lightly when she notices my presence. She doesn't move away, and I find the idea that she might be just as affected by me as I am by her extremely gratifying. Besides, I'm simply introducing myself, right?

"Welcome to the party, I'm Jaxon Avenier," I greet Trey's date.

"Oh! The infamous Jaxon Avenier." She smiles politely. "Thank you, lovely party. Truly," she gestures around the room. "Trey did tell me you always throw quite the event, and seeing really is believing."

"So when did you meet Trey?" Hadley asks. Her tone is curious enough, but there's something about the way she purses her lips, a slight frown between her eyes. Her gaze darts towards Trey, eyes narrowing briefly, before returning her attention to his date. Is she...*jealous?*

It is unclear to me what it is, but there is something there. I've always had a good read on people.

As the women make idle chit-chat, I find my own

thoughts spiraling. Why would Hadley be jealous? Did something happen between her and Trey? He hasn't said anything. Has she developed feelings for him? They work together so closely, but he would *never* act on that. I am positive I made it quite clear the *boundaries* I expected him to keep.

This anxious feeling of betrayal is ludicrous. I'm not jealous of *Trey*. I need to get a grip.

Genevieve is right. I am allowing this to become a problem.

I need to get away from everyone for a minute. A moment of solitude to calm my mind. My father may be retired, but he is the founder of the company, he was the face of AVC for decades, and he should have been here. Instead, he's enjoying his first year of retirement, off on some luxury vacation with Colleen, leaving me to deal with… everything.

To clean up the messy Cipher acqui-hire.

To mingle with all our accounts and all of our clients at tonight's soiree.

To rub shoulders with all the *important* people, the *right* people for the social and political bullshit that I have no tolerance for.

And, perhaps most painfully of all, I admit to myself, avoid the hell out of Hadley.

Suddenly, it's all too much.

I excuse myself and make my way quickly towards an exit, any exit. Alastair is hot on my heels. He means well, but I don't even want to talk to him right now. I need to be alone and to get the fuck out of here long enough to calm my racing heart.

"You can't leave, Jax." Alastair's tone is soothing but authoritative.

"Watch me," I say as I walk towards a discreet door in a shadowed alcove, praying it's a staircase.

The sign is there, clearly embossed on a shiny brass plate. *Restricted Access: Private Terrace.* It doesn't matter. I don't give a damn about the rules tonight. I need to escape, need to get away, just for a minute. I shove the door open.

The cold shocks my system the second I step outside, it's sharper than I expected, cutting straight through the fabric of my Zegna tux, but I welcome the chill. Alastair isn't stupid enough to follow me out here, but I have a feeling he'll be standing guard, waiting for me when I finally decide to return.

It's quiet out here, countless stories above the bustle of lower Manhattan. The air is crisp and bites as it whips across the private, rooftop terrace. The lights of Manhattan sparkle below, twinkling like stars in a universe that doesn't give a shit about my first-world problems.

I close my eyes for a moment, letting the wind hit my face, relishing in the feeling of being this far removed from everything and everyone. I try to clear my head, but even out here, I can feel her presence, the pull of the tension between us. It gnaws at me, a constant fucking ache that I haven't been able to ignore.

And seeing her tonight. Wearing *that.*

She deserves so much more than me. So much more than what I can give her. But damn if I don't want to give her *everything.* Because it's so much more than physical attraction I feel for her, and that's the fucking problem.

If it were lust, I could *compartmentalize* it. I've done that before. Too many times to count. That kind of delicious heat that burns fast and clean, and when it's over, you walk away without ash on your hands. That, I am familiar with. But that's not what this is.

I can't snuff this out: this is something that has already burned straight through me, and then somehow settled deeper, like coals that never stop glowing. But I also *care* about her. Too much. It's the only thing stopping me from making a colossal mistake. I don't know how to box this away, lock it behind some door. And truthfully, I don't want to.

What I feel for Hadley, what she *does* to me, isn't something that knocks. It seeps. It seeps into the spaces I didn't think were vulnerable. It slithers under doors I thought had long been shut.

I tell myself I'm still in control. That I'm watching from a distance.

But I'm not.

She's in the room even when she's not. She's in my head like a pulse. In the moments between meetings. In the silence after a call. In every fucking erratic beat of my heart.

And every time I try to draw the line, to *be* the line, I watch her toe right up to it with that determined fire in her eyes, and I realize this isn't something I'm going to outrun. Because it's already made its way inside.

I am hers, whether she realizes it or not.

That much, I know. I just don't know what to do about it.

I let the wind bite at my skin; the chill feels good, like a shield, tempering that fire that burns within.

Just as I'm starting to realize I can't last out here in the cold, not tonight, the door to the terrace opens. I'm about to bark at Alastair or whoever the fuck is coming out here to demand I act like the responsible person I'm expected to be and go back inside.

No.

My heart stops when I watch the silhouetted figure gracefully step out into this secluded space. It's *her*.

"Hadley?" I ask, more for my own benefit than hers, wondering what the hell she's doing out here.

"I was curious where you went," she says. "I saw you rush off and –"

"And what?" I don't even know what I want her to say.

"Come back, Jaxon. Back inside. To *your* party. It's freezing out here." Her eyes plead with me to join her. I have no idea how she found me, *why* she found me, but I know I need her to leave right now, or my resolve is going to break. I'm hanging on by a thread, and every second I spend around her, that thread thins and frays a bit more.

"What are you doing out here?" I demand, ignoring her request. And when I look into her eyes, that thread pulls more tightly, and I feel it, the slow unraveling of my resolve to stay away from her. "It's freezing, and you're not dressed for this weather."

"I mean, you're not exactly dressed for the wind chill either," she offers me a shaky smile. Then her expression hardens into one of determination, and I know this is an argument I am going to lose. She followed me out here, bringing with her all that defiant, tenacious fire. And I completely melt.

But no. I can't, we can't. This. This is exactly what I came out here to avoid.

"Hadley," I don't intend it, but the words come out raggedly, like a growl.

"I know why you said last week there's no future for us," she insists, surprising the hell out of me with the direction she just took this conversation. "But the thing is, I'm realizing that I only want to be wherever you are."

"Do you?" I ask as I take a step closer. Because she needs warmth, I tell myself, as I remove the jacket of my tux, draping it over her exposed shoulders.

"I know you feel it too," she says, staring directly into my eyes in a way that pierces my soul. "I wouldn't have said it if I didn't believe you felt the same way. You might not admit it, maybe not even to yourself, but I see it. I see it every time I catch your eyes lingering on mine, and I *felt* it in that kiss, Jaxon. Don't you dare try to deny it."

She's right. And she knows that I know she is. I stiffen, using every remaining sliver of my control not to reach out and touch her. Because goddamn, I want to.

"And I see it every day. In the way you've *observed* how I take my coffee, assuring the fridge is always well-stocked. And in the way my favorite Thai takeout appears on my desk on the nights I'm working late, or there's an oat milk latte waiting for me the following morning. It's also the way you share things with me, about you, about your life, your past. I know you don't do that with most people."

I could tell myself, tell her, that those are just common courtesies. That I'd do the same for anyone who matters to the company.

But the lie doesn't even form properly.

Because she's right. I don't catalog anyone else's habits the way I do hers. I don't notice when their hands shake if they skip lunch, or the way their noses scrunch when their coffee is too bitter. I don't worry about how anyone else is going to get home on dark, stormy evenings either.

I don't soften for anyone else.

This isn't generosity, it's intention.

And the most dangerous part about it is that it never felt like effort. "I can feel it *now*, in the way you're standing too still, in the way you won't touch me but your eyes say you want to."

I clench my hands into fists at my side to stop myself from reaching out and proving her right. "We can't, Hadley. You know we can't." I can barely get the words out, afraid that pushing her away again might be the very thing that breaks me.

"Don't shut me out again. Because I *know* you want this, whatever *this* is." She never takes her eyes off me, and I can't respond. I only swallow. Hard. She just stares back at me, and that look in her eyes - it's not just a challenge, it's an invitation. She knows what this is. She feels it. She's not running from it; she's confronting me head-on.

And she's going to win.

I take an involuntary step closer. Because she's right, I haven't been able to stop thinking about her and I do feel it too, whatever *this* is. This burning, aching desire to be hers. And only hers.

"Maybe you're afraid of how it will look, how *we* would look, or what people might think, what they might say about me. Maybe you're protecting me." She tilts her head slightly. "Or maybe you're just afraid that *I* don't want *you*. But here I am, telling you that I do."

I can't deny any of it, because she's not wrong. So I just stare at her in silence as my heart pounds beneath my ribs, my pulse racing, my head reeling.

This stunning, brilliant woman.

"The thing is, I can't deny my feelings or this attraction. To *you*, Jaxon... and I get it, you're scared to let me in, to see where this could go. You worry about what people might think, how it looks. And I'm scared too, I can admit that. But here's the thing, if we let caution rule our hearts, if we continue to willfully ignore whatever this is, were our hearts ever really worthy of it to begin with?"

I still don't say anything; instead, I take another step closer, closing the gap between us as my hands gently grip her waist and pull her against my body. I tell myself it's because it's too cold for her to be out here dressed like that.

"You don't mean it," I say it because I can't admit out loud that she is right, even as hope inflates in my chest like a balloon.

"I mean every word of it, Jaxon." Those words. That affirmation. That promise finally snaps whatever last strand was holding that thread together.

"Okay." I'm barely able to catch my own breath.

"Okay." She repeats my own words back to me, extending her hand.

I take it, and for the first time, I don't try to tamp down the hopeful feeling rising in my chest. Instead, I smile as I lace my fingers with hers and allow her to lead me inside.

"Wait," I say just before we reach the door. "If you really want this, if we're going to do this, whatever *this* is, you need to be prepared. Because people *will* talk, Hadley. About us. About *this*. And I need to know, are you really ready for that?"

She pauses for a moment, looking at me like she's trying to find answers I'm not sure I can give her. "Do you want this?" She asks, her eyes burning with desire, though there's an undeniable vulnerability there.

That question I *can* answer. Of course, I want this, more desperately than I've ever wanted anything.

"Yes," I sigh. "I'm tired of fighting it. It's just…" fuck I've already said too much. But then I look into her eyes, and the tenderness that radiates from within, and that look of longing fucking destroys any lingering shred of doubt I once possessed. "It's always been you, Hadley. Since the first moment I laid eyes on you, there's been no one else," I admit.

"Let's go back inside," she says as she tightens her grip around my fingers, tugging me through the door. "Together."

I follow. I'd follow her anywhere.

CHAPTER 28

JAXON

There's no one on the other side of the door as we reenter the building. How am I expected to go back to this party and work the room after *that* conversation? Because Goddamn, I don't even have the words to describe the cocktail of emotions that Hadley Aldridge just served me.

Whatever she poured into me wasn't alcohol, but it has a similar effect - a blooming warmth in my chest, a slight loss of equilibrium, and the unsettling awareness that I'm no longer fully in control. My fingers are still linked together with hers, and now that I have her hand wrapped in mine, I don't want to let go of her for a single fucking second.

"This way," I tell her, as I lead us back towards the main ballroom.

"Jaxon," Hadley whispers, her eyes falling to our hands. I squeeze gently, refusing to let go. "What are you doing?"

"Something I should have done a while ago," I respond, my voice low. "As long as you're sure."

Her teeth catch her lower lip, one of her tells. She's

thinking. I feel the tension in my shoulders ease when she finally lets it go. She pauses, her eyes dipping downward before they come to meet mine, a fiery determination blazing behind them.

"I've never been more sure of anything." And the certainty in her tone offers all the confidence I need.

"Okay," I give her hand a gentle squeeze before letting go. "Then let's head back to the party." I make a point of holding out my arm to her. "Together." She takes it, hands wrapping around my bicep as we head back towards the ballroom, looking very much *together.*

"Where the fuck have you been?" Of course Alastair finds me immediately. "You know what, don't answer that." His eyes fall to my jacket, possessively draped over Hadley's shoulders, narrowing even further as they hone in on her hands wrapped around my arm in a way that very much says I am hers.

"I don't want to hear it." I glare at him, making sure he is fully aware I am not open to whatever criticism he is about to deliver. Outwardly, he's judging my brief disappearance. Though I know what he's thinking, and I really don't give two shits what he has to say about Hadley wearing my jacket while her fingers dig into my bicep.

"A conversation for later then," he acquiesces. "But a conversation for now?" He raises his brow as if asking permission, and I nod, allowing him to continue. "Russ just arrived, eager for an audience with you. And of course, Barnaby Mordrake readily offered himself in your stead."

"Noted." Of course my *well-intentioned* board chair swept in to entertain one of our greatest assets. No doubt *Barney* is hoping I'll fail to show my worth, but I'll make damn sure to prove why I'm indispensable.

"Show me the way." Alastair smiles somewhat triumphantly as I gently remove Hadley's hand from my arm.

"You should probably take this back too," she slides my jacket off her shoulders and I hate the way she suddenly looks less like she belongs to me.

"Don't go too far," I murmur, leaning closer than is probably appropriate as I slip into my coat. "I'll come find you once I wrap this up."

I force myself to focus as Alastair steers me through the crowd. I grab a cocktail off a passing waiter's tray, sipping as I nod, smile, and pause occasionally to say hello to those I need to take a moment to acknowledge. It's exhausting, playing the role of CEO in the charming way my father always did. Only, there are more eyes on me now - and a much bigger target on my back.

I lose Alastair somewhere along the way as I continue to make polite conversation with AVC's guests. I act like I *want* to be engaged in superficial chatter with every client, investor, and strategic partner I come across. Talking to them all as though they have my undivided attention. As though I came here hoping for the opportunity to personally connect with each of them. Like every instinct I have isn't pulling me back toward Hadley - toward the promise of taking her home instead of parading through a room full of people who don't matter to me.

But this is the role life cast me in.

And for now, I play it.

Even with Russ.

Especially with Russ.

"Russell, delighted you could join us." I approach the pair, cutting off the snake of a board chairman, Barney Mordrake, from whatever it was he was sharing with Russ.

"I haven't missed your holiday party in years, Jaxon, you know this. Glad to see you haven't scaled back since taking over." I'm not clear on whether that's a reference to the guest list or the event itself, but either way, leave it to Russ to be keeping tabs.

"After the performance of Catalyst, I'd say tonight is a cause for celebration." I don't miss the opportunity to prove myself once again in front of both Russ and Barney.

"I was hoping to share a celebratory toast with you when I first arrived," I had a feeling this dig was coming my way. "But you were nowhere to be found. If I didn't know better, Jaxon, I'd think you were maybe avoiding me. Luckily Barnaby over here has been keeping me *well* informed." His tone makes me uneasy. As does the smug look on my board chair's face.

"Well, it's an awfully big party, Russ. I've been making the rounds. Though I think we can both agree, I've saved the best for last." I raise my drink to him in a toast, and this calculated bit of flattery seems to placate him for the moment.

"Yes, where were you?" Barney cuts in. "I was also hoping to have an early word, and hopefully meet the founder of Trueno. I hear you've been quite taken by the company's potential."

"It is exactly the type of scalable technology we are looking to fund." I offer no more, refusing to give Barney even an ounce of satisfaction. One thing I've learned about Barney is that if you give him an inch, he will take a whole fucking mile. And then some.

"Is she here?" Russell is practically chomping at the bit.

"She was invited," I offer my own calculated response.

"Well, do make a point to introduce us, won't you, Jaxon?"

"I'll do my best," I promise. I see Alastair waving towards me from across the room. "If you'll excuse me, it appears I'm being summoned for remarks."

My eyes scan the room, searching for Hadley as I make my way over towards Alastair. He stands with Joe - *Beau*, I remind myself - a copy of my printed remarks in my assistant's hands. My father is the one who always handled this, delivering the recap of our year's successes with a commanding presence that drew everyone in. But he's not here. He prepared me well, however. For this moment. For the eventual takeover of his carefully constructed empire. And AVC had a record-breaking year thanks to the performance of the Catalyst fund. Which, I remind myself, I spearheaded from the beginning, even before I was voted in as CEO.

Catalyst's success makes my remarks easy, along with a few other windfalls we've had this year; the message is overwhelmingly positive. I've made almost every person in this room richer this year, in one way or another. I don't deny myself the sense of pride I feel, even as I scan the room for Hadley, delivering the last of my remarks - hopeful words about the year to come, with my eyes locked on hers.

Now that the formalities are over, I venture back into the crowd and head straight for Hadley as the band starts up, signalling that the dancing has begun for the evening. She lets me take her hand in mine as soon as I reach her.

"Dance with me." I start guiding her towards the dance floor. I want to keep her away from any possible interactions with Russ or Barney and have her to myself as much as I can in a room full of hundreds of people. Besides, the event organizers are always imploring me to set an example at these kinds of things. *If the CEO takes to the dance floor, everyone else will too.*

If anyone asks, I'm just leading by example. I know people will be watching, clocking *who* it is I'm dancing with. But I decide that I don't care anymore. This is exactly what I made sure Hadley was prepared for too.

"You were brilliant up there." She smiles back at me, and I can feel my hand at her waist instinctively pulling her closer. "I had no idea you were such a strong public speaker."

"Thank you." It's a casual compliment, but it still means more to me than it probably should. "My dad had me speaking in front of crowds before I was ten. Honestly, it doesn't even phase me anymore."

"I wish I could say the same," Hadley leans into me, bringing her mouth closer to my ear, and I tighten my arms around her. "I know you warned me, but people are already looking."

I can feel myself stiffen, but I don't break our dance. "It's probably because I am not exactly known for my presence on the dance floor at these sorts of things."

"It feels like maybe it's more than that." Her voice dips to a whisper as I watch her cheeks flush crimson.

"Are you okay?" My first concern is Hadley's comfort. "We don't have to keep dancing."

She raises her chin defiantly and looks me in the eye. "Of course I'm okay," she gives me a conspiratorial smile. "They're probably just jealous."

My God, I want to kiss her.

"Let them be jealous." I spin her around as the music picks up, and the way she laughs, her eyes sparkling with joy, nearly brings me to my knees.

"I don't care what they think." Her voice drops, her words carrying more weight than she realizes.

"I don't deserve you," I whisper, my breath catching in my tightening chest. "But I'm yours as long as you'll have me." The confession slips effortlessly past my lips. I mean every word, and that's a fucking promise.

"Good," she replies as she rises higher on her toes and brushes her lips against mine, as she says, "because I think I'm already falling for you."

I reflexively squeeze her so hard, my fingers dig into the flesh of her waist, afraid, no, fucking terrified to let go as, I swear to God, my heart stops beating in my chest.

I have to ask. I need to know. "You think?"

Is that what this feeling is? The tightness in my chest every time I see her, every time I even fucking hear her name? The shortness of breath, the erratic beating of my heart, the way I feel incomplete when she's not there?

"I don't just think, Jaxon." There's conviction in her tone, and her voice drops before she adds, "I know." Two words that land like a key, turning in a lock somewhere inside my heart. "And I know I probably shouldn't have said that, because sometimes it feels like we barely know each other, and the intensity of this connection probably isn't normal, but I can't explain it any other way. I feel safe with you in a way I can't articulate, and I can't help but open my heart to you. So if we're going to do this, that means we are going to admit to each other and to ourselves how we feel. How we *really* feel. And that's how I feel."

I don't even respond. I can't. Her words just unlocked some part of me that's been hidden away, buried beneath layers of self-control, and the walls I built to keep myself safe. But it's there, it's fucking *here*, and it's very, very real. It's her. She's the one with the key.

I don't think, I just react as I drop my hand from her waist and pull her off the dance floor mid-song, her other hand grasped tightly in mine. I drag her to a secluded corner of the room, on the far side of one of the bars.

I pull Hadley close and cup her face in my hands. "Hadley," I gasp, taking in her open expression. I'm not even in control of what falls out of my mouth right now. "I need you," I tell her. "And I've never *needed* anyone, not like this, not like I need you. It's dangerous, how much I need you. You've undone me in ways I didn't know I could unravel."

Her eyes grow wide for just a fraction of a second before I see the blue in them burn bright with desire. "I'm not going anywhere."

"You are so perfect."

"Jaxon –" She starts, but I cut her off, fusing my mouth to hers with a kiss as I pull her against me.

My name. On her lips. The most perfect fucking sound. Goddamn, I need her right now.

My Hadley.

Fuck. When did I start thinking of her that way?

Probably after she confessed that she's falling for me.

"Come home with me." I sound wrecked, probably because I am.

She blinks once, then nods.

Holding her hand firmly in my grasp, I haul her around the edges of the crowd in an effort to slip out unnoticed, shaking off my jacket and throwing it over her shoulders on the way out of the ballroom.

We are less than twenty feet from the exit when Calvin Thornton steps inside, effectively blocking our path. The man has always rubbed me the wrong way, and in this particular moment, my patience for him is nonexistent. I halt abruptly, causing Hadley to stop pressed up against my side.

"Cal?" she says before I can acknowledge the son of one of the city's most affluent businessmen. Calvin is the son of Rex Thornton, owner of the New York Riders hockey team and one of the Catalyst Fund's limited partners. I briefly consider asking after his father, which would be the expected thing to do in this situation. Though right now, all I want to know is how the fuck Hadley knows him well enough to call him *Cal.*

"Hadley? Wow!" Calvin's face lights up, but his smile feels more devious than genuine. "I didn't expect to see you here..." *with him* is left unspoken as his gaze purposely rests on me and his eyes fall to our intertwined hands, my jacket draped over her shoulders.

"I could say the same," Hadley smiles back at him,

seemingly oblivious to the uneasy undercurrent simmering between Calvin Thornton and I. "I'd say we should catch up, but umm..."

"You were just leaving," Calvin's knowing smile leaves me with an uneasy feeling in the pit of my stomach. But Hadley simply nods as she tugs at my hand, and I'm right back on track. Yes, we *are* leaving. The hum of satisfaction rushes back through my veins.

"Another time then." I hear Calvin, now behind us, as we exit into the cold air. Emilio had better be ready and waiting.

CHAPTER 29

HADLEY

This is reckless.

I just told Jaxon I'm falling in love with him.

Because I am.

Which is crazy.

I shouldn't have done that.

No, I should have.

This is …

… exactly what I want. After Beau bought me this dress, I had to admit to myself what I wanted. What I *really* wanted. I came here tonight with every intention of capturing the attention of Jaxon Avenier. I want this. I want him. All of him, no holds barred. I'm not one to lie to myself, and I won't lie to Jaxon.

At least not about my feelings. And really, I've never *lied* to him.

I've just never told him about that night with Trey. A night we shared before I'd even met Jaxon.

I instinctively tighten my grip around Jaxon's fingers as an unexpected thrill races through my body at the thought of Cal seeing us together. Of Cal *knowing*. Of anyone knowing, really.

Of being *his.*

An expression of recognition crossed his face when he looked at Jaxon. I didn't miss it. I also noticed it was not a friendly one. I wonder how they know each other, but then again, everyone in Manhattan apparently knows Jaxon Avenier, or at least *of* him.

I saw the way Cal's eyes widened at the sight of my hand in Jaxon's, as he took in the implications of our leaving the party early, of us leaving *together.*

Will he tell his father? My mother? Honestly, who cares?

"Emilio should already be waiting," Jaxon tells me, pulling me into the quiet street and pointing towards an SUV halfway down the block with its hazard lights on. Emilio must be expecting us because the black Escalade pulls out of its illegal parking space and begins driving towards us.

Jaxon's arm wraps around me at that moment, and he turns my body towards his, leaning over me and gently kissing the top of my forehead as he does.

"Hadley …" he whispers, his voice trailing off. Words aren't even necessary; my entire body shivers delightedly in response as my heart flutters erratically. Maybe I'm crazy. Maybe Jade's right, and this is the worst possible thing for me. But I'm so sick of fighting my traitorous heart, of fighting *this.* Apparently, finally, so is he.

The car pulls up, and Emilio jumps out to open the door for us, activating the sidebar, which gracefully extends from the vehicle. That is something I'm still not used to, and likely never will be. Jaxon helps me into the SUV as I take a shaky step in my heels, his hands never breaking their steadying contact with my body.

"Third row," he growls softly. "Now that I have you, I'm not letting go."

My skin immediately prickles in response to his words, his touch, every inch of me alive with a sudden awareness that this is really happening, something I'm simultaneously not sure I'm ready for, and have been desperately craving.

And just like that, as I climb into the back of Jaxon's SUV, settling onto the rear bench as Jaxon practically lands on top of me, the entire world tilts, the ground beneath me suddenly feels a little off-kilter as my center of gravity shifts towards him.

"Before I start jumping to any conclusions," Jaxon says, "I need to know, because the way he looked at you, at *us*, you've dated Calvin, haven't you?" It's not an accusation, it's an invitation for honesty, for complete transparency.

Trust.

If I'm going to do this, I want to answer his questions truthfully. He asked, and he almost hit the nail on the head with that one. There's no way I can lie to him, nor do I want to.

"Let's not ruin tonight by talking about our pasts," I offer.

"So you have dated him then." He seems a little flustered, and is that a hint of jealousy?

"Maybe," I respond, a small smile turning up the corner of my mouth into a smirk. He's definitely jealous, and for some reason, that makes my heart skip a beat. "But we all have exes, Jaxon. Are you jealous?" I can't help but ask, as I nuzzle my cheek into his chest.

"He knew you," Jaxon accuses. "Pretty well, it seems."

"I dated him, yes." I sigh.

I feel him tense beneath me, but he doesn't say anything.

"We were over well before I met you," I reassure him, placing my hand on his thigh as I sink deeper into his chest, his arm around me pulling me closer.

He begins to say something else, and I cut him off. I don't like this line of questioning, and not only because my relationship with Cal is firmly in my past. "Jaxon," I sit upright, cupping his face between my hands and gently guiding his forehead so it's pressed against mine. "Are we going to have to spend the next few hours talking about Calvin Thornton?"

"No." I can feel the tension melt from his body as his lips gently brush mine. "Not unless you'd like to spend them talking about all my previous exes."

An irrational knot of envy starts twisting in my stomach at the mere mention of his exes, the beautiful vixen in the red dress flashing across my memory. I never mentioned my interaction with her from that night, and I'm not about to bring it up now, as much as it still bothers me.

I feel Jaxon smile against my mouth and all the tension, that cold, jealous knot, just... fades. Like a shadow retreating with the first light of dawn, it melts into something lighter and more forgiving until I forget about it entirely.

In this moment, Jaxon Avenier is mine. Or maybe I'm his. Who the hell cares? All that matters is that his lips firmly press against mine, eager and insistent, and I gently part mine as he groans against my mouth.

God, that's hot.

My heart skips a beat. It starts there, a quiet hum of awareness, and then crawls down my spine like a sly, forbidden secret. I can feel the air between us shift, charged with something totally and completely undeniable. There is no turning back now.

The kiss is slow and delicious and holds a certain amount of delicacy, as though he's trying to savor it, to keep it *controlled*. But there's something in the way his fingers trace the edge of my jaw, the way his hand grips my waist, the way his lips press deeper into mine, that speaks of restraint *barely* held together.

The car jerks to a stop.

Oh my God.

We're not alone.

We're in the back of Jaxon's car. But I can't stop, *we* can't stop, so we continue this delicate dance between decorum and desire as everything inside me burns with the *need* to succumb to the electric heat crackling just beneath the surface.

I hear Emilio clear his throat, informing us we have arrived, and I gasp in relief; this fire that burns between us cannot be contained, threatening to consume us both whole. I need to get out of this car before we both burst into flames.

Jaxon helps me out and onto the sidewalk, offering me his arm as he guides me towards the entrance to his building, nodding goodnight to Emilio as we go. Every place my body touches his feels aflame; I'm hyper aware of every point of contact, yet somehow it is not nearly enough.

More. I need more of him.

My breaths are shallow and quick, and I struggle to steady them. I feel like I've just run a marathon, my heart threatening to beat itself straight out of my chest as it pounds against my ribs. The world around me blurs, and the only thing that remains in focus is *him*. I can barely hold on to any sense of time or place as we make our way into his elevator and the doors quietly close behind us. All I can think of is how much I want to feel the heat of his hands, his touch, his body against mine, the soft press of his lips on my skin, how I can't seem to escape the pull of this *magnetic* ache inside me.

The doors open with a quiet ding, and the penthouse looms ahead, silent and waiting.

But none of it feels real anymore. Just him. And the intensity of the heat that burns between us.

I allow my eyes to take in his massive apartment as he guides me, hand linked with mine, deeper into the chic, contemporary living room. Holy crap, this place is pristine, polished, almost sterile. Does he actually *live* here? The first thing I notice is a grand spiral staircase made of concrete; it's an artistic masterpiece, and is both masculine and imposing. Just like Jaxon. It's perfect. I cannot get over the fact that he has a staircase in what I'm quickly realizing is a multi-story penthouse apartment.

Damn, and I thought Trey had an impressive place.

Trey's home is warmer though; it feels more lived-in. But here, inhaling the scent of expensive leather, taking in the contemporary polished concrete, the monotone color palette, save for a massive piece of abstract art that adorns the wall in an expanse of navy blue, I can't shake a strange sense of foreboding, that maybe *something* is lingering here with us, like the past is waiting to catch up with me.

Trey.

The memory of our night together comes crashing across my memory in the most unwelcome way. That night. That one night that somehow changed everything, but also changes nothing.

If we aren't talking about Cal, my *actual* ex-boyfriend with whom I had a literal *relationship*, it's certainly not worth bringing up a meaningless one-night stand. I left without even learning his name. It *was* just a one-time thing. I was looking for something reckless, something spontaneous, something temporary. *It was nothing.* Nothing at all compared to what I've found with Jaxon.

It's all in the past. It's all from *before*.

Before I met Jaxon.

It feels like a lifetime ago, really, so what's the point of dredging it up now? I'm here with Jaxon, and nothing else matters. Right?

Right.

This – what I'm standing in, this moment, this connection – *this* is real. This is what matters. This is where I am supposed to be.

It's like he can read my thoughts, because right then, at that very moment, Jaxon's hand squeezes mine, the pressure both comforting and possessive, and I feel a tingling sensation all the way down to the marrow of my bones. I glance up at him, and he leans in just enough to let his breath ghost over my ear.

"Do you know what you're doing to me in that dress, Hadley?" His mouth is hot against my neck. "You're driving me insane. I haven't been able to take my eyes off of you all evening, and I certainly can't now." He pauses, the corner of his mouth gently rising into a smirk as his gaze rakes over my body, and every one of my nerve endings fires in response.

"I've never brought anyone here before, to my home," he continues, and I struggle to breathe. "I'm not even sure how we wound up here," he confesses. "It just felt right. I can't explain it, but every rule I've ever created for myself somehow changes around you. It's a new, unfamiliar feeling for me, but I'm trying here. I'm trying for *you*." He's rambling, and the way he says everything is so raw, so... *honest* that it shatters the last remnants of anything that doesn't belong in this moment. Because this moment, it belongs to no one but the two of us.

His warm breath stirs against my skin as he whispers in my ear. "How's that for sharing how I feel?" The words are simple, but they hit harder than they should, twisting through me.

We're standing so close now that I can feel the heat of his body, and it's almost suffocating, yet at the same time, absolutely electrifying. His breath is hot against my neck, his lips barely grazing the skin, causing goosebumps to rise, and I know he's not asking for permission. He's just *waiting*, waiting for me to grant it.

I don't say anything. I can't. There's no need. The tension, like a string pulled taut, speaks louder than words ever could. It's in the way he's looking at me, the way his chest rapidly rises and falls in sync with my own, the way his gaze drags across my face like he's trying to memorize every one of my features, to burn me into his memory. My skin prickles, every nerve alive with the ache of desire.

It's been weeks of this, of barely restrained *want*, and now the space between us feels impossibly small, like a fuse burning faster than I can stand. I didn't ask for this. I certainly didn't plan for this. I didn't think *this* would happen so fast – *too fast*. But here I am, standing in front of him, every part of my body and my heart drawn to him in ways I can't explain, in ways that feel almost *dangerous*.

It shouldn't feel this intense. It shouldn't feel so *right*, but it does.

Silently, he tugs on my hand, beckoning me to follow. My heart drums in my ears, the rhythmic ringing drowning out the sound of my heels clicking on his polished concrete floors as I allow him to lead me through the apartment, up the stairs, and towards what I assume is his bedroom.

I know it's too soon. I know it's *reckless*. I know we shouldn't. But I can't help how I feel. I feel it, deep in my chest, this longing, this desire, this undeniable connection.

I love him.

Some love, I'm realizing, doesn't build slowly. Instead, it arrives like a storm - unexpected, and already fully formed.

I'm falling, fast, and for reasons I cannot explain, I trust him to catch me.

"Hadley…" his voice trails off as he pauses in the doorframe of his bedroom, and he suddenly looks uncertain of what to do next. Is he *nervous?*

"There's no one else for me, Jaxon," I step closer, closing the distance between us and slipping my arms around his neck. "I don't want anyone else," I confess. It tumbles out of me before I even realize I've said it out loud. The words come out raw, unexpected, but they feel true, so fucking true.

I'm already all in, and maybe that's the scariest part of it all.

My heart pounds in my chest, ringing in my ears. Surely, he must feel this too? Either way, there is no turning back now.

My arms slide around to the back of his neck, my fingers gently grasping the loose curls that hang from the base of his skull. His arm wraps around my body, pulling me flush against him so I can *feel* how much he wants this, wants me, as our bodies fuse together.

Desire pools between my legs as my entire body heats.

"I need to know that you want this, Hadley. That you *really* want this." His voice is soft, his words breathy.

"More than anything," I admit, my eyes locked on his as those dark sable depths turn molten with desire.

He doesn't respond right away, but I see it in the heat of his gaze: the same hunger, the same *certainty*. We've both already crossed the line, and neither of us is looking back.

"Good," he breathes, his lips hovering near mine, just a whisper of a kiss, a warning, a promise. "Because I'm not in the habit of letting go of what I want. And you, Hadley Aldridge, are *everything that I want*."

My breath catches, and for a moment, everything around us blurs. The intensity in his eyes is undeniable; dark and focused, like he can see straight through me, into places I didn't even know existed. His gaze burns with a hunger I can almost taste.

And you, Hadley Aldridge, are everything that I want.

I'd think this might be some type of well-practiced line he uses to bed women, but behind the heat burning in his eyes, a raw vulnerability shines through. He almost looks scared, and my heart bursts open with the same feverish need that suddenly heats my body.

The tightness in my chest makes it hard to breathe, love and fear tangling into a knot that pulls tighter with every passing second. My breathing grows ragged as my unguarded heart pounds desperately in my chest, fully aware of the risk it's taking. My skin feels like it's on fire, my body on the edge of something I've been avoiding but can no longer resist. Fuck, I don't *want* to resist it.

He doesn't move, his eyes wide and still locked with mine, unblinking, and that challenge in his eyes, overpowered only by flickers of fragility, ignites something that burns fiercely. I swallow, trying to steady myself, but I can't. There's something raw about this moment, something *real*.

I can't explain it, but I can feel it. The words he wants to say, his desire to reach out and touch me, his own insecurity and uncertainty. The intensity of this, whatever *this* is, is terrifying; like we've stepped into the eye of a storm, calm and chaotic all at once, and I don't know if I'll survive the aftermath, but part of me doesn't even care.

Then, I make the choice. I don't need to respond; I allow my body to do it for me. I rise onto my toes until the heels of my shoes lift off the ground, and I kiss him.

He stiffens for one beat, and just as panic begins to set in, just when I begin to think that maybe I managed to misread the situation, and he isn't willing to take this risk, he unleashes.

With one swift motion, he whirls me around so quickly that for a second, I swear my head is still spinning as my body slams into the wall, pinned between the cool drywall and Jaxon's heaving chest.

"Shit. Are you alright?" he gasps, his lips hovering just above mine. I can feel the warmth of his breath in this faint touch of a kiss.

"I'm fine," I tell him, my voice barely above a whisper

as I struggle to fill my lungs with air. "You're not going to break me."

He pulls away, his chest rapidly rising and falling as he chokes out. "I need you, Hadley, more than I've ever needed anything."

I couldn't speak right now if I tried, so instead, I allow my fingers to rake through his hair, tugging him towards me as I fuse our mouths back together.

His mouth begins to devour mine, and it's absolutely delicious. He tastes like maple, and bourbon, and everything I shouldn't crave. There is nothing shy or vulnerable about this kiss. No, in the absence of words, it captures the raw, wild need that now consumes us both.

His hand cups the curve of my neck as he angles to deepen the kiss, and I'm desperate to be closer to him as heat erupts from between my legs; I'm desperate for *more*. Instinctively, I lift one leg, bending it at the knee, and slide it against his side, the fabric of my gown shifting with the movement. His hand slips beneath my thigh, fingers pressing gently to hold it in place, and my skin burns like fire where his hand makes contact with the sensitive skin there. The slit in the dress climbs higher, and the dark silk falls away from my leg, pooling at our feet.

His tongue traces the seam of my lips, silently demanding entry, which I readily grant, parting my lips as he eagerly explores every corner and crevice of my mouth. We're all tongues and teeth and roaming hands, but I still need to be closer, I still need more.

My leg wraps around him as, I grind against his thigh, and he groans into my mouth in response. The friction is delicious, and I shiver with pleasure.

"Patience, Hadley," he growls as his fingers trail upwards between my thighs in exploration.

I've never been like this, so out of control over a single kiss, over a man, over, well, *anything*. The craving within me is all-consuming, like it's a fire that cannot be contained, I can't put out, and it's growing hotter with every second, threatening to burn me alive.

His fingers slip beneath the lacey fabric of my underwear, making slow, tantalizing circles, and I moan as I roll into him.

"Jaxon, I need —"

"I know. I've got you," he cuts me off as he slips a finger inside, followed by another.

"So tight," he growls as my back arches in pleasure and I thrust my hips against his hand.

Every nerve is on fire, and I feel like I'm going to shatter. The pressure builds inside me with every stroke and every thrust of his fingers, a tight coil that feels like it's going to snap if I don't give in soon.

"Let go for me, Hadley," his breath is hot against my neck. And right then, at the moment the tension inside me becomes unbearable, like I'm about to explode if it lasts another second, I come undone. *Completely* undone.

My head falls back as pleasure arcs through me like an electric current, each pulse sending warmth rippling throughout my body. I've never felt so aware, so *alive*, as electricity pulses within me, vibrating along every one of my nerves with a sharp, thrilling pleasure.

"Shit," I gasp. I have no other words.

"I'll take that as a compliment," he smiles as he cups my ass, hoisting me up as I automatically wrap both legs around his waist, before making his way towards what is presumably his bedroom.

Chapter 30

HADLEY

Jaxon Avenier just got me off without removing a single article of my clothing. And the way he's gracefully carrying me into his bedroom just now, with a quiet determination, I know we've only just begun.

"I'm never going to get enough of you, am I?" He asks as he drops me at the side of his bed.

I reach my arms up, behind my neck and with one gentle tug, I release the ties of my top. The fabric gently falls forward in loose ripples before I cross my arms at my waist, delicately pulling it over my head.

He breaks our gaze only momentarily to run his eyes over my half-naked body, and when his eyes once again find mine, there is an intense desire there that mirrors my own.

I gently unzip my skirt, allowing the fabric to fall to the floor before stepping out of it, stepping closer to him, wearing nothing but my stiletto heels and my lacy black bottoms. I picked out the lingerie with the hope that *this* might be a possibility tonight.

"Fuck, Hadley," his voice is shaky. "Look at you, you're beautiful."

His thumb brushes the side of my cheek as he cups my jaw in his hand, tilting my face up towards his. His breathing is shallow as his fingers graze the line of my jaw, the touch so light, it sends a shiver down my spine. The warmth of his hand lingers, as if his fingertips leave a trail of fire in their wake. He moves upward, slowly, tracing through my hair, brushing the strands above my ear and sending tiny sparks of electricity everywhere he touches. It's almost reverent, as if he's handling something fragile, something precious.

Me.

My breath hitches when his hand cups the base of my skull, his thumb lightly brushing my neck, guiding me closer. Time feels suspended in this moment, everything still except for the heat between us, everything quiet except for the beating of my heart and our ragged breaths. He tilts my face up to meet him, his touch firm but tender. It's not forceful, but there is an undeniable power in it as his mouth finds mine.

The moment is both intimate and intense, as if we're giving ourselves to each other completely, in the quietest of ways. But there's a hunger beneath the tenderness, an urgency, like a beast pacing in the dark, only a breath away from uncaging itself. And I'm about to turn the key and watch him break free.

My hands begin roaming, a gentle exploration that grows more frenzied, more deliberate as the kiss intensifies. My hands find his belt, frantically working to unclasp the buckle.

"Hadley," his voice is ragged as my fingers dip beneath his waistband, tugging his shirt loose.

"I need this off," I gasp. "Now."

"Fuck, Hadley," he growls as he grabs the edges of his top and yanks it open, the fabric tearing with a sharp sound that makes me gasp. The studs along the front of the formal shirt spring free, flying in every direction as the crisp white material splits apart, buttons snapping off in the process.

That was easily the hottest thing I've ever seen.

The pristine, white shirt is shredded in an instant, and he doesn't even care. My hands frantically pull at the hem of his undershirt, pushing it upwards, exposing the chiseled dips and grooves of his abs.

In one swift motion, he pulls the shirt over his head, exposing every ridge and valley of his bare chest heaving before me. His *perfect* chest.

I think about running my tongue along every single one of the hard lines of his body, and in particular, the muscles just below his abs that form a deep, enticing V. Those sharp lines that disappear into his waistband make it impossible to look anywhere else.

I push him down so that he's seated on the bed, and he grasps my waist in response, pulling me towards him as I stand, settled between his legs. I run my fingers through his hair, and he closes his eyes, groaning softly as he leans into my touch. I'm about to push him onto his back and climb on top of him when I realize he still has his shoes on. So do I, but mine aren't standing in the way of my access to what he has going on inside those pants.

A teasing smile forms on my face as I sink to my knees and watch his eyes grow wide. "Shh," I press my index finger to his lips. "I'm just taking off your shoes."

I feel him watching as I slowly untie one shoe, and then the other, before looking up to meet his gaze, rising slowly as I do.

"Fuck, you're killing me, Hadley," he pants, and I watch his perfectly sculpted pecs rapidly rise and fall.

My fingers slowly begin to trace each one of the valleys of his chest, the sharp contours of his abs, the faint trail of dark hair that disappears just below his waistband.

He moans something inaudible as my fingers gently unclasp his pants, and it unlocks a primal instinct I didn't know I had buried within me. I give in to the instinct, the sudden urge to taste him, and push Jaxon onto his back, climbing on top of him as I murmur, "I want to taste every part of you," my voice soft but heavy. His body instantly stiffens beneath me, and I watch his hands curl, gripping the edge of the bed.

My tongue begins tracing a deliberate trail along every hard line of his chest, exploring every taut, defined muscle of his abdomen, and my pulse quickens as my tongue reaches the deep valley of that defined V, dead-ending at his waistband.

"Well, these are in the way," I say, grasping his pants at the waist, my words breathy. He fucking groans, his hand moving from the bed to grip my ass and squeeze. Firmly. "Luckily, this can easily be remedied," I smile, preparing to strip him bare.

Already unbuttoned, I slowly pull, removing both his pants and the black boxer briefs he wears beneath with a satisfying amount of ease, leaving him naked. Finally.

I take him then, leaning into this carnal desire to taste every part of this exquisite man who lies on his back before me. I sink to my knees, gently part his thighs as I settle in between his legs.

"Fuck, Had —"

"Shh," I cut him off, and he gasps as my tongue makes contact.

This isn't something I have a lot of experience with. My exes never gave, and rarely received, but my lack of experience doesn't seem to fucking matter as I let desire drive me. As I weaponize my tongue against him, driving him closer to release.

"Hadley," his voice is raspy, a guttural moan. "I need you to stop, now." His tone is insistent, urgent.

"But I'm not —" He cuts me off.

"Your mouth is … I have no words," he pauses between heaving breaths, "but if you keep that up, I'm not going to last, and the first time I have you, well, I want more. I need all of you, Hadley."

"Then have me, Jaxon," I demand as I rise from the bed, my eyes met with a ferocious intensity as they lock onto his dark, sable depths. Subtle amber flecks dance in his irises like flames, beckoning me.

A moment of understanding passes between us as I slowly step out of my black lacy underwear. I'm still in my stilettos, but I can't be bothered to deal with the straps; he can fuck me in them as far as I'm concerned. And apparently, he feels the same way.

Time seems to slow down and speed up all at once as he grabs my waist, pulling me towards him so that I land astride his lap. I can feel the firmness of him pressing itself between my legs, demanding entrance, and I grind against it.

He reaches between my thighs, and I shudder as pleasure ripples through me when he grazes that overly sensitive spot. "So ready for me," he growls as his eyes narrow, mouth pressed against mine.

"I don't want your fingers again, Jaxon, I want *you*." I gasp before quoting his own previous demand, "*All* of you."

He leans over me, one arm wrapped firmly around my waist, holding me in place as he reaches into his nightstand, pulling out one of the unopened, neatly arranged boxes of condoms he apparently stores there.

"Let me," I tell him, ripping open a box and removing a tiny packet, tearing it open before rolling it down his length

I rise then, positioning myself just above him and

lowering myself onto him as he guides himself into my entrance. I gasp at the sensation of that first, tight inch.

"Are you okay?" He asks, his hand moving to gently cup my face.

"More than okay," I murmur against his lips. The feel of him, the fullness, everything leaves me short of breath as we begin a slow, gentle cadence. Our mouths immediately fuse together, and the kiss is insistent but tender. I roll against him, slowly rising and falling with the rhythm of our breaths as his hands trace gentle lines across my back, running through my hair.

I need more.

I once again draw on this carnal need, unlike anything I've experienced before. I didn't know this feeling could exist, this deep, raw hunger inside me. It's like a door that's been locked for so long, and now, with the slightest touch, the key is turning, and it's all rushing out at once.

I've never taken charge like this, but then I've never wanted anyone like *this*. I've never experienced this; this wanton, primitive desire that now pulses through my veins like fire, demanding to be fed.

"Oh, God!" I shriek as his thrusts meet mine, activating some sensitive spot buried so deep within me that's never been discovered.

Until now.

"Unless you think it's divine intervention, causing you to quiver and moan like that, then you've got the wrong name, Hadley."

"Jaxon," I choke out.

"Good girl," he breathes. "I want to hear my name on your lips when you come for me." My whole body shivers deliciously in response.

He pulls me towards him and claims my mouth in a reckless kiss that's fiery and demanding and filled with every bit of the hunger for him that I feel; in the absence of words, it conveys every desire clawing at me from the inside, striving for release.

Jaxon throws me back on the bed, pressing me deeper into the mattress as he kisses his way up my body until he is settled firmly on top of me. By the time his lips reach that sensitive spot where my neck meets my collarbone, I'm burning alive as I writhe beneath him.

"I have to have you, Hadley." His words are surprisingly tender, and there is a softness behind his wild eyes that causes my heartbeat to stutter.

"You do." I smile before arching up to claim his mouth in a kiss. A kiss meant to convey that I am undeniably *his*.

"There's nothing left of me that you don't already have," he gasps as he enters me in one smooth thrust. "I'm yours, Hadley." And fuck if my entire body doesn't tremble in response. I'm not sure whether it's his words that do something to my heart or the physical sensation of the fullness of *him*, but I am on the verge of coming undone.

He is *everything*.

Hard. Deep. Fast. He sets a brutal, almost feral pace that has me aching for more as our bodies join and come apart again and again.

"Don't close your eyes," he growls as my lashes begin to flutter shut.

"Jaxon, I can't, I'm, I –"

"You're so fucking beautiful, Hadley. I need to see you as you let go for me." He knows I can't last, that I'm too far gone, and he braces himself on his arms, hovering above me, eyes locking onto mine as he drives his hips into me, maintaining the pace.

"Jaxon, I –" And I can't even get the words out before I fucking shatter.

"Fuck, I'm never going to get enough of you," he groans as I come apart around him.

Heat, charged and electric, radiates from every bone,

every pore, every fiber of my being as a blazing, forceful sort of pleasure erupts from my core, setting my entire body aflame.

"I love you," I gasp.

I'm so completely lost, so totally consumed, that I don't even realize I've said the words out loud.

His eyes widen, then darken, his gaze intensifying as something shifts.

Then, suddenly, he's collapsing on top of me as he growls my name, at least I think that's my name; his voice is gravelly and barely audible, riding out his own release as the aftershocks of mine continue. I'm left clinging to him, my fingernails buried in the flesh of his back as my body quivers with the last lingering waves of pleasure.

Neither one of us speaks as we lie, tangled up in one another, hearts pounding, breathing labored.

The silence wraps around us, laced with the intimacy of what we just shared as we both try to process what happened. And while my words silently echo in the air between us, imbuing this moment with a tremor of fear, there is also something that feels beautiful and just so completely *right.*

He rolls onto his back, pulling me with him so that my head rests on the sweat-slickened tawny skin of his chest. I can hear the pounding beneath his ribs, thrumming rapidly, in sync with the metronome of my own unguarded heart.

His fingers find my hair, gently running through the sex-tangled strands of my locks, and I nuzzle into the warmth of his chest.

"Stay," he whispers, and I can hear the cadence of his heartbeat change, his pulse quickening at the implication of his own request.

"I shouldn't," I respond, but my words carry no conviction. Who am I kidding? I'm not going anywhere. Not tonight. Not ever, if I have anything to say about it.

"Do you need me to offer you another reason to stay?" He teases, pulling me tighter against his body. "Like I said," he reminds me, "I'm not in the habit of letting go of what I want."

And Jaxon Avenier wants *me*.

"Well, maybe I could be convinced." I smile against his chest. "Assuming your offer is compelling," I giggle, feeling content for the first time in a long time.

"Is that a challenge?" He asks, rising on his elbow, "Because I've never backed down from a challenge a day in my life. I don't like to lose." His gaze heats as he rolls me onto my back, pinning me to the mattress beneath him. I hum softly, biting my lower lip.

"Challenge accepted," he says as a sly smirk spreads across his perfect fucking face.

CHAPTER 31

ACCORDING TO ARIA

NOT ALL THORNS SPILL BLOOD...

...SOME SPILL SECRETS.

A STAR-CROSSED TALE FOR THE AGES

BY: ARIA THORNE

Move over, Romeo and Juliet, it looks like there's a new power couple in town, and this one isn't waiting for a tragic ending.

Forget Verona, we're in Manhattan, where anything is possible, and I'm here to offer you a new twist on an old tale.

The stage is set, the players are in place, and it's looking like we may be witnessing the beginning of a real-life drama that rivals Shakespeare himself. But this time? That infamous, tragic ending might instead be something far more... explosive.

You heard it here first, folks, Jaxon Avenier, New York's most eligible bachelor, suddenly appears to be ineligible, as in off the market.

Jaxon Avenier.

The name alone is enough to make anyone sit up straight. He's the heir to the Avenier fortune and current CEO of AVC - one of the city's most powerful venture capital firms. He has access to billions, he's a player, and the kind of man who could buy your soul and still leave you wanting more.

Grab your tissues, ladies, because the bomb I'm about to drop is going to break your hearts.

Jaxon's reputation as Manhattan's most sought-after bachelor is certainly nothing short of legendary. But now? Well, it seems Jaxon may have finally met his match. And before you ask, no, it isn't Kit D'Vesle. It appears that flame has been snuffed out. So who exactly was responsible for this unexpected turn of events?

It turns out her name is Hadley. And yes, she has a last name too. Aldridge.

But who exactly is Hadley Aldridge?

So glad you asked, because this is where the plot begins to thicken and things get a little more interesting for our main male character and his current leading lady.

Hadley, daughter of infamous political heavyweight Elizabeth Aldridge, whose career is as fierce as it is controversial, has mostly stayed out of the spotlight - until, apparently, right now. She was spotted spending much of the evening on Avenier's arm, sharing the first dance, and even leaving the exclusive annual AVC Holiday party wearing Avenier's tuxedo jacket, causing the jaws of the city's most powerful insiders to drop.

I know, it's unbelievable, but before you go thinking she's just another name on Jaxon's seemingly endless list of trysts, let me tell you this wasn't just a casual walk to a waiting car. No, this was something more. In the attached photo that's already making its rounds on every Upper East Side socialite's inbox in this city, Jaxon is seen leaning down to kiss the top of Hadley's forehead as they wait for their car. A rather intimate gesture for this notorious playboy, don't you think? But here's the kicker — it's the way he's holding her hand, an oddly public display of affection for the famously private billionaire. Party-goers noted the way his fingers curled around hers like he was trying to keep her close - maybe too close.

Jaxon is suddenly rumored to not be playing the field. Is this love?

Or is this a Machiavellian move in a high-stakes game of power, politics, and money? AVC is presumed to be funding Ms. Aldridge's latest venture, after all. Could Hadley be using him to get ahead in a game her mother has been orchestrating for years? Has Jaxon Avenier finally been outmatched?

While this may look like an innocent case of love at first sight, things are rarely as simple as they seem, aren't they? Which begs the question — what does he want from her? Or perhaps, the question we should really be asking ourselves is - what does she want from him?

Stay tuned, my darling readers. After all, in Manhattan, there's no such thing as a quiet love affair.

Stay Sharp,
Aria Thorne

Chapter 32

Hadley

We must have drifted off because I don't even remember falling asleep. We were kissing softly, sharing quiet murmurs, exploring each other, but at some point, we must have succumbed to slumber. I have no idea what time it is, but the apartment is still dark, and the spot in the bed next to me is cold and empty. I can vaguely hear Jaxon's deep voice outside the bedroom; is he on the phone? He does *not* sound happy.

Shit.

My mind starts spiraling, I'm not forming any coherent thoughts about *why* or *how* I fucked things up, surely I've done *something* to make him leave the bed, to upset him. It's illogical, I know. Last night was *perfect*, but I can't help this pit from forming in my stomach.

It falls silent outside the bedroom, and I sit up in bed as Jaxon enters the room. It's dark, and he pauses for a moment, his silhouette outlined by the soft lighting from the hallway.

"You're awake," Jaxon's voice is infinitely softer than the tone he used on the phone only moments ago. "I'm sorry if I woke you." I exhale in relief. He doesn't sound angry with me.

He makes his way towards the bed, climbing in next to me and taking my hand in his. His brow furrows slightly, and I'd think it was actually adorable if he didn't look like he was gathering his thoughts in preparation to drop a bomb on me. My heart rate skyrockets with anxiety.

"Is something wrong? What time is it?" I glance around as I ask - wait, where is my phone?

"It's just past 6:00 AM." He takes a deep breath. "And it seems we were spotted leaving the AVC party together last night," Jaxon's tone is calm, but it carries an undercurrent of frustration.

"Okay," I squeeze his hand, still trying to read him. "By who?"

Jaxon sighs; he's definitely annoyed. And probably pissed off, but not at me. "Someone who snapped a pic, and clearly sold it to Aria Thorne. They made quick work of it, too." His expression shifts to one of concern as he squeezes my hand between his.

Oh.

Oh no.

"But like, are you saying… ?" Sure, I've always been adjacent to this stuff; my mom runs in some pretty influential social and political circles after all, but it's usually just local media and certainly nothing Aria Thorne would ever care to write about. And just because my mother rubs elbows with Washington's elite doesn't mean *I've* ever found myself anywhere close to becoming gossip column material. I don't think anyone noteworthy in D.C. could even pick me out of a lineup.

But Jaxon Avenier, he is a regular in that column. And I'd know, because over the past several weeks, I've spent more time than I'd care to admit googling the man. Like any sane woman in my situation would. Not that I give anything the tabloids say much merit.

"The column dropped about 45 minutes ago, and yes, *we* are the featured story." He gently squeezes my hand, eyes unable to meet mine as he says with so much sincerity it hurts, "I'm so sorry, Hadley." As if this is *his* fault.

But then the reality of it hits.

"Oh my God." I scramble out of bed, ripping my hand from his grasp. "Where's my phone?" I halt only a step away from the bed - I am very naked and very unfamiliar with his massive apartment.

"Hey," his voice is gentle, but still commanding as he follows me up out of bed. "At least let me get you a shirt to put on." He pauses, clearly, there's more he hasn't told me yet. "Alastair is on his way over."

"Lex?" I spend so much time with Trey that sometimes I forget Lex is a nickname that not everyone uses for Alastair Sterling. "He's coming here? Now?" I wonder why Jaxon's cousin is coming so early in the morning - just because some tabloid article came out?

"Yeah. Damage control. It may have an adverse effect on one of his accounts." Now I feel myself starting to panic, what could this article possibly have said about us?

Jaxon pulls me to him, and I gasp at the way my skin ignites where it meets his. My hands come to rest on his bare chest, and I have to tilt my head up to look at him. How does he do it? With just one touch, thoughts of the article fade into the background and all I want to do is tumble right back into bed with him. Instead of doing that, though, Jaxon guides me to another room. It's a closet, but it's bigger than my bedroom at Jade's place, and he opens one of the sleek drawers from the built-in organizational system, pulling an old, faded workout shirt with *Brawl &* *Order* written across it. I pull it on, it's soft and smells like him, and I smile inwardly.

God, I'm so fucked.

He pulls on his own shirt and a pair of sweatpants that look casual but I am sure are extremely expensive; I don't think I've seen him in anything besides a suit, a tux, or naked, and damn. The dressed-down simplicity of his attire, the intimacy of it, makes my heart stutter.

"I think your phone is downstairs in your handbag from last night. We have about ten minutes before Alastair is here, and there are some other business matters I need to debrief with him." His tone is apologetic.

"The column?" I ask.

"No." Jaxon doesn't say anything else, and I don't press. The way his jaw ticks, I know it's not good. This is not how I imagined waking up with Jaxon this morning.

I follow him downstairs and find my phone while Jaxon makes us coffee, or more accurately, takes out two mugs and presses some buttons on a fancy machine the likes of which I've only seen in high-end Italian bistros.

I sit down hard on the leather couch in the seating area adjacent to Jaxon's kitchen.

73 text messages, half of them from people I haven't talked to in close to a decade. 11 missed calls. Five from Jade, which has me wondering why the hell she's awake, though given her clientele, she probably has all kinds of alerts set to push through her *do-not-disturb* settings. Another missed call from my mother. It's not even 7:00 AM, and my head spins just thinking about what the rest of today is going to bring.

"The column dropped… an hour ago?" I call out, pulling up the article first linked to me by David, my ex-boyfriend. We finally broke up for good two years ago, but he apparently still thinks he should have a say in how I live my life. It was accompanied by a note expressing his disapproval of my involvement with a *guy like Jaxon Avenier*.

I decide his message doesn't deserve a response.

"About that, yeah." Jaxon walks over and places what appears to be a cappuccino down on the table in front of us before sitting on the couch next to me. He looks over my shoulder to see me scrolling and remains quiet for the minute or so it takes me to finish the article.

"I should text Jade at least," I sigh, resigned. "She's probably freaking out on my behalf."

"You can call her," Jaxon offers. "Your mother too." There's an edge to his voice at that. I place my phone deliberately in my lap and look at him.

"I'm not speaking to Elizabeth." I refer to my mother by her first name. "Not now, not ever," I watch his eyes as I speak, making sure he knows how serious I am. I'm not naive. Okay, maybe a little bit naive. But not *that* naive.

I know about the animosity between our two families at a surface level, and honestly, maybe that really is all there is to it. I know my mom isn't exactly thrilled that I've gone into business with the Aveniers. But I'm not happy about my mother's choices either, or her lack of support for literally any of my life choices. I've made a point to distance myself from her over the years, especially since Dad died, almost eight years ago now. I may be her only child, but we've never seen eye to eye, and we're sure as hell not about to start right now.

"I didn't realize you two… weren't close," Jaxon chooses his words tentatively, the hardness in his eyes fading a bit.

"Do you have a PR team on this?" I ask, changing the subject. I am done talking about my mother.

Jaxon nods. "Alastair looped them in right away. The photo isn't that scandalous, not really." He's right, it isn't. He's kissing my head. Which apparently is more newsworthy, given his reputation, than if he'd been photographed with his hand up my skirt.

And honestly, if I let myself admit it, I am a little giddy

about it. Not the article and its ramifications, obviously, but about forehead kisses, and being the only woman he's ever brought *home*. It would be so incredibly sweet if I weren't so anxious and paranoid about what it all means for me, my career, and the future of Trueno. Though I knew this was always a possibility, hell, I knew this was a probability when I said I was certain I wanted to be with him.

I reach for my coffee. I need some fuel before calling Jade, when Lex arrives, letting himself in.

Jaxon and I both stand up, and Lex's eyes grow wide as he glances at me, only briefly, before averting his gaze. If he has something to say about us leaving the party last night, or me standing in Jaxon's apartment wearing nothing but a well-worn t-shirt that obviously isn't mine, he's saving it for now.

He stops in front of Jaxon and crosses his arms over his chest. Jaxon's stance instantly shifts. This is CEO Jaxon.

"They fired everyone, Jaxon. Everyone." Lex's voice is even, but there's an edge to it.

What is Lex talking about?

"Slow down, Alastair. Who fired everyone?" Jaxon's tone is calm, but I can see how tightly his jaw is clenched.

"Ashlan Corp, the company that just bought Cipher Group. The *acqui-hire.*" He throws a lot of emphasis into that last sentence in a tone that borders on condescension.

"That's impossible." Jaxon is already moving towards a door I didn't notice until just now.

"It's possible, Jax. So possible that it actually just happened. That wasn't an acqui-hire; it was a strip job. They wanted the IP; that's it, never even planned to keep the Cipher team. And, thanks to your escapades in Aria Thorne's column, The Cipher Group is suggesting we didn't catch this because you've been too *distracted* by Hadley to do your job properly."

Damn. Lex can be almost as scary as Jaxon when he

wants to be, and he certainly commands even Jaxon's attention. Must be a trait that runs in the family. "Cipher is surely trying to build a bigger case against us, suggesting we applied pressure for them to go through with the acqui-hire for our own personal gain. The Aria Thorne article just dumped fuel on the fire, so to speak."

"It's not our fucking fault. We vetted the deal as much as we could, but it's not like I'm the one who signed off on it." Jaxon's voice is heated. How the hell is this even possible?"

Alastair doesn't blink. "Ashlan Corp. didn't want the company, Jaxon. They just wanted to eliminate Cipher as an emerging competitor of their *own* new product."

I follow the men into what appears to be a study. I suddenly feel very exposed and even more awkward in Jaxon's oversized T-shirt. And ashamed. Rationally, I know this isn't my fault, but still, guilt gnaws at me from the inside.

"Fuck." Jaxon slams his hand down on his desk. I haven't been able to follow the details of their conversation, but Jaxon is pissed.

"Yeah. Fuck. You know, we might have been able to head this off if we had locked down Echelon. Wasn't Cipher originally going to be part of the portfolio before we counseled them to go through with the acqui-hire?"

"That wouldn't have fucking mattered, and you know it, Alastair. Look, the acquisition was the right move. Cipher and AVC both did well from a financial standpoint. Even with the Echelon funding, Ashlan would've crushed them eventually - or picked them up for pennies on the dollar after bleeding them dry. This isn't on AVC." I suddenly understand why Jaxon is described as intimidating, along with being commanding and powerful. His voice brooks no argument, and Lex seems to defer to Jaxon, immediately cowed.

"Fine." Lex sits down hard on a chair by the window. "I have some ideas for solutions, but I'm not going to pretend like that fucking gossip column didn't just make everything more complicated." He sighs. "I suspect we will have a lawsuit on our hands, not that we've done anything to warrant it, but you know how it goes."

Jaxon scoffs, but doesn't say anything. Which means Lex is probably right. So far, I've been standing silently at the entrance of Jaxon's study, but I use the break in their conversation to take a few tentative steps inside.

"Is my... involvement with Jaxon an issue somehow?" My question is directed at Lex.

"No," Jaxon answers, way too quickly.

"Not exactly." Lex shoots Jaxon a glare. "It's complicated. But Cipher, one of the companies we've invested in, they make tech that operates similarly to yours, actually, was going through with an acqui-hire that AVC... well, we encouraged it." My brain starts putting the pieces together.

"But an acqui-hire means they acquire the employees too and..."

"They laid off everyone, almost everyone, the moment the ink was dry. " Lex finishes my line of thought for me.

"Can they do that?" I ask, probably sounding as naive as I feel.

He just shrugs.

"Cipher Group isn't our company, Hadley. *We* didn't decide to do this, nor did we predict this, but it's no longer within our control," Jaxon explains, with more patience than I probably deserve. "Ashlan is a big tech firm, Cipher's founders stand to make a significant profit off the acqui-hire, and as a result, so will we. Which is why, I'm guessing, they're blaming AVC, accusing us of knowingly putting profits before people." I pick up on the bitterness in his tone at the end of that.

"I don't understand. What does any of this have to do

with… us?" I feel my cheeks flush as I pointedly avoid looking at Lex.

"Cipher blames AVC for how everything went down. The founders never wanted to see their company absorbed in this way and always spoke of their employees, many of whom had been with them since the earliest days, as family. This is the exact outcome they were keen to avoid. So they're accusing AVC of pressuring the deal, *knowing* this would happen, or, arguably worse, negligence. After the column broke… they also started implying that Jaxon shouldn't be CEO if he is going to be so brazenly mixing business with pleasure. Well, they didn't put it so bluntly, but they're using it as an opportunity to question his integrity, his character, his judgment… things like that." Lex does not look amused.

I feel the color drain from my face.

"Jesus, Alastair." Jaxon moves to my side. Lex shrugs again; he's probably just relaying the truth, but I can't help but feel like there's a deeper undercurrent there, that maybe he *knows* something about us, or… about me. "Hadley, this isn't your fault. It's not even AVC's fault. This is angry, hurt people who feel an overwhelming sense of responsibility for their former employees suddenly losing their jobs, and they are lashing out." Jaxon's tone is calm, calculated, and I hang desperately onto every one of his words.

I throw Jaxon a beseeching look. "That doesn't make me feel better!" I feel awful. I lean into Jaxon's comforting embrace as he wraps his arms around my waist and gently kisses the top of my forehead, once again grounding me in a way I cannot comprehend.

"Jaxon?" Lex interjects. "We need to get to the Valley as soon as possible. If we can get in front of these *angry, hurt people,* as you call them, we might be able to avoid a lawsuit. Figure out some sort of way forward with them?"

Jaxon nods. "Okay. Let's call the jet center, see how quickly we can get a flight out this morning."

"I want to help." It's out of my mouth before I realize what I'm saying. Because really, how could I possibly be of any help in this situation? Jaxon frowns down at me.

"No offense, but how do you think you can help, Hadley?" Lex's tone lacks condescension and in fact, carries genuine curiosity.

I look at him, taking a deep breath, willing him to have faith in me. "You just said their tech is similar to mine. Trueno is working on some new initiatives, weren't you just asking about expansion?" This question is directed towards Jaxon, and he nods, encouraging me to continue.

"We just had a strategy meeting that would involve scaling up. A lot. We're still working on the business plan, but it will involve hiring new engineers. I don't know all the details yet, but we might be able to absorb some of the Cipher team." I'm grasping at straws, I know, but I can talk to my team, and the AVC associates who helped map out our strategic plan. "One of the barriers we identified was how difficult it is to find solid, qualified engineers. And retain them. I doubt we could take on all of them, but if you want to work something out with them, maybe Trueno can be of use."

Lex looks to Jaxon, who's looking at me with a small smile that makes me feel like my chest is too small for my heart. "Okay." He nods.

"Okay, so Hadley comes to California. We can work out the details about if or when she and Trueno enter the conversation, but it's worth fleshing out." Lex already has his phone out. "We can talk more on the jet. Trey's already working with the jet center. I'll make sure he knows to add Hadley to the manifest."

"Trey?" I ask, confused. Wondering why he will be there too.

Lex turns to face me with an expression I can't discern, and I suddenly feel uneasy, beneath his knowing gaze. I can't shake this feeling that maybe Lex knows something about me and Trey, though I have no idea how. "Cipher Group was one of Trey's accounts. Before Trueno." He explains with a pointed look.

"Oh. Awesome. That makes sense." I sound like an idiot, but I have no idea what else to say. I need to get a fucking grip, but this is a lot to process so early in the morning and after not nearly enough sleep.

"All right. Well, I'm going to go grab my shit, and probably apologize to Vera for so abruptly ending our… whatever, never mind. I'll see you two at the jet center. Wheels up at 10:00."

I don't fully understand what Lex just said, but I'm pretty sure it means that I'm about to fly on a private jet to San Francisco with the man I am in love with, the man I had a one-night stand with, and their cousin, friend, colleague, whatever the fuck Alastair *Lex* Sterling is to them. The whole situation is messy, and it seems like Lex quite possibly knows this. Or maybe he just hates me? I'm actually not sure which is worse.

CHAPTER 33

TREY

O f course I am the first one to arrive. Jaxon is almost always early, earlier than I am, but lately he's been distracted by Hadley. It's not that he's lost sight of work or anything; it's just that he's prioritizing her in a way he's never done for or with *anyone* before.

I'm not the only one who sees it, as evidenced by the gossip column last night, and this subsequent drama with Cipher.

I glance at my phone, 9:20 AM. Lex always shows up no more than fifteen minutes before departure, claiming that hanging around the jet center is a waste of his time. He normally takes a helicopter over here from the City; *efficiency is paramount*, as he always claims.

Hopefully he doesn't miss the flight.

Jaxon is on his way too, but I expect him imminently.

I take a deep breath and get myself a long espresso in the jet center's lounge. I don't *want* to be annoyed, not with Lex, Jaxon or least of all Hadley. I *am* still disappointed about my night, or should I say *morning*, being interrupted by this bullshit. It was embarrassing, having to wake up my date and ask her to leave. I didn't even offer her coffee, and I'd promised her breakfast.

Hopefully I haven't ruined my chances of seeing her again. Lex was right about moving on - I just needed another gorgeous, interesting woman to distract me, and Vera's colleague, Juliana, has more than captured my attention. She's stunning, yes, but she's also as charming as she is flirtatious. And she's great in bed. It's a relief to feel this way again.

But that fluttery feeling I get when I think about a potential *next time* with Juliana instantly evaporates, transforming into something more akin to jealousy as I hear a familiar voice entering the lounge.

Hadley.

For the entire night, with Juliana on my arm, and then in my bed, not once did I think of Hadley Aldridge. But now she's *here*, and I can't stop the lump from forming in my throat.

"Oh my *God*," Hadley's voice is reverent as she enters the lounge. She scans the room, her gaze only pausing on me briefly, giving me a shy smile. I smile back because, well, it's *Hadley*.

She's adorable the way she's taking it all in, of course, she's never been on a private jet before. Jaxon is right behind her, his hand grazing her lower back as they enter, because he apparently hasn't left her side since last night. I school my face into a relaxed smile. Calm and collected and not at all bothered.

Jaxon, who is usually bored as fuck and glued to his phone as we wait, smiles softly at Hadley and offers her a coffee. Really? Who even is this guy? Hadley is glowing as she accepts, staring at him longingly, and honestly, I can't even blame Jaxon. Her excitement is infectious. I even catch myself smiling at her enthusiasm, and the way she doesn't try to hide it.

"No word from Alastair?" Jaxon asks impatiently as he sits down next to me. Hadley looks over at us shyly and takes a seat on his other side. It's only 9:40 AM.

"You know Lex, he's always on our asses about timing, and he'll show up by helicopter with less than 5 minutes to spare." Not that Jaxon needs this reminder, but I say it anyway.

I watch as Jaxon puts his arm around Hadley, and she leans into his embrace like it's the most natural thing in the world.

I turn away, my stomach churning. Though I think that has more to do with the fact that I've just realized how hungry I am. I'll order breakfast on the jet.

"So nice of you to join us," Jaxon's voice cuts through my thoughts just as my mind begins wandering back to last night. Probably for the best because the last thing I need right now is my body remembering Juliana too fondly as we are about to board.

Sure enough, Lex is waltzing into the jet center at 9:50 AM, hair windblown from his chopper ride over, asking if someone has his flat white.

"You're late, they'll make you one on the plane," Jaxon barks at him, annoyed that he cut it so close. Though I can't help but smile as I watch Lex stride across the room, unaffected.

We make our way outside to board the jet, Jaxon and Hadley leading the way hand in hand. They pause on the red carpet that leads to the airstairs, where she insists he take her picture so she can send it to her friend Jade. When he patiently stops and agrees to do so, I share a look with Lex and shrug. Lex looks somewhat annoyed, though more confused than anything. Neither of us has ever seen Jaxon like this. But he fucking deserves this. Hell, he *needs* this. More than anyone.

Once on board, Jaxon and Hadley unsurprisingly take

one of the plush leather couches towards the front of the plane, presumably because Jaxon hasn't broken physical contact with her since they walked into the jet center, so why would he start now? I follow Lex further back and grab one of the leather recliners at the card table, sitting across from Lex.

The flight attendant, Naomi, hands me a glass of champagne, which I down in practically one gulp, earning me a warning look from Lex. I shoot him a look back that says I'm aware this is a *business trip.* Naomi informs us she'll take our breakfast orders shortly after takeoff, and my stomach grumbles in response.

Once we reach cruising altitude, I order an omelet, fully loaded, and another espresso. As tempting as it is to down a scotch on the rocks right now, I haven't forgotten why we're on our way to Silicon Valley.

"Wake me up after you eat," Lex says, as he moves across the aisle to an empty seat and reclines it fully. "I didn't exactly sleep last night. And I'm assuming you didn't either?" He winks at me and catches my wistful smile before closing his eyes. "I want to hear more about that," he mumbles before dozing off.

I'm finishing up my omelette, trying - and failing - to focus on work, when my thoughts are interrupted by Hadley getting up to refill her champagne. Naomi chides her, Hadley can't be pouring her own champagne.

"Actually, is there orange juice?" Hadley asks the flight attendant. "Maybe I should have a mimosa, I don't want to drink too much before we get there."

"*Is there* orange juice?" I hear Naomi mumble under her breath, but she's smiling as she prepares Hadley's drink. Hadley certainly isn't the type of passenger Naomi is used to dealing with; it must be nice for her too.

I look back to see Jaxon on his laptop, noise-canceling earbuds in, and the unmistakable tone of Jaxon Avenier,

CEO of AVC, talking assertively to whoever is gathered on the other end of the Zoom call. It sounds like he's dialed into the meeting Genevieve has convened with our legal team in NYC.

Just the sound of business happening must have woken Lex because he sits up with a stretch. Hadley is gushing to Naomi about the fact that her flute is actual crystal. Was she expecting a plastic cup? Lex glances between Jaxon and Hadley, apparently taking in the fact that they are currently on opposite ends of the plane.

"I know," I quip. "It seems they *can* stand to be separated." The corner of Lex's lip barely twitches. I guess he's still tired.

When Hadley passes our table on her way back to Jaxon, Lex throws his arm out to stop her. "Sit," he commands, gesturing to the empty seat across from mine. Okay, I guess he *has* woken up then.

"Hi." Hadley flashes me a smile as she takes a seat. Before she's settled, Lex hits us with a proclamation that I did not expect.

"You two need to fess up to Jaxon."

What the fuck?

Hadley's eyes widen, and she looks like a deer caught in the headlights, first looking at Lex, who is staring her down so fiercely that she quickly turns her gaze to me. I imagine my expression mimics hers.

"Tell him what, exactly?" She asks. I imagine she's smart enough to put two and two together, but she's also smart enough not to reveal anything unintentionally.

"You know exactly what," Lex deadpans. Hadley just continues to stare.

"No," she tries. "I don't."

She may not actually be sure what Lex is talking about, so she's right to have her guard up.

"He's talking about *us*, Hadley. That night we met at

the Bar Room and… well, I'm sure I don't need to remind you about the rest."

She leans towards me with her arms on the table, her eyes ablaze with accusation. "You remember?" She demands.

My heart plummets to my stomach, and it must show on my face because Lex sighs. "Christ, Hadley, of course he does."

"You told him?" Hadley whisper-shouts at me.

I realize I have to take control of this conversation, and I choose, for the moment, to ignore Hadley altogether, instead focusing my gaze on Lex. "Why? What good would that do?" Telling Jaxon is the *worst* thing any of us could do; surely, he must realize this.

Lex's entire body deflates as he lets out an exasperated sigh. "Are you fucking blind, Trey? Have you seen the two of them together? Did you not see them this morning? What about the Aria Thorne *article* about them?" He gestures towards Hadley, who still looks shell-shocked.

"Of course I've seen the column!" I'm trying not to raise my voice, but what the actual *fuck.* I confide in Lex, and now *this?*

"So, you want Jaxon to *finally* fall for a woman, then find out from someone else that you fucked her already?" He's talking about Hadley like she's not even here.

"Hey!" Hadley finally pipes up.

"He won't find out," I say with conviction before looking directly into Hadley's eyes. "Right?" I hold her gaze pointedly as I say it, daring her to challenge me. Her chest heaves and her breath hitches, but she doesn't respond to my question. "You are *not* thinking of telling Jaxon." I lower my chin.

Of course, Lex interjects. "You absolutely should tell him."

"Again, Alastair. Why?" He frowns at my use of his

given name. Or maybe at my question in general. God, I just want this whole mess over with, behind us, buried, gone forever.

"Who drove you back to your place that night, Trey?" Lex asks, his expression smug. Of course he already knows the answer.

"Emilio wouldn't breathe a word," I say it because it's the truth.

Hadley's sharp intake of breath brings my attention back to her. It seems she might finally have something to say on the matter.

Except, of course, Jaxon stands up at exactly that moment, making his way towards us.

Hadley jumps up to greet him. "Everything okay?" She asks, and I watch as the tension in his jaw releases just a little. Because of *her*. God, the concern, the affection in her voice. The way his arms reach out, and she just fucking gravitates towards him. I shoot Lex a glare, and he meets my gaze with conviction; he's not backing down on this issue. He really thinks we should tell Jaxon.

Well, Hadley and I seem to be aligned on *not* telling him.

At least for now.

CHAPTER 34

TREY

Twelve hours later, I flop facedown on the bed in my suite at the Nobu hotel, Jaxon's go-to for trips to Silicon Valley. I'm exhausted, but it was worth it.

We did it. Correction: Hadley did it. Her idea to absorb a key group of Cipher's tenured engineers may have saved us from a nasty lawsuit that would have tainted the AVC name, or at least Jaxon's.

And based on our recent strategy meetings about scaling up Trueno, this could potentially make AVC, and Hadley, a whole lot of money.

I'm pretty sure the entire Cipher team was fully prepared to serve us with a lawsuit, holding AVC responsible for Ashlan Corp. laying off the entire team only hours after the acqui-hire. Our legal team said Cipher has no basis for the claim, but ethically, they could still bring a pretty ugly case against us in the court of public opinion. It's bullshit, of course, but it would not have been a great look for AVC, especially since they accused Jaxon of negligence after that stupid Aria Thorne column. A story that broke at like 4:00 AM - damn, their legal team must work 24/7.

They really weren't interested in listening to any of our arguments, even our proposed solutions. It all sounded like a bunch of defensive bullshit, to be honest, and they saw right through it.

That is, until we called Hadley into the meeting. She'd spent the better part of her day working with her team on a possible solution - bringing a significant portion of Cipher's engineers over to Trueno - and while the plan was hardly fully fleshed out, she offered a compelling, viable proposition.

The Cipher team said they'd need to convene - make sure this is really in everyone's best interest and review the offer, but this is a significantly better outcome than we'd initially thought possible.

There's a knock on the door, and I groan into the mattress before getting up to answer. I check before opening it and see it's Lex. Begrudgingly, I let him in.

"Jaxon and Hadley are heading home on the corporate jet tonight. We get to hang back and meet with the team on Monday before flying home that night. I'm having Beau coordinate our return flights, unless you think we need more time."

I nod in thanks. Fuck, was it only this morning, sixteen short hours ago, that we were scrambling to get here to salvage what we could of this Cipher fiasco?

"Nah, I think we can get it done. Nothing is going to be signed this week, but we've at least opened the door for continuing this conversation." I sigh, not thrilled that we'll have to hang around for yet another series of meetings. "At least you and I are handling it together," I say as Lex makes himself comfortable on the sofa in my junior suite. "And at least Jaxon isn't sticking around, breathing down our necks."

"You know he would be if he wasn't so distracted by

Hadley." Lex sounds annoyed, and I wonder whether this has to do with the *situation* he brought up on the plane.

"So let him be distracted," I shrug, insinuating that I'm moving on.

Lex scrutinizes me, studying me intently before he speaks, "Speaking of distractions..." The corner of his mouth curls slowly upwards until he's flashing me a full, mischievous smile.

"Oh, here we go." I laugh as I flop down next to him on the sofa.

"Vera's friend, Juliana," he starts. "I couldn't help but notice she's the same woman you took home from Cubed the other night." He sits back, one arm now draped casually over the back of the couch as he leans closer, smiling. "And I definitely noticed that you two snuck out early from the holiday party last night."

"Yeah well, that will probably be the last time I see her." I sigh, recalling the disappointment and confusion on her face this morning as I asked her to leave.

"She couldn't keep up with you in the bedroom?" Lex jabs me playfully, but he's watching me intently.

"Oh no, that *definitely* wasn't an issue." I feel my cheeks heat as I remember one moment in particular from last night in my living room - before we even made it to my bedroom.

"So, you're saying you've met someone who can more than keep up with you?" He grins delightedly.

I feel my lips twitch into a shy smile. "I'm not saying it exactly like that. But yeah, she... definitely knows what she likes. And I'm *into* that." I admit, but that's all I'm going to say.

"So, what's the issue?" His eyes narrow before he adds, "And don't say Hadley."

"No, not Hadley. You were right, actually. I just needed to get back in the game. I was kind of stuck in a rut, spending so much time with Hadley, Jaxon —" I wave it off, "didn't exactly leave much oxygen in the room."

"And?" He looks at me expectantly.

"And what?"

"What's wrong with Juliana?"

"Nothing is wrong with her. God, she's amazing." I sigh, defeated. "Yeah, we left the party early together, and yeah, I brought her home with me. I'd offered her breakfast and everything..." I trail off for a moment, remembering how I promised to take care of her, to *worship* her. "And then I had to wake her up and ask her to leave my apartment while it was still dark outside with very little explanation."

Lex laughs. I fail to see the humor in the situation and tell him as much.

"Trey, I kicked Vera out too. I'm sure she can explain that to her friend if you want to see her again."

"Maybe."

"Maybe," Lex repeats, like he's testing out the word. Or like he's testing me.

I make my way over to the minibar. Mostly so that I don't have to sit pinned under that look Lex is giving me. "I'm just saying, I'm glad you pushed me back out there, okay?"

"Okay," he echoes.

I grab two glasses and hold one up to Lex in silent question. He nods. I make my way back to the sofa with the tumblers and a small bottle of bourbon. They stock Avenier Spirits in this hotel, probably one of the reasons Jaxon always insists we stay here on trips out to the Valley.

"Fine, I like her. I'd like to see her again," I hand Lex his drink and our fingers brush, brief but accidental as he slowly takes the glass from my hands. "Plus, she's uncomplicated."

"Uncomplicated," he says as he lifts his cocktail

without breaking eye contact. "That's a glowing endorsement if I've ever heard one."

I smirk back, "Don't sound so disappointed, Sterling."

"Oh trust me, I'm not." And there is something in the way he's looking at me, steadily assessing, like he's waiting for a crack in my answer.

I take a sip of my bourbon instead of giving him one.

The silence stretches until Lex finally breaks it, "I still think you should tell Jaxon." I place my drink on the coffee table with more force than is probably necessary and turn away.

"Not now Lex, please." Seriously, he really has to bring this up again right now? "It's been a long fucking day."

After a beat, he finally stands with a sigh, giving me a squeeze of my shoulder, his fingers lingering there before he slowly removes his hand. He gently shakes his head, as if thinking something to himself that he doesn't want to say out loud, before he finally takes his leave.

"Breakfast tomorrow, and then we will get working on the paperwork and shit."

I nod in acknowledgement, standing to see him out and making sure my *Do Not Disturb* sign is hanging on the door before climbing into bed.

CHAPTER 35

JAXON

I thought we'd stay the night in San Francisco, maybe I'd even take Hadley out to one of my favorite spots in the city for dinner, but it's been a long fucking day, and I just want to get home. And, I want to bring her home with me.

I don't know what I did to deserve her. I *don't* fucking deserve her. Yet somehow, inexplicably, she's here by my side. Holding *my* hand as we walk into the jet center. And the scariest part is, I never want to let it go.

I'm fucking falling for her, and I don't know what to do about it. Attraction, desire, *sex*, that I can deal with. I can manage it, compartmentalize it. But this, it's a strange kind of ache, a new kind of feeling for me - one that is constant and feels both impossible and inevitable at the same time.

I keep my hand on her lower back as we climb the airstairs of the jet, guiding her towards the couch again - no way am I letting go of her, not for an instant.

And as we board the plane, all I can think about is how lucky I am that she is mine. That she loves me.

Love.

Not something I'm familiar with, nor am I sure I'm

even capable of it, but whatever this is that I feel for Hadley, it has to be something. My heart fucking skips a beat as I watch her eyes light up, taking in the jet again. Realizing that this time, it'll be just the two of us on board.

"Welcome back, Mr. Avenier, Ms. Aldridge," Naomi greets us. "Can I offer you some champagne?"

"Please," I respond as I pull Hadley onto my lap, and she giggles in response.

"Just us," I whisper. "No work tonight." And I wrap my arms firmly around her waist as I press a gentle kiss to her temple, taking in her intoxicating floral scent as I do.

Naomi tries to be discreet, but I notice her appraise Hadley before she walks off to the back of the plane to prepare our champagne.

Technically, Hadley *is* here for work, but I don't tend to mix business and pleasure, so this is a first for Naomi. Not that I'm concerned. She, like all my regular staff, has signed an NDA.

Naomi returns moments later with two crystal champagne flutes, two perfect pours, the foam barely kissing the rim of each glass.

"I've taken the liberty of converting the beds for you towards the rear of the aircraft. I imagine you'll want to get some rest, Mr. Avenier?"

"Thank you," I respond, hoping she'll move on so that I can give Hadley my undivided attention.

"I'll stop by shortly after takeoff to check in with you about dinner," Naomi says before making herself scarce.

"You," I breathe against Hadley's neck as she turns to face me, still perched on my lap. "You are… brilliant." I swear I see her cheeks flush in response, and damn if that doesn't make my heart stutter beneath my ribs.

"Mmm," I feel more than hear her soft moan as she relaxes against me, and feel my body instantly respond. She seems exhausted though. Hell, I'm exhausted; it's a certain other part of my anatomy that failed to get the memo. It's almost 11:00 PM EST and we've been up since before dawn - without much sleep.

"You were amazing today," I press a kiss to the crown of her head. "Incredible. It took me ages to be able to command a room like that."

"It was kind of thrilling," Hadley's voice is suggestive, and her hand moves further up my thigh. We are encroaching on some dangerous territory here, and I reach behind me, grabbing a cashmere blanket to cover my lap. The last thing Naomi needs to see is my raging hard-on.

When Naomi returns to take our dinner order after takeoff, I decline, opting instead for a few fingers of Avenier 23 and a top off of Hadley's champagne flute. I tell her I'm not hungry… well, not for food.

Hadley must feel my desire, because she turns her face so that her mouth is on me, pressing hot, open-mouthed kisses up to my jaw.

I groan into her hair as I grasp her neck. Finally her mouth meets mine in a kiss that is intense and insistent and has me straining against my pants. Her tongue slips past my lips instantly; there is nothing soft or tentative about this kiss.

The blanket has slipped, and it's barely covering us when Hadley's hand dips between my thighs.

My head rolls back on the seat as she starts trailing kisses down my neck.

"Hadley." I try to keep my voice low, but I'm barely able to groan out the words.

She runs her hand down my chest, lifting the hem of my shirt as she traces the muscles along my abdomen until her hand finds my belt buckle. "It was so hot seeing you commanding that room too," she purrs just below my ear before she gently sucks the lobe into her mouth. I can only grunt in response.

"So powerful," she breathes, her breath hot on my neck as her hand begins to fumble with my belt. "So sexy," she whispers.

Her mouth finds mine again, and I groan into her kiss as I struggle to compose myself. "Not here, Hadley." I place my hand over hers, using every ounce of what remains of my resolve to gently guide it off my lap. God, I fucking want this so much it's quite literally painful, restraint scraping raw against desire. But we're on my corporate jet, and I need to at least *pretend* I am in control.

"I just wanted to take care of you after today," she pouts. The look of disappointment in her eyes is almost enough to undo me all over again.

"You're too good to me, Hadley." I pull her into a gentle kiss, "I don't deserve you." I know I don't, but I'm going to hold onto her, whatever this is we have, as long as she'll have me.

"You're sweet." She smiles, her eyes shimmering.

"I'm not," I tell her. Because it's the truth, and isn't that what we promised each other?

"Don't say that." She curls up beside me on the couch, resting her head on my chest and nuzzling into my neck.

"No, Hadley. I'm not." I sigh. "I'm not sweet." But damn if she doesn't make me want to be, at least for her.

"Well, you are to me," she sits up as she says it and fuck me, she looks at me like she sees something no one else ever has. My heart fucking explodes.

I try to swallow, but there's a lump in my throat that makes it impossible. It's not fear, or maybe it is. I don't know, but there's this ache, a pressure in my chest that I can't ignore.

You are to me.

I don't even know what I'm doing, here, with her. Every second I'm in her presence, every smile, every kiss, it makes me want to be someone else, someone better. But I don't know how to be better, I only know how to be me. I can't afford to be soft. I've spent my entire life building walls around myself. Hell, I've built an entire fucking fortress. Yet here she is, tearing it down, one touch, one word, one look at a time.

I don't know how to be what she needs me to be, what she *deserves*. But the one thing I do know with absolute certainty is that I can't fucking lose her.

I kiss the top of her head, drawing her in close and just close my eyes as I hold her against me, feeling her sink into my chest as I inhale the subtle, sweet scent of her.

"You deserve better than me," I whisper, wishing my conscience didn't demand I say it.

"Mmm," she just nuzzles closer, and I know she's not listening to what I'm saying. Not really. And that, that's what terrifies me most.

I'm already falling for her. Hell, I already fell.

"Come on," I tell her, gently pushing her off of me as I stand, offering my hand. It's late, and we need sleep. Desperately. "Let's try and get some rest," I say as she stands. She looks as exhausted as I feel, so I lead us to the back of the plane where the recliners have been converted into two neatly-made beds, folded AVC-branded pajamas placed at the foot of each.

I call down the galley to let Naomi know I'm changing and wait for her affirmative response before I slip out of my suit and into the soft cotton pants and tee folded in front of me. I slowly pull back the covers and climb into bed while Hadley slips into the bathroom to change.

Moments later, I feel her slide into the makeshift bed beside me instead of the one already made up for her across the aisle. This bed, if you can call it that, isn't even big enough for me, let alone both of us, but that doesn't stop me from wrapping my arms around her and pulling her to my chest as she settles in against me.

This. I think to myself. This is all I need.

"Get some sleep, Hadley," I whisper against her as I hold her.

"I love you," she mumbles, only partially conscious as she drifts off in my arms.

She's warm. Safe. *Mine*. And there it is again, that pulse of truth in my chest, stronger than anything I've ever felt. That undeniable feeling.

I love you.

I want to say it back. I want to tell her that she's everything. That I've never felt anything like this in my life. But I can't find the right words. It's like my mouth is locked, and I've forgotten how to speak.

It doesn't matter; she's already sleeping soundly against my chest, and I can't help but smile.

As I lie here beside her, unable to sleep, it hits me all at once, like a fucking lightning bolt – clear and sharp and undeniable. *I love her.*

I am fucking *in love* with her.

I don't know when it happened or how. But it's there now, and it's pretty damn real. Something I've never even believed in - at least not for me. Something I never thought I'd feel. But it's there, and it's mine.

She sleeps soundly in my arms, so damn perfect, tightly wrapped in my embrace. *She's mine.*

Mom would have loved her. The thought stings my eyes with tears. I don't know that I deserve a love like this. But God, I can't lose it. I'll do anything to hold onto it, to keep it. I can't lose *her*.

I need her.

And I don't *need* anyone. At least, I never have. But Hadley, she's everything, more than I ever thought I could want or have in a lifetime. An instant connection, and suddenly I can't fathom how I existed for so long without her. She's the reason my chest aches when she's not around. She's the first thing on my mind when I wake up, and she lingers there all fucking day, until I close my eyes, still thinking of her as I finally drift to sleep.

I'd never say it aloud; it's hard enough to admit it to myself, but I am fucking terrified. So scared of losing her. Scared of fucking this up, because I know I inevitably will.

I press my lips to the crown of her head. Gently, I don't want to wake her. She stirs just a little, nuzzling deeper into my chest, and I reflexively hold her tighter, like I'm afraid that if I let go for even a second, she'll disappear.

I love you.

I say the words in my head, and I smile to myself as my heart temporarily stops beating.

"I love you," I try the words out loud, so quiet it's barely a whisper.

It sends a thrill down my spine.

She can't hear me, already fast asleep, but a part of me wishes that maybe, just maybe, she'll hear it somehow in her dreams, and that when she wakes up, when she looks at me, she'll see it in my eyes. That she'll just *know*. That I'm hers. That I'm only hers. That I'll do anything to keep her, to protect her. That I'd burn down the whole damn world if it meant she'd never leave.

But for now, I just lie here, letting the feeling wash over me. I close my eyes, finally beginning to drift. And I fall asleep thinking about her. *Hadley.* Because she's mine now. And I'll be damned if I ever let her go.

CHAPTER 36

"We're landing," I hear Jaxon's voice, but it takes me a moment to gather my bearings. God, I was out cold. On a plane.

Oh shit, we're on *his* plane. And I'm in bed... sort of. I've never actually slept soundly on a flight before, even though it was just a few short hours.

"What time is it?" I mumble, still drowsy with sleep.

"In New York?" He smiles down at me, and my whole body tingles at the sight of him. This man, is he really *mine?* "It's just past 2:00 AM."

"Oh," I'm slowly starting to wake up. "I slept through the whole flight?"

"You did," he says as he leans over me, tucking a loose strand of hair behind my ear before his arm gently slips behind my back, pulling me into an upright position.

I take him in then. He's already dressed in his impeccably tailored black suit, not a wrinkle in sight. His soft, loose waves are perfectly styled. Does he just wake up looking like this?

I almost feel self-conscious, aware that I'm completely disheveled with sleep and in these ridiculous oversized pajamas, but then I catch his gaze – and the way he's looking at me. Something about it feels different, like he's seeing something in me, something deeper, more than whatever he usually sees, and as his eyes lock onto mine, I feel a subtle shift between us.

He's not quite smiling, but he looks… content? More relaxed. No, it's more than that. I can't explain it, but it feels like his eyes are speaking to me without words, and whatever message they convey is speaking directly to my heart.

God, I am so in love with him it physically hurts.

My breath catches as I stare back at him; his gaze feels less guarded, and there's a tenderness in his eyes that makes my stomach flutter. It's like something honed his edges overnight, and now he's softening, at least towards me.

I'm not sweet.

But he is. At least he can be. When he wants to be.

He is for me.

I told him as much last night, though I am not sure he really understood me, or maybe he did, but he just didn't believe me.

"Good morning," he says, smiling as his lips greet mine with a quick, gentle kiss that suddenly has me hungry for more.

The effect this man has on me. I will never get enough.

"My pilot just let me know we'll be on the ground in fifteen minutes, so if you need to use the bathroom or change, you've got about two minutes." He rises, extending his hand to me.

"Probably a good idea," I smile back sheepishly. "I'll just be a minute," I say as I stand.

He nods, gesturing towards the unused bed across the aisle, my clothing laid out neatly, waiting for me, presumably by Naomi. God, I don't think I'll ever get used to this lifestyle, and I really don't think I'll ever be entirely comfortable with it.

Twenty minutes later, we're back at the jet center.

"Emilio is waiting for us," Jaxon says as we exit the plane. "He can drop you off at home; you're probably exhausted." I try not to allow the pang of rejection I feel to show on my face, focusing on the reluctance I picked up on in his tone instead. I don't know why I'd hoped he'd invite me to come home with him. In the middle of the night. After a grueling business trip. Of course he needs to get back to his life, get some rest. We both do.

"Right," I respond, trying to mask the disappointment in my voice as I squeeze his hand a little tighter; I don't want to let it go. Not yet.

He leads me towards the black SUV that's idling outside, waiting. I watch as Emilio loads our bags into the back of the car as we approach. Jaxon opens the door for me, helping me into the large vehicle.

"I wish I didn't have to go home," I confess, the words just spilling out of me as I climb inside.

Ugh. Why did I just say that out loud when he just clearly told me he arranged for Emilio to take me home?

Because I can't stop thinking about the way he looked at me when I woke up, that's why. Because the thought of leaving him when I don't have to makes my heart ache in ways I can't comprehend. Because I'm exhausted, and there's nowhere I want to be more right now than asleep in his arms, with his body curled around me.

"You need sleep, Hadley. We both do," he says with conviction, but there's a hunger in his eyes that says sleep is the last thing on his mind.

"I can think of better ways to spend our time than sleeping." I hear his sharp intake of breath as I lower myself into my seat, praying we're on the same page here. But it's not just his body I crave. It's *him*. I crave his presence when he's not around, my chest feeling empty and hollow in his absence. Hell, I'm feeling it now just *anticipating* his absence.

"Hadley …" he growls softly. "Fuck, I'm really not ever going to get enough of you, am I?"

"That makes two of us," I tell him, the words coming out more breathlessly than I intended, and he reaches across the space between the two captain's chairs, placing his hand on my thigh.

"Then I guess we're both in trouble," he's smirking at me as he says it, but his expression quickly turns more serious. "Right now, though, you need sleep, Hadley. It's been a long day." His words sound forced. I can hear the hesitation in his voice, the longing, the door isn't closed, at least not all the way, and I decide to push it wide open.

"Not as much as I need you." I can feel my heart pounding in my chest, anticipating his response to my brazen confession. I hold his gaze and watch as his eyes grow wide, then narrow with focus and fire as the implication of my words sinks in. There, I said it. We did say we'd come from a place of complete honesty, right? And right now, I feel like I need him more than I need sleep, which, admittedly, I also need. Desperately.

"Fuck, Hadley. I'm really trying to do the chivalrous thing here, but when you talk to me like that… you know I'm taking you home with me now, right?"

"Good, I was counting on that," I say, the heat I feel behind my eyes mirrored in his own.

"I swear to God, you're going to be my undoing, Hadley Aldridge." I watch as he pulls the door closed and falls back against his seat. I can't stop smiling the entire way back to Manhattan.

Thirty minutes later, we're walking into Jaxon's Tribeca penthouse. This time, though, he doesn't take me straight to the bedroom. Instead, he takes my hand and leads me to his den, a small, cozy space off the main living room.

"I know we need sleep," he says. "But I'm exhausted and wide awake at the same time. I thought maybe a nightcap would help."

He gestures for me to sit on the leather couch, removing his blazer and tossing it onto a chair in the corner before he walks towards the beautiful - and obviously custom - wood built-ins. He opens a cabinet, revealing an elaborate and well-stocked wet bar.

He grabs two glasses, pouring a couple fingers of Avenier 23 – his favorite, I'm quickly learning – into one.

Just like Trey.

"What can I make you?"

The adrenaline of being in his presence is like a drug, heightening all of my senses. I'm physically and mentally exhausted, yet I'm wide awake, my mind racing as fast as my heart.

I'm here.

With *him*.

"Whatever you're having is fine," I say, knowing full well I'm going to struggle to drink a glass of warm bourbon.

He raises a brow at me knowingly, trying to conceal his smirk. I'm now more determined than ever to *enjoy* this glass, or at least act like I do. "Okay, if that's what you want," he says, the smirk still playing on his lips.

He pours me two fingers, identical to what sits in his glass, and joins me on the couch, effortlessly sliding his arm around my shoulders as if it's the most natural thing in the world. And honestly, it *does* feel natural. I can't help but smile as I rest my head on his shoulder, leaning into him so that there's no space between us.

This is exactly where I want to be.

"I'm glad you're here," he finally says after what feels like an eternal silence. And I nuzzle deeper into his chest.

"Me too," I mumble.

"You were incredible, Hadley. I know I've said it already, but I'm not sure how we would have made it out of the Cipher debacle without you."

"Shhh," I tell him. "No more work talk." Though there is one thing I have been meaning to talk to him about. "Well, actually," I continue, "there is one thing I was hoping we could discuss."

"Okay," he responds, "name it."

"Trey," I say, tentatively.

"Trey? What about him?" He asks so nonchalantly that it makes my guts twist. Jaxon sounds more curious than anything else.

"He's been great, particularly on the business development front. But now that we're taking a different approach, and might be acquiring some of the team from Cipher, I feel like I need a more seasoned liaison, someone who has more experience in navigating the nuances of more complex relationships, potential mergers, acquisitions, that sort of thing. It's not exactly his area of expertise." I hate that I sound so unappreciative of everything Trey's done for Trueno and for me, but I need Jaxon to take my request seriously.

"I see." He seems to ponder my request.

I can't tell him the real reason I want someone else on my account is because now that things seem to be getting serious with Jaxon, I think maybe some distance from Trey would be best.

I think about what Lex said. But whatever this thing is with Jaxon, it is so delicate. So new.

I'm not ready. *We're* not ready.

Maybe it was a bad idea to bring this up in my sleep-deprived state. I can't get my point across without either confessing or making it sound like Trey can't do his job.

"Forget it," I say softly. "It was just an idea."

"No, you're not wrong, Hadley." My heart swells and clenches at the same time. God, he's always believed in me and taken me seriously, even when nobody else has. "I'll talk to Alastair about it when they're back." Jaxon continues. "Get his take on it. New acquisitions *are* his area of expertise, so it may not be a bad idea to reassign him to your account now that you're likely absorbing the team from Cipher Group."

Even though Lex somehow *knows*, and might pressure Trey and I to tell Jaxon, I've seen him in action, and I know he will be professional. Most importantly, it will give me the distance I need from Trey.

Really, is whatever happened with Trey even something Jaxon needs to know about? Trey has a point. What does it even accomplish, Jaxon knowing about something that happened in the past? Something that's firmly in the past. I hadn't even met Jaxon then.

"Thanks," I tell him as he pulls me closer. I begin to drift, lulled to sleep by the gentle rise and fall of Jaxon's chest and the rhythmic beat of his heart. I'm doing the right thing, I assure myself, distancing myself from Trey.

Right here. With Jaxon. This is exactly where I am meant to be.

CHAPTER 37

HADLEY

"Come on, love, let's get you to bed," Jaxon's voice rouses me from a sleep I didn't realize had stolen me as his arms slip behind my back and beneath my legs, lifting me effortlessly from the couch into his arms. My body is still heavy with sleep as I burrow into his embrace, his arms wrapping around me like a soft cocoon.

Love.

Did he just call me *love?*

I bury my smile against his chest, soothed by the steady beat of his heart.

"What time is it?" I mumble, still drowsy.

"Quarter to four," he responds. "Way past your bedtime."

He carries me out of the den and up the stairs as I remain tucked against him, inhaling the scent of his cologne, something sophisticated and leathery with subtle hints of saffron.

"I'm sorry I fell asleep," I mumble.

"We both need sleep," he murmurs as he walks into the bedroom, and I nod against his hard chest, too tired to argue, too lost in the cozy sensation of being held like this.

He gently deposits me on the bed, his eyes finding mine as he releases me from the warmth of his embrace. The expression he so openly wears makes everything inside of me burn until it almost hurts, turning my insides molten beneath his heated gaze. But this is so much more than desire. It's so *clear*, the way he's looking at me, and I almost feel suffocated beneath the weight of it, like his eyes are saying more than words ever could.

And maybe he'll never find the words.

But I feel it, his love.

I feel it in the way his eyes trace every curve of my face, as if he needs to memorize every detail. I feel it in the way his fingers always find mine, entwining them like he's afraid to let go. It's in the way he just carried me to bed like I belong here with him, as if this is where I'm meant to be. It's in the careful way he protects me, driving me home, defending me, trusting me, giving me the floor in this morning's meeting, and having faith in me and my company when nobody else did. So while he doesn't say it, I feel it in all his quiet, intimate actions.

He momentarily disappears into his closet, returning with a folded t-shirt and hands it to me.

"Hopefully this will suffice for tonight." He sounds almost apologetic. Like he wishes he had more to offer me.

"It's perfect," I tell him as I slowly start to undress, slipping the soft cotton shirt over my head.

"You're perfect," he says, bending over to place a gentle kiss on my lips. Instinctively, I wrap my arms around his neck and rise to my knees in an effort to deepen the kiss, but he pulls back.

"Sleep, Hadley. There'll be plenty of time for that tomorrow," he smiles as he wraps a lock of my hair around his fingers.

As if underscoring Jaxon's point, a wave of exhaustion crashes over me, dragging me back towards the depths of slumber, and my traitorous body releases a yawn. "Fine, you win," I tell him as I collapse back onto the bed.

I watch as he pulls back the corner of his duvet, guiding me towards the pillow and carefully pressing me down into the sheets. The warmth of his hand lingers on my shoulder as he pulls up the covers, sliding into the bed beside me. The sheets rustle softly as he settles in, wrapping his arms around me and pulling me close, like I'm the only thing keeping him grounded.

He's not asleep yet, but he holds me in silence, making everything inside of me hum with awareness. And though I can't see it, I can feel his gaze on the back of my neck. I crane my neck, just enough so that I can meet his eyes in the dim light – there's something there, in the way he's looking at me that makes my chest tighten. I open my mouth to speak, but he cuts me off, his voice low and almost unsteady.

"I –" he pauses before leaning closer and letting out a shaky breath, its warmth gently caressing the nape of my neck, sending goosebumps dancing along my spine. "I ... I just want to hold you tonight," he breathes against my ear, "I don't want to let go." The words aren't a confession, but the *way* he says it carries a weight all on its own.

I can feel my heart beating faster, my body's response to the sweet simplicity of his request. His arms, gentle but firm, pull me closer as I settle in against him, and the way he's holding me, the way his fingers trace soothing patterns along the bare skin of my arms, is perfect.

This moment is perfect.

And then, almost without thinking, I whisper, "I love you."

His body stiffens for a moment, and his arms reflexively tighten around me, holding me like he's afraid I'll slip away if he lets go even for a second. I feel the faintest hitch in his breath and a shift in the rhythm of his heart, although maybe that's just my own erratic heartbeat. The silence that follows is interminable, but comfortable, and I let myself relax against him, my head resting on his pillow.

He lets out a long, slow breath, like he's been holding something in a long time. His fingers gently caress my hair, stroking slowly before, finally, his lips graze the top of my head with a tender kiss.

"Sleep, love." *Love.* "I've got you."

My heart stutters as a warm tingling sensation softly ripples through my body.

Sleep, love.

I replay his words in my head, a smile playing on my lips as I succumb to my exhaustion, tucked into the curve of his body curled around me.

CHAPTER 38

HADLEY

"Mmm," I stir awake, daylight peeking out from behind the blackout shades, a golden glow illuminating the perimeter of the windows. I am so comfortable, so cozy, and only vaguely aware I'm not alone.

Jaxon.

His arms are still around me, holding me close, and I can feel the slow rise and fall of his chest against my back. He's still asleep, and I let the quiet of the morning gently settle in around us, savoring the warmth of his presence.

I stir, shifting a little in his arms, and I hear him exhale softly, as if he is on the edge of slumber, on the verge of consciousness.

Last night slowly comes back to me. He brought me home. I'm in his bed. I'm wearing his t-shirt - his scent still clinging to the fabric, and for some reason, it makes me feel even more *his*. And I love being his; I love him.

"Morning," he mumbles into my hair, his voice still heavy with sleep. "Or is it afternoon? I don't have a clue what time it is. I haven't slept that well in, well, a very long time." He rolls away from me to grab his phone from the nightstand, and I immediately miss the feel of his body wrapped around mine.

"10:00 AM," he says, settling back in against me. "I love seeing you in my shirt," he murmurs against my neck. I can hear the smile in his voice, feel the softness of his touch as his fingers caress my bare arm. I roll over to face him, propping myself up on my elbow. "You look... perfect in it." He's staring at me now, like his world has just begun to make sense, and I feel a whisper of a blush heat my cheeks.

He lifts his hand, gently cupping my face, his thumb softly tracing the line of my jaw. And the way he continues to just look at me, almost reverently, it's the same way he looked at me on the plane, like there are a thousand things he wants to say, but he can't find the words.

My heart flutters in my chest, the air between us suddenly feeling charged as his eyes darken, steady and intense as they lock on mine. He inhales deeply, his jaw is tight, muscles clenching, as though whatever he is about to say will cost him something.

"I – " he starts, but pauses, his voice trembling slightly. "I love waking up next to you." His words are like a confession.

"There's nowhere else I'd rather be," I admit. And it's the truth. Right here, beside him, this is *exactly* where I want to be.

He cups the base of my skull, gently bringing his mouth over mine in a kiss that makes my toes curl. He kisses me slowly, but intently; such a simple gesture yet so full of promise that words feel superfluous.

"I love you," I sigh against his mouth.

He suddenly pulls away, his body stiffening as his breathing grows ragged. His pupils flare, eyes darkening as they burn all the way into the depths of my soul. I reach for him instinctively then, my hand finding its way to his chest seemingly of its own volition, my fingers brushing the fabric of his shirt before pressing gently against the steady, frantic thrum of his heartbeat. I can feel it – a pulse that's erratic, wild, almost desperate.

A heartbeat that matches my own in this moment, charged with an electric tension so thick it feels like it's holding us both.

"It's okay," I say, my thumb brushing lightly over the throbbing beat of his heart. "I know," I breathe, "I know how you feel. You don't have to say anything, Jaxon, because you've already shown me," I reassure him.

For a moment, I think he might pull away, his eyes flickering down before they once again meet mine, filled with the raw vulnerability of someone who's never let himself *feel* before. But then his eyes soften, his hand trailing along my arm until his fingers find mine.

With a breath so deep it seems to pull something from him that he's kept buried for far too long, he finally speaks.

"I –" he stops then starts again, "I love you, Hadley." His words are barely audible, but it doesn't matter. I hear them, and it's *everything*.

My fingers instinctively squeeze the hand that holds mine as I struggle to catch my own breath. "I love you, too," I remind him, unable to contain the smile that tugs at my lips.

Jaxon Avenier loves me.

He swallows hard, his gaze unwavering, his trembling fingers gripping mine, and I can physically feel his fear. The rawness of it. Something tightens in my chest then, because I know this isn't just an admission of love; it's an admission of everything he's never let himself feel, and the fissures that formed in my heart crack wide open.

"I'm in love with you," he says, "In a way I didn't know was even possible. But I can't deny it, not when every part of me is *yours*."

He's mine.

His gaze softens, almost like he's afraid of what I might do with this confession, but he doesn't look away. "I'm in love with you, Hadley, and I don't know what to do with it, but I need you to understand that it's *real*. Every second of my day, every one of my thoughts, every breath I take is filled with it."

His words sink in, so genuine, so earnest, so *vulnerable*, like he's carefully placing a piece of himself in my hands, and trusting me with it.

He reaches for me then, pulling me towards him so that our foreheads touch. His voice is low as he speaks. "If we're going to do this, *really* do this, we agreed we need to come from a place of complete candor. To be open. Honest. So, here we go. I am yours, Hadley. I've always been yours. I love you. I'm *in* love with you. Now that I have you, I'm never letting you go." His chest is heaving, and I can feel his breath mingling with my own.

"Jaxon …" I whisper, his name barely escaping my lips before he claims my mouth in a kiss, rolling me onto my back until he's positioned himself on top of me, bracing himself above me.

I can see it in his eyes now, in his expectant expression, this raw, unfiltered love, suddenly laid bare, and it's so much that it almost breaks me.

Because now I'm the one holding back.

Trey.

Every word Jaxon speaks feels like a burn and a balm all at once. It's everything I could have hoped for, soothing the part of me that has longed to hear him say what I've always known he feels for me, the ache in my chest that longs for not just his body, but *every* part of him.

The heat rises within me, all of me, my heart, my soul, suddenly aflame. But it's not just the heat of love, or of desire, or of the way his words make my heart race. No, his words fucking scorch me from the inside out, because I know the secret I carry will forever cast a shadow over this beautiful moment.

Every beat of my heart feels like it's stoking the flames that burn me from within, a burn that is simultaneously beautiful and excruciating. The way he's looking at me now, his deep sable eyes full of hope and tenderness, combined with the burn of knowing I can't be fully honest with him, not yet, not right now, but the desire to tell him the truth, the whole truth, suddenly feels both urgent and demanding.

I arch my back, reclaiming his mouth with my own as I fist the soft fabric of his shirt. He is mine. Jaxon Avenier is *mine*. And I'm his. I've always been his. And as I kiss him with everything I have, I make a decision. I have to tell him, *we* have to tell him.

Jaxon loves me.

And we promised each other *complete* honesty. Jaxon deserves that. Or maybe I don't deserve him.

And that act of deciding, definitively, that I will tell him, is like a release, giving permission for his love to act as a salve, healing the burns. His hands gently caress my skin as I lose myself in this kiss, in this moment, in *him*.

The kiss is slow, searching, and unrushed as we explore each other for what feels like the first time. It's a slow unfolding of *us*. He presses his body against mine, his hands carefully roaming, tracing every inch of my skin and leaving a trail of fire in their wake.

Slowly, gently, he pulls his shirt over my head, and we continue to carefully undress each other, as if unwrapping a set of cherished gifts.

His body is warm and familiar as he slips closer, and I part my legs for him, his hard against my soft. I let myself *feel* every part of him, every breath, every brush of his skin against mine, savoring the touch of his lips, the taste of his tongue, the sound of his gentle moans. Because the decision to tell him has already freed me. I'm here, with him, in this moment, and for the first time, I feel the full breadth of what it means to be loved by him.

"I love you," he gasps, his whispered breath hot against my neck.

And in that moment, I lose myself in him, in the simple beauty of his confession, in the safety of his arms, in the slow, steady rhythm of his hips. And as we come together, as I cling to his body, feeling both physically and emotionally as close as we've ever been, it is only him and me in this world. And that is *everything*.

CHAPTER 39

HADLEY

I'm still sitting in Jaxon's massive bed scrolling through my phone while he showers. An email pushes through from Lex confirming the agenda for the meeting with Cipher that he and Trey will be attending tomorrow.

Trey.

Another reminder of the secret I carry, and the guilt that looms, standing between us like a wall.

Lex knows about Trey. A sudden, second wave of guilt washes over me as I realize Lex is also keeping a secret for us. A secret he doesn't want to keep.

Jaxon loves me. And I love him. And as much as I hate to admit it, Lex is right. I chew my bottom lip, holding my phone with both hands. I should text Trey; we need to be aligned in this. Trey deserves that much. After everything Jaxon and I just shared, the need to confess everything to him feels almost urgent.

I hear the water stop in the bathroom and decide I will reach out to Trey later, not while I'm in Jaxon's bed. Another notification pops up on my phone as Jaxon steps out of the bathroom. Jade. I swipe it away in favor of perusing the hard lines of Jaxon Avenier in a towel. I still can't get over how exquisite he is. His body looks like it was sculpted expressly for my viewing pleasure. All smooth skin and chiseled lines, his deep, golden skin just inviting me to touch and lick every dip and crevice.

My phone pings again - probably another message from Jade, but I don't take my eyes off Jaxon's almost-naked body. I know we just made love, but I can still feel the heat pooling low in my belly.

"Everything all right?" Jaxon quirks a brow with a nod to my phone.

"Oh. Yeah. Just need to text Jade. I should spend some time with her today."

Jaxon walks slowly towards where I sit perched on the bed, and I don't hide the way my gaze travels down to that low-slung towel, riding so precariously on his hips. He stops inches in front of me, it's incredibly tempting to tug on the towel, invite him to tumble back into bed. "Lots to catch up on?"

I force myself to look up at Jaxon and let out a soft laugh. "Well, I jetted off across the country with no warning," I remind him. "She's mostly just checking in."

Jaxon's features don't harden exactly, but there is a stillness that settles over him. "She's protective of you." It's not a question, it's an observation.

"Always has been. Like a sister," I give him a wry smile. "Even though she's always been the wild one." I sigh. "Me, on the other hand? Not so much, I had one boring high school boyfriend for almost two years." I wrinkle my nose at the memory of Dave - I can't believe I thought I loved him. Or that he had the gall to text me after the Aria Thorne article about Jaxon and I came out. Though, until I moved in with Jade in the city, Dave and I never really had any closure, maintaining an on-again-off-again situationship when we reconnected after college. "And I already told you about Cal. I wasted more of my life with him than

I'd care to admit, but that's it as far as guys I've really dated. Pretty boring."

"That's it?" Jaxon's tone is gentle, but there is a certain possessiveness to it. I shouldn't like it, but *God*, combined with the way he grazes the back of his fingers down my bare shoulder, I feel like I'm on fire.

Except *no*. That's not *it*. Well, as far as actual relationships go, yes, it is.

Selective truths. I promised him everything, I promised myself honesty, and I will not lie to him. But the truth about Trey, I need to talk to Trey first. I owe that to both of them.

"Those are the only relationships I've been in. I mean, I've had a few one-night stands too, but I don't have a whole lot of experience with those either." There. It's the truth. Technically.

Jaxon leans in to press a soft kiss to my lips. It's chaste, and I move to deepen the kiss when my phone starts ringing. Jaxon's groan makes my toes curl, but he pulls back to look at the caller ID. I glance down to see that Jade is now calling me.

"Jade. She isn't going to let up now that she knows I'm awake," I give Jaxon an apologetic look.

"You should answer it." Jaxon pushes himself up off the bed and laughs as I pout, but he still turns towards his dressing room. Because it's a literal room, not a closet. I reluctantly flop back onto the bed and slide my finger across the screen, answering my phone.

"Hi Jade, I'm alive, don't worry."

"Seriously, Hadley! You told me you'd update me last night! It's been over 24 hours, and I check your location to find you're back in Manhattan. I assume Tribeca is where Jaxon lives?" So that's how it's going to be. She's worse than my mother sometimes, I swear, stalking me. Though at least I willingly gave Jade access to my location.

"We got in at 2:00 AM, okay, I passed out."

"Mmhmm, for ten hours. I saw what underwear you packed, Hadley. Ugh, please don't tell me you fucked that man on his jet." She's never been shy about sharing her opinion on my dating choices.

"Jade! No, we didn't *have sex* on the jet," I whisper-shout my response, but Jaxon must have heard because I hear a distinct grunt of amusement from the other room. But hey, it's the truth, despite my attempts to escalate the situation. Thank God she can't see the blush that heats my cheeks.

"Ugh, gross," Jade makes a gagging sound. I forgot she knows me too well; she can read between the lines. I climb off the bed and head towards the bathroom so Jaxon can't hear our conversation as Jade continues her rant.

"You should have at least texted me at some point, Hadley. You know I worry about you, sometimes." Understatement of the year. "You promised me you would."

I sigh, because she's right. "I know, I'm sorry. It was such a whirlwind day, it was amazing and successful, and I can't wait to tell you about it. And then Jaxon..."

What can I say about Jaxon?

Jaxon *loves me*. I want to tell her, but I know she won't approve.

"Hadley. What *is* going on with Jaxon? First, you two are all over the *According to Aria* column, and then you just jet off with him across the country and *then* when you land, you don't come back to the apartment, you stay at his place?" She sounds judgmental to say the least. Though I can't exactly blame her.

I sigh again and hope I don't sound like a lovesick fool. But maybe I am? At least a little bit. "Jade...Jaxon is, he's different from the CEO Jaxon Avenier that you and Bash know. He's...we're —"

She cuts me off with a groan of realization. "Oh my

fucking God, *Hadley*. Please do not tell me you think you're in love with him. Seriously?"

"Jade..." I won't deny it though. "He loves me too." I want to defend us - God, it gives me such a thrill to think of Jaxon and I as an *us*, but I somehow just feel more silly than anything else right now.

"Jesus, Hads! Look, I'm not here to interrupt a good time - we can talk more when you're back at the apartment, but try to remember this isn't Dave, or even Cal. This is *Jaxon Avenier* you're talking about." I sigh in frustration, and her tone softens a bit. "Tell me this, though. Does he even know about you and his stepbrother?" I gasp at Jade's accusation, somehow terrified Jaxon might have heard her through the phone. But she said it quietly enough, and Jaxon is two rooms away, with a closed door between us.

"No," I admit. "But he will, okay? I just want to talk to Trey first. He's still in California."

"Oh." Jade seems surprised that I agree with her. I frown, I'm not *that* unreasonable or disagreeable. "Good. Okay then. Well, we don't need to talk more right now since I know you are at his place, but get your ass back here eventually, okay? Bash is traveling with some clients to the BVI's, and I miss my bestie."

"I will, I'll be there for dinner." I shake my head as I end the call. I know she means well, and Jade has always been more confident and worldly than me, but sometimes my best friend can be too direct, and frankly, too opinionated for her own good.

Speaking of which, I open the Messenger app to text Trey, preparing for a little directness of my own.

> Hadley: Hey Trey. When are you back in the city?

> Hadley: We need to talk. In person.

Trey: Tomorrow night. But I have plans. Can it wait?

Hadley: I think Lex is right.

Hadley: I'm going to tell Jaxon.

I turn on the water for the shower as I wait for Trey's response. I see the three bubbles pop up and go away multiple times over the next few minutes before his response finally comes through.

Trey: Come over to my place at 8:00 PM tomorrow.

As I step into the shower, I let the scalding hot water wash away the tears that start to flow as I process the cost of the truth. I can't predict whether Jaxon will forgive me or hate me for what I've done. I finally have him, and now I'm going to hurt him. I might even lose him. All I can think about is the look in his eyes and the love he so freely and earnestly gave me.

I begin to sob as I think about how I'm about to rip it all apart, the hot water running down my face, blending with the salt of my sorrow. My heart contracts, squeezing like it's trapped in a vice, my conviction to tell him wavering. *How do I tell him?* How do I destroy what we just shared, so fleetingly perfect, with just one truth?

No, I shake my head, I have to tell him. He deserves better than this. And in the end, the truth is the only way forward. Even if it burns. Even if it breaks me. Even if it breaks *us*. Because he will never fully be mine until he knows the truth.

CHAPTER 40

JAXON

Alastair: Landed early. Bar Room at 7:30?

Jaxon: That works

Alastair: What did you need to discuss?

Jaxon: I'll explain in person

Alastair: Typical

Jaxon: See you at 7:30

I walk into the Bar Room. It's been weeks since I last set foot in here, not much time to socialize between work, life and *Hadley*.

Hadley. My heart stutters in my chest at the thought of her. It's been almost 24 hours since I last saw her, and I fucking *miss* her. My body craves her, her touch - always, but just being in her presence is intoxicating. The way she smiles up at me, leans into my embrace. It makes my heart fucking *flutter*. I'm never going to get enough of her.

I told her I love her when we woke up yesterday, and about one hundred times since then. I haven't figured out when it happened yet, but it doesn't even matter. All that matters is that she's mine. And I love her. I'm *in love* with her, and this is a new fucking feeling for me.

I see Alastair, lounging in the plush banquette of a table for two and make my way over to him. He's looking down at his phone, a soft smile on his face, and I wonder if he's texting Vera Norvelle. I subtly shake my head to myself. Was it just a couple months ago that Alastair and I were firmly bachelors, no interest in *love* or anything close to it?

He lays his phone face down on the table as I take my seat. "Hey man," he gestures to the place settings already arranged on the table's surface. "Hope you don't mind, I ordered us both steak frites. I'm starving!"

I raise a brow. "You didn't eat on the jet?"

"Yeah, breakfast. Five fucking hours ago. It wasn't even eleven when we left the Valley. You're welcome for staying by the way, an extra two nights for one fucking Monday morning meeting." Alastair gives me a discerning look as he takes a sip of his drink.

I want to say something about how he didn't really have a choice, but he's right. Normally, I would have stayed to wrap things up, and coming back with Hadley Saturday night was *everything*.

"Thanks," is all I say as our waiter approaches to take my drink order. When I look back at Alastair, he is frowning at me. "What?"

"You just thanked me," Alastair narrows his eyes further. "Are you okay man?"

I feel my lips twitch with the urge to smile and finally

give in, offering Alastair a grin. "I'm...great actually." And I am. I feel lighter than I have in ages. Why the fuck was I so afraid of falling in love? "I told Hadley I love her."

His jaw drops for a moment, but he quickly pulls it together. "Fuck, congrats, I guess?" He raises his bourbon cocktail in a toast to me.

I try to school my smile, but I can't fucking help it as I think about Hadley. The waiter returns with my drink then, and I take a sip as I watch Alastair absorb the news. He looks as surprised by my revelation as I am that I shared it. I can't explain what Hadley does to me; even when she's not here, I can't help but talk about her. And smile.

He's studying me, really looking at me, and his expression is anything but celebratory. He doesn't look angry, but his features exude something more like disapproval. Is he *jealous*? Anxious? Maybe he thinks this is unprofessional, that it complicates things. He's not wrong; it absolutely does. But I need him to just come out and say whatever is bothering him because he is really starting to frustrate me.

"Want to tell me what's going on with you?" I ask, hoping he'll just come out and say it if he has some kind of problem.

"What do you mean?" That act of naïveté is not going to fly with me. In fact, it's pissing me off. I tell him I'm in love, and he - what? Finds fault with it, clearly. If he isn't going to hide his disapproval, then the least he could do is tell me what his issue is.

"The stick. Up your ass." I tell him, "Either remove it or tell me what the fuck is going on with you."

"Nothing." He responds way too quickly. I narrow my eyes at him and notice he shifts nervously in his seat. It's subtle. Nobody else would notice it. But nobody knows his tells as well as I do.

"You have a problem with Hadley?" It's more of a statement than a question because I'm certain it's about Hadley, I'm not fucking stupid.

"Not a *problem*." Seriously? I glare back at him. "You just told me you're in love with her," Alastair continues, "so Jesus fucking Christ, maybe I need a minute, okay? Dude, do you know what you're doing? Does *she* know what she's doing?"

For fuck's sake.

"Well, she's the reason I wanted to talk to you," I tell him, prepared to discuss Hadley's request.

"To tell me you're in love? I mean, look, I'm sorry for my reaction. I'm happy for you, really, I am, it's just –"

"I know," I cut him off.

"You do?" He asks, looking uncomfortable, but oddly relieved?

"Yeah, I get it, it's not a good look."

"Right," he sounds resigned. What is going on with him tonight?

"But I can't help how I feel, man." I need him to understand, no, I need his *support*. "Look, we talked. Hadley and I. About *everything*." God, I feel myself losing control just talking about her. It's like I need him to know everything, like I need to say it all out loud again to someone just to prove it's real. "This isn't some fling, Alastair. It's not some fleeting romance. Fuck." I sigh. I feel like there aren't any words in existence that relay how *big* this feels, how significant this is. "I really love her, okay? I don't know when the hell it happened, but here we are."

Alastair sighs, but I can't help myself, and I continue, "We talked all night, so much that I hardly slept. All weekend really. She stayed over Saturday after we landed, then spent most of the day at my place on Sunday, until Jade threatened to drag her home herself. We talked about our pasts, and I *shared* things with her. Things I haven't shared with anyone just came out of me. Shit about my mom. About Dad and Colleen, and how much it messed with me. I told her all about my past relationships, if you can call them that, because they weren't anything even close to what I have with Hadley. I even told her about my arrangement with Kit."

"Oh?" He asks, encouraging me to go on. And so I do, because when it comes to Hadley, I can't seem to shut up.

"And yes, she told me about her difficult relationship with her mother, coping with the loss of her father, and how, in the absence of siblings, she's had to lean on her best friend Jade. She told me about her exes." Alastair's eyebrows raise at that - does he expect me to be some jealous asshole? I don't care about her past, okay, maybe I do care, but it doesn't fucking matter. Her present, her future, that's with me. She's mine. And I'm hers. "We talked about work," I continue. "Her work, and the complicated feelings with Trey and everything that happened there."

"She told you that?" His eyes widen, and he studies me closely, as if I'm some kind of specimen beneath a micro-scope, and suddenly I feel fucking uncomfortable. Yes, I'm mixing business with pleasure, but even if I think about it objectively, this is the right thing to do. Trey served Hadley well at first; she appreciates it, hell, I appreciate it, but it's time for a change. This is business.

"That's why I wanted to talk to you tonight, actually. I'm going to ask for your discretion here." I watch the color drain from his face. I make a note to circle back and ask what is going on with him once I get Hadley's account sorted.

"About what?" Maybe it's just me, but it seems like his voice cracks a little.

"Well, I'm reassigning you to Hadley's account, for

starters," I tell him, preparing myself for his inevitable argument against this.

"Okay," he says, not putting up a fight. "That makes sense."

"Of course it does." Thankfully Alastair is as sharp as a fucking tack, because I'm really not in the mood to explain what this situation with the acquisition means for Hadley's company. This is his specialty; he just gets it. Was he worried I wouldn't see it?

"Okay," he says again, digesting my request.

"I'll deal with Trey," I tell him. He's my brother, and losing the account might feel like a blow.

"Okay." Alastair seems really distracted. That's the third fucking time he's said nothing but "okay."

"Alastair, what is up with you tonight?"

"I mean, it's just," He pauses, scrutinizing me as his brow furrows, "Dude, are you sure *you're* okay?" Is this about Hadley again? Is it really this hard for him to accept that I've fallen for someone? I'm trying to be professional here, and he's acting like I hit my head on a fucking rock.

"I'm fine," I respond through a clenched jaw.

"Just … go easy on him, okay?" Is he talking about Trey?

"It's not his fault. He didn't really do anything wrong," I reassure Alastair. What does he think I'm going to do? Fire Trey?

"You're just... Shit. You're taking this too well." He eyes me suspiciously.

"Shit happens, Alastair. We deal with it, and we move on." He really looks at me then, and it's making me very uneasy.

"Okay then," he says with a heavy sigh. "I mean, I told them they needed to tell you. I knew you'd eventually understand, but I didn't expect you to be so chill about it. I know it was before you'd even met her and all, but fuck man, you're taking it *really* well. I mean, I –"

"Them?" I cut him off because now I need to know what the fuck he is talking about.

"I'm glad she told you, but you need to hear Trey out, too. Jesus, he's been such a wreck since that night when, well, you know."

I feel my heart rate pick up as a deep sense of foreboding settles into my limbs. Every muscle tenses, the weight of the dread pinning me in place. "Hold on. Clearly I don't know. I have no idea what the fuck you're talking about, Alastair, but you'd better enlighten me right now." I grit through clenched teeth. If he is implying what I think he is - no, that is not a possibility I'm even going to entertain, even though my mind automatically jumps to the worst.

Alastair looks like a deer caught in the headlights. "Nothing," he mumbles. "Shit. What are the odds you can just forget I said anything?"

"Exactly zero," I tell him as my fingers grip the edge of the table so hard I legitimately might crack the wood. "So I suggest you tell me what the fuck is going on." I pause, "Right. Now." I glare at him so intently that I swear to fucking God I can see him physically shrink in his seat.

Good.

He'd better be cowering.

"Oh shit," Alastair falls back against the plush velvet of the banquette, and his pallor is starting to complement the green fabric of his bench.

Whatever this is, it's bad.

"Alastair …" My gaze intensifies, and my fingers curl around the steak knife sitting in front of me. I watch as his eyes, wide as fucking saucers, dart from mine to the knife in my hand, and back up to meet mine again.

"Fuck," he says. "I fucked up. This isn't my business,

this isn't my news to share. You need to talk to them, Jaxon. *Both* of them."

"You just made it your business," I snarl. I'm not letting this one go.

I've never seen Alastair look so uncertain, so uncomfortable, so *terrified*.

What kind of secret has he been keeping from me, and who the hell else knows? He implied that Trey and Hadley, but *no*, I refuse to allow my mind to go there. That is not possible. And the longer I sit here, without answers, the harder that is going to be.

Stay calm. Breathe.

Alastair just continues to silently stare, my blood pressure rising higher with each beat of my pulse which is quickly reaching a dangerous rate.

"Well," I demand, "fucking say something!" I can feel my voice rising, and despite the din in the atrium, I can feel the curious stares from nearby tables. I don't even care. My own flesh and blood is harboring some kind of secret, and it has something to do with the woman I just fucking fell for.

"I don't know what to say!" He's not shouting, but his words are heated. "I'm in a bad spot here."

I scoff. "Oh, *you're* in a bad spot here? Are you fucking kidding me right now, Alastair?" His face contorts in pain, and I cannot bring myself to care.

"I just —"

"You just said you told *them* they needed to tell me. So you are clearly in possession of some piece of knowledge that you believe should be mine," I spit.

"Jaxon, I can't. Just, you need to talk to —"

"Fuck that, Alastair," I throw my chair back as I stand to leave. "Since you won't say shit and insist on keeping my business from me, I'm going to track down Trey, wherever the fuck he is, and I swear to God I'll kill him myself if I have to, because, since you won't say shit, I'm now assuming the worst."

"Jesus Christ, Jaxon. Sit the fuck down."

"Are you going to tell me what the hell is going on here?" I demand, because if he isn't, I'm going to make good on my promise.

"I'll tell you what you need to know, yes," Alastair says, his tone firm but calm. "Besides, based on what Trey said yesterday, he's on a date right now anyway."

I sit, pulse racing, my jaw involuntarily ticking, as I wait for Alastair to compose himself. And just as he looks like he's about to say something, and I'm on the verge of eruption, the cocktail waitress appears with two fresh glasses of bourbon.

Thank fuck because I need a drink. I throw mine back in one long swing, slamming my glass down on the table.

"By all means," I tell Alastair, my tone cruel and sharp, "enlighten me."

He sighs, clearly trying to collect his thoughts while mine are swirling, screaming with the volume of a gale force wind inside my head.

"It was before you even met her," he finally says, as if this is supposed to mean something to me.

"*What* was?" I lean closer, my hand curled into a tight fist.

"That night," Alastair says, voice shaky. "That night, a couple of months ago, here, at the Bar Room. The one when Trey met that mystery girl that had him so fucked up."

"What does that have to do with anything?" I ask, refusing to read between the lines. Refusing to process what he's saying. If he's implying what I think he is, I'm going to make him fucking say it.

"It was *her*, Jaxon," he finally admits. "Trey's mystery girl. It was Hadley." His words hit me like a fist to the stomach. A painful punch I didn't see coming – it knocks the air right out of my lungs.

"Say that again," I demand, "because I don't think I heard you correctly." But I don't want to hear it again. I know I heard him right. Trey. My own fucking stepbrother. And Hadley.

My Hadley.

But she was never really mine, was she? Not if she was keeping something so significant from me. And what hurts the most is that I have only ever been hers.

"I'm sorry," Alastair genuinely looks it.

Pity. He fucking pities me. And that somehow cuts deeper than the knife that Trey and Hadley just plunged into my fucking back.

I don't hear the sound of my glass shattering as I throw it onto the floor, the sound of my chair crashing to the ground as I abruptly rise to my feet, I don't hear Alastair yelling after me as I storm out of the Bar Room, I don't hear the door slamming behind me or the horn that blares as I walk straight into oncoming traffic.

I hear none of it, I hear nothing but the words that just fucking *shattered* me.

I don't even know where the rage starts, but it's there, bubbling over, frothing and boiling in my veins, flooding my mind, distorting my vision. It's acidic, eating me from the inside out, like a poison is running through my blood, stinging, burning, *destroying*. It's not just anger. It's *desperation*.

Fuck, I wish it were just rage, that I can deal with. But this, this is so much deeper than anger. And as I gasp for breath, the physical pain so acute, I know that this is much, much more. This is fucking heartbreak.

I want to scream. I want to go back in time. I want to make everything *disappear* – make it all go away so I don't have to feel this *crushing* pain in my chest.

I don't care about the cars, I barely see them, just streaks of light in my periphery as I charge forward. I don't care about the people shouting at me as I storm ahead like a wild, enraged beast on the hunt. I don't even hear the traffic anymore. All I can hear is the blood rushing in my ears, pulsing and pounding with every step I take.

I know exactly where I am going.

Chapter 41

Jaxon

I'm not thinking, I'm just moving, my feet slamming against the pavement, each step carrying me closer to his place. I don't even know what I'm going to do when I get there. But I *have* to see him. I have to make him look me in the eyes and *feel it*. I need him to see the depths of this pain. This betrayal.

It's unforgivable.

I trusted him. I trusted both of them, in a way I've never trusted anyone. I believed in his loyalty. But that trust is gone and I can feel my entire world crumbling around me. And Hadley, I let her in. I finally let someone in, and she fucking destroys me from the inside out.

I don't alert anyone when I get to his building, entering the code and riding the elevator up to his sixth-floor apartment.

"Trey!" I roar the moment the doors open into his living room, storming inside. "Trey, where the fuck are you?"

"Jaxon?" I hear him before I see him turn the corner from his kitchen. His bright smile quickly fades, and the light drains from his blue eyes when they meet mine, the ire I possess undeniable.

"Tell me it isn't true," I seethe, "and don't fucking lie to me." My stomach churns as I await his response.

"That *what* isn't true?" He asks, cautiously. But I can see it in his eyes. The guilt. He *should* feel guilty.

"You know *exactly* what I'm –" and my words catch in my throat as Hadley walks into the room.

Hadley.

"Jaxon!" She rushes towards me, eyes bright, smile wide, radiant and genuine joy spreading across her face. I reflexively step forward to embrace her, to hold her, to kiss her perfect –

No.

I step back, recoiling. What the fuck is she doing here?

Trey has a date.

Alastair's words come rushing back. This has got to be some kind of cruel joke. She's here. With *him.*

It's too much. Too fucking much. I feel so exposed, like I've been flayed open, my shattered heart on display for them to examine. The pain is as visceral, acute, and as searing as a raw, exposed nerve.

"No." I choke out the words as I back away. Somehow, I manage to keep breathing, which is a miracle given my heart feels like it just shattered into a million fucking pieces.

My stomach drops as my mind races, grasping for anything but the obvious, devastating truth. That she is here. With him. His first fucking priority after landing was seeing her. I never saw it. I was so goddamn lovestruck that I missed it, whatever this is, unfurling right in front of me.

I can't believe I fell for her.

The warmth, the heat, that fleeting bit of happiness. Of love. The flame in my chest that burned so brightly has been suddenly and swiftly snuffed out, leaving nothing more than a trail of cold, suffocating smoke curling and dissipating in its wake.

Alastair. Trey. Hadley. Everybody knew but me.

My gaze tears back and forth between them as my thoughts spiral. Alastair said it was one time, before I met Hadley, but she's *here*. Maybe Alastair didn't know *everything*, but the harsh reality of it all is pretty damn clear to me now.

This. This is why I was rightfully wary of falling in love. Because when it all inevitably goes to shit, all that remains is a hollow echo of what could have been.

I let my guard down, and I risked everything. I gave her my fucking heart. And here I am, standing in the wreckage, feeling the pull of self-recrimination. *I should have seen the signs.*

"And you call yourself my brother," I spit.

He takes a step forward, reaching out to put his hand on my shoulder. "I am, Jaxon. And if you'd just give us a chance to explain –"

Us.

And just like that, anger surges forth and overpowers the hurt.

"You knew I was falling for her," I shove him off me, "But when were you going to tell me you were fucking her?"

"Woah," Trey holds his hands up in surrender, but I choose to ignore him, turning towards Hadley instead, watching her expression bleed from joy into pain as the gravity of my revelation settles in. I can't help but notice how small and lost she appears, the pain she wears so plainly, and fuck my shattered heart for still feeling protective, for wanting to reach out and hold her, to soothe her hurt, to comfort her. It makes it that much more agonizing.

"Please," she says, her hazel eyes large, pleading, and glassy with tears. "Please, let me explain." She takes a step forward, her hand reaching out to caress me, but if I let her touch me, I know I'll break.

"Don't touch me," I spit, my words laced with the very venom that fuels my rage.

She looks shocked, confused, and hurt, but I have no room in my heart for compassion right now.

"Jaxon …" She begs, tears pooling in her eyes. "This is not how I wanted to tell you. How *we* wanted to tell you."

I have no words for them as I turn towards the elevator. I need to leave. Right now.

"Jaxon, please!" I hear the desperation in her voice as the doors open. I step inside and press the button for the lobby with a trembling finger. "But you love me and I lo–"

"Not anymore." I cut her off with that one, cruel statement as the doors close, muffling the sound of her cries as I disappear behind them.

Not anymore.

CHAPTER 42

HADLEY

He can't be gone. This is not how this was supposed to go.

Not anymore.

He doesn't mean it. He *can't* mean it.

I rush towards the elevator button, frantically pressing it, praying by some miracle the doors will open in response to my touch.

They don't. I hear nothing but the mechanical hum of the elevator descending as air rushes past.

"I'm so sorry," I hear Trey say from behind me.

Irrational anger heats my blood as hot tears sting my eyes, blurring my vision.

"Are you?" I spit, swirling around to face him.

His soft blue eyes are full of so much remorse, so much pain and sadness that my anger instantly fades, dissipating until I'm left feeling numb and hollow. This is *Trey*. My anger is misplaced. He didn't do anything wrong.

"Of course I am, Hadley." His voice cracks as he opens his arms, inviting me into the comfort of his embrace. I know he is sorry. And God, I forgot how damn *good* he smells. Woodsy, but warm and comforting at the same time.

The elevator dings, drawing me out of Trey's arms as I momentarily forget I hit that button, calling it back. The cruel irony of it, undoubtedly returning empty. As I instinctively turn towards the sound, I watch the doors open, revealing Jaxon, watching us, watching *me*. His eyes are now black as coal.

Time slows. Or maybe it stops. I watch as his eyes drop to Trey's arm around my waist.

"Looks like you wasted no time getting cozy." There's an edge to his words, but they're softer, more honed than they were before.

"Jaxon, it's not what —"

"Not what I think?" He cuts me off. "Then please, enlighten me. I'm listening." And I watch in disbelief as he walks over to the beautiful trunk that serves as Trey's bar and pours himself a few fingers of that Avenier bourbon he loves so much before slowly, deliberately, walking over to the sofa and taking a seat.

Suddenly, I am at a loss for words.

"Jaxon, she came over here to tell me —"

"I want to hear it from Hadley." Jaxon's voice is more commanding than I've ever heard it. But it doesn't scare me. Trey fades into the background as I slowly approach Jaxon. He sits impossibly still as I climb into his lap and wrap my arms around his waist.

"Trey and I hooked up once, Jaxon." I decide to start at the beginning. "The week before my pitch to AVC. I'd never even met you yet, and I had no idea what we would become. We didn't keep this from you intentionally. And I was here tonight because now that things have grown more serious between us, I knew we had to tell you. I wanted to tell you."

I can feel him start to relax in my embrace, and I can

feel the hope flaring in my chest. "I love you, Jaxon," I say it with all the conviction in my heart.

"And you were every fantasy I'd ever had, Hadley Aldridge."

Were?

I clutch at his jacket, but my hands keep slipping, and I feel like I'm falling through the floor. I can't tell up from down, and I'm suddenly overcome by a deep sense of foreboding; something is wrong.

I'm falling, he's slipping away. I'm thrashing wildly as darkness falls over the room.

"Jaxon?"

I'm kicking now, the sheets tangled around my feet, my body clammy with sweat

The sheets.

Oh God.

I sit up in bed, *my* bed, completely still, completely silent. The only movement, the rapid rise and fall of my chest, the only sound, my ragged breaths as I fight down the sob that burns my throat. The air instantly chills my sweat-slicked skin, causing me to shiver from the sudden cold. I glance at the clock on my bedside table: 4:00 AM.

I'm in my room. And I'm alone.

Alone, the same way I've woken up every morning for the last nine days following some version of this recurring dream. This fucking nightmare. A nightmare my trembling body refuses to shake.

I'm wracked with guilt. I'm drowning in regret. And I hate myself for it. But the guilt was never sharp; it started slow, like water rising. We should've told him before the water got too deep. *I* should have told him, but before I knew it, we were all in over our heads.

I fucked up. And it cost me *everything.*

So I'm tormented by this dream. The nightly manifestation of a secret I tried to bury. And I have no one to blame but myself as it replays over and over in my mind. The part where I reach for Jaxon, the man I love, the man who holds my heart, the one I *chose*, and he slips away. Because I've lost him. That's what hurts the most. The dream isn't just about the past; it's about how the truth, and my inability to confront it, shattered everything. It's me realizing, over and over, how much damage my silence has done. And now, I'm left with the wreckage, alone in a bed that feels colder with every passing night.

Alone.

The same way I've gone to sleep - *cried myself* to sleep every night since Jaxon walked out of Trey's apartment and out of my life. He still won't answer my calls.

It's the first day of a new fucking year, and I'm still alone.

I never got my midnight kiss.

And tomorrow, I have to face reality. Tomorrow, I have to return to AVC.

Happy fucking New Year, Hadley Aldridge.

CHAPTER 43

TREY

"Still no word from Jaxon?" I ask Beau, passing him a latte.

"Oh my God, for me?" He looks at me like I just handed him a winning lottery ticket. "Low-fat, salted caramel latte?"

"For the hardest working executive assistant in all of Manhattan? Of course." I flash him a dazzling grin.

Beau smiles back at me like I just hung the stars and moon, which makes me feel pretty damn good about myself. "It's just a latte." I wave it off. "Jaxon?"

The real reason I'm supplying this man with lattes - I know the asshole has undoubtedly sworn Beau to secrecy, but luckily for me, his enthusiastic assistant is as pliable as Play-Doh. Given the right amount of steamed milk, sweet caramel syrup and espresso.

"Ugh, he's killing me, Trey." Beau sags in his chair, but clutches his latte with two hands as he takes a sip. "It's been a week and a half, how much longer is he going to stay there? He has three social engagements this week that are really more like business appearances and I can only make up so many excuses for his absences."

"Hmmm," I pretend to ponder. "Where, is *there*, exactly?" Shit, that wasn't exactly subtle.

Beau raises an eyebrow. "Nice try, you know I've been threatened with my *job* if I tell anyone where he is." Though he looks desperate to share, the man isn't as much of a vault as he'd like to believe he is.

I sigh. "Honestly, I have no idea how long he'll be gone. Knowing where he is probably wouldn't help." I perch on the side of Beau's desk and sip my own coffee.

"Can I ask you something?" Apparently, now I'm the one with information *he* wants. "What could you have possibly fucked up so badly that Mr. Avenier would be this closed off? I haven't been here that long, but this reaction doesn't seem normal."

"It's not. And yeah, you could say that I… fucked up."

Beau's eyes sparkle as he hones his gaze on me. "Genevieve said she has no patience for his 'broody betrayed billionaire shit'?"

I turn to face Beau. "Look, I didn't know I was *betraying* him when I… betrayed him."

"That doesn't make any sense." I can see the wheels in his head starting to spin.

"What else did *he* tell you?" Enough about me, if he won't spill his exact location, surely he must have something useful to share.

"He is refusing calls from everyone basically, specifically stating that you and Hadley have been designated as absolutely no contact allowed, under *any* circumstances. So unless you fooled around with her behind his back, I don't see what could be the reason."

I shift uncomfortably on my perch.

"*Trey Eskridge.*" Beau practically falls over his desk before dropping his voice to an actual whisper, eyes wide. "Did you and Hadley… I can't even say it! But did you?"

I glance around the office, making sure no one is nearby and sigh. "Look, it was before she and Jaxon met."

"Oh shit."

"Yeah, no shit."

"Okay, so you and Hadley, then Mr. Avenier enters the picture and…" I see the pieces click into place for him, "so the betrayal is you two not telling him."

"To be fair, it was just a one-time thing. I didn't even know her name, and then she walked into that conference room and –"

"Oh! This is even more scandalous than I thought!" He claps his hands together. "And you must have been so shocked to see each other again. And then to work so *closely* together while she and your boss…" His brow furrows for a moment before he continues, "Wait, you were working *so* closely, did it … oh! Tell me it didn't happen *again?*"

"No, nothing like that." I clarify. This is exactly how rumors start. "So what, you just decided to pretend like it never happened? Take the secret to the grave with you?"

"We were going to, but then he kind of caught us together," Beau gasps at that. "Not like *that*," I say again, shooting him a look before heaving a sigh. "We were actually talking about how we need to tell him. Anyway, the timing was *awful*." I groan.

"Hmm," Beau takes another sip of his latte. "So much drama." I think he is trying to sound sympathetic, but it sounds more like he is relishing it. If I weren't firmly cemented in the very vortex of said drama I'd roll my eyes at the way he is clearly thriving amongst it. I'd probably even find it amusing.

Suddenly he sits up in his chair, latte sloshing over his lid, but he manages to stop it from spilling on his well-tailored suit. "Wait! What about you and that girl! I heard a rumor you were dating one of Vera Norvelle's friends.

An up and coming model!" He waggles his brows at me conspiratorially.

"Juliana," I grin, letting my mind focus in on her, and the drama-free situationship we have. Because it really *isn't* a relationship - not exactly, anyway. "Yeah. We're kind of seeing each other."

I don't know how he does it. I came here, bribing him with his favorite beverage in order to pry information out of *him,* and yet somehow I ended up sharing all the details of my own personal relationships with him.

"I don't give a shit whose dick was in Hadley Aldridge, this is fucking unacceptable," Genevieve's voice carries towards us as she stomps around the corner from the elevator bank.

The look Beau gives me, teeth bared in an *oh no this is bad* grimace, almost makes me smile. But unfortunately, I'm one of the dicks she's referencing.

"Seriously, Gen? Shouting it so the entire office can hear isn't exactly *professional.*" Oh great, Lex is with her.

They both stop short when they see me at Beau's desk. Genevieve lets out an exasperated sigh of frustration.

"Trey," Lex's eyes are pleading. I have spoken to him no more than once over the past week, outside of obligation, that is. He's called and texted me multiple times, apologizing profusely for his slip up. I appreciate that he's been giving me the space I asked for after texting him back and telling him I don't blame him. And honestly, I *don't* blame him. But it doesn't mean I want to grab drinks or hit the gym together right now either.

It really isn't his fault. He kept my secret when I told him about me and Hadley. And now he's handling her account. He's become intimately entangled in drama that he didn't create. He could be as mad as Genevieve, but he's not. I meet his gaze as I give him a nod, and I see him visibly relax. We might not be totally good yet, but we will be.

"Oh look, it's one of the *dicks*." Yup, I knew Genevieve was thinking it, but that doesn't mean she had to *say* it.

"Hi, Gen, have a nice holiday?" I wear my best *kill her with kindness* smile.

"You mean cleaning up your Cipher mess? Or hearing about the latest drama you fucking men have created by thinking with your dicks instead of your brains?" Genevieve gives me a very dazzling, very insincere smile. "I had a lovely holiday, thank you for asking."

"God, she's terrifying," Beau says softly, which causes Genevieve's eyes to sparkle with satisfaction.

"Glad you think so," she smiles genuinely, turning her attention to Beau. "You'll connect me with Jaxon then. Since you are the only one he will answer. He needs to do his fucking job."

Beau gapes at her, opening and closing his mouth like a guppy without actually saying anything.

"You know he's threatened Beau with his job, right?" Lex tells Genevieve. "You can't ask him to do that."

Genevieve narrows her eyes at Beau. "Fine. Give me something to write on." She taps Beau's desk, and he moves hastily to oblige her request.

Genevieve quickly writes out a couple sentences and slides it back to Beau. "Next time that angsty asshole calls you, I want you to read this to him. Word for word. Got it?"

I watch as Beau's eyes widen while he reads her loopy scrawl. "Umm..." he looks up to meet her gaze and simply nods. "Okay."

Genevieve taps the desk, apparently satisfied with that response. She gives Lex a smug look. "There. Everyone's job is secure. Except... everyone at AVC because we have an AWOL CEO." She sighs. "Okay. I'll take care of this.

Once again, leave it to the woman to clean up your mess." She looks around as if she's assessing whether there is a single exception to her blanket statement. "Well, except maybe you," she nods at Beau. "Just make sure you read him that message. *Verbatim.*"

"Yes … uh, ma'am?" He replies uncertainly.

"Don't ever call me ma'am again." Genevieve spares me one last look and exhales a groan of disgust before spinning on her black stilettoed heel to stomp off.

Unfortunately, Hadley arrives at that exact moment for our transition meeting - the meeting I've been dreading all week. I send a plea to whatever God might listen to me that Genevieve will go easy on her. They must have mercy on us all because Genevieve simply gives her head a shake, refusing to step around Hadley, forcing Hadley to stumble out of the way, catching herself on the wall as she dodges Genevieve's advance.

"Hi, um, thanks for agreeing to work with Trueno," she pauses awkwardly in front of Lex, wringing her hands.

"No problem," he jumps in. "Shall we get started?"

Lex gestures for the three of us to head into the meeting room we've reserved. Hadley takes the seat on the far side of the room, Lex takes the head of the table, leaving me sitting across from her. Once again, she looks up, her blush deepening further. I want to take her hand and tell her it will be okay, but I'm not sure it *will*. I have no idea what my stepbrother is thinking, where he is, or what he's doing. I want it to turn out okay for them. I really do.

"Hey, Hadley," I get her attention. "It doesn't have to be weird. We all feel bad about everything that happened." Lex grunts at that, and I give him a half smile to show I'm grateful for his support. "Jaxon's… reaction, well, none of us could have anticipated he'd disappear."

"Kind of a dick move actually," Lex chimes in. "No

opportunity for any explanation, just a lot of assumptions and anger." Lex shakes his head.

Clearly our counsel isn't helping though because Hadley's expression of concern only deepens. "He hasn't talked to either of you?"

"Only Beau," I sigh. "And maybe clients or investors, but strictly work-related."

"We don't even know where he is," Lex adds.

Hadley visibly deflates.

"He'll come back eventually, he has to. He's the CEO," Lex sounds somewhere between desperate and angry as he says it, like he wants to expect the mature response from Jaxon - the one where he comes back, we have a conversation, and things get back to some semblance of normal - but like he doesn't actually believe it will happen.

"Okay," Hadley looks anything but *okay*. I want to offer some sort of reassurance, but I'm the absolute last person who should do so right now. Lex takes pity on her though.

"It will be," he says. "Look, we are going to proceed with the transition of your account. That's a good step; hopefully, Jaxon can recognize the efforts we are all making here."

We go through my involvement with Trueno over the last two months, reviewing the strategic plan we built together and the ways Lex's expertise will lend further support.

At the end of the meeting, Hadley is standing at the table putting her laptop away just as I'm leaving the room, and she stops me at the door, calling out, "Hey, Trey..."

I turn back to face her, though she doesn't look up from her bag. She starts chewing her nip nervously, and I step back into the room, though I don't go to her. "Hadley?"

She looks up at me then and tries to smile. "Lex said you two are okay? I feel so guilty about putting him in the middle of this, and if it affected your friendship..."

"We're good," I tell her. "We've never let a girl come between us, and we're not about to start now." I try to crack a joke, then wish I hadn't, realizing it really didn't land well as I watch Hadley's eyes widen as though I'm accusing her of something.

"My friendship with Lex is also way more chill than literally anyone's relationship with Jaxon," I quickly add. That gets me a tentative, nervous laugh. "And Jaxon shouldn't have reacted the way he did, no matter when or how he found out." I try to reassure her.

"Thanks." She lets out a sigh, but I think her shoulders look slightly more relaxed. "You're probably right."

"Oh, I am," I hold the door open for her, instinctively placing my hand on her lower back as I guide her out the door, causing her to jump.

"Sorry." I quickly drop my hand; it was an involuntary gesture. I didn't even realize I was doing it, but fuck, I'm going to have to check myself with that kind of behavior.

Hadley glances back at me, her cheeks clearly flushed. *Shit.*

"My bad," I give her a contrite smile. She nods awkwardly and races towards the elevator bank, leaving me standing alone just outside the meeting room, feeling uncomfortable and perplexed.

I hate how awkward that was.

Genevieve: Meet me at the bar at Slice. 7:30. This is mandatory.

Trey: Fine. See you there.

When I arrive at Slice later that evening, Genevieve is already sitting at the bar, with half a glass of brut rosé champagne - rim marked with her signature pink lipstick - sitting in front of her.

"Hey." I slip into the open seat beside her.

"Look, Eskridge." Oh, so she's using *last names* now. "I really don't care about whatever girl drama you and Jaxon have going on. I swear to God you boys are less mature than middle-school girls."

I open my mouth to defend myself then promptly shut it when she cuts me off with a death glare.

"Jaxon is acting like a baby. I'll give you that. But you should have told him sooner."

"Is this seriously why you called me here?"

"No, but I saw an opportunity to offer you my unsolicited advice and took it. Sue me." She rolls her eyes, then takes a sip of her champagne before she continues. "I swear this is the last mess I'll clean up for you boys. You don't typically cause trouble, so I'm disappointed in you, Trey. Jaxon, on the other hand, it's technically not my job to save his ass, but my professional reputation is kind of tied to AVC, so who do you think is the one with our PR firms on speed dial? Including one that specializes in damage control. For your *personal image*."

"I'm not sure our interpersonal drama warrants a PR firm's involvement."

"Not yet, but if Jaxon keeps up his brooding in hiding, we're going to need more than a carefully constructed PR spin to save face. He's missed his last two scheduled appearances. Granted, Beau was easily able to weave a story about a brutal strain of the flu, and things are typically slow around the holidays anyway, but that'll only last for so long."

She has a point.

"So what do you need from me?"

"If you have any plans tomorrow night, cancel them. Jaxon is supposed to accept an award on behalf of AVC at some fundraiser, and Beau offered you up in his stead."

Fucking great. "Why can't Lex do it?"

"First of all, Trey, it's the least you can do given your actions are the reason we're in this mess in the first place. I get it, Jaxon is being a fucking drama queen. So you licked her first, I still fail to see what the big deal is." A surprised laugh escapes me at Genevieve's extreme candor.

"Besides," she continues, "Lex is heading out west to go bring that fucker back to Manhattan."

I almost fall off my barstool at this revelation. "What? You found him? Where is he?" It's been almost ten fucking days that Jaxon has been evading us.

"He's at his place in Aspen," Genevieve looks smug. "I'm not sure how anyone didn't think to check in with the staff there sooner."

"Oh shit, I forgot about that place." I remember the one time he brought me there a couple of years ago. Apparently, it was once his mother's - she left it to him, and he assumed ownership of it when he turned eighteen. One of the few places that not even Ken and my mom have access to. Jaxon hardly goes, and he rarely invites anyone to join him. It's a ski-in-ski-out mountainside chalet. I'm surprised he doesn't take more advantage of it, now that I think about it. Maybe he does, it's not like I track his every move.

"Yeah, well, he's not as mysterious as he thinks he is. In fact, he's pretty fucking predictable," she scoffs as she throws back the rest of her champagne, signaling to the bartender she'd like another round.

I offer her a relieved smile in a show of gratitude. "Okay, I'll handle the award and the fundraiser."

Genevieve smirks. "I know you will. Beau will send your written remarks tomorrow." She fills me in on a few key logistical details, all being sent by Beau as well, before finishing her champagne and taking her leave.

I nod and pay for her tab, feeling more than a bit guilty that she apparently did have to swoop in and do damage control. "What would we do without you?"

"Best not to think about it," Genevieve gives me a wink as she stands. "Now if you don't mind, I have a date."

CHAPTER 44

JAXON

The wind whips across my face, stinging my cheeks as I carve tracks into the fresh powder. The world around me is nothing but a blur of white as I barrel down the secluded mountainside, off piste. I push myself harder, faster down the mountain, as if I can somehow outrun this ache in my chest.

My lungs burn, my thighs are on fire, but still I continue to test my limits.

No distractions here. No crowds. No calls. No chance of seeing someone who reminds me of *her*. Who sounds like her.

For ten fucking days I've tried to forget her, tried to seal off my heart, tried to heal its jagged fractures, but I can't, because there's a fucking Hadley-sized hole in it now. I close my eyes, embracing the bite of the wind as I fly down the empty mountain, the last bit of the sun's warm rays sinking beneath the peaks in the distance. This will be my last run of the day, I tell myself, as I ski towards home.

I can almost feel her here, beside me. I can see her smile, feel her touch, hear her laugh, the way she says my name. Every time I close my eyes, all I can see is her beautiful smile, her perfect fucking face. All I can hear is her saying those three little words that caused my heart to crack wide open and let her in.

I love you.

I fell for her. Hard. I told her I *loved* her, something I've never said to any woman, never *felt* for any woman.

And I still do. I probably always will.

No. I can't go there. Not again. Not today. Not ever.

My eyes fly open. Just in time to see the tree.

Fuck.

Her face is the last thing I see flash across my mind before everything goes black.

Chapter 45

Jaxon

My nose stings. No, it fucking *burns*. What is that smell? Whatever the hell it is, it slices through this distant, floating haze and forcibly drags me back to reality.

My body jerks instinctively, and I gasp for air, like I've been holding my breath underwater for way too long. Have I been underwater? I feel - no I felt, like I was floating, suspended. My eyes snap open and everything is blurry, and dark.

The cold hits me.

I'm fucking freezing.

And wet? I feel something warm trickling slowly down my face.

Is she here? She has to be. The image of her face flashes across my vision.

"Hadley?" The words slip out before everything comes into focus.

"Mr. Avenier," a voice cuts through the fogginess, deep and serious and distinctly male. Well, that's not her. Of course, it's not fucking her.

The sound, the voice. It makes no sense at first. I try to

collect myself, gather my bearings. Why am I so fucking cold?

"Hadley?" I ask again, hoping this is just a dream. Some terrible nightmare. It has to be.

"Mr. Avenier?" That voice again, it's closer now as the fuzzy world comes into focus, slowly, like watching a Polaroid develop. He's in a familiar red jacket, his face is blurry, drifting in and out of focus. I can't quite tell if that's one person or two.

I blink, trying to gain control, and I'm once again desperately aware of the cold. I shiver as hands press against me and I try, unsuccessfully, to figure out where the hell I am. There's a bright light preventing me from fully opening my eyes - at least not without a shooting pain boring deep into my skull.

Wasn't the sun setting? I hear other voices too - people talking in hushed tones. About me, presumably. I'm definitely not on the mountain anymore, so where the fuck am I and how did I get here? I finally manage to open my eyes, just slightly. Everything feels so far away. Familiar and unfamiliar all at once.

The red jacket.

Ski patrol.

I'm on my back.

Oh. Shit.

The tree.

Fucking hell.

And then *he's* suddenly there. Where the hell did he come from?

"Hadley isn't here." Alastair's face suddenly materializes inches from mine as he practically shoves the nameless man in the red jacket out of the way. God, I'm so fucking pathetic. Of course, she isn't here. I'm in Aspen. I know where I am, but how the hell did I end up *here*?

"Jesus, you scared the shit out of me, man." Alastair's expression is one of both relief and concern.

"Sir, I'm going to have to ask you to step aside so we can do our job." The words are directed at Alastair. "We need to transfer him to the hospital."

"I'm fine," I grumble, attempting to prop myself up into a seated position. I groan, blinking back a sudden wave of dizziness at the attempted movement. No fucking way am I going to the hospital to be poked and prodded.

"What the fuck are you doing here?" I ignore the man from ski patrol and shift my gaze towards Alastair.

"What the fuck am I *doing* here?" His tone is incredulous. "They called your emergency contact. Trey. Who called me, because I was already here."

Well, fuck.

I shake my head, trying to clear it, but that only makes it worse. Everything in my field of vision moves a moment after my head physically does. The smell of salt still stings my nose and burns my throat, pungent and sharp, and I suddenly feel like I might be sick. An eerie sense of foreboding settles in my bones; I feel like I've woken up from something I don't want to remember, and honestly, I probably fucking don't.

"Mr. Avenier, just please try and relax. We need you to wait here until the hospital transport arrives."

Here appears to be the small, but serviceable, patrol hut.

"I'm not going to the fucking hospital," I snap. My resolve is back. I swallow back the bile threatening to rise in my throat and sit up fully. There is no way in hell I'm going to be taken away by ambulance. I repress the shame I already feel at the thought of my unconscious body being taken down that mountain strapped to a board and trailing behind the ski patrol's snowmobile.

"Christ, Jaxon. Let the man do his job." Alastair levels

me with a glare that says he'll help them restrain me if he has to. And I don't doubt he will. "You took a hell of a hit, and you probably need stitches for that cut above your eye. It's still fucking bleeding."

"You're lucky we found you when we did our last sweep of the mountain," if the ski patrol is looking for acknowledgement or gratitude for *doing his fucking job*, he's going to be sorely disappointed.

Eventually, we compromise. I manage to stand without assistance and agree to have the ski patrol escort me back to my house on the back of one of their snowmobiles. Despite their insistence, I decline a visit to the hospital and instead defer to Alastair, who arranges for a doctor to make a discreet home visit. I'm diagnosed with a concussion, bruised ribs, and I receive four stitches, suturing the cut that now sits above my left eyebrow. Let it scar, I decide. I don't fucking care.

Two hours later, I'm sitting on the couch with Alastair, a fire roaring in the stone hearth as the forecasted snow falls outside. I want nothing more than to sit alone outside in the hot tub, a Campari and orange in hand, hidden from the world by a veil of steam as the snow falls, then melts away as it lands on my body.

But no. I have a concussion. I allowed myself to get distracted. I hit a fucking tree. And now my damn cousin is here watching my every move, like he's worried I'll do something stupid. I'm a prisoner in my own home.

So much for solitude.

Took him long enough; I probably should have expected him sooner than almost ten days into my self-imposed exile, but I'm not surprised he found me.

"Are you sure it's a good idea to have that?" Alastair eyes the two fingers of Aretian Reserve I just poured myself.

"Does it look like I care?" I shoot back. It's been a

fucking day, and Alastair insisted we follow the doctor's instructions, so here we are, awake, for the entire night if he gets his way, but all I want to do is go to sleep and forget any of this ever happened.

"Well, if you can't beat 'em, join 'em I guess." He shrugs and rises from the couch to pour himself a glass. At least he knows not to start an argument he has no chance of winning. Smart man.

"You want to tell me what the hell happened out there?" He asks as he takes a seat on the opposite end of the oversized leather sofa. "Because there was only one tree in that open bowl, and it seems like you were aiming for it." He eyes me warily, and suddenly his presence, the depth of his concern, hits me like a fucking punch to the gut.

"What? No. Jesus, Alastair. It was nothing like that." Is he serious right now? I refuse to feel guilty when he's acting like a mother hen.

He gives me a look that says he's not buying what I'm selling, and I groan before continuing. God, my whole fucking body aches.

"I got distracted on that last run and just kind of… zoned out, I guess."

"You just zoned out straight into the only fucking tree in sight?" He narrows his eyes, like he's trying to assess whether I need further medical attention.

"I wasn't aiming for the tree, Alastair. I just, fuck. I was thinking about *her* okay? Are you happy now?" He's really going to make me fucking talk about this, isn't he.

"No, I'm not happy." His tone is gentler now, but he's still worked up. "I feel awful about what happened."

"It wasn't your fault," I give a defeated sigh. He looks like he wants to say something, but thinks better of it.

We sit in companionable silence for what feels like an eternity. The only sound is the crackling of the fire, though its heat is doing little to numb the cold emptiness inside of me.

"I fucking loved her," I finally say, even though he already knows that. "I fucking *loved* her. What a joke."

Alastair is silent for a moment and keeps his gaze fixed on the fire as he contemplates my words. "Loved… or love?" He asks, but he already knows the answer. And so do I. He's just going to make me say it.

I sigh. "I love her. I don't want to, but –"

"But you can't help how you feel." He cuts me off. "I know. It may seem easier to run. But in the end it always catches up with you. Trust me, I know. I get it."

"Are you fucking kidding me right now, Alaistair? *Trust me*, you definitely don't *get it*." I spit. For one thing, he's never had any serious woman in his life. Ever. Vera Norvelle is the longest-standing relationship I think he's ever had, and even that feels performative as fuck sometimes.

"No, I don't get your *particular* situation. But you know what else I don't get? Why the hell aren't you fighting for her if you love her? Why are you just hiding like a coward?" He throws up his hands in some kind of dramatic gesture that I assume is supposed to make a point, then rolls his eyes and adds, "and skiing into fucking trees."

"Fuck off." His words sting because there's too much truth in them for my liking. Doesn't give him the right to act like a patronizing dick about it, though.

"Nope, that shit may work with everyone else, but it doesn't work with me. I'm your family, Jax. I'm not fucking going anywhere. Doctor's orders." He lifts one of his feet from the floor and crosses it so that his ankle rests gently on the opposite knee, then he leans back into the couch, indicating he is very much settling in and is indeed not fucking off.

Great.

"There's nothing left to fight for," I try.

"Oh? Enlighten me. Because from the way I see it, you're so fucking in love with Hadley Aldridge that you can't see straight." He gestures to the bandaged wound on my head, alluding to the fact that I just ran right into a fucking tree. Which I did. "And from what I understand, she's heartbroken and confused and actually *trying* to fight for you, but you're, what? Too allergic to any form of emotional discomfort to talk to her? To give her a chance to share her side of the story? To, I don't know, *apologize?* At this point, man, I'm thinking maybe you're the one who owes her an apology and not the other way around."

"Enough!" I feel my chest tightening with rage. He doesn't know how I feel, how their actions fucking destroyed me, how I opened my heart, this one and only time, for what? To have it completely fucking shattered. To be fucking humiliated. They betrayed me, *she* betrayed me. And he thinks I owe either of them an explanation, or an *apology*?

"You have no fucking idea how I feel, Alastair!" I'm raising my voice now, the turmoil swirling within matched only by the acute physical agony of my bruised ribs, and the throbbing in my head as I abruptly rise from the couch, storming into the kitchen, pouring myself another glass of bourbon, desperate to numb the pain.

"Jaxon —"

"No," I cut him off, spinning around to face him. "I'm glad you're content with your surface-level relationships. Fuck I wish I could go back to that. It's more than just Hadley." I can feel the bitterness in my words. "It's that something happened between her and my *brother*, Alastair. My own fucking stepbrother. So don't you dare sit there and tell me you have any understanding of how this fucking feels." My words are sharp, filled with vitriol as I try to choke down the fury bubbling up from within.

He opens his mouth to speak, but I don't let him.

"Honestly, fuck you, Alastair," I rage on. "You don't get to tell me you understand. You *can't*. What do you know about being blindsided like this? About giving *everything* to someone only to turn around and find out they'd already given it to someone else? How can you sit there and tell me you understand what it's like to be *destroyed?*" I seethe, my words fueled by every bit of the betrayal I feel.

His face is tight, but his eyes are sympathetic, which only amplifies my anger. *Pity*. The same fucking way he looked at me ten days ago in the Bar Room when he let slip the secret everyone had been harboring.

"Look, Jaxon, I only –"

"No, just shut the fuck up, Alastair!" He does. "You think I don't know what I'm feeling? You think I don't *know* I've been shutting her out? I've been trying to figure this out, trying to understand how the hell this fucking happened. How can I ever trust her again?"

Uncomfortable silence hangs in the air between us. I feel my anger slipping into something far more dangerous, something that leaves me feeling empty, and raw, and so goddamn exposed: grief.

Then he says it. Quietly, gently, but steadily, "You still love her, Jaxon. So fight for her."

He still doesn't get it. "Fight for her?" I stare at him like he just slapped me. "Are you serious right now? Did you hear *anything* I just said?"

"Every word," he responds evenly. "And you know what I hear?"

"Tell me, Alastair. What is it you *hear*? Because I'm not sure we're even having the same conversation."

"I hear you telling me you're still hopelessly in love with Hadley. I hear you saying you're so caught up in your own little pity party that you've lost sight of the bigger picture. Nobody *betrayed* you, Jaxon. Yeah, it's messy and you need some time to lick your wounds. Fine. So Trey had her first, before you'd even met her, you can't tell me you believed she was a virgin before she walked into your life. And from what I see, she's yours now, so long as you get your head out of your ass and fight for her. You're Jaxon fucking Avenier, I've never seen you give up on something you want. Ever. I'd really hate to see you start now."

I'm speechless. We stare at each other in silence, neither one of us knowing what to say next. His words fucking cut, like a knife to my gut, because he's right. It's everything I need to hear, and it's exactly what I don't *want* to hear.

And Alastair. My cousin. My best friend. He's the only one who can deliver the message.

I feel the fight loosen its grip, slowly, silently slipping away.

It hits me then, all at once. The dam fucking bursts, and the emotions rush in at once, flooding my system. The grief, the remorse, the anger, the heartbreak. I let it all wash over me.

I don't want to break. Not in front of anyone, not even in front of Alastair, but I can't help it. The pressure has built up for so long, and I'm fucking sick of holding it all in. Everyone has their breaking point, and apparently, I've just hit mine.

The tears come before I can stop them, hot and fast and before I even realize they're falling, I'm clinging to the counter for support, gasping for air as I heave out one pained cry after another.

I collapse against the stone countertop, burying my face in my hands. I can't regain control as the sobs overtake me, my shoulders shaking as I cover my face in shame. It's not just the anger anymore, or the betrayal. I'm angry at myself too, and the world, for finally fucking putting myself out there, and somehow feeling like I've come up empty.

I hear Alastair move, and I don't even think to try and stop him as he comes up beside me, lifting my head and arms from the countertop and pulling me against him as I sob into his chest. I'll never admit this aloud, but I fucking *need* him. I need someone to hold me while this storm of emotions works its way through my system.

"Fuck, Alastair." I moan between sobs, clinging to the back of his sweatshirt. "I don't even know what the hell to do anymore."

I'm too exhausted and too broken to keep fighting it. I want to push him away. I want to scream. I want to fucking punch something… or someone. But instead, I let my cousin, my best friend, hold me and soothe me. And for once, I don't worry about being judged, and just let myself fall completely apart.

"I need some fucking ibuprofen," I finally break the silence as I slowly regain my composure, pulling myself away.

"You need a hell of a lot more than that, but that's a good place to start," Alastair chuckles.

I wash down two pills with the remainder of my Aretian Reserve as Alastair side eyes me from the sofa he's returned to. But he doesn't say anything; instead, he just pats the couch and shakes a box of tissues at me. I make my way over there and take a seat beside him.

"Look, what happened today – what happened here, tonight, stays between us. Promise." So much for not feeling fucking judged, though I appreciate his pledge to keep my breakdown confidential.

He looks at me expectantly, like he's asking permission to continue, and I offer a small nod of approval. "So, I know you think I don't know anything about being blindsided."

I watch him intently, because no, I do not know about any such occurrence in Alastair's love life.

"Almost a decade ago," he says tentatively, "remember I did that semester abroad in Switzerland my sophomore year of undergrad?"

"Yeah." I'm not sure where he's going with this.

"Well, I met someone. While I was there." I can feel my eyebrows shoot up in surprise. He never mentioned anyone.

"I remember, you were pretty fucking angsty when you got back. I figured it was just a symptom of being twenty and forced back to reality after your throwaway time partying in the Alps."

"That probably didn't help," he lets out a humorless chuckle. "But I was actually heartbroken. My… the person I met, we were just friends, except we *weren't,*" Alastair sighs. "I'm not explaining this well. But my point is, I felt things I had never felt before. *Real* things."

I nod. I've never heard Alastair talk so openly about his feelings before.

"We kept it quiet. There were… reasons why we didn't really want people knowing about us. So it was just the two of us, in that little world we'd made behind closed doors. But when I tried to make it real and move beyond the secrecy, I was shut out. It wasn't just a rejection; it was complete devastation. They acted like everything we had, everything we'd built over those months, never even happened at all. Like it was nothing. Like *I* was nothing to them. After that… I stopped even *trying* to find love. Because I thought then that maybe I had found it, but clearly I'd misread everything. So I stopped letting myself hope that what I felt back then was something I'd ever be allowed to find again."

Okay. I admit, I did not see that one coming.

"Why didn't you tell me?" His confession stuns me, yet in the simplicity of this admission, after I just screamed at him, accusing him of not understanding how I feel, reminds me why he's more than family, he's my best friend. And he really does understand me better than anyone.

"I don't know, you were in NYC preparing for your summer internship anyway, deep in the AVC shit with your dad. And I was heartbroken and ashamed. I just wanted to move on. Forget it ever happened," Alastair gives a wistful smile. "It may not have been a happy ending for me, but I promise you, I barely think about that person anymore."

"Well, respectfully, fuck her," I offer.

Alastair chuckles in response, opening his mouth like he's going to say something, then shakes his head instead.

I'm not ready to admit it yet, not even to Alastair, but his story actually gives me hope that I can get past whatever the fuck this is. *Hope.* It's a fleeting thing, and I never allow myself to embrace that emotion, but fuck me, it's just wormed its way into my desiccated heart, and so I cling.

"Thanks, Alastair," is all I say. But I know my words hold weight by the way he nods in acknowledgment, before his expression turns more serious and he looks me directly in the eyes.

I have a feeling I know what's coming.

"So one more thing ... " he takes a deep breath before he continues, "I booked you on a flight home tomorrow afternoon. This was, obviously, before you decided to fling yourself into a tree, but assuming you're cleared to travel, I think it's time for you to head back to New York, Jax." I roll my eyes at him, even though deep down I know he's right.

"I'm not sure I'll be up for flying tomorrow," I try, pointing at the bandage wrapped around my head, though I know I'm only delaying the inevitable.

"I figured you might say that," he smiles like he knows something I don't and I wonder what kind of ace he has stashed up his sleeve. "So Gen told me to tell you," he pulls a scrap of paper out of his pocket and I immediately recognize Genevieve's loopy cursive as he begins to read from the note. "Russ Artanza has been poking around the Trueno account. He's invited Hadley to attend the gala he is being honored at in three days as his personal guest – she accepted the invitation so he'll be hosting her at the head table."

The fuck he will.

I instantly sit up straighter. Suddenly, I'm feeling well enough to fly home tomorrow, even if it's fucking commercial.

CHAPTER 46

HADLEY

I take a deep breath as the elevator doors open onto AVC's floor, smoothing my skirt to occupy my nervous hands, running them down my hips. I thought about texting Lex, or Trey, or Beau, anyone who might know if Jaxon actually came back this past weekend, but I was too terrified of what the inevitable answer might be. What if he's still gone? Or what if he's back, and he never reached out? Honestly, I'm not sure which is worse.

I can tell from Beau's expression as I approach his desk that Jaxon is in fact *back*. He's on the phone confirming something about a premiere sponsorship, but his eyes widen at the sight of me striding towards him, before darting back and forth between me and Jaxon's closed office door.

He's in there.

My steps slow as my heart starts to race, my gaze locked on the solid wooden door to Jaxon's office. He could step out at any moment. I'm torn between wanting him to do exactly that and terrified that it might actually happen. I've been agonizing over what I want to say to him for almost two weeks, but now that I might have the chance, I feel frozen.

"You know what, let me send you all the details in an email.... Yes, I agree that would be best....Thank you so much, you're amazing." Beau is staring daggers at me, and is on his feet as soon as he ends the call, before he even removes his headset. It's only then that I realize I've stopped halfway between his desk and Jaxon's door.

"Don't you *dare* try to go in there," he hisses at me as he comes tearing around his desk. He wraps an arm around me and guides us towards the ladies' room - the same one he followed me into on my first day at AVC. He does the same thing today. Does anyone actually *use* this bathroom?

"Hadley," Beau drags my focus back to him as he takes my hands in his, a look of concern etched into his face.

"He's back." It's not a question, and it comes out very matter-of-fact.

"He is," Beau answers in a cautious tone. "But he was very firm about not letting anyone in without his *express* permission. So please, Hadley, for my sake and yours, just wait until the gala on Thursday."

"He's coming?" I'm not sure if that's hope or anxiety that's fluttering in my stomach.

Oh shit.

Lex and I decided to accept Russ Artanza's invitation as a show of good faith to try and secure his support in the Echelon fund - it's not something I'm privy to, but Lex said he'd take care of that part of it, and I just have to represent Trueno, which is now officially part of Echelon. Russ Artanza has apparently taken an interest in my budding product.

Beau tilts his head to one side and works his jaw as if considering his words first.

"Oh no," I sigh, resigned. "Is he angry that Lex and I

agreed to go? Lex said he needs this deal, AVC needs this deal." Shit, I knew this might be a bad idea.

"Angry? Uhh, that's not exactly the term I would use. Not at you, or Mr. Sterling. Or - not about *this*. He actually asked me to secure a table for a *sold-out* gala, three days before the event." He leans closer and says, in an exaggerated whisper, *"No matter the cost."*

"What? Is that even possible?" I'm speechless and so out of my depth here.

Beau rolls his eyes at this. "Of course it's possible. Money talks. And so I made it happen, obviously, because I'm the best. And now you don't have to sit at Russ's table. You get to sit at the AVC table! With me!"

Jaxon got a *table*. And wants me there. "But Lex and I told Russ we'd join him. Jaxon wants me at *his* table?"

This is too much.

Of course, I *want* to sit with Jaxon, even if I have no idea where I stand with him. I've been dying to see him, to talk to him, just to be in his presence. But if the first time I'll get a chance will be at a *gala?* How am I supposed to just be calm about this?

My mind starts spiraling. How am I supposed to act around him? The world, well, *his* world, thinks we're an item thanks to that *Aria* column from a couple of weeks ago. Is this why he needs me there with him? Are we supposed to act like a couple?

My expression must betray my uncertainty about all of this because Beau squeezes my hands. "Hey, it's okay," he reassures me, locking his eyes onto mine. "This is good. Mr. Avenier wants *you* at the table with him. With us. Because I'm coming too. He put *me* in charge of filling the table. His only requirements were that you and Lex both be there, instead of with Russ. Obviously, my partner Victor is coming, I had him clear his evening for this!"

"Okay. Yes. You're right." I force a smile. "This is

good." I nod at Beau as his words sink in, and my smile grows genuine. "Oh my God, Beau! I'm so glad you'll be there too. Seriously, thank you."

"Of course babe. I may just be a temp here, but our friendship is *not* temporary. And don't worry about Mr. Artanza. Jaxon already spoke with him."

"He did?"

"Yep. No idea what went down, but he came in before I'd even had a sip of my latte and was all *'get a table for the gala'* and *'get Artanza on the phone'* and *'no one even think about disturbing me.'* Scary man. But he's stopped calling me Joe, so I'd say that's progress."

"He did?" I don't know why, but I am hopeful. Maybe even excited?

If Jaxon is coming around, if he wants to see me, maybe even sit next to me, then he must be willing to talk to me, to hear me out. And that gives me a small sliver of hope that his love, his heart, is still tethered to mine. Regardless, I'm not done fighting for him, for *us*. Just like I never gave up on the idea of us in the first place.

"Beau," I turn towards him, a mischievous smile spreading across my lips. "I might need your help with a dress again."

"Oh, Hads, I think your dress is already taken care of." He winks.

Chapter 47

Jaxon

Trey is already in the ring waiting for me when I arrive at Brawl & Order. Good. He knows better than to be late when I've given him the fucking opportunity to explain himself. As I get closer, I can see the apprehension in his face, but he also looks so fucking hopeful. My anger doesn't dissipate though, and I clench my fists at my sides.

"Jaxon," he steps towards me as I remove my sweatshirt and join him in the ring.

"Let's go."

Trey hesitates a moment before nodding. We begin the dance of sparring with each other. I know he won't attack first; he's going to let me have this, so I don't waste any time, coming in low and fast. I manage to graze his shoulder, but he steps back before I can land a real blow.

"I'm sorry, okay." Trey says as he moves back on the balls of his feet, bouncing in place for a few moments. "I never would have kept it from you if I'd known how serious it would get."

I grunt again. "You should have told me day one." I don't have to tell him which day one I mean - the day he was assigned to her account. He pretended like he'd only just met her that day.

So did she. The depth of their betrayal lances through me again like a fucking dagger. "You *both* should have." It comes out as an angry growl.

"I know. You're right."

Fucking right, I'm right. I catch Trey with a kick to the ribs, and he stumbles sideways, but doesn't go down.

"Come on, Eskridge. Stop playing defensive." I want him to at least try to hit me, so I can hit him fairly. "I'm not going to go easy on you." I leave it unsaid that he shouldn't go easy on me either. I don't need a pity win.

Trey hesitates only a moment before he finally goes on the offensive. Thank fucking God. Trey is a good boxer - and I need a challenge right now.

"She's yours, Jaxon."

She's *mine.*

"There was never any question about that. It was a one-night stand. We didn't even exchange names. Obviously. You, though..."

I let his words wash through me. I know, logically, I know there is nothing between them. But there is one thing that I can't let go of. I go on the offensive, advancing on him driven by my anger, forcing him back as he deflects blow after blow.

"Then why was she at your place that night?" I demand. Trey frowns at my question and barely changes to block my punch to his jaw, my knuckles grazing his ear instead.

"Oh my God, Jaxon. Haven't you talked to her? We were talking about how we needed to tell you! She insisted on seeing me to discuss how we were going to tell you as soon as I came back. She refused to wait another day, said she could never really be yours until you knew the whole truth, something about promising you complete honesty.

She was really torn up about it - I cancelled my fucking date so we could talk through it. Jesus, Jax, we were deciding *how* to tell you." Trey takes advantage of my shock at this revelation, and lands a blow that has me stumbling back towards the middle of the ring. I lean into the momentum and take another few steps back, gathering my bearings.

"I haven't talked to her," I admit.

Trey lets out an exasperated sigh. Is this fucker seriously annoyed with me right now? "You're an asshole, Jaxon." He advances on me, and I bring my arms back up. *I'm* an asshole? Fuck that.

We spar in silence for a few minutes, both of us getting in as many hits as we block.

"Talk to your fucking girlfriend, Jaxon," Trey finally pants, dancing back away from me after an especially intense melee. I got a couple good hits in, and I see a drop of sweat drip down his temple. It feels good to take out some of my aggression this way. But something about what he just said feels even more satisfying.

My *girlfriend?* Trey just called Hadley my girlfriend. I think back to the AVC party, the *According to Aria* column, our trip to Silicon Valley.

As far as anyone knows, Hadley is mine. And I am hers.

I nod to Trey before walking off the mat.

"Seriously, dude?" Trey calls out to me. I look back over my shoulder, and Trey is smiling. I keep walking towards the showers as I raise my arm above my head, flipping him the middle finger. I roll my eyes as I hear his laugh behind me.

CHAPTER 48

HADLEY

"Hadley! Why is a courier at the door with a giant box from Bergdorf's wrapped in an oversized bow? He says it's for you!" Jade calls from the entryway, where she is presumably signing for some sort of package that just arrived for me.

The dress.

"Oh! That must be for tomorrow." I try to say it casually, meanwhile I'm dying to tear it open and see what's in the box.

"Seriously, Hadley, this better not be from Jaxon. What is your deal with him now?" She asks as I pull a long, slinky black gown out of the box. It is *gorgeous.* So much so that it renders me speechless.

I hold it up against my frame, and watch as Jade's jaw drops to the floor. *Holy Shit.*

"Christ, Hadley. That is obviously couture." It takes a lot to impress Jade, and clearly, this dress has achieved the impossible.

She runs her fingers along the delicate satin straps, their intricate design intertwining with the bodice where they meet, which flows and drapes to the floor like ribbons of shadows.

"Hadley." She gives me a stern look as she picks up the tiny envelope accompanying the gift. "The card in here says this is from Jaxon Avenier, and his note implies there's plenty you aren't telling me."

I snatch the card from her outstretched hand.

Black suits you, but then again, so does everything.
For tomorrow.
– J.A.

"Is there something I'm missing? Because the last thing you told me was that he still hadn't spoken with you like the asshole I warned you he is." Her voice is dripping with disdain, and I don't blame her; she's only being protective after watching me cry myself to sleep over him for the better part of two weeks. Like any best friend would do.

Ignoring her, I take a moment to finger the delicate fabric of the dress, deciding how to tell Jade how hopeful I am for this gala. It's hard when I'm not even sure how *I'm* feeling right now.

"I'm honestly not sure, Jade." I let out a long, slow breath. "We still haven't talked."

But sometimes actions speak louder than words. And if this dress is a message, I am reading it loud and clear. I can't help the hope that rises like a tide within my chest, my excitement for the event, for an evening at his side, finally outweighing my nerves and apprehension.

"Well. I don't know how I feel about him trying to buy himself back into your good graces with this dress," she groans. "But I'll give it to him, the man's got taste. Not bad as far as apology gifts go." She says this as though it pains her to admit it.

My gaze flies up to look at Jade. "*He's* apologizing?"

"As he should," Jade frowns as she fingers the deep V of the gown.

"Jade. I'm the one who slept with his stepbrother. Granted, I didn't exactly know that at the time. But once I did, I never said anything. I hid it from him." Part of me hates that I'm defending Jaxon right now, because I do agree with her; his reaction was… I'm pretty sure *unhinged* is the word Jade used to describe it.

"Oh please." She scoffs. "Do not make excuses for that man's behavior. It was before you even met him, and you kept it professional with Trey." Her eyes narrow in disapproval. "If you'd been able to keep it professional with *Jaxon*, then you wouldn't be in this mess." She lifts the dress again, running her hands down the length of it. "Honestly though," she can't hide the admiration from her tone. "If this," she gestures to the gifted designer dress, "is what a messy working relationship gets you…" Jade trails off as she heads towards my room to hang the dress.

"Come on, Hadley," Jade calls out. That's when I realize I haven't moved, frozen in place in the foyer, analyzing all the possible scenarios that might play out tomorrow. "Let's talk about what you're doing with your hair, and make-up. I'm clearly not going to be able to dissuade you from pursuing this *thing* with Jaxon Avenier, so at least let me help you show him exactly what he's been missing."

Admittedly, I was disappointed when Beau sent me the itinerary for tonight. I'm scheduled to be picked up promptly at 6:00 PM by a car and ride to the event with Lex. I can't say I'm surprised that Jaxon is avoiding one on one time with me on the way to the gala and honestly, I hate to admit it, but it makes sense. Tonight is about networking and AVC. It's not about us, but God do I want it to be.

The buzzer rings at 5:59 PM, just as I begin anxiously pacing around the kitchen, already wearing my coat and absentmindedly holding the glass of champagne that Jade poured for me while helping me get ready, as if hiring her hair and makeup artist to do my glam wasn't enough. She may not approve of Jaxon, but she also knows when to step down. My nerves are firing on every cylinder, my stomach rising and falling in the same way the bubbles dance in my glass. I can't even bring myself to take a sip.

"You look amazing," Jade gushes as I move to answer the door.

Lex stands on the other side, looking as uncomfortable as I feel. But damn if he doesn't wear that tux well.

"You didn't have to come all the way to my door," I say. Though I'm grateful he did as he extends his arm to me for support. My legs suddenly feel like wet noodles as reality sets in. I'm about to see Jaxon for the first time in over two weeks, and I have no idea how he's going to react.

"Shall we?" He says, like some dashing gentleman in a Regency novel, guiding me out of the building and into the idling black sedan where his driver, Saul, stands holding the door open for us. Well, there's no turning back now.

Lex offers me one final reminder as we pull up to the venue. "Don't disclose anything about your technology to Russ Artanza," Lex issues me a warning as we pull up outside the venue. "Trust me on this one, Hadley. Honestly, just try not to find yourself alone with him."

Before I can get in a word, ask a question, protest, anything, he turns towards the door that Saul just pulled open for us and steps out, once again offering me his hand for support as he helps me out of the car.

After a brief stop at the coat check, I walk into the

event on Lex's arm, and maybe it's just me, maybe I'm just paranoid or hyper aware, but I swear I can feel heads turning, eyes on us as he escorts me up the red-carpeted stairs.

"It's the dress," he whispers, sensing my unease. "You look beautiful, Hadley. And if I'm noticing, trust me, he will too."

"Thanks," I mutter, hoping it doesn't sound as pathetic as it feels.

"Speak of the devil." Lex nods towards the open ballroom as we climb the last stair. And there, amid the sea of elegant ballgowns, dapper tuxes and high-top tables dressed in plush fabrics, stands Jaxon. I find him instantly, and I watch with eager eyes as he moves towards us.

Has he been watching the entrance? Waiting? I can't help it, my heart skips a beat at the thought.

My eyes are fixed on Jaxon's tall frame, purposefully striding toward us across the ballroom, his expression unreadable. My heart momentarily stops beating, then, without warning, pounds rapidly in my chest, but I hold my ground, refusing to look away.

The other partygoers blur into the background. I can't look away from him, can't take my eyes off of him. As complicated as our situation is, it's also unbelievably simple. He is *it* for me, our connection is so undeniable, something I doubt I'll ever find again. I've felt it in my soul since the moment I met him, and I *know* he feels it too.

"Alastair," he says, nodding at his cousin. "Hadley," he greets. Polite, but curt, his expression revealing nothing.

My heart sinks.

"I'm going to see if Vera's arrived," Lex excuses himself.

Suddenly, I'm struggling to breathe. Jaxon is here, in front of me. This isn't a dream; he is *real*. And I'm not sure what the next move is. I'm completely frozen.

"Can I get you a drink?" He asks plainly, the

mundanity of his question jarring. So, I guess that's the play. We're just going to act like things are okay between us for the sake of appearances, without actually discussing anything. Honestly though, we're at a gala, how did I expect this to go?

"Sure." My response feels awkward, though I watch his gaze narrow as he allows himself to take me in, his eyes lingering on the deep V of the exquisite black gown he purchased for me before slowly returning to meet mine.

My breath catches as I see a spark, a sudden fire reignite in those deep sable depths as they lock onto mine.

"This way then," he moves to escort me to the bar, his hand resting gently on my lower back like it's the most natural thing in the world.

We've taken not even two steps, when out of the corner of my eye, I see that woman Collette - *Kit*, charging towards us.

Shit.

"Jaxon," I stop us in our tracks, feeling brazenly possessive. "I'm going to have to ask you to do something you may not be ready for, and I'm sorry."

He turns to look at me, brow furrowed, "Oh?" His mouth turns up in a curious smirk, "And why is that?"

"Kit." The name tastes like acid on my tongue.

"What about her?" He grits out through his clenched jaw.

"She's spotted you and is storming towards us as we speak."

He releases an exasperated sigh. "Of course she is, I don't know how to make it any more clear –"

"Kiss me," I cut him off. There's no time for discussion.

"What?"

"Now, Jaxon." My words come out in a harsh whisper, but I need to convey the urgency of my request. "Unless you don't want to." I hold his gaze, my heart pounding in my ears - this is not how I pictured us having this conversation. "You took back your words without giving me a chance to explain myself, but we can talk about that later. We can argue later. Don't do it unless you actually want this, but I can't think of a clearer way to send the message that she's not welcome." I watch him ponder this for a half second before I add, "even if it's just for show."

"Just for show," he whispers my words back to me, before he pulls me hard against his body and fuses his mouth to mine, his other hand gripping the back of my neck as he deepens the kiss.

The moment his lips meet mine, I wonder how I've survived the past two weeks without the indescribable feeling of kissing Jaxon. I wind my arms around his neck as my body instinctively arches against his, finding that perfect angle without even trying. It breathes life into my lungs, into every cell of my body. This. Things may be messy, but we just make sense. There's nothing like this in the world. When nothing else matters but the press of his lips against mine. My heart flutters and my body floats as my hands slide between the soft locks of his hair.

"Good God, have you forgotten how civilized people behave in public? It's sad, really, to see you've lowered your standards so quickly, Jaxon." Damn, she's more persistent than I gave her credit for.

I turn to face Kit and find her eyes narrowed in a challenge. Not far from her stands my ex, Cal Thornton, watching the scene unfold a little too intently for my comfort. Though it really shouldn't surprise me that he's at a flashy society event like this one.

Oh God. We're at a gala, and I was so lost in this moment, in *Jaxon,* that I almost lost touch with reality. I melted into that kiss, fading into a world where only the two of us exist. And for a moment, it was sublimely perfect.

"Interesting," Cal drawls, seemingly unaffected as he takes a sip from his cocktail glass. "I thought you disdained public displays of affection even more than you hated these, what did you call them, Hads? Oh right, *performative little vanity fairs.*" He emphasizes my nickname, as if trying to prove some kind of point to Jaxon.

"Well —" I start to defend myself, but Kit cuts me off before I can get another word in.

"Some of us actually try to maintain a bit of propriety at these things. Though I must admit, seeing how you handled yourself at the last event was… enlightening."

I am now more convinced than ever that the woman did drug me with something.

I lean into Jaxon as he pulls me more tightly against him, his arm already wrapped around my waist. We just gave them one hell of a show, and apparently it's not over yet.

"Sorry," Jaxon offers a thin lipped smile to Cal. "I struggle to control myself around Hadley sometimes." He's addressing Calvin, but he's looking at Kit as he says it and I watch with an embarrassing amount of satisfaction as her features tighten and her body stiffens.

"We both do," I add, my hand wrapping around Jaxon's wrist at my waist. I make a point to look pointedly at Calvin as I say it.

"Well then," Jaxon addresses everyone because the crowd is still staring, "I could use a drink. Let's go, Hadley."

"Word of advice?" God, that woman really doesn't know when to quit. "Keep an eye on your drink, I'd hate to see anyone tamper with it." And the saccharine smile she gives me feels anything but sweet.

Jaxon stiffens at my side, and I notice his jaw clench.

Just as he opens his mouth to speak, a bright flash captures everyone's attention.

Oh shit.

The photographers.

Cal winks at us before walking away, and my stomach sinks like a stone as I ponder the smug expression on his face.

CHAPTER 49

JAXON

"*I thought you disdained public displays of affection, Hads.*"

Calvin Thornton's words replay in my mind as I try to erase the image of Hadley ever having shown him any kind of affection, public or otherwise. And I hate the way he called her *Hads.* The use of that nickname sounded intentional, and if he was trying to get under my skin by reminding me that she was once his, it's working. I have plenty of choice words for him, but the camera flash keeps me silent. Barely.

Though I don't disagree with Hadley's assessment of these performative little *vanity fairs*, tonight's event being one of the season's greatest offenders.

I need to get Hadley alone. Away from the photographers and the prying eyes of Manhattan's elite. Because even more troubling than Hadley's past relationship with Calvin, is Kit's insinuation about tampering with Hadley's drink and the malicious way she smiled as she offered her *advice.*

Leaving my hand on the small of Hadley's back, I guide her away from the onlookers, away from Calvin Thornton, and far the fuck away from Kit. I look for a quiet corner, somewhere tucked away, because I have a lot more questions, and I'm demanding answers.

But as we walk, my fingers graze her soft skin. The familiar feeling of her by my side soothes me and as she leans into me subconsciously, it hits me. I *need* her. She hurt me. She *burned* me and scarred my bleeding heart. Yet, here I am, drawn to her as if my very existence depends on it, and on some level, it feels like it does because I don't feel whole without her.

I remove my hand from the small of her back, letting it gently fall, my fingertips caressing the silk fabric of her gown before brushing against hers. And as if on instinct, her hand gently curls around mine. Her presence, her touch, heals the very wound she inflicted, and I instantly regret every moment I've spent hiding. Every moment I've spent away from her.

You're an asshole.

I hear Trey's words from the other day in the ring play in my mind. And honestly, maybe I am.

Speak of the fucking devil …

"Jaxon, Hadley." Trey tentatively greets as he falls into step beside me - because I'm not stopping until I find somewhere more private. "Our table is over there." Trey gestures in the opposite direction.

"Noted." Just because we're okay does not mean we're *okay*.

I know I'm doing the whole *asshole* thing right now, but I want answers, and I am not willing to wait.

"Jaxon?" Hadley squeezes my hand as I move us to a secluded cocktail table just past the far end of the bar. Somewhere quiet, where we won't draw attention to ourselves.

"Did Kit slip something into your drink?" I ask Hadley in a low, commanding voice, meanwhile I keep my gaze on

Trey's face. The way his eyes widen, one of his many tells, I fucking knew it.

"You didn't tell me?" This is directed at Trey, my voice dropping lower as my tone grows more accusatory.

"Jaxon," Hadley draws my attention, but not before I shoot Trey a glare that says *this isn't over.*

"It was at Russ's holiday party," she cuts in. "I didn't say anything because there was no way to prove what happened. Trey, along with Jade, got me out of there as soon as they realized something was wrong. I'm not even sure it was Kit until… well, I'm still not sure… but after what she just said I'm starting to believe that, maybe…" She stumbles awkwardly through her explanation.

Trey's grunt tells me he's pretty damn sure, but she's right, we probably will never be able to prove anything.

"Start talking, Eskridge. Were you there?" I narrow my eyes at him. I still have more questions than answers.

"Look, I was going to tell you-"

"How many fucking secrets do you two have?" I'm so sick of hearing this *we were going to tell you* bullshit.

"There aren't any other secrets, Jaxon," Trey says it so calmly, almost patronizingly, the way you'd talk to a child about to have a tantrum and photographers be damned, I actually consider finishing what we started in the ring and punching him in the face.

"You sure about that? Think really hard, because -"

"I wasn't deliberately keeping this from you, Jaxon," Hadley interrupts, and as much as I hate it, I force myself to take a deep breath and turn my gaze to her. "I promise." I want to believe her, more than anything, and her words are so genuine, I think I do. "I wanted to bring it up, but then everything blew up with the Cipher group and…" She looks at me beseechingly, and fuck if the ice doesn't start to melt. "And I thought maybe I'd just had too much to drink or something. I was so nervous and hadn't eaten much, and I had no proof that she actually did anything."

I still cling to my anger though. A part of me wants to storm out of this gala, straight back to Aspen. But this time, I want to take Hadley with me. Take her away from these wolves, away from Manhattan, away from everyone. How the fuck am I supposed to fight for her, when every corner of the room is filled with people looking to threaten us, threaten her.

"Look," Trey starts, and I roll my eyes. I'm still pissed at him. "As much as I'm enjoying this conversation… You picked a rather public hiding spot, and Russ is already on his way over."

Damnit.

"You three aren't waiting for drinks are you? Sir!" Russell's voice is now directed at the nearby bartender. "Get Jaxon and my distinguished guest Hadley here a drink." He waves his arm with a ridiculous flourish that probably makes him feel more important than he is.

"As previously discussed, Hadley is now sitting at my table." I don't miss the way he just referred to Hadley as *his* guest.

"Nonsense, *she* told me she was looking forward to talking. Whenever will we get another chance after all?" He sounds like a pouty teenage girl as he makes an exaggerated sad puppy dog expression. His little charade has zero effect on me.

"That's not my concern, Russell. The matter is already settled. She's sitting with me tonight."

"I would love another chance to talk. Mr. Artanza," Hadley interjects. What does she think she's doing? This whole fucking night is going completely off the rails and I feel about ready to murder someone. I eye the corkscrew the bartender is currently using to open a bottle of wine, and imagine how easy it would be to jam it into Russ's pudgy neck.

"I'm sure we'll figure something out." Russ gives Hadley a smile as his gaze roams the length of her body in that revealing dress. The dress that *I* bought her. "Especially since I'll now be playing a significant *financial* role."

I can feel myself seething as a quiet rage builds within me, coiling tightly like a snake in the grass, ready to fucking strike. And the hungry way he is looking at Hadley? Yeah, I'm growing closer to striking with each furious beat of my heart. But he just signaled that he intends to invest in the Echelon fund.

Typical Russ. He *would* choose now to drop a bomb like that.

"I was going to ponder it a bit longer, but I think it's about time I confirmed my commitment." The insufferable man is practically glowing with self-satisfaction. "But really, Jaxon, I expected a more enthusiastic response from you."

"My *enthusiasm* is reserved for the moment the wire clears." It's about all I can manage, but it earns a hearty chuckle from Russ.

"A smart man knows you can't count those chickens until they hatch!" He claps me on the back, and I feel my entire body seize.

I've been patient, but I'm wound so tensely that Russell Artanza's games may just be the provocation that causes me to finally lash out. Just as I start fantasizing about the feasibility of using a corkscrew as a murder weapon, Trey nudges me and hands me a drink.

"I see Lex and Vera at our table," he says, using their sighting as an excuse to make our exit.

"Oh, is that *Vera Norvelle*?" Russ' tone is now gleeful. "At the gala honoring *moi*? My, my you've really outdone yourself this time, Jaxon." I note the unmistakable glint in his eye, and I know I made the right call in strong-arming Lex into bringing her this evening. "I'll let you go entertain your *exquisite* guest, but if you're going to steal Hadley from me, you must at least bring Vera Norvelle by the head table to say hello. I do enjoy having the opportunity to thank *all* attendees for their generous support." What a load of shit. He's a fucking celebrity collector. He's just after a photo opp and we both know it.

"Of course, I'm sure she'd be delighted to meet tonight's honoree." I draw on every last remaining ounce of my control to speak the words I know will placate him before excusing ourselves, guiding Hadley over to our table. Russ's funding is finally on the table; I refuse to blow this now.

An hour and several mind-numbing speeches later, there's a break in the program. As the tuxedo-clad wait staff streams into the room to begin serving the entrees, I nod at my cousin, and Lex takes the opportunity to excuse himself and Vera, who has graciously agreed to say hello to Russ on our behalf.

As soon as their seats open, I can *feel* someone watching me.

I smell her before I see her, the overpowering, animalic accord, laced with that sultry vanilla tincture I've come to associate with her. I'd recognize it anywhere, and after that very public altercation earlier, I am in no mood to deal with her antics.

I'm turned towards Hadley, half listening as she engages in conversation with Beau's boyfriend, some Broadway investor, or producer, something theater adjacent.

I refuse to acknowledge Kit's presence, but then I feel her fingers firmly gripping my shoulder.

"Jaxon! It's been months since we properly *caught up*." She is practically purring, and my skin crawls.

I need Lex to hurry the fuck up, why does the seat

next to me have to be empty right now? I'm still facing Hadley and I watch her eyes widen in fear as she catches sight of Kit's looming presence. I'm hit with a surge of protectiveness towards her. If Kit thinks I'll let her get anywhere near Hadley or her drink again, she is sorely mistaken. I'm not letting Hadley out of my sight. Not here, not ever.

"What are you doing here, Kit?" I don't even try to be polite, shrugging her hand off my shoulder. She can fuck right off with her tail between her legs for all I care.

"Uncle Russ sent me, actually." I shudder at the way she calls Russell *uncle*. "He wanted me to formally invite you to a private dinner at his club next weekend. *Both* of you," I note the strained way in which she forces out that last sentence and subtly smirk.

"No thanks."

"Oh?" She flutters her eyelashes as if that's going to make a lick of difference, and I brace myself for whatever's coming next because, just like her godfather, she isn't one to take no for an answer. They may not be blood-related, but those two have a surprising amount in common. "I guess I'll just tell him you aren't interested in celebrating doing business with him again."

This is his play. He knows he has me.

I reach for Hadley's hand that rests gently on the table, well aware that Kit's eyes follow my movement, watching intently as I lace my fingers with Hadley's. "Fine. We'll *both* be there."

Kit leans forward. "Wonderful," she purrs, placing a hand on my thigh. "I'll be sure to tell him you're looking forward to it."

More like I'm looking forward to his money. I grab Kit's wrist, removing it from my leg forcefully enough that she lets out a small gasp. "You should go now." I ensure my tone leaves no room for debate.

"What the fuck did *she* want?" Lex asks, as he and Vera return to their seats

"We have been *graciously* invited to dinner at Russell's private supper club. Russ oh-so-casually mentioned that he's all in for Echelon. Evidently, this is a mandatory celebration dinner."

Alastair glances between Hadley and I, our hands still clasped on the table. "We?"

"Hadley and I. But I want you there too." Alastair nods in acknowledgement before turning his attention back to his date. I know I can count on Alastair to get something in writing before the *celebration* dinner, but now is not the time to discuss business.

We sit through another hour of the insufferable program, including a twelve-minute-long tribute video to Russ Artanza that grates on every last one of my nerves. I can't take another minute, and I thank the stars when the formal program ends, giving way to dessert and dancing. Before they even serve our dessert, I lean into Hadley and whisper, "Let's go home." The way her eyes flare with hope, the way her lips part, I know this is what she wants too. And I can't help it, my heart fucking soars.

"You want me… to come home with you?" I know I haven't told her I want to fight for her, but I was hoping my actions tonight might have shown her as much. Buying this table, not leaving her side, then that kiss.

God, that fucking kiss.

"I want you with me," I tell her. And I mean it, in every way possible. I know we need to talk, and we will, but right now I just want us to *be* together.

"Okay," she smiles back at me, guarded but hopeful. And I stand, offering her my hand, which she readily accepts.

I nod at my table's guests, acknowledging my impending departure. Everyone else looks just as ready to leave, except for Beau, who is already halfway to the dance floor, sequins of his dinner jacket catching the light like a thousand tiny prisms as he drags his partner with him. Glad to see at least someone from AVC seems to be enjoying their evening.

I avoid so much as looking in the direction of the head table as I guide Hadley towards the exit. I need to get her out of here before anyone can corner her again.

I texted Emilio when we were ready to go, and he's already standing at the bottom of the steps, waiting to open the door for us. I keep Hadley's hand in mine the whole ride home, not talking yet, just letting her presence, her touch, ground me.

I do everything I can to delay the inevitable talk that Hadley and I need to have once we make it back to my place. I turn on the eleven o'clock news, pretending to pay attention. I need the distraction, the noise to counter the interminable silence stretching between us. I offer her a drink, and mix one of my own before settling on the couch beside her.

God, she is so fucking beautiful. And it's not just the dress, though she is stunning in it. No, it's *her.* I can't take my eyes off of her. She's here. And she's real. And I'm prepared to fight for us.

"Jaxon …" she reaches for the remote, muting the television. I swallow. I know that I can't avoid this conversation forever.

I look into her eyes, but I don't say anything, not yet. I can't. I nod once to indicate she has my attention. I'm listening. I need her to keep talking, to explain, so I can make sense of it all. I need to hear her, and I need to know she's not just apologizing for the truth they kept from me, but for how deeply it cut when I found out. I need to know she *understands*.

"I intended to tell you," she begins. "I swear. *We*

intended to tell you. It's just… what happened with Trey, it was one night. Before I'd ever met you. And it meant nothing compared to what we have, Jaxon." I let that sink in, allowing the silence to hang between us, this isn't anything I haven't already heard.

"As things got more serious between us, I just didn't know how." She confesses, and I don't miss the way her voice wavers. "I compartmentalized it, shoved those memories in a box, hoping if I willed them away, I could pretend that night never happened, because the truth is, the harder I fell for you, the more terrified I became that what happened that night might cause me to lose you, and that wasn't something I could take." Her voice quivers, and every tremor feels like a punch to my chest. I pull her against me, wrapping my arms around her back.

I sigh. I know I am going to forgive her.

"I broke down after you told me you loved me." She pulls back to look up at me. She's crying, her breath hitching as tears fall, causing her mascara to form dark trails down her cheeks. "I cried in the shower that morning because… because everything was so perfect with us, except one thing. This thing I kept from you cast a shadow over what was otherwise the best night of my life. Because I knew, right then, that I couldn't have you, not all of you, if you didn't know the truth. And I knew it had already gone too far, telling you would hurt you, it might even make you leave. I didn't want to lose you. I was so scared, Jaxon. I didn't want to hurt you, and it just…" The cracks in her voice transform into sobs, but she continues as I keep my arms loosely circled around her. "It got harder and more complicated the deeper I fell for you." I pull her against my chest, holding her as she cries, wanting nothing more than to fix this, to take away her pain.

She fucking burned me. They *both* did. Yet somehow, that no longer matters. Her presence, having her here in my arms, is like a gentle rain falling softly on my scorched heart, washing away the ash and dust, bringing back life where only desolation once existed.

"But you *didn't* tell me," I whisper, because I can't fucking let it go. "You didn't trust me enough to share the truth." I watch her wince at my words, but if we're going to have this conversation, *really* have it, then I need to speak too. I need her to understand how much it hurt me.

Because you fucking love her.

"I know," she says softly between sniffles. "And I hate myself for it."

"Hadley –"

"No, you're right." She tells me. "I fell in love with you, Jaxon. And I thought about telling you so many times, but I was so terrified of losing you. It was selfish, and I regret it. And then… then you told me you loved me, and it was everything I wanted to hear, and that is when I realized in not telling you, I'd never allowed you to wholly and completely be mine, and it broke my heart."

"We promised each other *complete* honesty, and you hadn't –"

"I never lied to you, Jaxon." And with that one sentence, she stokes the embers of my waning rage.

"Fine, you offered me *selective* truths." I raise my voice, and she recoils. I instantly regret it. I don't want to be the source of her pain, only her comfort. But she fucking *broke* me.

"And you disappeared. You don't walk on people you love, Jaxon." She bites back. Fair. "And when you stormed out, when you walked out of my life without even giving me a chance to explain myself, when you assumed the *worst*, my world shattered. I cried myself to sleep for an entire week."

I hurt her too. Godammit. I don't want to be the one apologizing right now. But I fucking am.

"I'm sorry, too," I whisper, my voice unsteady. I'm not used to apologizing, for anything. But I think back to everything Alastair said back in Aspen. This is how I fight for her, for us. "I shouldn't have left you. I shouldn't have… shut myself off like that. You didn't deserve that." She didn't, not if I fucking love her.

She pulls back slightly to look at me, her large almond eyes swollen and red, and I can see the pain that's still living there, still raw. "But you're angry with me."

"I am." Honesty, I remind myself. "I need some time to heal and to learn how to trust you again. In case it wasn't obvious, you fucking *wrecked* me, Hadley."

"I'm so sorry," she whispers, a fresh tear making its way down her face. And despite the jagged gray lines marking her face, she's still the most beautiful thing I've ever seen.

"I need you to know," I take a deep breath, carefully choosing my next words, "I'm not sure I'm ready to say those words again… not yet." I can't, and I need her to understand that.

She nods, slowly comprehending what I'm saying before leaning into me, her head resting against my chest as I hold her. We stay there in silence, and while the silence is heavy, it isn't uncomfortable.

"I still want you to stay," I murmur, my face buried in her hair as my fingers gently fist the hair at the nape of her neck.

"Of course I'll stay," she whispers against my chest. Her posture relaxes as her arms gently encircle my waist. "And I'll wait for you, Jaxon. As long as it takes." We stay there, holding each other, and I realize that maybe, we can fix this. We can both heal. One piece at a time.

Slowly I stand, scooping her up and holding her against my chest. I carry her to bed, offering her one of my shirts to sleep in and leave her to change as I complete my nighttime routine, placing a spare toothbrush and a clean washcloth on the vanity for her. It's a simple gesture, but it feels like so much more.

She emerges from the bathroom and slides into bed, instinctively snuggling against me. And all I can think about as I curl around her, holding her body tightly against mine, is that I've been given a second chance, a courtesy I grant no one. I refuse to fuck it up this time. She is *mine*. And if I have my way, she'll be mine forever.

I place a gentle kiss on the top of her head, inhaling the sweet floral scent of her hair as I drift off, not even bothering to suppress my smile.

I love her.

It's my last thought before I surrender my mind and body to sleep.

Chapter 50

ACCORDING TO ARIA

Not all thorns spill blood…

…some spill secrets.

THE KISS THAT CLOSED THE MARKET

By: Aria Thorne

Manhattan's glitterati gathered beneath the vaulted ceilings of the Astor Conservatory Ballroom last night, honoring philanthropist Russell Artanza for his unwavering support of the Empire Trust for Historic Preservation. But while the chandeliers glittered and the Ruinart champagne flowed, it wasn't the historic architecture that was turning heads last evening.

That distinction belonged to Jaxon Avenier.

The reformed - or perhaps I should say redirected - billionaire heir arrived characteristically early, but uncharacteristically very much not alone. At his side (and, later, quite literally in his arms) was Hadley Aldridge, the evening's most talked-about guest in a form-fitting black satin gown that left very little room for subtlety.

If there were any doubts about the nature of their relationship, they were erased somewhere between the second pour of Dom Ruinart and a brazen, incendiary kiss delivered with the kind of authority usually reserved for closing mergers.

Witnesses say the pair were inseparable. Avenier, long considered the city's most elusive bachelor, ignored the usual orbit of admirers - most notably, a certain Ms. Colette (Kit) D'Vesle, who was seen lingering among the marble columns looking as though she'd swallowed something far more bitter than stale champagne. He never once approached her.

And why would he? Avenier spent the evening glued to Hadley Aldridge's side, whispering in her ear, hand at the small of her back, gaze unwavering. Dare I say, many partygoers went so far as to claim he was looking very much in love.

A statement that would have been laughable mere months ago. After all, no one ever thought they'd see the day Jaxon Avenier would settle down.

Mere months ago nobody had ever heard of Hadley Aldridge either. Yet here we are.

Sources have confirmed Hadley was previously linked to Calvin Thornton, the dashing son of New York Rangers owner Rex Thornton. Though, apparently he quietly ended things with her last fall.

Hadley and Jaxon weren't the only ones in the Avenier contingent out last night. Jaxon's cousin and business counterpart, Alastair Sterling, made his own entrance with his habitual showstopper, famed supermodel Vera Norvelle, draped elegantly on his arm. The pair posed dutifully for photographers, making sure they were seen visiting the head table occupied by the night's honoree, Russell Artanza - Alastair Sterling ever the strategist, Vera Norvelle ever the vision. If Avenier's display was fire, Sterling was ice: controlled, polished, and impeccably timed.

And speaking of icy things, last night's public appearance by the duo lacked any spark. Sterling's level of interest in his stunning date appeared more dutiful than anything - hard to fathom, really, when you've got someone like Vera Norvelle on your arm. He's always been the private type, however. Maybe Sterling just appeared a bit frosty when compared to the electric heat of his cousin, Jaxon Avenier and his new, dare I say, girlfriend?

This journalist can't help but wonder, though, if Sterling's relationship is merely for show, a front, or some sort of elaborate PR stunt. Either way, it's certainly caught the attention of this journalist. Well played Sterling, well played. But that theory still begs the question: what or who has something to hide from the public eye?

Avenier, however, was certainly not hiding his feelings for his love interest last night. And make no mistake, the night belonged to the two of them. Between Avenier's uncharacteristically public shows of subtle affection and that headline-worthy kiss, the pair didn't just attend a gala. They staged a declaration.

And in this city, darlings, declarations are never accidental. This journalist is wondering, are they truly in love... or does this duo simply have something they're trying to prove?

Stay sharp,
Aria Thorne

CHAPTER 51

HADLEY

I wake up wrapped in the warmth of Jaxon's embrace, and we spend the morning lazily tangled together in bed. His fingers comb through my hair and draw slow, gentle circles along my back, reaching beneath the fabric of his well-worn t-shirt.

Eventually, we both roll out of bed in search of coffee, and I'm delighted to find my favorite almond croissants in a ribbon-wrapped box on the kitchen counter.

Jaxon smiles as he sees me eyeing the box from my favorite bakery.

"I had them delivered yesterday, hoping this morning might start exactly like this." And once again, though he may not be ready to say it again, his actions speak louder than his words ever could.

I cross the room, throwing my arms around his neck, and press up onto my toes so I can kiss him.

"Thank you," I murmur against his lips, smiling.

He chuckles softly, brushing a stray hair from my face. "Anytime," he says, and I know that he means it.

We pull apart just long enough to unwrap the box, and we share a quiet breakfast, bathed in the morning light.

Eventually, I glance at the clock and sigh. "I should probably get home to Jade's."

Jaxon's hand lingers on mine as we stand before it moves to wrap itself around my waist, pulling me closer. "Already?"

"Yeah," I turn in his arms so I can bury my face in his chest, finding it hard to leave. "I promised Jade I'd spend the day with her."

"But did you promise her you'd spend the night with her?"

I laugh softly, nuzzling deeper into his chest. And even as I pull away, I already know I'll be back here tonight, tangled up with him all over again.

Jade is waiting for me when I finally arrive back at her place a little after noon. I expected as much, and I'm glad to see Bash is out, giving us some much-needed time to talk, just the two of us. She has been my rock these past few weeks, even sleeping in my bed with me that first night after Jaxon found out about what happened with Trey.

I know she's still angry at Jaxon, and I totally understand her misgivings about last night, but she's smiling and holding out her phone in my direction. The screen is open to the Aria Thorne article that came out this morning.

"Oh, look, you're famous." She sticks her tongue out playfully before making her way towards the living room and flopping herself down on the sofa.

"Hardly," I laugh.

"I know you saw the Aria Thorne article, and you're trying way too hard not to gloat. So I guess I'm happy for you," Jade sounds resigned, but there is a softness in her expression.

"Thanks, Jade," I throw myself down on the sofa next to her.

"No, really," she continues. "Look, about last night… damn it. I still kind of hate him. And I definitely don't trust him. And I absolutely want to fucking throttle him for breaking your heart. But I get it, Hads." She holds out her phone again, nudging it closer. "Look at him in this photo. The way he's looking at you like you're the only person in the room. The way you *deserve* to be cherished. Damn it, I hate that I can see it now."

"He's not Cal, Jade. They may run in overlapping social circles, but they're nothing alike." Jade never thought Calvin Thornton was good enough for me, and it took me longer than I'd care to admit to realize it, but she was absolutely right.

Cal and I met at a fundraiser in the city that my mom dragged me to when she was in town. I got swept up in his charm and his undeniable good looks. It was convenient, and he was well-connected, always offering to help set me up with the 'right' people to get Trueno off the ground. There was never any follow through. Eventually, I realized what he wanted wasn't a woman with ambition - but someone who was impressed *by* him. That was never going to be me.

I won't forget what he said to me the night I broke up with him: *I'll give you twenty-four hours to reconsider your position on the matter, Hadley. Remember, you can make more money in a marriage than in a lifetime.*

And yet somehow, Aria Thorne got that one wrong, suggesting that he was the one to end things with me. The columnist never paid him much attention before, so I'm sure he's relishing his little mention today.

"You mean the *dashing son of New York Riders owner Rex Thornton?*" She recites Aria Thorne's description of Cal while pinching her nose.

"The very one who allegedly dumped me," I snort, rolling my eyes.

"Whatever happened to reliable journalism?" Jade feigns incredulity. "Though I suppose credibility doesn't get clicks."

A slow silence settles between us as I sigh with a smile, my mind wandering back to the same place it always does. Jaxon.

Jade gets up to open a bottle of wine and pour out two very generous glasses. We spend the next couple of hours debriefing the gala, talking about Jaxon, and gossiping about the Aria Thorne column before deciding to order pizza from our favorite spot down the block for dinner.

There's still a lot to work out with Jaxon, I acknowledge this to Jade, but the point is, we have something to work on, period. And right now, that's enough for me.

I also tell Jade we need to stick to pacing ourselves with the wine, because I won't be staying here tonight. I'm going back to Jaxon's.

"You're leaving me *again?*" She whines, but she's grinning as she does. "Damn, the sex must be good." I roll my eyes.

"Bring your wine," I gesture for her to follow me to the room I've been staying in. "I need to pack a bag before we drink too much and I forget."

The second we enter my room, Jade beelines for my dresser, pulling open the top drawer and rifling through it.

"Definitely pack this," she says with a smirk, tossing a black lacy bra onto the bed.

I can feel my cheeks heat and I look away, avoiding her discerning gaze as I grab my weekender travel bag.

"Yeah, well..."

The next thing I know, Jade is helping me pick out all my sexiest undergarments, and we are sprawled on my bed, giddy and giggling. It feels *good* to share everything with her. Jaxon and I are together, it's not perfect, and it's more than a little terrifying. But as Jade says, *that's love, babe, you risk your heart, and it's worth it.*

She's right. And I'm no stranger to taking risks. Trueno was a risk. A risk that led me to Jaxon, and a world that I never imagined for myself.

I squeeze Jade tight as I hug her goodbye. Today was exactly what I needed. "When are you coming home?"

"I'll be back Monday evening," I promise. "Takeout from Carlina's?"

"Deal," she says it with a smile, but the silence that lingers after feels heavy.

I take a beat before I leave, realizing that it feels a little different, and a little more final as I prepare to walk out the door. I'm not moving out, but I'm also not coming straight home. And, I made *plans* to be here, rather than to be out.

Jaxon sent Emilio to pick me up, and as I pull up to his building, I see him waiting for me at the entrance. I can't help feeling in my heart that this is it. That *he* is it. *This is where I belong.*

I step out of the car and into his arms, and that's when the truth settles in me: wherever he is, that's the place I most want to be.

He holds me a little tighter as his voice drops so low that I'm certain his words are meant just for me, "It's only ever been you, Hadley Aldridge."

It's the only truth that matters.

To be continued …

Two Encores
The story continues …

Jaxon and Hadley fought hard for their second chance, but love doesn't protect them from what comes next.

When tragedy strikes, everything that once seemed whole begins to fracture. Relationships shift. Secrets surface. And truths that can no longer be ignored are finally confronted.

For Alastair *Lex* Sterling, the unraveling hits differently. Because while some people are fighting to hold on to what they have… he's beginning to question everything he thought he knew about himself.

Some love stories survive the storm, others are forever changed by it.

Jaxon and Hadley's journey continues in *Two Encores*. And Alastair's… well his is just beginning.

Releasing summer 2026.

Acknowledgments

If you've made it to the end, thank you. This book would be nothing without our readers and all of those who encouraged us along the way.

Getting here was not without significant effort, and we couldn't have done it alone. We've learned so much throughout this process, and we are grateful for every member of our hype squad who helped us bring this project across the finish line.

It's important to recognize the individuals who have been here since the beginning and those who have joined us on this journey along the way.

To our amazing beta readers - thank you for the candid feedback, the encouraging comments, and all the care you showed with each round of reviews. And a special thank you to Lauren, for the insightful line edits, and your meticulous copy edits. This story is ten thousand times better thanks to the collective input of our beta and editing team.

Thank you C. Jackdaw for finding inspiration in our story and sharing your art with us. I think it's safe to say we all learned a lot about book cover design together and we are so appreciative of your willingness to figure it out with us.

Thank you to the friends and family who encouraged us.

And finally, a tremendous thank you to those of you who have been with us since the very beginning, back when this story lived in its earliest form on Archive of Our Own, before it was developed into what it is today.

About the Author

Tenley Seré is the pen name of two friends and co-authors Tegan and Sara (yes, just like the pop duo, but sadly no relation).

They met online through a writing server in 2024 and quickly started collaborating. Not even two years later, they have written over half a million words together, starting with their debut novel, *One Manhattan*.

They met in person for the first time *in* Manhattan (neither of them even lives in the state of New York), and have enjoyed many adventures traveling together, writing together, and of course, drinking Manhattans together.

Follow them on social media: @AuthorTenleySere

www.ingramcontent.com/pod-product-compliance
Lightning Source LLC
Chambersburg PA
CBHW051258130726
47987CB00004B/1577